PAIGE MORGAN

THE ANCIENT NEXUS

SOUL EMPIRE SERIES
BOOK I

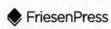 FriesenPress

One Printers Way
Altona, MB R0G 0B0
Canada

www.friesenpress.com

ISBN
978-1-03-831213-6 (Hardcover)
978-1-03-831212-9 (Paperback)
978-1-03-831214-3 (eBook)

1. YOUNG ADULT FICTION, FANTASY, DARK FANTASY

Distributed to the trade by The Ingram Book Company

To my mother and father, who helped me construct my imaginative mind at such a young age, who encouraged me to look beyond our own world, and who told me stories before I fell asleep so that fantasy blended with actuality....

Thank you

There's another world out there just beyond the world we're in. It's just on the other side of that translucent, semitransparent surface.

— Bill Viola

To those whose dreams invade their waking moments...

Chapter I

She'd be dead if she hadn't moved out of the way. Just as the clenched fist came hurling towards her, she swiftly ducked.

"Bitch!" the man growled.

Over six foot three and thick, he was slow to swing, slow to move, and slow to think. However, Luna still couldn't manage to knock him out. So, she did what she often had to do: she took out her taser rod and slammed him in the back. The man let out a howl and toppled to the ground. Luna was so concentrated on what she was doing that she hadn't noticed the alarms above her blaring loudly and blinking red. A group of her fellow prison guards ran into the hallway. So much for backup—she would've been dead before they got here if she hadn't known how to fight.

Her hands were shaking. She put her taser rod away before someone saw them trembling. Adrenaline always pumped Luna up, but she had a difficult time calming down. She wasn't afraid; all she felt was anger towards the prisoner who attacked her. Just because she was a female Elf didn't mean she couldn't hold her own. She tightened her long bright red ponytail, which had loosened during the fight. Multiple guards were already on the prisoner she'd tasered, who was still shaking on the ground as the electrical current ran through his body. Luna smirked.

A voice pipped up behind her. "Luna?"

She turned around to face Edric, her friend from the prisoner guard program she had taken a few years ago. They were similar in age and had become friends quickly. Now they were slightly older than a lot of the new recruits: Luna was now nineteen, and Edric twenty-three. His cute pointy Elf ears stuck out from his freshly cut light-brown hair. Luna studied his new haircut. His hair was wavy; the top, longer, tapered down to a buzz cut below his ears. He looked good. He always looked good, with his square-set jaw and striking blue eyes. Many Elven women found it hard to resist him. Luna had never gone for him, though. He flirted with her at times, but while they were at the prison guard program together, she had been in a serious relationship, which ended about a year ago. Luna had taken the breakup worse than she'd expected.

Her stomach gurgled, begging for food after all the excitement.

"Nexus to Luna, you in there?" Edric asked again.

Luna forgot she still hadn't responded to him. "I'm good! Sorry, just lost in thought... feeling hungry. Mind if I go and eat lunch?"

Edric raised an eyebrow and gave her a quick scan for any wounds from the fight. "Sure, as long as you're sure that you're all right."

Luna nodded and took a deep breath. "Just fine," she said, and began to walk down the hallway. She could feel

Edric's eyes on her until she disappeared into the shadows of the prison.

Luna flicked on her flashlight, which was screwed onto her chest protector plate. The prison guards here wore a full set of metal armour, which was heavy, weighing about fifty pounds in total—it was a good thing Luna was strong. She had an athletic build, her breasts weren't necessarily small but large for an athlete, and she had big strong thighs and a small but sturdy waist. Elven prisoners liked to comment on her ass, and she liked to follow that with a "fuck off."

Luna had to deal with men all the time at work, and she'd become slightly distrustful of them. There were a lot of sickos out there, and she had to work with the worst of the worst. Rapists, murderers, serial killers—you name it, they were there. She wished she could get rid of them all. She didn't understand the point of spending resources to feed these men. There were some women prisoners too, but not as many, and they were in a separate building, far away from the men.

The prison was kept dark for a reason: to create a dungeon-like experience for the prisoners. Not only that but Nexus had a wet climate, like a rain forest, and the prison's roof had multiple holes to let rainwater into the cells so that it was constantly damp in the prison. Damp and dark. In the quiet of the night, all you could hear was the scurrying of the rats and the dripping of the rain.

The Elven prison was the only prison on all of Nexus, the inmates came from the two large clans of Elves. Luna belonged to the Ancients, the oldest known clan on Nexus; the other, named after the large expanse of desert in their region, was the Plains clan. The Elves of the Plains had more animalistic features than the Ancients: their pointed ears were rimmed with hair, and some grew tails. Both clans took great care in mending the land and sustaining its ecosystems. They didn't overpopulate their planet. They grew their food naturally and walked everywhere despite there being other ways of travel, though some Elves rode on horses if they needed to go a long distance. And most Elves ate a more plant-based diet; they still ate meat, just not as often.

Luna felt a cold drop of water hit her forehead as she walked through the corridor. She shivered and wiped it off quickly. That water was probably full of rat droppings. She reached a door and used her fingerprint to unlock it, then ran up the stairs and into another hallway. This hallway was much nicer than the prison one below. Instead of cement blocks as floors, it had beautiful wooden ones that smelled like pine, and bright lights hung from the ceiling. As Luna continued walking, her boots clicked on the floor and she left a set of wet footprints behind. She got to another door and opened it; no fingerprint needed. It was the staff lounge, and it was empty. A nice surprise.

Luna went to the cooler and got out a stir fry she had made the previous night. She placed it in a water steamer, then waited as the system reheated her food. After a little while, she turned the steamer off and carefully took her food out using a towel to protect her hands from the heat. She set it down and began to eat it slowly, appreciating every bite.

She could hear the pitter-pattering of rain on the roof above her. It made her think of all the times she used to lie in bed as a child and listen to the rain as she fell asleep. It also made her want to cozy up by her fire and read a book, but she wouldn't be able to do that until later tonight. She got off work at seven p.m. Here, the prison guards had to work twelve-hour shifts, two days and two nights. She got five days off, which was better than most.

The staff lounge door creaked open; Edric stepped inside. His eyes brightened at seeing her. Luna smiled, then turned her eyes down towards her meal to continue eating. Edric went to his locker and grabbed a lunch bag. He threw it on the table and pulled out a bunch of different packets of food from it: crackers, nuts, jerky, and dried fruit. Their silence wasn't awkward for her. Edric and Luna often worked the same shift and spent a lot of time together. They had grown to know each other well.

"You busy tonight?" Edric asked.

Luna blinked a few times before responding. Did he just ask her out on a date? Couldn't be. Not Edric. "Me?" she asked dumbly.

Edric laughed. His laugh was deep and masculine, and now that he had asked her out, his laugh made her blush. She didn't like to get involved with other Elves at work and hadn't expected Edric would ask her out. She wasn't sure what men thought of her, although she'd been told by previous lovers that she was beautiful. Most Elves are naturally beautiful, so was it even a compliment?

"Yes, you. I figured you could come to my place for dinner?" His eyes had fully focused on hers. Weren't they just friends?

"I-I… um, sure, I guess?" she replied with a stutter.

It had been a few months since she'd gone on a date. After the breakup, she went through a phase of going out with a few different guys, but that ended fast.

Edric gave her a sideways smile, which made him look badass but also cocky. "You seem… surprised."

Luna's face had now turned beat red. She was not easily embarrassed, but this was a weird situation. Her skin was naturally whiter than others, which she inherited from her father, along with his brilliant red hair and freckles.

"I guess, I just didn't think you would want to," she replied abruptly. Not sure if that was the answer he was looking for.

Edric let out another laugh, this one coming more from his chest. He was a large dude, at least six foot two, and had a muscular build. Elven men usually sat around five foot eleven to six feet. At five foot eight, Luna was taller than most women on Nexus.

"I think you'd be surprised with what I want to do," he said.

As soon as those words left his mouth, Luna almost choked on her saliva. She had no idea how to respond to that. Thankfully, she didn't have to because the lounge door opened and another male prison guard stepped in. Luna didn't know the guy well, but she wanted to say his name was Gabriel. He was younger and one of the new guys.

"After work then, come over," Edric said.

Luna's eyes caught Gabriel glancing over at them. She nodded to Edric and began to eat her lunch again. Edric kept sneaking glances at her. Whenever they made eye contact, he would wink, which he often did before, but now that he had asked her out, it was making Luna's heart race. Why hadn't she seen the signs before? Had he always been this obvious? She finished up her meal and left the lounge.

She pressed a button on her radio as she was walking. "Luna back on duty," she said. The radio fuzzed, and then a second later, a male voice answered, "Luna, go relieve Rem off his posting in section three, floor two."

"Copy that," Luna replied before letting go of the button.

She walked all the way over to Section 3, which was the farthest and biggest section. This was where she did most of her work. It had the lower-risk murderers and rapists; one might say she was put here because she was a woman and young. The prisoner who had tried to punch her earlier was from Section 1, where the highest-risk and most dangerous criminals were kept. They usually didn't put her there, but, of course, the one time they did, she got attacked. Either way, she handled it well, so what did it matter?

"Rem?" Luna asked as she approached a slim male guard.

He was standing by one of the cells, talking to a prisoner. He turned around, and Luna did indeed see it was Rem, aka Remmy. Hard to tell when the only light around was coming from the odd candle lit on posts along the brick walls.

"Hey, Luna, I'm heading downstairs to help out with some things. Can you take over this floor for me?" he asked.

Luna nodded. "Sure thing." He left at a quick pace back towards the stairs.

"What's a pretty thing like you working here for?" a creepy, raspy voice asked from one of the cells nearby.

Luna usually ignored comments, but for some reason, she turned towards the voice and looked at the prisoner.

He was clutching the bars of his cell and staring at her. He was older, maybe in his mid-seventies, and had a long beard and ragged dark hair. His skin was so dirty that she had a hard time seeing where his shirt started and ended. She continued to not respond as the prisoner stared at her. "I'm talking to you miss," the man said.

Luna exhaled, not realizing she had been holding her breath. "What are you in for?" she asked nonchalantly.

The man laughed, then wheezed. "For a crime I didn't commit," he said.

Luna rolled her eyes; she heard this all the time. She turned away and began to walk down the hallway.

"Wait!" the man said.

She heard a few other prisoners scurry up to the bars of their cells and saw a few trying to peek out to see what was going on. Luna stood in the hall, listening to water drip, one drop at a time, into a puddle beside her.

The silence grew toxic and made her want to run.

"Closer," the man said.

She stepped a bit closer to the cell, but not close enough for him to grab her. A musty aroma wafted into her nose from the prisoner's clothes.

The man's dark eyes studied her for a moment before he whispered, "He's coming for you, and he will find you."

She furrowed her eyebrows, wondering what he was talking about. The man backed away into the shadows of the cell. Luna took a few shaky breaths before continuing to walk down the hall.

Part of overseeing a floor was pacing around and making sure that all prisoners were behaving. Besides that, and many other tasks, prison guards served the prisoners their meals, which was Luna's least favourite job. She hated that she had to act as a waitress and give them their food. Her favourite job was making the prisoners clean their cells and the hallways. Every day, from each floor, one prisoner was chosen to clean all the hallways and walls as two guards watched them. At this time, each prisoner had to clean their room and were allowed to shower. Luna didn't like to think she enjoyed other people's pain, but when it came to the sickos in this prison, she very much enjoyed watching them suffer.

The rest of her shift went by slowly, without any more exciting events happening. All the prisoners behaved, for the most part, which was rare. Luna had spent most of the shift thinking about how she was supposed to go over to Edric's house. She didn't really want to; she was tired and would rather go home and lie in bed. She worked nights tomorrow, so at least she could sleep in and maybe go for a run. She had to keep herself in shape to fend off these prisoners with the exercise program that the prison had set for the guards to follow.

She went into the staff lounge and strolled over to her locker. The lounge was packed with guards that were off for the night and were changing to go home. She'd gotten used to changing clothes in a room full of men. There was only one other female prison guard for the male prisoners, and she was off right now because she'd gotten assaulted. Most of the female guards worked with the female prisoners. Luna slid her armour off over her head to reveal a sports bra. Of course, her luck would be that she'd be wearing a sports bra to Edric's… not that they were going to do anything else… or were they?

A regular bra was stuffed in the back of her locker somewhere; she could change into that. After finding it, Luna looked around quickly before using her ninja-like changing skills to switch into the normal bra. She then put on a T-shirt and slid on the pair of joggers she had come to work in. She didn't look like she was dressed for a date.

Luna locked her locker and swung her bag around her back. The changing room was noisy. People were chatting away about their plans and their day. Luna looked up and locked eyes with Edric. He was waiting for her at the door. She walked up to him.

"You still coming over?" he asked.

She nodded. "Yep."

He smiled in return. They walked down the hallway together, chatting about their day. Edric often worked in Section 1 or 2, so he had the best stories to tell about the prisoners there. There wasn't one boring day that went by in that place.

***

The pair made their way outside. As the sun set, red and orange colours lit up the sky. Birds flew across their path, feasting on the bugs that came out when the sun went down. Luna breathed in the fresh air. Being in the prison all day often made her nose stuffy. The breeze tickled her cheeks. She loosened her hair and let it flow down her back. Edric glanced over, in awe of her beauty. She had brilliant purple eyes with speckles of blue. Her skin was smooth and healthy, making her glow and stand out from all the men at the prison. Her lips were full and pink, and her hair, long and thick, flowed down to her hips, which swayed back and forth as they walked.

Luna caught Edric staring at her. "What? Do I have something on my face?" she asked sheepishly.

Edric shook his head and smiled. Though they talked a bit as they walked, Luna mostly tuned into nature, enjoying the singing of the crickets. After about twenty minutes, they arrived at Edric's place. His house wasn't far from hers, which was only another ten-minute walk eastward. All the homes were made of wood and stood around ten to fifteen feet above ground. Many were attached to trees like treehouses; Luna's house was in a tree, but Edric's was not.

They climbed up the ladder and into the home. It was cozy inside. Most homes had a combination of a fire and a sun-powered heating device. It never got too cold on Nexus. Luna had never actually been inside Edric's place. She had only ever seen the outside. His home was surprisingly neat for a bachelor. He had lots of fur rugs over his furniture. She could smell something woody and citrusy in the room. His walls were painted grey, and his flooring was stained a dark walnut brown. From where Luna stood, she could see another set of stairs, which likely went up to his bedroom. She gulped, wondering how many women he'd had brought up there.

"Well, what do you think?" Edric asked.

Luna slowly started to nod her head. "Honestly, you're a clean freak. Who knew?" she said as the corners of her mouth curved up.

It was the first time that day she'd allowed herself to tease him a bit. He nudged her side. "What, you imagined me to be messy?" he asked.

Luna laughed. "No, but I didn't think you'd be so… clean. Your place looks like nobody lives here. My place is definitely messier."

Edric shrugged. "I like to be organized."

He ran over to his couch and sprung up with a jump, landing on his back on the couch. Then he sat up and asked with a wink, "Wanna join?"

Luna cleared her throat and tried to keep her blush from rising. "What's the plan? You got any board games?"

Luna walked over to the couch and sat next to him, but not too close. His eyes were watching her, and it was giving her butterflies. He opened a wooden box next to the couch and pulled out a board game. Luna couldn't see the name of it.

"Let's play this one," he suggested.

He pulled the board out and the pieces. It looked like something Luna had played before, but she couldn't remember the name. Basically, you had to roll the dice, go around the board, and land on different places. The places made you pay fines or gave you certain abilities.

"Sure, let's play," she said.

They played for over an hour. Luna was competitive, unlike Edric, who was super chill and laughed at her whenever she got frustrated after he'd won something.

Luna was beginning to feel tired. It was probably close to nine, and she still had to walk home. She yawned.

"You getting sleepy?" Edric asked.

"Yeah, I think I'm going to head home now," Luna replied.

Edric jumped up quickly. "We never ate any snacks!" he said. They both started laughing.

"I guess we got too carried away with the game," Luna said still giggling.

Edric dipped his head down and kissed her softly on the lips. Her heart skipped a beat—she wasn't expecting that. Edric pulled his face away and looked at her eyes. She stood up and straightened out her shirt, which didn't need to be straightened.

"Um, I should go," she blurted.

Edric grinned. "Too soon?"

Luna took a deep breath before saying, "Maybe?" She paused. "I think so.... I enjoyed everything, though! I had fun!"

He looked at her for a moment longer than what felt comfortable. Luna tore her eyes away.

Edric let out a breath. "Let me walk you home," he suggested. Luna nodded.

They went down the ladder and made their way over to her place. The outside lights strung around her house made it inviting; she loved that.

She turned to face Edric. "See you at work."

He nodded and gave her a sad smile. Luna could tell he was disappointed; he probably thought she would be all over him. As much as he was inhumanly attractive, it was hard to see him that way. And what did he expect? They'd been in the friend zone for a few years. She'd thought she would be able to step out of the zone, but it was more difficult than she'd imagined. Or maybe she was just awkward? But she could try, right? Just might take some time. He turned around and started walking away.

"Edric?" She called. He turned and looked at her. His eyes were so bright in the moonlight.

"I really did have fun," she said.

He gave her that sideways cocky grin. "Me too," he replied, and then left.

She climbed up the ladder and into her cozy home, which smelled like old books and painting supplies. Unlike Edric's, her house looked like she lived there. She had lots of books on her tables, papers with her journalling everywhere. She liked writing and drawing, so she had her paintings everywhere too. She flicked her lights on. Her house had lots of browns and greys in it, mainly due to the natural wood furniture, walls, and floor. Her place was smaller than Edric's. Her bedroom was in the living room, separated by a big fur curtain. The only thing that had a separate door was her tiny bathroom. She didn't have heated water, as she never wanted to buy a boiler, so she took cold showers and always had her fireplace burning.

She threw some wood into the fire; the coals were barely there, so she spent some time stoking it. She grabbed some yogurt her neighbour had made and threw some berries and granola in it. She devoured it at her kitchen table before going off to her bedroom to read a book. She was exhausted. She thought she wouldn't last more than an hour reading. Luna was very wrong; she lasted maybe twenty minutes before falling asleep. Her soft snores carried throughout her house. Above her, the pitter-pattering of rain started up again.

Chapter II

His breathing hitched in his chest. His thighs were burning, and he could feel the men behind him fast on his heels. He ran down the empty stairwell, his heavy footsteps clunking with each stair. The goal was to get to the rocket before they caught him. His hands were covered in blood. Underneath his fingernails was dark red and dried blood. He smelled of mint and iron; an aroma that he'd gotten used to. He relished in the moment that he had killed the man whose blood this was. He had felt the life slip through his fingertips and then drip onto the floor. The thought sent shivers down his spine. He ignored the feeling and kept running.

He could hear the men behind him; their footsteps were like thunder echoing on the walls. He flung open the door. Sweat poured off his skin. He wiped his forehead and continued sprinting. His legs were beyond sore, the lactic acid was building up, but he had to keep pushing. He got to the last door before reaching the hangar where the rockets were housed.

"Where do you think you're going, Darick?"

He recognized the voice behind him, calling for him down the hallway, but he ignored it. He was leaving.

He opened the door and ran to one of the rockets. He pressed the discharge button, and his journey began.

Chapter III

Luna yawned while stretching her arms and legs out in bed. She had slept well and didn't feel like moving. She looked at the time: eight thirty a.m. Pretty good. She usually didn't sleep in. She got up and changed into some fresh clothes for the day.

She liked to wear T-shirts or long-sleeve tops with cargo pants—her go-to. She often wore hiking or running shoes. Luna went to the kitchen and made herself some oatmeal. She sprinkled seeds in it, added cinnamon, and threw in a mixture of fresh berries that she had picked from the community garden. Each neighbourhood had a shared garden, and each neighbour was allotted certain days to care for it. They also had a farm with animals, such as chickens, cows, goats, and sheep, next to the garden that the neighbourhood cared for too. Luna wasn't a fan of farming, so she spent extra time in the garden. She had a deal with one of her neighbours.

Luna ate her oatmeal outside on the deck, enjoying the beautiful, quiet morning. The rain had seized, and the sun had risen. All the dew glistened in the light. Luna took a big breath of the fresh air, smelling the healthy dirt and vegetation. The best smell. She finished her oatmeal and decided to go for her jog. She gave herself a good half hour before going out, just to let her stomach settle.

Luna jogged up to the exercise facility, which was about four kilometres away, mostly uphill. She was breathing hard by the time she got there, and her legs were shaky. Even though she did this four to five times a week, it never got easier. Her times did get faster, though, so she was always pushing herself.

For Luna's height, her muscles were very lean; she wasn't bulky, but she had a fit runner's body. She enjoyed lifting weights but tended to do higher reps at a faster pace; she liked to sweat. When she walked into the facility, it was packed as usual. Elves liked to exercise. She went to her gym locker and changed into a pair of inside shoes, then began her workout. Today, she was focusing on shoulders and biceps, with some more light-weight training at the end. She spent about an hour there before cooling down. Sweat was dripping off her forehead and onto the floor below her. She could taste the salt in her mouth.

"Hey, Luna," a deep masculine voice said from behind her. She was stretching her arms against the wall. She turned around to see Edric standing there. He had some friends with him, but they were pretending to mind their own business.

"Morning," she replied. Her voice came out breathless; she was physically exhausted.

Edric wore a pair of dark-grey joggers and a blue muscle shirt. His arms were massive, and he had impressive veins popping out of his muscles. He hadn't even exercised yet.

"Nice to see you. I'm about to start my workout but just wanted to stop by and let you know you look good, being all sweaty and stuff," he said.

"That's not weird at all." She laughed.

He shrugged. "What can I say? I'm bad at flirting."

Luna rolled her eyes as a tease. He chuckled before strolling away to begin his exercises. Looked like he was starting with squats. No wonder he had a nice ass. She packed up her stuff and changed into her outside shoes. Her sweat had dried up, making her feel sticky.

She left the building and found herself taking the longer way back home. It had gotten cloudy out, and the sky was dark like it was going to thunder. She began to wonder why she took the long way home. What if she got soaked? It wouldn't be the end of the world; at least, she'd get a natural shower out of it. The trees cast shadows across the path, leaving it dim. A breeze picked up, sending chills down Luna's arms. There were no signs of other Elves in the area, and she was beginning to feel isolated. Suddenly, she heard a loud crack. It wasn't a crack that you would imagine coming from a tree branch snapping, but more like a crack of thunder, and it came from the sky.

She looked up towards the sky and saw a ball of flames hurdling down towards her. Voices shouted from somewhere in front of her. The ball of flames disappeared through the trees ahead, and the ground suddenly shook from the impact.

A group of Ancient Warrior Elves came running down the path. All dressed up in fancy gold armour, they had their bow and arrows drawn. Luna hid behind a tree. They didn't see her; they had turned into the bushes before glancing her way. She followed them towards the object that had crashed. What the hell was it? A meteor? She remembered the little things Aywin taught her about space.

She arrived at the place where the object crashed. The trees around it were simmering and smoking, but it was too wet for them to catch on fire. The object was no longer in flames—and it was not a meteor. The Warriors surrounded it, talking and sending commands to one another. The oval object, a large metal-looking thing, looked as though two people could fit in it. It had a small window on its top, which she couldn't see through, and a latch on its right side. One of the Warriors opened the door with the latch, and it swung upwards.

The Warrior stuck his head in and then shouted, "There's something here! A man! He's unconscious!"

Luna ducked down behind a bush just as some of the Warriors looked her way. She knew they would tell her to go if they caught her watching. The Warrior hauled a body out. Luna studied the man. He was pale, paler than her, and he looked sickly. He had jet-black hair, which flowed down past his ears. His ears? They weren't pointy. What the hell did that mean?

She couldn't see his face well, as it was covered in blood. He must've hit his head. He wore a T-shirt and pants, which looked foreign to her; she'd never seen clothes like that before. Suddenly, the man's eyes popped open. They were a bright-gold colour—unlike any colour she had ever seen before. His mouth opened to reveal sharp fangs just before he turned and bit into the neck of the Warrior dragging him out of the object.

The Warrior screamed as his neck gushed blood, and… the man… She couldn't believe what she was seeing: Was he drinking it? Luna panicked. Her heart rate picked up, and she started to back away. The other Warriors were already on the man, but he was growling and trying to break free. She heard more voices coming from behind her and she sprinted away from the forest, down the path towards home.

She ran the whole way back home without stopping. As soon as she was home, she jumped in the shower. There, she could try to make sense of what she had seen. The cold water washed over her body and cleared her mind. She had never seen an object come out of the sky. Where did that man come from? He obviously wasn't from Nexus. Elves knew that there had to be other worlds, but they had never tried to investigate. As far as she knew, they were happy with staying on this planet and wanted nothing to do with any others. That man had killed one of the Elves; there was no way that Elf survived that neck injury. He likely bit the carotid artery. It had pulsated and squirted blood like it was. Her mind kept having flashbacks of the man's bloody face, and his teeth—they looked like hers except for his canines, which were much longer and sharp.

Luna got out of the shower and dried off. She peered at herself in the mirror. Her fair cheeks were reddened from scrubbing them, and her freckles were more prominent. She put on clean cargo pants and a loose-fitting tank top and went to the kitchen to cook a big meal. It was nearing two p.m. and she was getting hungry. Besides, making some food would get her mind off the man she'd seen. She fried up a bunch of vegetables with beans and made enough for her late dinner tonight at work. She usually ate around nine p.m. on night shifts and then didn't eat at all during the night. Unfortunately, the prison guards didn't get to have long breaks during the night. Without much time to fall asleep, Luna rarely napped on her breaks; instead she read. She put her leftovers in a container and her meal on a plate. As soon as she sat down at the table and started to eat it, her doorbell rang. She sighed, got up, and opened the door. She peered down to the ground at the bottom of the ladder.

"Fuck off, Aywin," Luna teased, and smiled.

Aywin was her brother. He was two and a half years older than her, and they had been best friends their entire lives. Aywin shared Luna's red hair, except Aywin's was a deeper, darker red. His eyes weren't blueish purple like Luna's either, but a dark blue.

"Good day to you too, L." He smirked.

"What do you want?" she asked, leaning against the doorframe.

"I was just at Mom and Dad's place; they want us to come over the day after tomorrow for dinner. After your last night shift is what Dad said," he explained.

Luna raised her eyebrows. "Dinner again? We were just there on my last set off. Is Mom getting lonely with Dad being so busy all the time?"

Aywin shrugged. "You're the one that works for him," he replied.

Head of the prison, their father ran both the male and female departments. Luna had decided at a young age that she wanted to be a prison guard; for some reason, it was something that interested her. Aywin, on the other hand, preferred things with the least amount of violence. He worked as an environmental scientist at the Science Base, usually Monday to Friday.

Luna thought about talking to her brother about what she'd seen earlier, but she decided against it. There were too many eyes and ears lurking around. Too many neighbours. She wasn't even sure if the man from the sky would become common knowledge to the people. Maybe the Elves would just kill him for what he'd done....

"Did you come all this way to tell me that?" Luna asked.

Aywin played with the little string that hung down from the doorbell. "Nope. I've been stopping by the gardens and checking in. Apparently, there are some vegetables that aren't doing too good right now, and I think it's from all the rain. Anyways, better get going," he said. "Chow." He saluted and walked off.

Luna closed the door and went back to eating her cold food.

The rest of the afternoon Luna spent reading and doing the odd house chore. There always seemed to be something to get done around her place. She was never able to sleep before her night shifts, so she didn't even bother trying. Luna had always been a motivated person. She did not have difficulty setting her mind on something and completing it. Just like with her schooling. Her marks in school were good because she tried. Her father was big on that. He used to say, "If you don't try your best, then there's no point at doing it at all." She truly believed that. She felt that Aywin was that way too. He succeeded in what he did because he put in effort as well.

Luna's mother, Rose, was the opposite of her father. It's funny how opposites attract. Rose and her father, Arin, met when they were in high school, and they'd been together ever since. Luna was the same height as her mother, but her mom was very slim, almost brittle. A clothes designer, she had delicate hands and long fingers. Luna always hated the thought of looking brittle; she wanted to be strong like her father, who was a large man, about Edric's height and just as big. Though due to his age, his muscles weren't as defined. Aywin seemed to be in between her mother and father in height. He was around six feet but was lean and about the same as Luna in build. Her brother had long thin legs, though, not big thighs.

Luna spent another couple hours reading before getting ready to go to work. When it was nearing six thirty p.m., with the half hour walk to work, she decided she would get going so she wouldn't have to rush.

The sun was getting close to the mountains, ready to go to sleep. The sky was clear, with no clouds in view. It was a beautiful evening. Luna walked along the dirt path. She shivered from a breeze that picked up. The "colder" season was coming. In the Ancients area, the temperature stayed around twenty to twenty-five degrees Celsius for most of the year. Luna took in the forests that grew naturally around her. Little treehouses were tucked away, and she could see lights beaming from their windows. She shifted her lunch bag onto her back and tightened the straps. She was approaching Edric's house. A light was on inside; he must still be home. She went over to the string that hung down from the top of the house. It was attached to a bell like her own doorbell. She shook the string and the bell dinged like a wind charm.

A few seconds later, Edric poked his head out of the door. "Thought we'd walk together," Luna stated.

Edric smirked. "I knew you thought I was irresistible."

Luna laughed. "Get down here. We have to go." She smiled.

"One sec, have to grab my bag," he said before dashing into his house.

He came out again and had a backpack slung around his shoulders. He closed the door and climbed down the ladder. He smelled like fresh pine and peppermint. Luna tried to ignore the reaction she got from his familiar scent.

He playfully nudged her side. "Gosh, let's go. We are going to be late," he teased. They took off together down the pathway.

Chapter IV

"Fuck you," Darick spat out his own blood onto the cement floor.

Four prison guards surrounded him along with a man named Arin, who appeared to be their leader. For the last hour, they had been hitting Darick repeatedly, trying to get him to confess why he was on this planet and where he came from. If they were a little nicer, he probably would've told them, except for the fact that he had no memory of why he was there or of where he came from. The only thing he could remember was his name. The doctor who had seen him did say he had hit his head badly on his way down.

"Now, let's play nice. What are you? You aren't one of us?" Arin asked.

He was a large man with red hair and light-blue eyes. He knelt on one knee to get closer to Darick, who was chained to the floor so he could not escape or lash out. The prison door creaked open, and a woman stepped in. She was also wearing armour like the other prison guards.

***

Luna had been called to help with an interrogation. Her father had said it would be a good experience. She stepped into the prison cell full of prison guards. At that moment, some Elves dressed in white robes came in and moved in front of her before she could get a good look at the prisoner. They looked like the scientists from Science Base.

The guards swarmed the prisoner and held him down. He was strong, but he was chained to the floor, and all she could hear were the chains rattling as he tried to escape. One of the scientists took a needle out and stabbed it into the prisoner's arm. The scientists nodded their heads as if they had done what they needed to do and then left the room.

Luna wondered what that was all about. Maybe this prisoner guy had some sort of disease or illness she wasn't aware of. Suddenly, she felt the need to leave the room. The guards finally got off the prisoner and moved out of the way. She looked at the creature chained to the ground—the man from the sky. She could see his face better now, even though it looked like her father had punched him a few times. He didn't look as sickly as before. The man's dark hair fell around a handsome face. He had some stubble growing, which defined his jawline even more. He had full lips and sharp attractive features. Luna's breath was taken away by his golden eyes, which were staring right at her. He looked like he wanted to kill her.

She gulped. Could he taste her fear? His mouth was parted, and she could see the bottom of his fangs. They were bright white and looked deadly. She watched as the corner of his mouth lifted into a lopsided smile.

Arin's father kicked the man in the side. "Answer my questions! Who are you? What are you? Why did you kill those soldiers!" he yelled.

Luna jumped. Her father's voice had always been one of the most powerful voices she had ever heard. She watched as the man's head fell back and he began to laugh, his fangs showing fully.

"I guess I haven't been clear enough, have I?" the man said. "Fuck you."

Luna caught the hint of an accent in the man's words. It was foreign to her. Her father's temper exploded. He stood up and yelled while kicking the wall. Luna was proud of him for not booting the prisoner in the face. She slowly stepped out from behind the other guards; she hadn't realized she'd hid herself behind them. She moved close to her father.

"If you answer my father's questions, you might not need to be locked up," Luna said. Her voice sounded so feminine and sweet compared to her father's. Her father turned and watched her as she spoke to the prisoner.

"My name is Luna. What's yours?" she asked.

The man stared at her, for longer than what felt comfortable, his pupils widening in the darkness.

"Darick," he said. His voice was deep, almost raspy. Not a smoker's raspiness, more like the raspiness you get after your throat has been punched a few times.

Luna nodded, hoping that he'd keep talking. The vengeful look that had been plastered on his face the whole time was now changing into an expression of smugness.

"And you can also fuck off," he stated.

Luna narrowed her eyes. The man was vulgar. She thought she'd been getting somewhere. At least, they knew his name now, right? Unless he was lying. Doubtful. Why would knowing his real name cause any harm?

Her father gently pushed Luna to the side. "Take him to section two, cell thirty-three. It's far away from the other prisoners. That's where he will stay until he changes his mind." He paused, with one eyebrow raised, and then he gave Darick a stern look. "No food or water," he finished, then grabbed ahold of Luna's hand and took her outside the interrogation cell.

Once they were down the hallway a bit, he stopped and turned to her. "I'm going to put you in charge of this prisoner. He will need one-on-one. If he doesn't fess up, he will just become like the others: he will receive no trial. But I want you to try and get him to talk," he whispered.

"Thank you, sir. You won't regret it," she replied.

Her father patted her on the back. "I never do," he said, and with that, he left.

Luna could hear the other guards struggling with Darick. She turned and saw that they were bringing him down the hallway towards her as she was on the way to Section 2. She waited until they were closer.

"Arin has put me in charge of the prisoner for now. Let's take him to section two," she stated.

The others nodded. Luna couldn't help but notice Darick's face: he was staring at her again, his gold eyes flickering in the dark hallway. She shivered, thinking back to when she watched him kill that Warrior in the woods. As if he could read her thoughts, he moved with inhuman speed and elbowed one of the guards in the side. He sprung out and bit the other guard on the side of the neck, his fangs latching in. Then he tore a chunk of skin out and spat it onto the floor. His mouth was covered in blood.

Luna hadn't had time to react. But the other guards beside the prisoner did. They pinned him down onto the ground. Luna ran to the guard that had the neck wound. Blood was pouring out, and the smell of it hung in the air. She ripped a piece of her clothing off and pushed it against the wound to try and stop the bleeding.

"Call for backup!" Luna ordered. "And ask for a muzzle for his face," she growled.

She was furious. He had done that to piss her off. Within minutes, a doctor came running down the hall as well as a few more guards, including Edric. The doctor took the wounded guard away. Edric held the muzzle, which they often put on prisoners as a punishment, but in this case, it would stop Darick from biting. He went over to Darick and wrapped the muzzle around his mouth. Luna peered over. Darick was staring right at her again as Edric tightened the muzzle. Darick squirmed from the pinching on his face. They stood him up.

"Let's continue," Luna said.

Her heart was still racing from all the excitement. "From now on, he's to wear a muzzle around any guards," she ordered. The guards nodded in response as they walked down the hall.

They arrived at Cell 33, in Section 2. Luna wondered why her father hadn't put the prisoner in Section 1. He sure acted like a Section 1 inmate. Luna helped bring him in.

They carefully undid the handcuffs and then went out of the cell. Luna locked the door. Darick was able to slip the muzzle off quickly with his bare hands.

"You guys can go. We are good now," Luna said to the guards, who all left except for Edric. Edric stood with her by the barred cell door.

"I'm stationed on this floor, so let me know if you need any help with… it," he said, loud enough for Darick to clearly hear.

Darick was sprawled out on the futon bed, licking the blood off his lips. Luna had a look of revulsion on her face, which went away as soon as she felt a warmth on her hand. Edric's hand had reached out and touched hers for a moment. It was comforting. She looked up at his dark-blue eyes. Was that… desire?

She blinked a few times and took a breath. "Um, I'll be fine. I'll let you know, though."

Edric nodded and went down the dark hallway. Luna watched him go, listening to his footsteps echo long after. From in the cell, Darick let out a whistle.

Luna turned angrily. "You never mind," she spat.

The man let out a chuckle and turned to his side on the bed. In that moment, Luna regretted saying yes to guarding this guy. He was going to make her snap; she could feel her blood already boiling.

***

Hours went by in complete silence, other than the odd prisoner down the hallway screaming or shouting something. Darick just sat on his bed in the cell. Every once in a while, he would get up and start pacing. And then he would do some exercises on the floor. Currently, Luna was watching him do push-ups. His strong shoulders popped out from underneath his T-shirt.

She felt exhausted; nobody had come by to relieve her for a break, and it was close to one in the morning now. Why was this guy still awake? She tried to ignore his heavy breathing and instead focused on listening to the dripping water. She sat on the wet, cold ground and inhaled. The air here was stale. She coughed. Her eyelids were heavy, and it was difficult to stay alert.

She heard heavy footsteps down the hallway. Thank God—someone to relieve her. It was Edric. The way he walked made him look powerful: broad shouldered, thick strong legs.

When he reached her, he held out a hand to help her up. "Getting sleepy?" he asked.

It was very dark in the hallway now that it was the middle of the night, the only light coming from the odd candle along the wall. She accepted his hand and stood up. His grip was strong, and his hands callused. Her whole body pressed against his as she stood, and his smell and warmth were overstimulating. She couldn't help but feel goose bumps break out across her skin. They both stood there, staring at each other. Edric's chest heaved up in down, and she saw him shiver.

"Are you… here to let me go and have a break?" she asked, her voice coming out like a whisper.

They let go of each other's hands and took a step back. "I am." He turned and peered into Darick's cell. At some point, Darick had stopped doing push-ups and was now sitting on the ground, watching the two of them.

"That thing doesn't seem to sleep, does it?" he stated. Luna nodded in agreement. What was Darick anyways? Some sort of cannibal? Or maybe a complete sicko.

"I never got my first break. You okay if I take an hour?" she asked.

Edric nodded. "Yeah, no problem," he replied. She gave him a short nod and made her way back down the hall.

She went up the stairs to the staffroom. The lights were out, and she could hear snoring. Someone was on one of the couches. She took a timer from her locker and went to the other couch. She set the timer and then lay down. Usually, she didn't nap, but tonight, she was exhausted. Her body was aching from fatigue. Maybe she pushed herself too hard at the gym today. She also did a lot more running than usual. Within minutes, her mind shut off and she fell into a deep sleep.

A loud ringing noise woke Luna up. She grumbled and turned off the alarm. How had it been almost an hour already? She sighed and got up from the couch. Her mind was annoyed about being woken up from REM sleep. It was groggy and disoriented. She left the staffroom and began her short walk over to Section 2.

***

Darick felt a sharp pain on the side of his temple. It was piercing down into his brain and he felt like he was going to barf. His vision blurred. The last thing he saw was Luna coming back to relieve the other guard before his vision went black for a moment. Then it was bright. Really bright. Was that the sun?

He opened his eyes a little more and looked around. He was somewhere else. He was no longer in the prison cell. He knew this place. This was where he used to live. Darick was standing in his living room, staring out through the window at the mountains. It was late in the day, and the sun was beginning to set. Its rays shone through the window, creating streams of light through the house. His stomach growled. For some reason, he knew what he needed. His body moved as if this was a memory, something that had already taken place.

He watched himself walk to a door with locks. He opened it. The room was decent: brightly coloured, it had a small bed and a little window. What made his stomach squirm was the person chained to the bed. His body moved to the woman, and he watched her face pale as he got closer. She shook her head. "No... please," she begged.

His former self grabbed hold of her. She didn't resist; she was too worn out. He could smell her blood and fear; it made his cravings stir and gave him pleasure like nothing else could. It was addicting. He leaned in and bit her neck, the best spot. The carotid artery. It was easy access. He moaned as he drank the blood from her. If he wanted, he knew he could release hormones from his saliva to make it pleasurable for her, but there was no need for that since she was just going to be food for him, something to keep him alive. His saliva had healing properties. When he was done feeding, he could heal the wound. After a few minutes, he finished and she slumped onto the bed.

He stared at her with his gold eyes. His body hummed with arousal. He shook his head and left the room, locking the door behind him.

Darick gasped. He opened his eyes. Sweat dripped off his body. He was back in the dungeon-like cell on Nexus. He blinked a few times, trying to comprehend what had just happened. Was that what he was? Maybe that was why he bit those guards—it was instinct. Why did he feel sick about it? It felt… wrong.

***

Luna noticed Darick jump up. His body appeared to be all sweaty, and he looked panicked. She had already told Edric to go for his break, so it was just her there now.

"Everything all right?" she asked.

His eyes darted to hers. Was that fear? He wasn't scared of her—that was for sure—so what was he scared of?

"Darick?" she whispered.

With no answer from him, she stepped closer. He was taking some deep breaths and began to pace.

"I'm fine," he said; his voice sounded hoarse.

"You don't look fine," Luna stated.

He put his hands up to his head, clearly frustrated. "I just… I just wish I remembered everything!"

Luna raised an eyebrow in surprise. He was telling the truth. There was no way this was fake. He had no recollection of his past other than his name; of course, he would be scared. He was in an unknown place, with people who attacked him when he first arrived, and now he was their prisoner. This was wrong, Luna thought. Her breath felt like it had been taken away. She needed to talk to her father about this.

"Here, sit down," she said, and motioned towards the floor.

He studied her with a face of distrust. She sighed, walked closer to the bars, and sat on the ground. The cold, wet floor soaked through her pants, but she didn't care. His body went still. His eyes roamed her for a few seconds, and then she saw him relax. He took a step closer and kneeled. This was strange. Luna had never tried to have any conversations with a prisoner. She usually avoided it. The fear that she'd seen in his eyes, though, made her want to talk to him, to get to know him. To understand what had happened. And it was part of her role. Her father had asked her to question him and get answers.

She cleared her throat. "So, I'm thinking we could do this thing where I ask you questions about yourself and maybe it will help pop some memories up?" she suggested.

Darick's face was stern. "Sure," he replied.

"What's your favourite colour?" she asked.

His eyebrows raised. "My favourite colour?" He seemed confused.

Luna exhaled. "Yes, like a colour you like."

He sat there for a minute and began thinking hard; she could practically smell his brain burning.

"I think it's red," he replied.

She nodded. "Good! That's good. See, you do know yourself," she said. She was trying not to smile too much, but she couldn't help it. This was possibly working. "What about animals? Do you have a favourite animal?" she asked.

He didn't think hard about this one. "A horse, definitely a horse," he replied.

So, they had horses where he was from. "This one's a bit harder, but then we will go back to an easier one. Do you know if you have any hobbies? Like things you like to do. My hobbies are reading and art," she said.

He grew silent for a while. She was afraid he wasn't going to reply.

Finally, his gold eyes flicked up to hers. "I think I like to fight," he said.

Luna nodded. "What do you mean, 'fight'? Like compete in fighting?" she asked.

He shook his head. "No. An army. I used to fight in an army."

She nodded. "Okay. I'm going to ask you an easier one now: What's your favourite food? Mine are pancakes," she said with a small grin.

She saw Darick's face darken, and he shook his head. "I'm done," he stated coldly, and stood up. He walked over to his bed to lie down.

Luna stepped closer to the cell bars. "Darick?" she whispered, just loud enough for him to hear.

He didn't move.

"Darick? Do you eat other people? Is that why you keep biting us? Do you have a sickness?" she asked. She needed to know the answer. She needed to know if he was a monster.

He stayed silent. She grumbled and moved away from the cell again. So much for her interviewing skills.

The last few hours of the shift went by quickly. Darick slept the entire time, or at least pretended to sleep. When she left the building, Edric was waiting for her by the entrance of the prison. He was holding his bag, and the way he stood there and stared at her made her stomach flutter.

She smiled. "Aww, what a gentleman," she said while batting her lashes.

He winked at her. "Only for you."

They walked together down the path.

"What do you think of that… new prisoner?" he questioned.

Luna paused before giving her reply. Should she mention her conversation with Darick? No… she decided she shouldn't—not until she knew more. "I'm not sure," she responded.

"He's crazy. Taking bites out of Elves' necks—that's some fucked up stuff," Edric said heartlessly.

Luna nervously fiddled with a string that hung off her shirt. "Where do you think he's from?" she asked.

Edric shrugged. "Beats me. Some other planet, that's for sure. He's no Elf."

Luna nodded in agreement. He was not an Elf. He was something else entirely. The question was, what? "I wonder why he's here," Luna thought out loud.

"Apparently, he came down in some sort of metal object from the sky. That's what the boys were sayin'. Maybe he got lost up there in space? Elves don't mess with that shit; we stay close to the ground. There are things out there that we don't want to meet, and that creature is one of them," Edric said.

Luna shivered at his response. Things out there…. What other creatures could be living out there? How big was space? All she knew was it was dark empty void full of stars and planets and other galaxies.

They continued their way down the path, Edric whistling a tune. The morning was calming. No wind and no rain. Just utter silence. The birds hadn't even started chirping yet. The skies were lightening up with pastel colours. Wispy clouds had formed overhead. Luna relished nature.

When they arrived at Edric's place, he turned to her. He was so large and tall that as his body moved so close to her, it took her breath away. His arms gently wrapped around her and pulled her close. She let him hold her. They stared at one another. His eyes appeared an even darker blue today. He bent down and kissed her hard and she accepted it. His kiss was so full of need, he almost lifted her off the ground. As his hand went lower, cupping her butt, her hands began to explore him. All his hard muscles. They continued kissing until her mouth was sore and she could feel his lust. He pulled away first, his eyes dopey.

Her body hummed, and her stomach fluttered. "Have a good nap," she said breathlessly. She stepped away, gave him a wink, and began to walk down the path.

He smirked at her. "Such a tease," he said.

Chapter V

When Luna arrived at her home, she immediately crawled into bed. She thought it was going to be impossible to try and sleep after that encounter with Edric. She was beginning to have some strong, flirty feelings for him, and she wasn't sure how she felt about it. Did she want to enter another relationship? She didn't know yet. She rolled onto her side and took a few deep breaths. She felt her body relax. Her eyelids were already closing.

When she woke up, she was surprised to see it was nearly three p.m. She had slept quite a few hours, and she usually didn't sleep the greatest in between her nights. Her body still felt heavy, and her head ached like she was hungover— that was normal for shift workers, that feeling of tiredness. The night shift hangover. She rolled out of bed and changed into a loose top and joggers. She peered down at her pants, which stopped mid-calf. Her long legs never fit things properly. She pulled on a pair of long socks to cover her exposed skin; she was feeling cold today. She made some food and ate it while working on a painting. She was using thick oil paint to create a forest scene, the place where she often hiked with her friend Samara.

Thinking of her friend, she realized she hadn't got together with her or her other friends in a while. Samara was Luna's closest friend. She had grown up with her, and Luna considered her family. Samara was a bad ass and one of the commanders of the Ancient Warrior Elves Army. Luna bet she knew something about Darick. Samara started off as a Warrior Elf and was then upgraded due to her superior fighting skills and intellectual abilities. When it came to fighting tactics, she was one of the smartest Elves Luna knew. Samara was also beautiful with jet-black hair styled in a pixie cut and bright-green eyes.

It had been hard for her at first to have the men take her seriously when she had started off commanding. Luna remembered Samara venting to her about this during those times. Obviously since then, Samara has gained all their respect. But Luna bet that they all had crushes on her. As female Elves tended to be petite and delicate, most of Warriors were male, but that seemed to be changing slowly with more females joining. Samara was smaller than Luna, but she fought like a six-foot-three man. She had a strong, lean, muscular body and knew how to work it.

Samara had brought in another friend to their little group, a male she worked with in the army named Fin. Initially, Luna thought that Samara had a thing for this guy, but she found out later he had a wife, Shaela. Both him and his wife hang out with them sometimes, along with Luna's brother, Aywin. Fin's dark-brown hair was always tied up in a bun, but when he let it flow, it went down to his mid-back.

He was a beautiful male Elf, with high cheek bones, soft features, thick, dark eyebrows, and light-blue eyes. He wore a goatee at the moment; he always had some sort of facial hair growing. Fin was also a great fighter. For his size, he was fast and smooth; at least that was what Samara had told Luna.

Luna didn't know much about the army. She didn't really understand why they had one. They never needed to use them; they'd never had any trouble in her lifetime. All the army did was train, day in and day out. Even Samara had mentioned to Luna the strangeness of having an army when there hadn't been a war in years. The last war was with the Plains clan, and that had been over a hundred years ago.

As she painted, Luna thought of Fin's wife, Shaela, who was a cute little thing. At five foot nothing, she looked like a child standing next to him. She had white-blonde hair that was curly and flowed down to her low back. Shaela mainly worked in the community gardens, doing some other outdoor work for the Elf communities, and she was funny. Luna definitely needed to see her friends soon; she could use their warmth and laughter.

Luna added a stroke of light green to one of the trees. She hadn't always been artistic. She begged her father to put her in lessons when she was a pre-teen. She wanted to learn how to paint and draw. She didn't draw much now. Her preferred style was landscapes and realism; she liked to do both. She loved to capture natural elements. She was never able to create something that she hadn't quite seen before. Luna set the paintbrush down, then stood up and went to the kitchen to clean off her bowl and spoon.

For the rest of the afternoon before work, she read. She had thought about going for a run but had decided against it. She didn't feel like going to the gym today either; her mind was busy thinking about other things. Out of all the things to think about, her thoughts were on Darick.

What was he? Why was he here? Would his memory come back? All questions that she needed answers to. It was driving her mad. She wished she could explore space now. No matter how many times the Elves said it was dangerous, she didn't care. She was feeling her adventurous self coming out. The Science Base probably had hidden knowledge of space or even secretly housed spacecrafts of some sort. Aywin said he didn't know what other departments did, but she wondered if he might've heard something. Luna never tried to ask him about his work. To her, it would be unfair to put him in a position like that. Aywin hated lying, especially to people's faces.

She kept her loose top on and joggers and left the house. Time for work already. It was her last night shift, so she wasn't going to complain. She stopped at Edric's house around the time she knew he would be leaving. He was already outside, waiting for her. He smiled and strolled over. His hair was still wet from a shower he'd had after the gym. His shirt clung to his large arms and shoulders. His pants stretched out over his strong thighs. He dipped down and kissed her gently, his lips soft and tasting sweet. A strong, masculine smell of pine and peppermint wafted into Luna's nose.

"How did you sleep?" he asked as they made their way down the path.

"A lot better than I usually do. How 'bout you?" she asked.

He shrugged. "Not the greatest, but I hit the gym and feel better now. I had a hard time falling asleep after you left me."

She blushed. He obviously wanted to be intimate with her. Luna was aware of that during their little make-out session. It wasn't that she didn't want to; she just wasn't sure if she wanted to go there quite yet with him. It seemed too soon. He had literally just asked her out, and she didn't like to be pushed into things. Couldn't they just... take it slow?

"You'll just have to take a sleeping aid or something to help with the nerves," she teased.

He chuckled. "I'm not sure if that's what I need."

They continued chatting about their day. She told him about the different paintings she was working on.

"I'd love to see your paintings. How about tomorrow night?" he asked.

Luna almost said yes until she remembered she had dinner plans with her family. "I'm going over to my mom and dad's place," she replied.

He nodded, clearly disappointed. "The day after then? Let's go for a hike. I can meet you at your place. We can look at your paintings, and then we can go for a hike from there." He grinned.

The sides of Luna's lips curved up. "Sure, that sounds good."

They got to the prison and made their way to the staff-room. Luna's locker was in a separate row than Edric's, which was probably a good thing, or else she suspected he'd check her out as she changed. Or maybe he wouldn't… but knowing him, he would.

The two of them met at the door to the staffroom and turned on their radios. The guard in charge told Luna she was still responsible for Darick. Edric was placed in Section 1 today; he was going to have a fun night ahead, full of psychotic, dangerous, and gross Elves.

Luna walked down to Section 2. She relieved the guard that was standing by Darick's cell. The man left without saying more than a few necessary words to her. Now it was just her there. With a lack of airflow in the prison, the hallway smelled especially ripe today. She was told that Darick had been awake and pacing in his cell for most of the day, but when she came to the cell door, he was sitting on his bed. He peered up at her with those intense gold eyes.

"You're back," he stated.

Luna nodded. "Unfortunately."

She swore she saw Darick smirk. His dark mischievous look had faltered for just a second. She looked down at the food tray on the floor. They must have decided to start feeding him already. He hadn't touched it.

"Don't like the food?" she asked.

She didn't blame him; it was disgusting mush. He stared at her and didn't answer. She tore her eyes away. "So, do you remember anything else about yourself?" she asked, but he remained silent. His eyes now staring down at the food.

"Darick?" she questioned, her tone more forceful.

He looked up. "You're the only one that calls me by my name," he stated. His voice sounded hoarse.

Her chest fluttered. "What do you mean?" she said, the words a whisper.

"They call me 'the thing,' 'it,' 'monster,' 'creature'... I guess they aren't wrong. Why do you call me by my name?"

Luna hadn't realized she was the only one doing this; she was humanizing him, feeling pity for him. She had never felt that way or did that for a prisoner before. She didn't respond to Darick. She wasn't sure what to say. Instead, she turned and looked down the hallway. The cells were at least twenty feet away from each other. Not all of them were full. There weren't that many sickos, thankfully. The distance between them was so prisoners couldn't talk without yelling, and if they yelled, then the prison guards would hear. Twice a week, certain prisoners were allowed to go to the courtyard, where they could interact with each other, though they were heavily guarded.

"So, you like to read and draw?" Darick's voice pipped up from the cell.

Luna was so busy staring off into the darkness that he jolted her out of her trance. She must have been more tired than she thought; so much for the "long" sleep she'd had. "Yeah," she responded, unsure why he was asking.

He nodded. "I think I remember liking to read. Books about true things, nonfiction," he explained.

Luna raised her eyebrows. He liked to read? He didn't come off as a reader to her.

"I like fiction," she said, "but I read nonfiction every once in a while."

Darick nodded. The expression he wore was still stern; he was always alert. His eyes flickering into the darkness around her. She swore his eyes glowed at times.

"So, are you going to eat?" she asked again. Darick glanced up at her. He looked hungry. She wondered if he'd eaten today at all.

"I don't eat that," he said, and had a look of revulsion on his face as he peered down at the tray. He stood up and pushed the tray hard. It slid under the cell door and to Luna's feet. She sighed and picked it up. The indistinguishable food reeked of something pungent. She set it closer to the wall.

"I don't know what you ate on your planet, but we likely don't have it. So, you're just going to have to deal with eating our food," she stated clearly. He scoffed.

"What?" Luna asked while narrowing her eyes. She was annoyed with his attitude. He grumbled and shook his head.

"Are you going to try and kill yourself through starvation?" she questioned in a snarky tone.

She was right up to the cell's bars. Darick moved quickly. He had grabbed her by the front of her armour before she even had time to comprehend. Her reflexes were fast, but she stood there frozen as this man's strong hand gripped the armour between her breasts. He was breathing hard. She hadn't been this close to him yet. His mouth was parted enough to see the bottoms of his fangs. She wondered if his kind developed the fangs for fighting purposes. He smelled like a morning after it rained—surprising for a guy who hadn't showered for who knows how long and was covered in dried blood. She could smell a hint of that too, which made her stomach lurch.

His eyebrows were clenched, and he appeared to be in pain, like he was fighting something. His eyelashes were dark and thick; his pupils dilated. The hand that was holding on to her was trembling. He let go of her and stepped back into the cell. He was shaking. She was shaking too. Why didn't he kill her? She knew he could've. She stepped back, her legs wobbling, and she fell back onto her ass, then scooted against the wall on the other side of the hallway.

He let out a deep roar; it echoed. Luna felt it rumble through her, and it terrified her. What was he? What was wrong with him? Darkness and power radiated from his being as he stood in the cell, furious. Should she tell the other guards what happened? Frankly, she was embarrassed that she'd trusted him and been so close.

"Darick? Are you… okay?" she asked.

He really did look unwell. He was all sweaty. His face shot a look of rage towards her.

"You need to leave," he growled.

Her legs had gained their strength back and she stood up, her heart pounding wildly in her chest. "I'm not leaving. I'm stationed outside your cell." Her voice boomed with authority.

Darick bared his fangs at her and growled, "I said, you need to leave!"

Luna jumped back. She flicked on her radio. "Someone available to come to section two. It's Luna. I need a break," she said.

The radio fuzzed out before a voice spoke back. "Yep, I can head over." Luna put her mouth close to the speakers and said, "Send two."

***

Two guards arrived within a few minutes. One guard eyed Luna as they got closer. "Everything all right?" he asked.

They both peered over at Darick in the cell. He was huddled in his bed, ignoring them.

Luna nodded sternly. "Fine. Just safer if there's two of you."

Why had she lied? There was obviously something wrong with Darick. And she was worried to leave just one guard there. Her body felt on edge from fear. She needed to go and eat something to separate herself from him.

"I won't be long," she said, and left.

Luna went up to the staffroom; the lights were still on. Too early for nap breaks, she thought. She grabbed her snacks and almost ate them all. Her mind was racing. What the hell should she do? She didn't want to look after Darick anymore. He officially freaked her out. She spent a few more minutes taking some calming breaths and creating a plan in her head. She decided she was okay. She could handle it. It was not like she hadn't dealt with fear before. She'd seen some horrific things in this prison. She was strong. Her father had trusted her to deal with this, and she would.

When Luna returned to Darick's cell, the two guards were chatting away. They hadn't noticed her.

"Okay, I'm back," she said.

One of the guards jumped. "Ah shit, you're quiet." He laughed.

Luna forced a half smile. "Uh-huh. You guys can go. Thanks for coming."

The two guys exchanged a look of confusion and then left. She wondered if they were suspicious. She slid down against the cold wet cement wall and sat down on the floor. Her head felt pressured; a headache was certainly coming on. This was going to be a long night. Usually, she could do rounds and deal with the occasional yeller, but with just having one guy to watch, the night was going to be painful. She groaned and rubbed her eyes. She better not fall asleep on the spot.

A few hours went by, and she had taken out some cards and was playing with them in the dark. The closest candle to her was down the hallway, too far to be of any help. Luckily, an Elf's eyesight was decent enough in the dark, so she could see the cards well. As she played, she heard footsteps clicking towards her. She turned to the right and saw Edric coming over. He made eye contact with her and gave her a wink. She stood up and patted down her pants; they were covered in dirt.

He studied the playing cards on the ground.

"Bored much?" he stated.

Luna shrugged. "When there's only one prisoner and you can't leave, you resort to playing games to stay awake."

He grinned. He had a mischievous look in his eyes as he pulled her into an embrace. The warmth of his body collided with her cold armour.

"Edric... not here," she whispered.

He gave off a playful smile. "What are the prisoners going to do? Tell on us? Besides, I've been thinking about you none stop," he whispered back.

He reached around with both hands and lifted her hips up on his. He spun around and pushed her against the wall. He was so strong that she felt weightless in his grasp. His mouth met hers and he kissed her passionately. Her core heated and she kissed him harder, their tongues tangling. Luna then realized what she was doing. What was wrong with her? She was at work.

She broke their kisses. "Edric, we have to stop," she said firmly. He shook his head and began to kiss down her chest.

She put a hand on his chest. "I'm serious," she stated.

He continued to kiss and grind against her, his hands exploring her body. He reached one hand up to try and cup her breast. She shoved him, but he didn't stop. "Edric stop," she said again, her voice coming out shaky. He was strong; he wouldn't budge. The feeling of his hands on her body now revulsed her. At this point, she could hear him unzipping his pants. She was becoming mad—she had told him no. She was about to shove him again when a voice caught her attention first.

"How 'bout you get the fuck off her before I tear your throat open," Darick snarled.

He was standing right by the cell bars, gripping onto them, his knuckles white and his teeth bared. He was furious. Edric let go of Luna and turned towards Darick.

Edric let out an arrogant laugh. "How 'bout you shut the fuck up and mind your own business?" he replied; his hands were clenched into fists. "What are you going to do from in that cell, huh? You can't get out, and even if you could, I'd kill you within seconds."

Luna stayed against the wall, shocked at the situation.

"Let me out and we will see who kills who first," Darick growled.

Edric let out another laugh, which got on Luna's nerves. He turned towards Luna. "When did IT start talking so much?" he asked.

"Edric, I think you need to go," she said, her voice sounding stronger than she thought it would.

Edric scoffed. "Seriously? You're asking me to leave?"

Luna sighed. "Edric, just let me do my job. We'll talk later," she said.

Edric stared at her for a few seconds. She couldn't tell what he was thinking. He looked annoyed, but there was a mix of emotions. He scoffed again and took off walking angrily down the hallway.

Luna burst into tears. She never cried; why was she crying? She shook and sobbed for what felt like forever, her whole body vibrating. Would he have forced himself upon her? Edric? Her friend? She sobbed some more. Her body began to relax. Her eyes felt puffy and red. She took some deep breaths. She finally lifted her gaze up to the prisoner's cell.

Darick was standing there; his eyes looked sad. He was watching her with a look of concern. She looked down at her watch; it was nearly seven a.m., almost time for the end of her shift. She heard a guard walking down the hallway. She rubbed her eyes, hoping that he wouldn't be able to tell that she'd been crying. When he reached her, it was too dark for him to see her face, even with Elven eyesight. For that, she was thankful. She handed off the report and then left. She was scared that she was going to run into Edric, but she never did. She left work and walked home quicker than normal.

She huddled into her bed sheets; her chest felt tight and her heart cold. A strange numbness had fogged over her brain.

Luna had fallen asleep for a couple hours and woke up around noon. Her eyes were dry and heavy from crying. She took a shower and dressed in joggers and a baggy T-shirt. She didn't want to go to her parents' today. Her heart was aching, and she was so upset about what had happened. She couldn't believe Edric had done that. Was she overreacting? Maybe she was overthinking things and shouldn't be so upset about it. She sighed. She wasn't hungry but felt nauseous. She grabbed one of her many books she had half-finished and began to read. Reading helped her escape. Reading provided her with a different reality.

She sat for what felt like hours, reading until her mind was distant and she had no more brain power left to take in information.

She looked at the time. "Ah shit," she mumbled.

She had to be at her parents' place in a half hour, and it usually took her at least an hour to walk there. She could use a run anyways. She changed into a set of tight, breathable exercise pants and a loose top. She tied her hair back into a bun and headed out the door with a pair of runners. It was a dry and sunny day outside; no sign of rain. Thank God. She didn't feel like getting soaking wet.

A faint smell of flowers bloomed in the air, likely from her neighbourhood garden. She stretched quickly before setting off at a good pace up the trail. Her parents' place was towards the prison, but instead of heading straight on the trail, you had to take a hard right into the forest. They had a large treehouse that weaved around the trees. It had a big deck that circled the whole house and came down to the ground.

She turned right and onto the trail, continuing her jog. She was there in a few minutes—not too shabby. She walked up the ramp to her parents' home, breathing heavily from her run, her skin glistening from sweat. Strings of light, connecting the deck to the trees above, lit up their home, making their place look magical. She had to admit her mother had good taste. Her father was outside, leaning against the railing of the deck and smoking a cigar. His large body looked wrong with all the petite décor around him. His hair was fiery red.

He was looking at her, smiling. "Nice of you to come by, my daughter," he said.

Luna smiled back. She went over and gave him a big hug. The smell of his cigar reminded her of childhood. It comforted her so much that she almost began to cry. Her emotions had been running ramped. She pushed back the tears.

She let go. "Is Aywin here yet?"

Her father nodded. "He's inside, helping Mom with dinner. You know how he loves to cook."

Luna rolled her eyes. "Ugh, what a weirdo," she replied.

They both laughed and stepped inside. Unlike Luna's home, her parents' house had high ceilings and big windows, making the place look ten times more spacious than it was. The design of their home was open concept, so when the pair walked in, Luna saw Aywin and her mom in the kitchen frying vegetables and laughing away. A rich aroma of spices wafted into her nose.

Her mom caught her eye. "My sweet daughter, nice of you to join. Why on Nexus are you so sweaty?" she asked, raising her eyebrow.

Luna laughed. "I jogged here," she replied.

Her mom sighed. "Always exercising."

Her mom looked even more petite than usual. She was wearing a black dress that flowed down to her knees. She truly was a beautiful woman. Her father went and stood beside her mom to give her a kiss on the forehead.

"Of course, you show up when the work is all done," Aywin called out from the kitchen.

Luna sauntered over to him. He was resting his forearms on the counter and leaning forward. He looked too tall to be in this kitchen. Luna's mom had made the counters for her height.

"When did you get here?" Luna asked.

Aywin shrugged. "Around a half hour ago."

Luna gasped dramatically. "You? Early? What happened? Are you okay?" she asked sarcastically.

Aywin let out a little laugh. "Now, now, L. We both know that you aren't known for your timing either." He winked.

"How about we sit down and relax," her mother suggested. "Dinner will be ready shortly."

Luna and Aywin went into the living room and sat down on one of couches. Their parents followed them in and sat down as well. Luna's father leaned forward and rested his elbows on his knees.

"So, I hear you had two guards come out to watch the prisoner," he stated.

Rose gave Luna's father a playful smack on the side. "Now, no work-talk during family dinner," she retorted.

Luna did want to talk to her dad about it; she was curious about what they knew about Darick.

"I just don't trust him," Luna stated.

Her father nodded. "You afraid he's going to escape or something?"

Luna shrugged. "I just think he's capable of a lot more than we know. We don't even know what he is," she explained. Her father nodded.

Her mother gasped. "What do you mean, you don't know what this... prisoner is? You put our daughter in charge of a prisoner that's dangerous?" she asked with astonishment.

Luna sighed. Her mother had always been so protective. "Mom, it's fine. I can fend for myself. Besides, all the prisoners are dangerous. This guys just a mysterious dangerous since we don't know what he is," Luna said dryly.

"I just don't agree with it," her mom stated flatly. She crossed her arms and leaned back on the couch.

Aywin cleared his throat. "So, who is this prisoner?" he asked.

Luna waited for her father's response.

"It's… we aren't sure. He came from the sky, and that's about all we know. He's attacked a few guards, so we decided it'd be safer for the Elves if he was in the prison," he replied.

Luna shifted in her seat, suddenly unable to get comfortable. Why was she so nervous? "Have they found any info on the object he came down in?" she questioned.

Her father cracked his fingers, one by one. "I'm not sure. I don't think so," he said.

Luna leaned in closer. "There must have been something in there that would give us some info, right? Like, where he's from?"

Her father stopped cracking his fingers—thank goodness; she hated that sound. "Luna, you know our kind doesn't study other worlds. What would we find that would give us anything useful? He is obviously from another planet," he said.

Luna's mother looked at her. "What does he look like? Does he look like us?"

Luna nodded. "Yeah, other than the fact that he doesn't have pointed ears. His are rounded, which is strange." She decided to leave the part about his teeth out. She wasn't sure if her father wanted people to know that.

"Huh, weird," Aywin said, more to himself than anyone else. Although, his quietness astonished Luna. Usually, he would be all over something like this. Aywin was interested in absolutely everything. Luna had decided he was a genius since he was constantly studying books about all sorts of things.

Her mother jumped up. "Well, I believe dinner is ready! I'll put everything on the table." She forced herself to smile.

Luna and Aywin got up and helped her serve the food. She had made a delicious casserole dish with some home-made buns and a salad. Luna was practically drooling at the smell and sight of it all. They dug in right away. Luna ate way more than she should have; her stomach felt like it was going to explode. Her mother was an amazing cook. Aywin was a great cook as well. Whenever she went to his place for lunch or dinner, she tended to eat more food than she should.

They spent a while chatting about Aywin's work and how things were going. Her mother talked to her and Aywin about how they both needed to find a good relationship so she could have grandchildren. Luna laughed at this because she knew that Aywin was a workaholic and would rather have one-night stands. She, on the other hand, seemed to have bad luck with relationships. The conversation brought up memories of what had happened with Edric, which made her almost throw up. She needed to go home. She wasn't feeling well. She stayed for another hour or so before leaving. She was tired and needed to go to bed.

Thankfully, her stomach settled down right before she left. Nevertheless, the jog home was painful. Her legs were sore, and she felt like curling up in bed and passing out—which was exactly what she did once she got there.

***

Darick's head began to hurt again. Right at his temples. He'd had a few more of these weird memories popping up lately. Short and not sweet. His last one was of him as a child.

He was playing with this other male child, perhaps an older brother. They had been out in a field, laughing and throwing rocks. It had been a bright summer day. In the memory, he had heard a woman screaming. The brothers turned to see their father dragging a woman into his barn shed, her blood smearing a trail behind her. Her arms were stretched out as she called for help. Her voice carried out into the forest, where nothing could help her. Her eyes met with Darick's. They were full of fear.

The look of fear in another could either give one delight or sorrow. And Darick wasn't sure what he had felt, but his brother had stopped looking at the screaming woman. Instead, he had gone back to throwing rocks. It was just part of what their kind did. They killed things.

Darick's vision was blurring. No, not again.... He blacked out. His body swirling around, making him gag. He opened his eyes, but he was not in the cell. He was somewhere else.

Of course, another memory. This time, he was on a battlefield. There was blood everywhere, and his fangs throbbed to taste it. The smell was intoxicating. There were hundreds of bodies on the ground. The skies above were dark like a storm cloud, and the wind howled, whipping his hair from side to side. He felt pity within himself. He was grieving.... Why was he so sad? He was ashamed as well. What had they done?

He looked down at his hands; they were covered in blood. He held a blade in his left hand. Huh? Who knew he was left-handed. He felt a figure approaching him from the side, but his memory ended almost as quickly as it started.

His eyes fluttered open, and he was back to the cell. Back to reality.

His head still ached. He rolled onto his side and cursed. His stomach ached; he was so hungry. If he didn't eat something soon, he was going to break.

***

Luna yawned. She had woken up this morning with a bunch of energy. It had been her day to do garden work, and she'd finished it all by nine a.m. She stood on her little deck, drinking a coffee. She grabbed the radio that she had brought outside and dialed it to Samara's number.

Samara answered immediately. "Yo, what's up?" she asked.

Luna sipped her coffee. "Well, I was bored and thought I'd see what you're up to today."

Samara laughed. "How about you come over to my place? We can maybe go for a hike or something from here?"

Luna thought for a second. Did she feel like hiking? Not really. But she should get out and get some fresh air.

"Sure thing. Be there in twenty," Luna replied.

She finished her coffee and rinsed out her cup. She changed into a pair of cargo pants and a breathable tank top. It looked like it was going to be another nice, non-rainy day. She walked to Samara's house at a quick pace.

Her house was smaller than Luna's. It stood by itself, without a tree, and sat up high on a hill. It overlooked one of the many lakes that covered Nexus. Luna liked going over to Samara's because of the view. It was utterly gorgeous. She stood there in awe.

"Hey, jackass," Samara called. "Stop staring into space," she teased, and jumped down from the ladder up to her place.

She wore a white tank top with a green pullover and a set of cargo pants. They dressed very similarly. Luna pulled her into a big hug. Samara felt cozy and warm against Luna's chest. Her touch took away the hollowness inside her. Another image of Edric popped up in Luna's mind, and she pushed it aside.

"How's things been?" Samara asked. Her earrings reflected the sun behind Luna. They broke the hug and smiled at each other.

Luna scratched the back of her head. "You heard about that guy that came down from the sky?" she asked.

Samara nodded, her expression turning serious. "Yeah, killed my men."

Luna shuffled her feet nervously. She didn't want to say too much. "He's a prisoner now. I'm in charge of him," she said.

Samara narrowed her eyes. "Okaaay…" She dragged out the word.

Luna felt tense. She wasn't sure what she was trying to say to Samara, but it wasn't wanting to come out. Luna sighed. "I just—I know he killed them. It's just… there's something strange about him and he lost his memories, and there's got to be a reason he's here, right?"

The reason she felt so nervous talking about this to Samara was because she knew how loyal Samara was to her Warriors, and there would be no pity on Samara's part for Darick. Luna also didn't want to tell Samara about what had happened to Edric. She was still questioning the encounter herself. Had he done something wrong, or had she been overreacting? Samara didn't even know that she and Edric had a thing for the last couple days.

Samara held her hand up. "Luna. I know you've always been empathetic, but I also know you're a level-headed gal. This guy's bad. Real bad. Nothing EATS Elves. He's dangerous," Samara explained sternly. Luna could see there was no arguing about the topic.

She continued to talk despite the tension and nodded. "I'm not saying he isn't dangerous. He terrifies me. I'm just... I don't know... never mind," Luna said in a flustered tone. She had gotten herself all worked up and needed to calm down. "Let's go for a hike and talk about something less... dreary," Luna suggested.

Samara snorted. "I don't think I know how to do that." She gave Luna a playful shove.

They went up the trail they often went to. It led up behind the lake and to a waterfall. Once you climbed up to the waterfall, the view from there looked over many communities. They chatted as they walked. Samara told Luna about how things have been at the army base; they were going well. She was teaching the Warriors, and they'd been creating new tactics and training programs. The fact that she was a big deal there made Luna proud of her. She had accomplished so much at such a young age.

They continued to hike up a steep part of the mountain. Luna's legs were burning from all the work she was putting them through. At one point, they were practically climbing up the mountain on their hands and knees—that was how steep it was.

Luna was covered in mud, which she didn't mind. She smelled of sweat and dirt. They reached the top and peered down at the waterfall. Heaps of fresh water gushed out of the mountain side. Luna smiled out at the view; her breathing had calmed down. The light breeze felt cold against her sweat. The two of them stared off at the town for a while. The silence was peaceful. Lush green forests covered the area; it was hard to see each neighbourhood due to the houses being built among the trees. Most of the communities were inside the little bowl of the land below them. The mountains surrounding the town for protection. Other communities were built beyond this cluster of Elves; the ride to those places took days.

In the distance, Luna could see the line of the scarred, burnt trees where Darick had landed. Samara caught her gaze, and they both stared at this spot.

"Do you think there will be more?" Samara whispered. Luna almost couldn't hear her, it was so soft.

"I sure as hell hope not," Luna replied honestly.

They climbed back down from the mountain. Their shoes were caked in mud. Luna felt like her feet had two-pound weights attached to them. They got to Samara's place and left their shoes outside. They went into the house. Both stripped down at the front door. Samara went to her room and came back with a baggy shirt and joggers; she threw them at Luna. Luna changed into the clothes, which smelled like fruit. Samara changed as well. They both plopped down onto the couch.

"Who knew we would get so muddy?" Samara laughed.

Luna scoffed. "Um, I'm pretty sure we both knew." And they laughed again.

Samara got up and poured some wine for the two of them. Red wine was Luna's favourite. Samara handed Luna a glass and then sat down with hers. Luna took a long sip. The sweet taste glided down her throat like honey. Samara rested her face on her arm propped up against the couch.

"So," Samara said. "Who's the guy?"

Luna choked on her wine and started coughing.

"Sorry, didn't mean to almost kill you." Samara laughed, and sipped her wine.

Luna shook her head. "Why do you think there's a guy?" she asked.

Samara shrugged. "I can just tell. You seem… distant? I assume it's guy problems."

Luna grumbled. Of course, Samara had good instincts; her job was to analyze others and train them. Luna shifted herself on the couch. She snuggled into the warm fur blankets and got comfortable before going into her Edric thing.

"Uhm… Edric and I," she started, and then Samara squealed. Luna sighed. Samara's eyes widened and then calmed down.

Luna took a deep breath again. "Edric and I had a bit of a thing going for a few days. Nothing really. It ended quickly," Luna explained.

She didn't want to talk about it; she didn't even want to think about it right now. The thought of Edric made her stomach sick. He wasn't who she thought he was. At least, not at this moment. Samara could see the hurt in Luna's eyes, and then she became angry.

"What did he do?" Samara questioned, rage boiling in the back of her throat.

Luna threw her hands up. "Nothing. I just got uncomfortable; that's all. I guess, I'm just not interested in him."

Samara took another sip of wine. "Luna, you are going to have to explain this a little better. How could you not be interested in Edric? If you look up gorgeous in the dictionary, his face is there. He's one of the hottest Elves I know. Fuck, I'd get with him if I could; he's just never made a move."

Luna felt stupid now. Was it just her? Was she being weird? She had also just outright lied to Samara about the entire situation.

"I'm not sure. He kissed me, and I didn't like it," Luna said.

Samara frowned. "Like, the first time he kissed you? When did he kiss you?" she asked.

Luna looked down at her wine glass and realized she had almost finished the thing. She felt tipsy already from the lack of food. "No… like, I did like it when he kissed me. You know what? Never mind. I don't want to talk about it. I'm still fresh out of the situation, and I still need to think about… him," she said. Luna watched as Samara contemplated saying more; she could see her thinking, her hands tapping against the side table.

"Okay, fine. I won't push it. But you'll have to tell me at some point… once you figure your shit out. When was the last time you had sex anyways?" Samara asked.

Luna groaned. "Oh my goodness, Samara," she complained. She did not feel like talking about her sex life.

Samara laughed. "What? I'll tell you when I did: last month with that guy who works at the bar. But you already know that. And I hate getting involved with guys from my work because that doesn't play over well, so I have to find them… elsewhere."

Luna chuckled at Samara's words. Samara didn't actually get around much. The guy from the bar was the first time she'd had sex in months. And she probably would go awhile without it.

"I'm not interested in sex with Edric," Luna said. She didn't really mean for the words to come out, but they did.

Samara gasped. "Um, say what now? You really don't find him attractive, do you?" Samara asked.

Luna finished off her wine. "I find him extremely attractive. He's just a friend, though. Always has been. We work together, Samara. He and I work together. We can't be screwing around anyways." She narrowed her eyes at Samara. "You just got me to talk about him again. Let's go onto another topic…. How about how you need to clean your place better?" Luna said while looking around Samara's house.

It was bad. She had clutter everywhere, and it made Luna anxious just looking at it all. It was worse than her place. Samara wasn't dirty in the sense of gross food and unclean dishes and dusty tables. It was more about her organization skills—they were horrific.

"You know what," Samara said, "I think you are jealous at how I know exactly where everything is and it's all organized in my own way." She finished her wine and smacked her lips together.

Luna laughed. "Yeah, I think we both know that's not true," she joked.

They talked for a few more hours before Luna decided that she should get going. She was tired and a little tipsy after finishing her second glass of wine. Samara poured big glasses. Luna didn't drink much either, so she was a light-weight.

***

As Luna walked back to her place, she hummed a song to herself until, only a few feet from her ladder, she heard a male's voice behind her.

"Luna?" he said.

It was Edric. Luna swung around to face him. He walked up to her; his strong pine smell filled her nose. The smell revulsed her now. His face was a picture of perfection, though his expression was stern. He appeared pissed off. Was he drunk? She could see him swaying a bit, and she could smell whiskey. She was also tipsy, so maybe she was just imagining things, although you normally don't hallucinate when drinking alcohol. At least, not to Luna's knowledge.

She put her hand on her hip. "What can I do for you?" Her eyes narrowed.

He had stepped closer; his height was overwhelming. His arms came around her waist and pulled her tight against him. His mouth found hers, and he began to kiss her with a force she'd never experienced. She was shocked and didn't move at first. His hands explored her body, pushing her up against him.

"Edric," she protested.

"I know you want it," he groaned against her mouth.

She pushed against his chest just like in the prison, but he wouldn't budge. "Edric, I said stop!" she said again.

He pushed her up against the ladder. "I'm going to take you right here," he whispered harshly into her ear.

She was still in shock, but once the shock dissipated, she stepped back and swung her fist. It landed firmly against the side of his face. He stumbled backwards and fell on his ass. She looked at her knuckles, which were bleeding and throbbing.

"What the fuck?" he said, holding his jaw.

Luna narrowed her eyes. "What's wrong with you? Coming here and trying to pull that shit on me again? I'm not interested, Edric!" she snapped, then climbed up the ladder to her house.

She closed the door and locked it, then began to sob. In that moment, she knew what he did was wrong. He would've continued if she hadn't sucker-punched him. Her face was tight from the salty tears. She washed herself in the shower, trying to get the smell of pine and whiskey off her skin.

For the rest of the evening, she worked on a painting, one she'd never done before. It was dark, inspired by the forest at night. She shivered thinking about Edric. He scared her. He scared her more than any of the prisoners ever had. Because he was free.... He was free and he disguised what he was so well that he'd tricked Luna.

Chapter VI

The rest of Luna's days off went by quickly. She spent a lot of time at the gym or out in the gardens. She was trying to distract her mind, but nothing helped much. She often woke from nightmares about Edric in the night. She did end up getting together with Samara again, along with the rest of the group. They went out to the bar and had some food. She didn't have anything to drink, just water.

The night of her last day off, Luna groaned as she thought about having to get up for work the next day. She was nervous about seeing Edric and hoped they wouldn't run into each other. He hadn't stopped by since the last incident, and she was hoping he'd keep it that way. He was the only friend she had at work, and now he was gone. She grieved this a bit. She hadn't realized what type of man he'd been. She almost wished they hadn't taken the steps to starting a relationship because then she never would've seen that side of him. He hid it well. Too well. She closed her eyes and fell asleep.

Her alarm blared at her to wake up. She spent some time eating breakfast and enjoying the peaceful sound of rain.

She made sure to put on a rain jacket before she left for work. It was a cooler morning. She could see her breath in the air. When she passed Edric's house, she made sure to speed walk by it, just in case he came out, though she had left earlier than usual so that she wouldn't run into him.

After she arrived at the prison, she went to her locker and changed. Today was the day that certain prisoners got their free pass to the courtyard. She still had to talk to her father about whether Darick was going to be allowed out for that. She went to the prison kitchen and grabbed some food for Darick, as that was part of her job normally on her day shifts.

One of the other guards had given her a report about how Darick was doing. Apparently, he was acting well-behaved and hadn't caused trouble. They even let him out yesterday to shower and clean his cell. The only thing was he still hadn't been eating or drinking. Luna thought that was strange; it worried her. He was probably trying to starve himself, just like she had suspected. It wasn't a foreign thing to her; they'd had prisoners do that in the past. Usually, dehydration took them first.

She took the food up to Section 2. Darick was doing exercises in his room. He looked sicklier for sure; lack of nourishment did that. He caught Luna's eyes and stopped his exercises. His striking features shocked Luna. He had showered, so his hair and body were clean. The dried blood was gone. He looked… good. Actually, he was really good-looking, but Luna was trying to ignore this. His eyes were intense, and his face seemed always fixed in an expression of vengeance.

"You're back," he stated. His voice was deep and coarse. Luna smiled and slid the food tray under the cell.

"I am," she replied. "I do work here you know."

Darick made a manly grumbling sound as if he was agreeing with what she said.

"I hear you still aren't eating," she stated, and cocked her head to the side.

Darick growled—he actually growled.

"Okay then," Luna mumbled, thinking he was so strange. She stood closer to the cell and glared at him. "If you are going to kill yourself, at least do it quickly," she suggested.

Darick spun around and moved with lightning speed. He moved so fast, he looked a blur. Before she knew it, he had her hand in his and he was staring down at her bruised scabbed knuckles from punching Edric. She snatched her hand back. His eyes met hers, and they narrowed. It was like he was processing her thoughts.

She gulped. "You can't touch me," she said softly.

He took a deep breath before continuing with the different exercises he was doing. Luna frowned as she took a few more steps back. Why did he care about her hand? She took some relaxing, deep breaths to calm her heartrate down. Darick didn't seem to care or notice her behaviour.

A few boring hours went by, and Darick ignored her entire time. He slept for most of it. Luna had gone on a lunch break during one of his napping times and had gotten a guard to watch him. She hadn't bothered to get him lunch since he wasn't eating anything. The time was coming to let the prisoners out to the courtyard. She still hadn't heard back from her father, so she decided to click the radio and contact him directly.

"Sir?" she said. The line was silent for a few seconds.

"Luna, my daughter, what can I do for you?" he asked.

Luna pressed the button again. "Is the prisoner… Darick—is he allowed out to the courtyard?"

"Yes. He's been behaving himself. But you'll have to keep a close watch on him," he explained.

Luna nodded. "Okay. Copy that. Thank you." She let go of the button.

She handcuffed Darick and took him down the hallway towards the courtyard. She had given him a quick rundown of the rules—rules that were obvious to most, but for a lot of the prisoners here, they needed to be reiterated, the most important being no fighting unless someone attacked you first and you needed to defend yourself. It wasn't rare for fights to break out in the courtyard. Sometimes, she wondered why they allowed it to even happen. I guess, long ago, when the rules were made for the prison, they had decided they should be fair in some ways to the prisoners. Their life was terrible, and they needed some sort of social interaction or else they'd die from isolation. Or maybe it was to keep them alive longer so they could suffer longer?

Luna was walking behind Darick. He was a big guy, tall and muscular. She couldn't help but notice the power and stealthiness of his walk; it was like he was prepared for anything. When they arrived at the courtyard, she unlocked his handcuffs, but then put a taser necklace on him. This was for safety measures, just in case things got nasty; she hadn't enforced the muzzle on him. Darick just stared at her while she did this. The other prisoners were out walking around, some playing basketball, some standing in groups. Most of them looked forward to this day. The sun was out, but the ground was still wet from the rain earlier that day.

"Go on," Luna said.

She motioned for him to go and socialize; she wasn't sure what that meant for him. She felt like she was releasing a dog into the wild. His striking golden eyes scanned her again, making her feel exposed.

"Do I have to?" he asked. He looked annoyed.

Luna sighed. "No, but I'd rather you didn't just stand there and look lost. At least, go for a walk."

He gave her a stern nod and left. Other guards were all lined up around the fenced perimeter. Luna became one of the many guards watching.

Darick sauntered around the courtyard. She saw him taking deep breaths of fresh air. It made her think about how she did that every time she went outside. Hell, she was doing it right now. Luna didn't take her eyes off him. He was circling around towards her again. As he did so, she noticed movement from his side. A large man was walking towards him: one of the prisoners. She recognized him. A big, burly man, with a shaved head and tattoos covering his arms and chest. She swore the planet moved with every step he took. She couldn't quite remember what he was in for. Murder and theft, maybe? Drug dealing too. Her body began to release adrenaline, and she felt her chest tighten. She needed to warn Darick. She sprinted towards him. The other guards watched her go, not realizing what was about to happen.

The large man swung at Darick, who gracefully dodged the punch. Darick didn't retaliate. Instead, he stood there with a smirk on his face. Luna got out her taser, ready to whack the large man. She wondered who had the taser for the other prisoner's necklace. She had no control over him. He took another swing and then another at Darick, who was dodging them all. But Luna knew the big guy would get him eventually.

Darick saw Luna running towards them. She saw him open his mouth, probably to tell her to stop, but she was already pointing her taser at the man, who, at the same moment, noticed her coming. His foot came up and knocked the taser out of her hand before he contacted her chest with the same foot and booted her a few feet in the air. She skidded against the ground, her arms and hands tearing on the cement. The wind was knocked out of her and she couldn't breathe. Luna choked and gasped for air that wouldn't come. She tried to make a sound with her voice, but nothing came out but wheezing. She heard yelling and voices around her, but her body was screaming for oxygen or else she was going to die.

Finally, her chest released the tension from the blow, and she was able to inhale. She gulped the fresh air down like water, then sat herself up, her arms burning in the process. They felt wet too. Her eyes found Darick. He was on top of the other guy, beating him so hard in the face that she could hear the other guy's jaw snap.

The guards were on Darick, zapping him and holding him to the ground. He stopped fighting them and just let them electrocute him until he couldn't feel his body. The pain was worse than anything he'd ever experienced before. Luna finally caught enough of her breath to speak. She stood up and ran for Darick. He'd done nothing wrong; he'd helped her.

"Stop!" she yelled to the other guards.

They had surrounded him and were still tasing him. One of them was Edric, and out of all the guards, he was using the most force. Anger boiled in Luna's veins. They were hitting Darick repeatedly, which would kill him if they kept going. She wasn't even sure he was going to live with the number of times they had already tased him.

"Stop!" she screamed again. They all paused, and a few looked at her. Edric booted Darick one last time in the side of his ribs.

"I'll take him back," she growled, her voice coming out with more authority.

The guards nodded. "You all right?" a guard asked. He peered down at her arms, which were covered in blood.

She didn't answer him. Instead, she helped Darick off the ground. He was heavy. His body was trembling from the tasers, and she could smell burnt hair. He stumbled when he stood upright.

Edric glared at Luna as she assisted Darick through the courtyard and back to Section 2. They arrived at his cell and hadn't said a word to each other. His eyelids were heavy. Four guards had tased him repeatedly, and just one zap could cause agonizing pain throughout someone's body, let alone multiple. More than one had even been known to kill a prisoner. Luna had seen it done before. She had no idea how Darick was still alive. Luna helped him onto his bed and to lie down. His eyes were clenched now, and he was still shaking. She took the taser collar off him, realizing she hadn't even handcuffed him on the way over.

"Darick, look at me. Can you open your eyes?" she asked.

She reached out her arm and saw him sniff the air. His eyes shot open, and he peered down at her hands and arms. Luna followed his gaze. Her injuries were gruesome; she needed some medical attention. The skin on her hands and along her forearms had torn off. She could see gravel and dirt embedded in her skin. It hadn't really started hurting until this moment.

Darick took her hand in his; it was the hand that she'd punched Edric with. The scabs on her knuckles had torn off and were bleeding too. The air smelled like iron. The blood had smeared all over her fingers and palms. He held her hand in his; his hands were callused but gentle. Her breath ceased. The way he touched her hand sent goose bumps across her body. He was looking at her with such intensity that she almost gasped. He took the bloodiest of her fingers and put it into his mouth. His bright-gold eyes closed, and she felt his tongue against her finger. It should have grossed her out, but instead she felt pleasure and her body tingled. His tongue licked off a few of her other fingers. The sensation was overwhelming.

He slid her finger out and opened his eyes. They were dark; his pupils dilated. "You need to leave," he ordered.

She pushed herself off the bed but didn't go.

"Leave," he said again, his voice shaky.

Luna hesitated. But she saw the darkness in his eyes. The need. Suddenly, a wind picked up around the room. It was so strong, it blew her hair out of her bun, and that scared her enough to leave the room. She backed away and closed the cell door. Darick stumbled onto the floor and began to shake. Luna almost began to unlock the cell when she heard guards coming down the hallway. She could see their shadows reflecting against the candlelight. There were a lot of them. Darick was huddled on the floor. He had stopped moving; his eyes were closed.

***

Darick opened his eyes. He was sitting in a chair staring at a man he knew was his father. He was young, just a child. His father had a stern look on his face. This didn't scare Darick; his father always had a stern look on his face, a look that told others that he could tear them apart in seconds. His father had sat him down to talk to him about something serious.

"Son," his father said in a deep and hoarse voice.

"Yes, sir?" Darick replied, not recognizing his own voice. It was so young and innocent.

His father was leaning against the wall of the room they were in. Darick recognized the room as his father's office. Well, his father's office for now. They were always moving around. Different planets, different homes. At this point in his life, they had only moved twice, but that was a lot to Darick.

"Your… abilities are beginning to surface, and it's time for me to train you," his father stated.

Darick nodded. He knew what his father was referring to. His abilities… the things that were happening that he couldn't control. The extreme cravings for fresh blood, for one. But also, the smashing of the windows without his fists having to go through them. The sudden gusts of wind. The darkness of the sky. The ability to get others to do what he wanted with some gentle persuasion. Darick noticed these things when his emotions got out of hand.

Darick opened his eyes gasping. He was back in the cell again. For the rest of the day, other memories of his childhood popped up, things that sickened him and made his heart feel cold. The taste of Luna's blood was still on his lips. So sweet, so addicting. It made his stomach cramp. He groaned for another taste of her, a proper taste. Shit… now just the smell of her was going to drive him wild.

***

The guards had surrounded Luna. Edric was one of them— yay for her. A man named Aaron held her arms; he was one of the doctors at the prison.

"Luna, you need some medical attention," he said with a worried look on his face.

She was still mystified about what had happened between her and Darick. "It wasn't his fault," she said too quietly for anyone to hear.

Aaron leaned in. "What did you say?"

The guards were still circling her. Luna paid no attention to Edric, but she could feel his eyes on her like daggers.

"I said, it wasn't his fault. Darick. He didn't start the fight. He was just… The other guy, he came at Darick, and I was just trying to help," she said, hardly recognizing the sound of her own voice. She was in shock. Aaron looked at the other guards.

Edric spoke first. "I'll stay and look after the… thing. He never should have been allowed into the courtyard. You go fix her up," he said to Aaron. His voice sounded calm, but she could sense the anger towards her. She didn't want him alone with Darick. What if he tried to kill him?

Luna shook her head, suddenly panicked. "No, you can't. Someone else needs to stay too."

Aaron tried to put his hands on her shoulders to calm her down. Edric gave her a sadistic smile. "She's in shock. You better take her Aaron," he said.

"No, I'm not!" she shouted.

The other guards stared at her with wide eyes. She realized now that she was acting bizarrely. Nobody there knew what had happened between her and Edric. They weren't going to take her seriously. She inhaled the stale air to lessen the panic. When she exhaled, her eyes tore into Edric's.

"Never mind, you're probably right," she said coldly.

Edric's eyes watched her like a predator. There was no way he would try and do anything to the prisoner; everyone would know it was him. Luna followed Aaron down the hallway. She noticed that another guard stayed with Edric and a wave of relief washed through her. Darick would be okay, she decided.

They got to the infirmary. Aaron guided her to a bed with white sheets. She sat down on it. Her brain still felt fuzzy, but her senses were clear now. Her breathing had calmed down. She watched as Aaron grabbed some medical supplies. He was getting water and disinfectant for her wounds when suddenly the door they had come through burst open with a loud thud. Her father stood there, his large body filling the doorframe.

"Luna," he said. He looked down at the torn skin on her arms. "I should never have let that… creature out in the courtyard! I should've known," he growled.

Her father came over and pushed a piece of hair out of her face. For such a large man, he was so gentle when it came to her.

She glanced up at him. "Dad it wasn't the prisoner's fault. He was about to be attacked by another prisoner, so I went in to stop it. I should've let the fight break out, but instead, I involved myself. It's entirely my fault I got hurt. I'll be fine."

She wasn't wrong. Prison guards were to leave fights between prisoners alone. If someone was about to die, then they would sometimes intervene, and then, they only intervened in a group. She had gone solo—against the rules.

Her father's eyes saddened. "Why put your life at risk for that… thing?" he asked. "I don't understand."

Luna shrugged and shook her head. "I'm not sure. I wasn't thinking to be honest," she said. "I just can't help but feel he's innocent in all this." She regretted the words as soon as they left her lips.

Her father's eyes turned to rage. "Innocent? Hardly! He murdered our people! For no reason at all!" her father snapped.

His anger pulsated through the room. Aaron froze in place over the counter where he had been assembling whatever medical stuff he was going to use on her arms.

"I was there! I saw them pull him out of that... flying object. He was probably scared! Thought someone was attacking him!" She pleaded for her father to understand, but all she saw was a deep hatred in his eyes for Darick.

"Normal people don't go around killing others, Luna. Would you bite someone's neck?" her father asked. The disgust in his tone was eminent.

"We don't know what he is," Luna said. At that moment, all the strength in her body dissipated. She felt weak, powerless, like nothing she could say would convince her father that the prisoner deserved something more than this.

Her father shook his head. "We know exactly what he is: he's a monster, Luna. He's just a monster that isn't from this planet. Do I need to take you off as his guard? Have you grown... attached?"

"No, I can do it," she replied.

With that, her father left the room. His rage was still felt after his exit. Luna exhaled and shook her head. What was she getting herself into?

Chapter VII

L una lay in the infirmary bed as Aaron worked on her arms. The process was anything but pleasant. She was wincing the entire time. The cuts were much deeper than she had originally thought. The chunks of skin the cement had taken out were gnarly enough to make her want to vomit. There must have been some jagged pieces sticking out of the ground in the courtyard that ripped her skin away as she slid across the ground. Her body shivered just thinking about it. Luckily, Elf medicine was highly advanced; her wounds would be healed within a week.

Aaron finished wrapping the bandages. "There, good as new," he said, smiling.

Luna looked down at her arms. "For fuck's sake, looks like I tried to kill myself," she murmured. Her lower arms were wrapped in white gauze and taped. "Thanks, Aaron. For everything. Sorry you had to listen to my father and I. We have… differing opinions sometimes," she said.

Aaron nodded. He was a bit older than her father. His hair used to be dark, but now tones of grey had set in. He was a nice man; always decent to work with. He had the jitters when he was too close to the prisoners, though.

Doctors always had guards with them when they worked on the prisoners anyways, but Aaron had dealt with a lot of stuff.

"You be careful," he said to Luna as she got up and opened the infirmary door.

"I always am," she said as she was leaving.

She walked back down to Section 2 as quickly as possible. The rain had picked up again outside and was pouring down the sides of the prison walls. As much as it sucked to work in, she liked the freshness it brought. Her boots were going to be soaked by the end of her shift. She pushed herself to walk faster; she had been gone too long and was worried about Darick.

When she turned the corner of the dark hallway, she could see Edric with the other guard. They were leaning against the wall, chatting away to each other. Thank God. She almost sprinted down the hallway. She hadn't really looked directly at Edric yet; she hadn't wanted to, but she decided to do it anyways. Her face tightened when meeting his, as perfect as it was. She immediately noticed the big swollen bruise on his cheek where she'd punched him and almost smiled at the thought. She hoped it hurt. The anger still simmered within her at what he'd done. Anger and guilt—a slow burning killer.

He noticed her staring at him and glared at her. "Prisoner's been quiet. Hasn't moved much. Unfortunately, we saw his chest rise, so he's still alive," Edric said dryly.

Vexation stirred up in her chest at the mention of Darick being dead. "Thanks. I can take it from here," she said with a coldness to her voice that she'd never heard before.

Edric scoffed. "Why does there need to be two of us, but only one of you? You should have another guard with you," he said sternly.

Luna took a step forward. She held her chin high and stared Edric directly in the eyes. "I don't trust others alone with him, but I trust myself. Arin put me in charge. Not you."

Edric gave her one last look up and down. "Come on, let's go," he said to the other guard, who had been dead quiet for their entire conversation.

The two of them walked away, and Luna couldn't help but smirk. Edric had turned into such an asshole as soon as he didn't get what he wanted. She flinched at the sudden reminder of Edric's slimy hands pushing her against the cold wall and not letting her go. She would never be able to look at that wall the same way again.

"Are you okay?" Darick asked. His voice didn't sound as hoarse as it usually did.

He was now standing up in the cell, leaning against the stone wall. He didn't look well at all. Luna couldn't believe he was asking if she was okay; he was the one who'd almost been tasered to death. At least, she just had some surface wounds that weren't even close to life-threatening.

"I'm all right. They'll heal up in a week," she said softly, and stretched out her arms with the bandages.

Darick looked down at the bandages, assessing how well of a job Aaron did. He gave her a slight nod. "Good."

A thought was clawing at Luna's mind. She stepped closer to the cell. "Darick?" She saw his body shake a little when she said his name and wondered if he hated her that much. She knew that she would hate the person who had her locked up. "What are you?"

There was a sudden stillness in the air, as if she'd said something wildly inappropriate and now no one knew what to say. She waited. Darick wasn't looking at her; his eyes were on the floor. His long dark eyelashes brushed gently against his cheeks. His raven hair was damp from the water on the wall.

"I'm not sure what you'd call me. I'm no Elf," he murmured.

It wasn't the answer Luna wanted. She wished he would tell her everything. She wanted to know everything about him. She was curious. What had he been through? What planet was he from? Why did he come here? All the things that troubled her and kept her mind racing.

She stepped away and looked down at the clock. She had a couple more hours of her shift left, but she wanted to go home now. She was exhausted, and her arms were throbbing now. She looked down the hallway on each side, and all was quiet and empty. She began to walk, then paced back, and forth, back and forth... It helped take her mind off the pain in her arms and the pain in her heart. She technically wasn't allowed to leave Darick alone, but there was no way he was escaping, and at the end of the day, she almost wanted him to escape.

As soon as it was time to go, she headed home. It was still pouring rain outside. The wind had picked up, and thunder and lightning lit up the sky in the distance. Luna walked down the path, smiling and listening to the power of thunder. She was always in awe of how much the planet shook from the power it created. A beautiful thing. She got home and showered before sliding into her cool, soft bed sheets. She pulled out her radio and dialled it to her brother's channel.

"Aywin?" she asked.

"What?" he answered within a few minutes.

She rolled over onto her back. "I think Dad hates me." She was upset about the fight they'd had. She had been upset about a lot of things lately. Her body was starting to feel too tight in her own skin.

"Dad could never hate you," he said with a caring tone.

Luna sighed. "He and I had a disagreement. And I still strongly disagree with him. I'm not sure what to do," she explained.

Aywin was quiet for a moment. All she could hear was the fuzz of the radio. "What was the disagreement?" he asked.

Luna hesitated. Should she tell her brother about the situation? He and Samara were the only two people she would consider talking to about it.

"You know that prisoner guy who came from the sky?"

"Yeah," her brother replied.

"I… I don't think he's as bad as we've been making him out to be. I think there's something bigger going on than we don't know about. I'm just not sure what. And he isn't telling us shit. But I wouldn't either if I was locked up. I also don't think he has all his memories because he injured his head on the way down," she explained carefully.

She was scared Aywin was going to interrupt her and say, "No way! Stay away from him!" But he didn't. He listened.

And then when Luna was finished talking, he waited a second to see if she had anything more to say.

"Luna," he said sternly, "you've always had good instincts. ALWAYS. Trust them. Stop second-guessing yourself. If Dad doesn't agree, there's not much you can do about that. He runs the place. But just do what you can do," Aywin said.

His response made Luna want to cry and hug her brother. She loved him so much; he was always helpful in situations like this. Any conflict she had in her life, she phoned her brother. He was calm and thought clearly. Just like Samara. Samara had been pissed about Darick, though, but he did kill her Warriors.

"Have I ever told you that you're my favourite brother?"

She heard him laugh from across the radio.

"Thank you, Aywin. I guess I better get to sleep now. Another day tomorrow," she said.

She rolled back onto her side just as Aywin spoke again. "Have a goodnight, L, and don't let your mind ruin your sleep. Everything works itself out with time."

She fell asleep with the radio static still on. When she woke up at some random point in the night, she turned it off and then fell asleep again. She didn't worry. She had peaceful dreams that she wouldn't remember when she woke up.

***

Luna's alarm went off, and she did her usual yawn and total body stretch on the bed. It was a new day. She could hear the rain on the roof again. She made a mental note to wear her boots so her runners wouldn't get muddy. She got up and got ready. She ate a small breakfast; her appetite wasn't around. She was thinking about Darick. Wait… Darick? Why was she thinking about him? She didn't even clue in until she realized she was thinking about his voice… and his eyes… and his mouth. Oh gosh. That wasn't going to happen. Her mind was just playing tricks on her. She must still be in shock with all the things going wrong around her.

Her chest still felt heavy, and the hollowness within was present. She shook her head and continued to get dressed. She wore a pair of joggers today and a big baggy hoodie— something to keep her comfy and warm. She pulled a light raincoat over top of her hoodie and then headed out the door with her work bag.

It wasn't pouring anymore but dribbling, the odd rain-drop hitting her little nose on the way down. A strong smell of dirt and earth hovered in the air. She speed walked to work, making sure to leave early again so she wouldn't run into Edric.

She walked into the locker room to change; there were others there too, some coming to work, some leaving. Luna realized she needed to make some other friends at work. Her only real work friend had been Edric. She had always been worried that any guy she'd become friends with here would eventually have a crush on her and it would ruin things. She must be psychic because that was exactly what happened. She decided to make the survival choice and be a loner at work—that would be best.

She was just heading out the door when she ran straight into Edric. Initially, he appeared apologetic, but once he saw it was her, his face turned sour. They both stood there in silence. Some others came in through the door, forcing Edric to move. She was thankful, as it was her chance to squeeze through the door and escape. Free from the situation, she took a few deep breaths. The tightening in her chest worsened, and she felt like her heart was having palpitations.

Today, she didn't bother grabbing Darick's breakfast; she had something entirely different planned. She had spent most of the morning thinking about him and was determined to make him talk. As she walked to his cell, her arms throbbed. They'd been hurting on and off. She was fine, though. Her pain tolerance was high. No blood was coming through the bandages, so her cuts must've scabbed well.

As she arrived down the hall to Darick's cell, she noticed only one guard there. Her father must've ultimately decided he didn't need two. Either that or they were short-staffed. She and the other guard did a quick hand-over report. Darick had been up most of the night apparently and was scheduled to see the doctor today because of how sickly he was becoming. Aaron was coming to assess him around ten a.m. Luna said her goodbyes to the guard, who gave her a little salute as he left.

"Good morning, Elf girl," Darick said.

Luna was surprised that he sounded so… boastful and playful. He was usually grumpy and angry.

She frowned. "I thought you'd be dead by now."

She wasn't even joking. By how unwell he was beginning to look, she wondered if there was something in the air that was slowly killing him. He had a constant sweat on his body now; his forehead always appeared damp. She heard him make a low grumbling noise. He had been sitting in his bed, but now he got up and walked over to the cell bars. His hands casually held onto them as he leaned forward. His dark hair fell over his face, and his bright-gold eyes flickered with mischief.

"I'm not sure if you've noticed, but it's hard to kill me," he said, an obstinate expression on his face.

Luna rolled her eyes and then walked right up to the cell. He let go and took a step back.

"What?" She furrowed her brows. Then she saw the darkness in his eyes and knew it was time to ask.

"Darick." She spoke gently. "You... don't eat food, do you?" It sounded stupid coming out of her mouth. She hadn't expected a response. Her mind began to race, and she decided she wasn't going to continue the conversation.

"No shit," he said. The way he looked at her made her think he wanted to devour her, which was slightly unnerving but also made her curious.

"Blood, right?" she said finally, her throat dry. "You... drink blood?"

His eyes darkened more. She was right up against the cell bars, but he had moved across his cell, pressing himself against the back wall.

"You need it, don't you? Or else you'll die?" she questioned. Luna wasn't sure what she was getting at, but she felt pity for this man. He had saved her twice, and she felt that he didn't need to be here. "That's why you attacked those Warriors, right? You were hungry?"

He still wasn't responding. Instead, he stared her down; his face had scrunched up into a look of need. She'd seen the same look on men's faces before.

Finally, he made a move: he nodded his head. Luna felt a heavy weight lift off her chest. Whatever he was, he was going to die unless she gave him her blood. Nobody else would understand, and even if they did, they wouldn't do it for him. Luna took a quick look down both sides of the hallway before she opened the cell door. She didn't really know what she was doing, why she was being so… irresponsible, but she did it anyways.

"Luna," he said. He sounded like he was begging her not to come in. But it was too late. She already had. She walked up to the large man. His body was still pressed against the wall as he stared her down.

He finally took a step towards her until their bodies were almost touching; the static between their clothes sent chills through Luna's body. He was breathing heavily; the warm air tickled Luna's neck. He was so close.

"You can, you know. I'll let you if you need it," she whispered.

"You need to go," he said, just like yesterday.

But she wasn't going to back down today. She turned her neck to the side. "It's okay. I want to help you," she murmured.

He let out a low growl. "Luna," he pleaded.

"You don't scare me," Luna replied.

Darick's mouth parted, his fangs visible. "Try saying that without trembling," he growled, and with that, his head came down and he bit into her neck.

He moaned at contact and began to drink from her. The initial bite was painful; her body stiffened up at the jolt. But a second later, she felt a warmth down the side of her neck, and it went through her whole body. It was the most pleasurable experience she'd ever felt before; it heated her core, tingled her breasts, and made her ache for more. She couldn't help but let out a moan.

Darick had grabbed onto her body and held it tight as he drank. The blood filled his body with the nutrition that he had needed for days. Would he control himself? But it felt so good. She felt so good. His body hardened against her, and he couldn't help but let out another growl. He was taking too much; he needed to stop. She could sense the feel of her body against his was throwing him over the top. He spun her around and pushed her up against the cell wall. She let out a moan in response. His hands slid down to her hips, and she pushed back into him, wanting more. His mind was crazed as her blood poured into his mouth and flowed into his body. Neither knew how much time went by, but her body began to sag slightly in his grip and it snapped him out of the frenzy. He stopped drinking from her, and then took his tongue and licked the two puncture marks on her neck. He had the ability to heal the cuts with his saliva, so he did. She shivered as his tongue glided across her skin. She was leaning into him.

"Luna?" he said. "Luna, are you okay?" he whispered.

His body was shaking with the strong urge to bite into her again. Her beautiful blueish-purple eyes lazily met his. He let go of her and backed himself up against the cold cell wall before he devoured her.

Luna had a hard time keeping herself upright. He'd taken a lot of blood, too much. Her vision was blurry. He had spoken to her, but she wasn't sure what he'd said. He was across the cell now looking at her. His chest heaving up and down. She stumbled towards him and caught her foot on an uneven stone. She fell forward. He caught her. He was so warm, so comfortable.

"I'm sorry," he said. "I shouldn't have fed from you." His voice sounded broken.

She tried to talk but felt so faint she was afraid she'd pass out. She heard Darick mutter the word "fuck" before lying her down on his bed. She must have passed out because she didn't remember anything that happened after that.

***

Luna opened her eyes. The memories of what had happened earlier came flooding back. She lifted her hand and felt her neck. No bite marks. Did he even bite her or had she imagined it?

She noticed she had been lying down. She sat up. Her body ached. She was on a bed. Her vision wasn't blurry anymore. She heard a shuffling sound and looked over. It was Darick. She was still in his cell. On his bed… with the cell door open. This was not good if someone came by.

She noticed there were a few cans of juice and food beside her on the bed. Her mouth felt dry, and she was so thirsty. She grabbed the juice and chugged it. She looked over at Darick. He looked… amazing. Even more gorgeous than before. His skin glowed with a radiance that even the Elves didn't have.

He was standing in front of her with a look of regret. "How are you feeling?"

Luna began to eat some of the crackers and cheese. "How did you get food here?" she asked.

Darick grumbled. "Luna. How. Are. You. Feeling?"

She sighed. Her energy level wasn't too bad, but she hadn't replenished all the blood she'd lost. At this moment, she was a hundred percent sure that everything she remembered happening did indeed happen.

"I'm… tired," she said. Then she looked up at him. "Darick, what are you?" She tried to stand up.

He gently grabbed her shoulders and made her sit back down on the bed. She saw his eyes flicker to the spot on her neck, and she swore she saw him sniff, which sent a shiver throughout her body, and she had to hold herself back from asking him to take more. Obviously, that would be a bad idea. But right now, her critical-thinking skills were a solid zero. He remained quiet for a few more seconds, avoiding her question.

"If you can walk okay, you should probably try and get out of the cell," he suggested. His tone had gone back to his normal stern, edgy self.

"You could've escaped," she said. "You still could."

She saw a small smile splay across his face, tugging at the corners of his mouth. It looked good on him. The arrogant grin.

"Don't you worry about that. Go take care of yourself," he replied.

She grabbed the rest of the snacks and slowly walked out of the cell. She locked the cell doors, then looked at the time. It was almost eight p.m. She gasped.

"Oh shit," she said, wide-eyed. She spun around. Darick was now sitting on his bed. "I've been out that long? Did anyone come to investigate? There had to have been someone! What about Aaron, the doctor?" She was almost hysterical.

If her father found out that she had let Darick drink blood from her, then Darick would be killed and she would be fired and sent off to who knows where. He would probably disown her.

"I told you. No need to worry. Your shift was over an hour ago. You should go home and rest," he said smoothly.

There was something about the way he said it that made her know that something had indeed happened when she had been "napping."

"Darick," she said in a serious tone.

He stared her down. "Luna," he responded in the same stern tone.

"Can you take me seriously for one minute!" she snapped.

His eyebrow lifted. "I'm not sure what you want me to say here," he answered casually.

Luna tightened her fists. "How about start with how you managed to get all this food for me and dodge guards for the entirety of my shift? Are there dead bodies around that I need to know about?" She began to look around at the floor to see if there were any traces of blood. She found none.

"No dead bodies," he replied.

Luna shoved some crackers in her mouth and chewed furiously. "Okay, so go on." She motioned with her hands for him to keep explaining.

He shrugged. "I went to the kitchen and got you food. Ran into some guards. Actually, a guard came here to check on you. Good thing I'm a smooth talker."

Luna almost spat her food out. Her heart rate picked up. So, someone had come by, and someone knew that she was just lying in this cell. She was ruined. She was going to get fired. And he was a hundred percent going to be executed.

Darick watched her with a look of pure amusement on his face. "Luna. You don't have to worry."

Luna threw a few crackers at him, which lamely hit his pants and then the floor. "Stop saying I don't have to worry! I'm going to lose my job! You are going to get killed!" she rambled.

"Ah, for fuck's sake," Darick grumbled. He placed his fingers on the bridge of his nose and took a few seconds to breathe before explaining himself. "I can make people forget things. I can do a lot of things. Turns out drinking your blood gave me a few more memories back and increased my abilities again. Although I didn't know I had the abilities until I remembered I did. That was a little while ago, and at that point, I was too weak to use them anyways," he explained.

Luna choked on a piece of cracker that had slid the wrong way down her throat while she was having her panic attack. She coughed a bit before drinking the rest of the juice.

"We need to get you out of here. You don't deserve this." She spoke the words without meaning to—how was she supposed to get him out? She couldn't break a prisoner out.

"You don't need to do anything. I could literally walk out of here right now. It wouldn't be hard," he said.

Luna widened her eyes. That would be perfect. She could go home. Then she'd have an alibi and he could just escape when she wasn't around.

"Where would you go?" she asked.

His dark eyebrows rose up. "I'd stay with you, obviously."

Luna cleared her throat. "Um, yeah, obviously," she said sarcastically. "You can't do that!"

But then she went silent and thought about the idea. He could stay with her; nobody would search her place for him. Besides, he could get his memories back and then hopefully find a way to get back to where he came from. It wasn't such a terrible idea. Other than the fact that she would be harbouring a criminal and breaking the law. Yeah. No big deal at all.

"Okay, fine. But you need to try and figure out a way to get some memories back," she said sternly. "I'm going to go back home then. I work tomorrow night. So, I'll see you then, and then we can figure out when you should escape."

He agreed.

Luna walked back down the hallway. It was nearly eight thirty p.m. now, and she still had to walk home. Her body was so tired. She ran into a guard on the way down the hall. He said he was relieving her for the night and apologized for being late. She was sure that he had come earlier; Darick must have used his powers to make him leave because it was an hour and a half past their usual shift changeover time. She told him not to worry about it.

When she got home, she climbed into bed and let out a long sigh. What a day it had been.

Chapter VIII

Luna sniffed the air. Bacon? And toast? Her stomach gurgled, and she was suddenly starving. She grumbled, wishing that she didn't have to cook. She did not enjoy cooking. Maybe she should ask Aywin to come over? She heard sizzling, like what oil sounds like when cooking. She frowned and then sat up in bed and looked directly at her kitchen. She had forgotten to close the fur curtain, so she had a clear view of the house. Darick was standing in her kitchen, frying food. Was she hallucinating?

"Darick?" she choked.

He looked even larger in her kitchen. She never pictured him as a cook if he drank blood. He turned and looked at her. He wasn't smiling; he just had that usual stern, pissed-off look on his face.

He raised an eyebrow. "That is my name."

Luna tried to get a hold of reality. She pinched herself. She flinched from her sharp nails digging in…. Okay, she was not dreaming.

"How did you find me?" she asked.

Darick took the bacon and toast and some fresh fruit and put it on a plate. He brought the plate over to her. "You have a strong smell," he said nonchalantly.

"I-I what?" She narrowed her eyes.

He placed the plate of food on her lap. It was warm and felt nice on her thighs.

"I can smell you. Your blood. Your scent," he explained. He leaned against her couch and stared at her.

She suddenly became self-conscious. She was only wearing a baggy T-shirt, and the material was thin. Her breasts were prominent, and it was hilly in the house.

She crossed her arms over her chest. Darick watched the gesture, and Luna saw a small smug grin sneak onto his face. Her face heated up.

"I thought we had decided that you were going to escape another time?" she said, and gave him a dirty look.

He shrugged. "I didn't really this it was necessary. Are you going to eat that food? It's getting cold."

She looked down at the plate. The bacon looked delicious. The toast was buttered, and the fresh fruit looked yummy. Her mouth watered because of how hungry she was. She used her fingers to eat since he hadn't brought any utensils, and she really didn't want him digging around her place.

"Thanks for the food. Didn't know you knew how to cook."

He got up and reached over to her, grabbing a tiny piece of bacon, and throwing it in his mouth. He chewed it. And swallowed. She watched him lick his lips, which shouldn't have been an interesting thing to watch, but that tongue of his was something else. She gulped.

"I can eat food... technically," he said. "But it makes my kind sick if we eat it. The small piece of bacon shouldn't do much, though eating it raw would be better for our stomachs."

Luna made a gagging sound and laughed. "Aw nasty! You're like an animal, aren't you?"

His facial expression remained stern and hard to read. "Nope, no animal," he said.

"So, do you drink animal blood? Why even drink blood," Luna asked as she ate her breakfast.

Darick scratched his chin. "No, animal blood makes us sick. Only humans, or human subtypes, like in your case, since you got"—he paused and pointed at her pointy ears—"those things." From the memories of his past that had resurfaced, that much he knew.

Luna played with her left ear. "You obviously don't have pointy ears, so you aren't an Elf. What is your kind called? Are you a human?" she asked.

Darick crossed his arms lazily across his chest. "We are a subtype of humans too. They call my kind Vampires. I've never met... an Elf. Or at least from what I remember so far, I haven't come across one," he explained.

Luna furrowed her brows. "So, if you've come across so many different... humans, is your planet quite large?"

Luna noticed that Darick's face tightened, and his body stiffened. She was getting better at reading his emotions, even through his gruff exterior.

"From what… I remember, I moved around lots… to different planets, I mean. Not sure why. In one of my memories, I was older and there was a war of some sort. Maybe that's why I left," he said.

Luna eyed him. There was something he wasn't telling her. He had gotten nervous initially, and now he seemed back to his smug self. Darick turned around and began to scan all of Luna's paintings and drawings. She blushed. People often didn't come over, and she had all her artwork out. She got up and put her empty plate in the kitchen. She felt uncomfortable with him sauntering around the room, studying her things like he was a detective.

"Find what you're looking for?" she asked.

He picked up a book and flipped it open. His eyes turned to her and then back to the book. Great, he was ignoring her. Luna sighed and went back to her "bedroom." She took the curtain and closed it. She needed privacy to change. She slipped on a bra, a T-shirt, and a pair of cargo pants.

When she opened the curtain, she found Darick sprawled out on her couch, reading. It was the strangest scene ever: a large, muscular, deadly man doing something as innocent as… reading. Luna appreciated the moment for a minute. A man whom she'd seen just last week kill Elves without a second thought was in her home, sitting on her couch, relaxing. She shook her head in disbelief. Her doorbell rang, startling her. Darick continued to lounge on the couch.

"Shouldn't you like… hide or something?" she whispered in a panic.

He flipped the page in the book and let out a little man grumble. She speed walked over to him and snatched the book from his hands.

"Darick," she said harshly.

He glared at her while standing and went over to her bedroom. He grasped the curtain firmly and closed it. She heard her bed squeak, then sighed and went to the front door and opened it. Down below was her father with a few prison guards.

"Luna," her father said, "can I come in?"

Luna hesitated. What if they decided to pull back her bedroom curtain?

"What's this about? Everything okay?" she asked, trying to pretend that she didn't know exactly what was going on.

Her father appeared grim. He spoke softly to the guards beside him, then climbed up the ladder. The ladder bent from the weight of her father. He ducked in through the doorway and walked into her home. He sat at the kitchen table and motioned for her to sit. She joined him and waited for him to speak.

"I have bad news. The prisoner. The… creature, it escaped last night on a prison guard's watch. Claims he doesn't remember a thing. We are assuming he fell asleep. I'm a little worried the prisoner might come for you. We've contacted the Warrior Elf base, and they've sent a bunch of troops out to search. Do you want me to ask if they can have a few guards stand by your house and keep watch?" her father asked.

"I'm not scared that he will come for me. Doesn't seem like that type of guy. He's probably trying to figure out a way to get back to where he came from," she replied.

She was trying to keep the shakiness out of her voice. She was very nervous that Darick was going to do something stupid and reveal himself. Her father gave her a pat on the shoulder.

"I'm sorry about our… disagreement the other day." He peered down at her still bandaged arms.

She needed to change the dressings. She smiled at her father. "Dad, I know we don't agree on everything, and I know the prisoner's escaped, but I still want you to think about what I'd said," she answered.

He nodded and got up. "If you change your mind about wanting a guard, let me know," he said. And with that, he left.

Luna took a few deep breaths. Her chest felt so tight. She walked over to her bedroom and flung open the curtains. Darick was lying on her bed, reading some other book he must've found. She looked at his dirty clothes and thought about her clean bed sheets.

"You need to wash your clothes," she stated.

His eyes didn't leave the pages. "I do," he replied.

He stayed still, continuing to read on her bed. She grumbled. She went into her drawers and tried to find anything her last boyfriend had left here. Since they had lived in this house together for a while, she was bound to find something of his. She made a little happy "ah-ha" sound and pulled out a shirt and a pair of joggers that were his. She had also found some socks, underwear, another few shirts, and some athletic pants. She threw the clothes at Darick. Her last boyfriend, River, wasn't as big as Darick so she hoped the clothes fit.

"There's a shower in the back room. Go shower and choose which of these you want to wear, and I'll wash your current clothes… although they are pretty torn up. I think I'll just throw them out," she said, giving Darick a once-over.

He growled and put the book down. The growl caused instant butterflies in her stomach, and she had to tell herself to calm the fuck down. He got up, grabbed the clothes, and walked over to the back room. She watched him close the door and then heard the shower going. She peered down at her bed sheets; they still looked clean. Then she leaned down and sniffed where he had been reading—and oh, it smelled so good. Why did it smell so good? This guy had showered once since being in that cell. But his smell was masculine…. In reality, it just smelled like his sweat, which was kind of weird that she liked it. Maybe him feeding from her made her think strange things. She gave her head a shake and went into the kitchen to wash the dishes from breakfast.

She wondered how long Darick had been in her house for? Her father said he escaped during the night, but she woke up this morning and he was here. So, either he had been here the whole time, or he'd gone somewhere else first. To get out of her head, she spent some time tidying up the house; it made her feel relaxed. She hummed as she did it. She was so caught up in cleaning, she hadn't heard Darick finish showering. She had forgotten about him being there at all, so when she turned around, she ran straight into him. He was so quiet.

He smelled even better than before, with a hint of mint for some reason, even though she didn't use mint in her body wash. She stepped back. His dark hair was wet. Droplets of water dripped from a piece that was hanging down over his forehead. She desperately wanted to swipe it to the side. But he was intimidating. A dark aura surrounded him, and she couldn't help but shiver in his presence.

He handed her his dirty clothes. "Do what you wish with them," he said in a coarse, edgy tone.

The clothes he wore fit okay. The shirt seemed fine, though it was tight around the biceps. He chose to wear the joggers, which were a bit snug in the ass and thigh region. Didn't look bad; Luna would just have to keep her eyes off that area. She cleared her throat. She took his clothes and put them into her garbage.

Darick went over to the couch and sat down. He let out a gruff sigh and leaned his head back. Luna sat down on the opposite couch and snuggled herself into the blanket she had there. Darick opened his gold eyes and stared at her, which made her feel insecure. Whenever he looked at her, it felt like he was reading the very depths of her soul. Her beautiful red hair flowed down the front of her and onto the blanket she was snuggled in. He probably had never seen her with her hair down, since she had to wear it up at work. She had to say something to break the awkward silence.

"How long can you go without feeding?" she asked.

"Not sure exactly," he responded dryly, clearly not wanting to talk about it.

Luna sighed. "Well, how hungry were you when you fed from me?"

His eyes darkened. "Starved." His voice had taken on a low, dangerous tone.

She shifted herself on the couch. "So, when do you need to feed again?" Luna wondered when he was going to get pissed off and annoyed with all her questions.

"I don't know. I don't want to... do that to you again," he said with a serious expression on his face. She thought back to when he drank from her, and how he'd taken too much of her blood.

"Shouldn't you feed now then? Don't let it go too long, and then you won't be so hungry?" Luna wanted to help keep him alive.

They needed to figure out how to get him back home before the Warrior Elves somehow tracked him down, and he couldn't risk going out and feeding from another Elf. It had to be her.

"I suppose," he replied. He had leaned closer to her, and his eyes had taken on a look of need.

"You can feed now then... if you need to. Better to do it early in the day before I have to work tonight," she explained, but her voice came out as a hush because he had already gotten up and walked over to her couch.

He sat himself beside her, and she watched him the entire time, not moving. Waiting. Waiting for him to lash out his teeth. His head came down to the nook of her neck, and her whole body tightened waiting for him to bite. But he breathed in, inhaling her sweet, addicting scent. She shivered.

"Someone clearly wants me to bite them." His voice was husky and deep in her ear.

Darick gently pulled down the blanket that had been pulled up past her collar bone, exposing her bare skin. His mouth found the sensitive spot at the side of her throat. Luna quivered. Darick's fangs scraped lightly over her skin. She felt the sharp pricks of his fangs against her flesh. The pain was quick, soon replaced by a pleasure unimaginable. She could feel the blood leaving her body, but a new magical feeling seeped into her very core. Her head fell back, and she let out a sigh of intense euphoria. Her knees felt weak. She never wanted the feeling to end. She melted against Darick.

Just as quickly as the bite had started, it ended. He lifted his head up and carefully licked the spot on her neck. Her skin was red, but the inflammation would go down before she went to work. Luna looked up at Darick. His eye lids were heavy and full of lust. She wanted him to kiss her in that moment. Instead, he tried to pull away. She reached out her hands and touched the stubble along his jaw. He held still. His eyes hadn't left hers. She took a hand and wrapped it behind his neck and pulled him towards her. Their lips met in a fierce kiss, a kiss full of unsaid need. She felt his fangs scrape against her bottom lip. Darick was now on top of her, his weight not fully on her. One hand was on her hip, and the other against the couch to hold himself up. Luna moved the blanket to the side and arched herself against his large body. He let out a deep growl and began to kiss down her neck and across her chest.

Then out of nowhere he sat up and moved away from her. Her chest was heaving up and down; her skin flushed and on fire for more. He had closed his eyes and appeared to be in pain.

"What's wrong?" she asked.

***

Darick grimaced. He felt a stabbing pain on the side of his head, his memories tearing through into his reality. He blacked out.

When his eyes opened, he was standing in the middle of a street. It was in a city, one of the human cities they had decided to raid. One of his close friends, Karn, was standing next to him.

"I can't do this anymore," Darick said suddenly. His voice sounded crackly and broken.

Karn had a dark, menacing look on his face. His shoulder-length blonde hair had droplets of blood in it. His piercing green eyes were wild with bloodlust. "Can't do what, man? Get it up anymore? There's pills for that," he joked.

Darick growled. "This!" he yelled. With his power, his voice shook the ground beneath them.

Karn's face became serious. "This is what we do," he answered.

Darick shook his head. "I will no longer follow him. I hate his orders… his plans," Darick raged. His hands were tightened into fists.

"Come on, man. You can't be thinking what I think you are," Karn protested.

Darick gave off a dark smile. "Don't tell a soul."

Darick opened his eyes. He felt sweaty and shaky. His vision was blurry but then began to clear the more he blinked. He looked up to see Luna on top of him, stroking his arm. Her face was the face of an angel—the most beautiful woman that he'd ever come across. And she was here with him. The monster.

***

Luna backed away as Darick sat up. He was pale. His gold eyes appeared dimmer than usual.

"Are you okay?" she asked.

He took a few seconds before responding. He was massaging his temples. "I am now. Pain seems to have subsided," he replied with a groan.

Luna wanted to scoot closer to him. Just because they had made out a little didn't mean she should be so clingy, so she forced herself to stay away.

"I had another… vision. Or memory, I guess. Something that happened in the past. I think I might know why I came here." Darick wore a solemn expression.

Luna covered herself in the blanket that she had thrown on the floor earlier. She let the soft fur warm her chilled body; turned out losing some blood made you cold. Darick noticed her shivers. He got up and went to her cooler and grabbed some juice and water. He put the juice jar in front of her as well as the cup of water. "Drink," he said, then sat down next to her, the heavy weight of his body sinking her closer to him.

She opened the jar of juice and began to sip it. "So, why do you think you're here then?"

"The Vampires, they go to other planets, and they take from them. They also feed from the humans there, killing them too. I think the Vampires are coming to this planet.

And I think the reason I came here was to warn your kind about it," he explained.

Luna gulped the last little bit of juice down. Panic spread through her veins. How was she supposed to convince the Elves that Vampires were coming to kill them? She technically could tell Samara what Darick had just told her, and Samara would possibly take her seriously and get the army ready. But even then, what would she do about Darick?

"I might have a plan," Luna said. She went to her work bag and pulled out her radio. She dialled it to Samara's frequency. "Samara?"

The radio fuzzed for almost a full minute. "Hey, Luna, just on my lunch break. What's up?" Samara asked.

Luna smiled. "Anyone with you? Like, can anyone hear me?"

"No, I'm alone. Why? What's going on?" Samara suddenly sounded worried.

"I need to tell you something, but you can't freak out," Luna said in a serious tone.

"Ha. Great way to start. Just hit me with it. I can handle anything," Samara teased.

"That guy, the prisoner? The one that escaped. He's what you call a Vampire. The reason he came to our planet was to warn us about other Vampires. Apparently, they invade other planets and kill the people living there. They are coming to ours," Luna explained.

As soon as the words came out of her mouth, she felt stupid for saying them. It sounded ridiculous. But someone who drank blood was something entirely unbelievable, and here he was in her living room. Samara was silent. The radio fuzzed; Luna could only wait for Samara's response.

"What in the actual fuck," Samara said finally.

A grin played across Luna's face. She looked up and saw Darick was sitting there, listening to the conversation with intensity.

"You aren't pulling my leg?" Samara asked.

"If I had the ability to make shit up like that, I would be a writer. And we both know I'm not," Luna replied.

"Point taken. Looks like my lunch break is going to be cut short. I'll stop the search party for your little Vampire buddy. I'm assuming he's with you. I won't let anyone know. But I will get the armies ready. Does the prisoner know how to kill his own kind?" Samara asked.

Luna turned towards Darick, who explained, "You can only kill us by ripping our hearts out or decapitating us. Stabbing me in the gut isn't going to do much other than slow me down." Luna recited the words back to Samara.

"So, stab them in the heart or cut their heads off? Sounds like foreplay," Samara responded.

Darick shook his head at the comment. "Not stab. You must take our hearts out of our bodies. If you stab it, it'll heal. If you rip my arm off, it'll grow back. Your heart and mind can't grow back if you take it out of the body," Darick said. Luna nodded and explained that part to Samara.

"When are they coming to attack?" Samara asked.

Luna looked to Darick for an answer. He shrugged. Luna put the radio to his mouth so he could answer Samara. He gave Luna a "fuck off" look, but she rolled her eyes and pushed it towards him.

He took the radio in his large hand and pressed the button. "I'm not sure when. Probably anytime. I got here last week to warn you. They must know I have left."

"Hot damn. Sexy-ass voice," Samara said.

Luna let out a little laugh, and Darick glared at the radio. Luna snatched the radio from him. She was surprised that Samara was so understanding of the situation, given her response on their last hike. "So, you'll work on the army?" Luna asked.

"I'm going to have to contact the Plains too. I'm assuming if these Vampires take over other planets, there's got to be a lot of them… with a strong army," Samara said. Luna nodded. "I'll get back to you either tonight or later tomorrow about everything. I'm going to get the armoury stocked and ready. Our planet isn't going out without a fight. I'll also talk to Torion," she added.

Torion was the leader of the Ancients, and he would be able to prepare their planet for the fight of their lives. Torion was a powerful Elf. Some Elves on the planet had abilities like clairvoyance, or strength, or speed. Torion had it all. He had dark-brown skin and bright-blue eyes. He was around Luna's father's age, maybe slightly older.

Luna turned off the radio. She fidgeted with the antenna before setting it down on the coffee table. Darick got up and started moving her furniture around to make more space in the living room.

Luna raised her eyebrows. "Um, what are you doing?"

He ignored her and finished moving the other couch over. He reached out his arms and began to stretch. He was exercising in her living room.

She sighed. "Can you at least try to not breath so heavy?"

He glanced up at her and then went back to his push-ups. Great, back to not talking again. Luna looked at the time. It was nearly one p.m. She still had time to exercise at the training facility. In her bedroom, she changed into gym clothes and then tied her hair up into a tight bun. Before she left the house, she turned to look at Darick who had started to sweat.

"I'll be gone for a couple hours. Don't kill anybody," she said.

He gave her a curt nod. She nodded back and left the house. She jogged to the exercise facility, taking the short route. After she arrived, she started working her legs. She had long, strong legs that could lift a lot of weight. She also worked on her triceps and forearms. Before she knew it, an hour had gone by. She was sitting on a bench sweating when she heard a voice behind her.

"Hey, Luna!"

She turned around and saw Shaela, Fin's wife and Luna's friend. Although not best friends, they hung out every once in a blue moon. Shaela had a big smile on her face. She was a petite Elf; her short, curly white-blonde hair bounced as she walked.

"Hey, how's a going?" Luna asked.

"I'm good! Just waiting for Fin to finish up showering. He was here, exercising too! I was sitting over at the front and saw you," she said.

Her voice was high pitched and far too happy. Luna never understood how Shaela could be so cheery; no one's that happy. She wondered if it pissed off Fin sometimes, especially since he could be a bit of a grump.

"So, how have things been? I heard about that prisoner escaping! Did you ever have to guard him in the prison?" she asked.

Luna didn't want to be short with Shaela, but she wasn't keen on talking about this with her. "I may have. How are things with you? I haven't seen you for a while."

Shaela didn't seem to mind the change in topic. Her white teeth gleamed with her smile. "Well… we are trying to have a baby!" she said excitedly.

Luna's eye widened with shock as well as joy. She was happy for them. They would both make great parents. Fin and Shaela were older than Luna by five years. Elves often had their children when they were young if they had a partner.

"That's so amazing. I'm excited for you two," she said, and smiled.

They chatted for a few more minutes. Luna looked down at the time and noticed it was nearly four p.m. She was starving since she never ate lunch.

"I better get going. I work tonight," Luna said.

Shaela leaned in and gave Luna a big hug. "Okay! I'm sorry if I've kept you too long!"

Luna assured her that she did not and she'd missed seeing her. She didn't visit with Shaela as much as she wished she did.

Luna left the building and walked back home as her cool down. She had gotten distracted when talking to Shaela and had never stretched. She rounded the path back to her place

P. Morgan

and looked up just as she was turning the corner. She saw two Warrior Elves outside her home, as if they were guarding it. Her face fell, and her heartbeat quickened. She ran over to her house.

The Elves looked at her but didn't stop her when she climbed up the ladder and opened her front door. In the living room sat a man she didn't know as well as Torion and Darick. They looked like they were having a serious conversation, and she had awkwardly walked in at a bad time. She forced a small smile and closed the door behind her.

"Um" was all she got out of her mouth before Torion spoke.

"Ah, Luna! We have been waiting for you. Come sit," he gestured; his voice sounded deeper than she remembered.

She felt strange about the matter since it was her home and her couch that he was sitting on. She didn't need permission to come in and sit. She tried not to shoot daggers at Torion's eyes as she walked into the living room and sat close to Darick.

She wasn't sure what emotions were filling the room; she couldn't tell if this was a good or bad situation. Torion was a powerful man. He was tall, lean, and had an authoritative glow about him. His brilliant blue eyes scanned Luna for a second before he spoke.

"Darick has caught me up with the Vampire situation. Samara informed me first. From this moment, you and Darick will be staying with Samara, closer to the base. Not at her house, but you'll be sharing one of the places I own near the river. It's quite high up and allows for a good view of the base and the sky, which, to my understanding, is where these Vampires will be coming from. Samara has agreed to allow Darick to train with our fighters," he explained calmly.

Luna nodded. Relief flooded through her at knowing that the Elves were taking the Vampire situation seriously. However, she was skeptical at how easily they'd believed the scenario. She was worried that they were going to try to either lock her up and kill Darick or kill them both. She wondered why they were being so trusting, knowing that Darick had killed two Warrior Elves. Maybe it was the fact that they trusted Samara's judgement, or maybe it was because they knew that they would need Darick's help if they wanted to win against the Vampires. She was a little annoyed that Samara told Torion where Darick was.

Torion got up. "Well, you better pack your things then."

Luna frowned. "Oh, we're leaving right now?"

"Those Vampires could come down any minute. We need to get working on this," Torion replied.

"Fair," Luna stated.

She grabbed a bag and threw some clothes and other supplies in it. She could always come back and grab things if she forgot them. The base wasn't too far away. Luna noticed that Darick had come over and was hovering over her as she packed her things.

"Something you need?" she asked with a raised eyebrow.

"No," he stated coarsely.

Luna sighed and continued to pack. She didn't have time to argue with him. She wasn't sure why he was being all weird, but she needed to be quick since Torion was outside, impatiently waiting for them. Luna swung her bag over her back.

"Okay, I'm ready to go," she said.

She paused and looked at Darick. He seemed… stressed. Actually, his face was tight, and his posture stiffened.

"Darick?" she asked. He looked down at her but didn't reply. "Is everything all right?"

He let out a big sigh/growl; Luna wasn't really sure how to describe it. And then, he said nothing. He just stood there, all puffed up and annoyed.

"Okay then," Luna murmured.

The two of them went outside to meet Torion. Luna noticed that Torion had brought horses. She hadn't seen them earlier, but she had been in a rush when she ran in. He had four of them. The two Warrior Elves were already up on their own horses. Torion hopped up onto his.

Luna glanced at Darick. "So, you know how to ride, right?"

Darick gave her a slight smile. "Yes. However, horses are much bigger on your planet," he said, staring at the horse.

She mounted the horse, and then Darick followed suit, sitting behind her. He put her bag on his back. The horses went into a steady trot down the trail. The cool air blew against Luna's face. She noticed that her hair was whipping back into Darick's face. She was surprised he hadn't complained sooner. She had time to tie it into a low bun without him grumbling on about it.

The feeling of his front pressing against her made her think back to the kisses they had shared earlier. With the motion that trotting caused, she couldn't help but blush. She tried not to overthink the kissing; it had been in the heat of the moment. They couldn't possibly like each other that way, could they? He probably just thought her blood tasted good.

"Luna?" Darick's low, deep voice whispered into her ear, snapping her out of her thoughts.

"Yes?" she asked.

"Do you trust these men?"

She thought back to how Torion had acted in her house, and she wasn't really sure.... She had strange feelings about the situation but couldn't point to anything in particular. The only thing she could think of was Samara and how she would always believe her best friend had the best intentions for her.

"I trust Samara. And Samara trusts these men," Luna replied. It wasn't really an answer, but Darick seemed to be okay with it because he remained quiet.

They continued down the trail, following the turns of the path that led them up the mountain and into the forest. About an hour passed before the climb became steep, though the horses were strong and steady. The path opened onto a large, open field leading up to the Warrior base. Hugging the side of the mountain, the base overlooked parts of the community below; a river ran down from the mountain above along one side of the base, disappearing into a cluster of trees.

Luna noticed a bunch of tree huts along the cluster of trees. The horses continued through the field and to the houses. A strong scent of flowers wafted through the air as they made their way to a group of three homes in the trees. The sun was shining brightly but would soon be setting behind the mountains. Once the group arrived in the shade of the trees, Luna looked up at the huts.

The homes were small like her own, with ladders leading up to each one. They all had a wrap-around deck, which looked out to a beautiful view of the forest. Luna looked at the colourful field behind her, which was dotted with the many different species of flowers and herbs.

"You and Darick can get off here. I'm staying at the base. The other two homes here are taken, so you will be sharing that first one there, with Samara," Torion said while pointing his finger out at the closest home.

"When do we go to the base?" Luna asked.

"Samara will be here shortly; she will let you know some more details about that," Torion replied.

Torion and the Warrior Elves trotted off with their horses towards the base, which Luna and Darick could no longer see, as the mountain and the base had curved away from them. Darick jumped off the horse first, his heavy feet thudding the ground. Luna stared down at the grass below her; it was going to be a far jump. She slid off the horse and hopped down, which went smoother than she had imagined. She grew up riding horses, but she didn't ride very often anymore; she never needed to. Darick grabbed her bag from the horse and threw it at her.

Luna yelped as she caught the bag. "You could have at least warned me!" She glared.

Darick ignored her as he took the horse over to a little barn under one of the trees. The barn had some hay and water in it. He tied the animal up there. Luna was too busy staring up at the sky; she was imagining what it would be like to see more of those space objects coming down. Would there be thousands of them, like little fireballs shooting down?

Darick took a brush and combed the horse's mane and body while the horse munched on some hay. Luna walked over and leaned against the side of the barn, watching Darick. He seemed to be at peace. Ten or twenty minutes went by before she eventually turned away and began to study the field.

"Do you think we can stop them?" she asked softly.

"What?" She heard Darick say. He sounded a far away.

She turned around and noticed the horse drinking water but no sign of Darick. She peered up and saw that he was sitting in a chair on the deck of their new house. She must've been daydreaming longer than she thought. She walked over to the ladder and climbed up to the top. With the massive trees here, these homes were a lot higher up than the ones in town, at least thirty feet above ground. Luna imagined that getting furniture into this place would have been a pain in the ass. When she reached the top, she sat next to Darick on a wooden chair. It was a bit breezy up there, so she pulled a jacket from her bag and swung it around her shoulders. Darick only had his T-shirt and joggers on.

"Are you warm enough?" she questioned.

He had been staring out at the mountains before his eyes found hers. The butterflies in her stomach suddenly started up again. "I don't feel the cold the same way you do. Doesn't bother me," he stated.

Luna gave him a nod, then took a deep breath. She had a lot of questions for him that she had thought about on the ride here.

"Go on," he said suddenly.

Luna frowned. "What?"

He grumbled, "I said, 'Go on.' I can tell you need to say something. You are being awfully quiet." His accent sounded stronger when he was frustrated.

How had he gotten to know her so well in only a matter of days? Luna fidgeted with her nails. She had a bad habit of peeling the ends of her nails off and giving herself hang nails.

"What do you remember about the wars? Do you think we have a chance?" she asked. She thought about her brother, and her father and mother. "Dammit," she mumbled; she needed to radio them and talk to them.

"I don't remember much. Just pieces. I'm not sure what you Elves have for weapons, but Vampires carry swords and knives. We tend to like to kill with our teeth. That way, you can drink some blood to give you strength as you're fighting," Darick mentioned nonchalantly.

Luna's eyes widened. "Seriously?" she croaked.

Darick nodded. Luna suddenly felt awkward; her cheeks began to blush as she thought about a Vampire biting her. "But… how does that even make sense?" she asked.

Darick raised one of his dark eyebrows. "I don't understand what you mean."

"If being bitten by a Vampire… feels good, and if a Vampire feels good biting someone, then why would you do that and potentially distract yourself in a war zone?"

Darick let out a deep laugh that caught Luna off guard. She had heard him chuckle but never laugh like this.

Once he stopped, he gave Luna a dark, bold look. "Vampire bites don't feel good unless we make them feel good," he said vainly.

Luna's jaw dropped. "Wait, you can actually control what it feels like? So, like with me…" Her voice trailed off, as she wasn't sure what she wanted to say.

"I can release certain hormones into your system. Makes the experience more… enjoyable," Darick finished.

"But what about for you? Doesn't it feel the same every time?" Luna asked.

Darick's expression went from casual to his sterner, serious self. "No. It doesn't," he said with finality.

The two of them stared off at the sunset. The first few minutes of silence were awkward, but Luna had a hard time with silence. Darick did not seem to mind silence, since he ignored her most of the time. After spending time watching the sun set, Luna's stomach growled. She hadn't had anything to eat for lunch and was starving. She shifted in her seat and began to push herself up, but Darick's hand came down onto her thigh. She paused and looked up at him. Her entire body went still, and it felt like the world stopped around them.

His eyes went from hers, then down to her neck, and then down to her breasts before he slowly trailed them back up to meet her eyes again. She took his hand and gently pushed it off, then got up and spun herself over to him. She sat onto his lap so that she was cradling him. His large hands had gone down to her hips. She leaned in and kissed him softly on the lips, just like she had imagined doing.

"Luna," he said into her ear after they broke the kiss.

"Yes?" she replied.

"I just wanted to say your name on my lips so that you know you're mine," he whispered, and then his mouth locked on hers with a needy urge.

Chapter IX

"What in the heck are you guys doing up there?!" Samara called down from the bottom of the ladder.

Luna panicked and got off Darick's lap. Her face was flushed, and her body tingled from the kisses they'd just shared. Too bad it had been over so quickly. Darick remained in the chair with a casual expression. Luna peered over the edge of the deck. Samara was now climbing up the ladder.

She motioned for Darick to follow her inside the house. He nodded lazily and got up. They went into the cozy home. It had two double beds in one corner, and a little living room space next to that. There was a tiny kitchen and a separate door that led to what Luna assumed was the bathroom. The home was quite warm from the high temperatures that day, but Luna assumed it would get chilly overnight. She went over to the kitchen and found some dried fruit to snack on while she waited for Samara to come up. Darick went and found a spot on the couch. There weren't any books around, so he just lay there, staring at Luna. Luna blushed when she noticed his eyes.

Samara burst into the room, filling it up with all her energy. "Well, well, well," Samara said as she looked from Luna and to Darick. Then she gave a sideways, back-and-forth motion with her pointer finger. "Naughty, naughty, you two. I didn't realize I interrupted something. Should I come back later?" she asked with a grin.

Luna sighed. "Samara," she said, shooting daggers with her eyes.

Samara smirked. "I'm KIDDING, obviously." Then she turned to Darick. "You're a quiet one, aren't you? They do say psychopaths are quiet, especially ones that kill my Warriors," Samara said casually, with a big hint of passive aggressiveness.

Luna choked on a piece of fruit.

Darick's eyes narrowed. "Oh, sorry. It's not like I had a massive head trauma and was delusional and had been travelling for days without a food source, so I was starving," he replied in an edgy tone, and with a whole hell of a lot of sarcasm.

Luna coughed. She had never heard Darick respond in such a sassy matter. She looked at Samara to see if her top had been blown off yet.

But Samara was smiling. "I like him. He can stay," she said, then turned to Luna. "By the way, Aywin and your dad are staying in one of the houses. They'll be here shortly."

Luna's heart dropped. Her father was going to be coming out this way? He often trained at the base since he was obsessed with sword fighting. In another life, he would've been a Warrior Elf. Luna knew for a fact that her father hated Darick, so their interaction would be interesting.

"Why is Aywin coming out?" Luna asked.

"He heard about what was happening and wanted to be here with you," Samara explained.

"How did everyone find out?" Luna questioned.

"Luna. If we are taking this seriously, which we are, then this whole Vampire invasion thing could mean the end of our planet as we know it. We are telling everybody to prepare. Tomorrow, we will be going over the details at the base. We hope we have until tomorrow, or else we're fucked," Samara said plainly.

Luna went over to Darick and sat next to him on the couch. She watched as Samara went into the kitchen and poured herself a glass of red wine. She held one of the empty glasses up to Luna, who nodded in response to their silent conversation. Samara poured her a glass, then brought the two glasses over to the living room. Luna took the wine from Samara.

"You want anything?" Samara asked Darick, who shook his head and stated, "I don't drink."

Luna knew what he meant: only blood, not alcohol or any other drink. Samara just raised her eyebrows and sat down. "Good for you. Hard to pass on a good cup of Elf wine. We make the best," she said, and winked.

Luna took a sip of the thick red wine, which was starting to look a lot like blood. Maybe she was just thinking about it too much. She swallowed down her nausea.

"So, tell me about yourself, Darick," Samara said casually. Wearing her armoured pants and a loose black top, she leaned back into the couch. Her jet-black hair was smoothed back today, which made her striking green eyes more vivid.

129

Darick grunted, then shrugged. "There's nothing to know," he said with a hint of edginess in his tone, although Luna noticed he always seemed to talk that way. Mysterious, pissed off, annoyed—they were all words that described him; Luna wondered why he hated the world so much.

"Oh, come on. You're a being from another planet. How can you not have anything interesting to say about yourself?" Samara teased.

"What do you want to know?" he asked with an alert expression.

Samara grinned and took a sip of her wine. "What do you eat with those set of sharp canines?"

Darick's eyes darkened; he was not in the mood to talk about blood, especially with someone he barely knew. At least, he trusted Luna now. Luna noticed his mood change.

"Blood, he drinks blood. End of story," Luna replied. She tried to make it sound like something that wasn't a big deal, but it was difficult to do that when someone drank blood to live.

Samara's brows drew together. She didn't look scared, though, just curious. "Do you drink other Vampires' blood?"

Darick furrowed his brows. "No, you can't do that. It must be from another species, hence the reason why Vampires go to other planets."

Samara frowned. "Why the need to change planets, though? You can just live with the people and figure out something for survival together? Like mutual blood drinking or whatever?"

Darick's face darkened, and his gold eyes flashed with something that Luna couldn't quite recognize. "Vampires are hunters, Samara. Not just predators but hunters," Darick replied coldly.

Both Samara and Luna's faces paled. "So… you guys can't help yourselves and end up killing off everyone on a planet after a certain amount of time," Samara stated.

Darick nodded, and his eyes drifted over to Luna's neck. He pulled them away and focused back on Samara. "We can help ourselves if we really want to. It goes against our instincts, but it's possible… at least, I think. Remember, I have a memory issue here, so I'm only telling you what I've recalled so far. The way my father led our race was wrong. There have been too many generations brought up in his reign," Darick explained with a look of disgust on his face.

"You're different then? You were able to break out of the societal norms?" Luna asked. She felt warmth in her heart for him as well as sadness. It must have been hard for him to not follow his kind.

"I don't think I did it until recently. I was just like any of them. Although deep down, I think I've always felt it was wrong. It's hard to know. My memories are… jumbled," Darick explained, thinking back to how he remembered his father murdering women in front of him. How had he really felt about it?

"Are the female Vampires the same way?" Samara asked.

Darick was silent for a few seconds, trying to dig back into his discombobulated memories. Luna and Samara watched Darick patiently. Luna saw his face grimace and she put her hand on his shoulder.

***

131

A sharp pain stabbed Darick's temples. Not again.… He winced and closed his eyes. The pain became a throbbing sensation that filled his whole head and neck. Eventually, he blacked out from his current reality, returning to his memories.

His eyes shot open. He was sitting at a kitchen table. His mother was there, smiling at him from across the table. She was holding a clear cup with thick red liquid in it. Darick somehow knew this was blood. He looked down and in his hands was a cup of blood.

"Darick honey, everything all right?" his mother asked.

Darick nodded. He lifted the cup and had a sip. The taste exploded in his mouth; it was hard not to close his eyes and enjoy the flavour. He looked back up at his mother, who had always seemed so calm and collected. She had smooth pale skin and long dark hair that was curly and went down to her waist. He shared at her gold eyes. His father had dark eyes that reminded him of what a monster would look like.

"Mom? Why are you okay when you drink blood? I notice dad gets weird when he does," Darick said, careful not to dishonour his father. Parental respect was important. Darick watched as his mother's face flashed with sadness; when he blinked, it was gone and his mother's same calm demeanour returned.

"Hun, it's not just your father that gets like that. All male Vampires do," she explained smoothly.

Darick didn't want to take another sip of blood. He ignored the sudden increase of saliva in his mouth. His mother wasn't wrong about how all men were like that, although Darick was still a child, only seven years old. "Why does dad drink from those women?" Darick asked.

His mother sipped some more blood and turned her head so that she could stare out the window. Their home overlooked a little village. "You will too one day, Darick. When you're old enough," she replied, her voice almost a whisper.

Darick frowned. "Why don't you?" he asked.

His mother smiled sadly. "Because I don't need to, my dear. I'm fine with harvesting the blood. It's safer that way." As soon as those words left her mouth, she went still. Darick saw the regret in her words. He knew what she had meant, though; she had already said it.

***

Darick's eyes flickered open. Luna took a cold cloth that she had grabbed and wiped his damp warm forehead with it.

"It's okay, Darick. You're back; it's me Luna," Luna murmured.

She saw recognition flash across his face, and then he relaxed. He took a few deep breaths before sitting up on the couch. Samara was watching from the other side of the couch.

Luna put the wet cloth down. "You okay?" she asked softly.

Darick grunted, then blinked his eyes a few times. "I saw my mother," he said.

Luna smiled. He cleared his throat and looked between Samara and Luna. "My mother didn't kill people to drink their blood. She harvested from someone, in a way that didn't kill them. Apparently, female Vampires do that because they don't have the same instincts as the men do," he said coldly.

Luna could tell he was pissed off that the males didn't do that as well.

"When I was young, I never fed from a human. I just drank harvested blood from a cup," he explained.

Luna noticed that his complexion had gone back to normal; he wasn't pale and sweaty anymore. A loud knock on the door interrupted their conversation, and the door swung open.

"Rude! Start the party without me!" Aywin beamed from the doorway. His dark red hair was ruffled from the wind. He walked into the room but stopped dead in his tracks when he made eye contact with Darick. "Hi, there. You're the neck-biting guy, right?" Aywin said.

Darick cursed underneath his breath. Aywin walked over and put his hand out to Darick, who stared at the hand, then back up at Aywin.

"You shake it," Aywin stated with a grin. Darick frowned before grabbing Aywin's hand. They shook awkwardly, then let go. "I'm Aywin, L's brother!" Aywin said.

"Oh really? The red hair didn't make it obvious," Darick said dryly.

Aywin burst out laughing, then sat next to Samara. "He's funny," Aywin said.

Luna laughed. "So, where's Dad?"

"He's getting set up in the other house. He'll be over shortly," Aywin replied.

Luna's heart rate picked up. "Is he… okay with everything?"

Aywin sighed. "L, is Dad ever actually calm about things? He's got the manly temper of a bear."

Luna grumbled and slouched deeper into the couch. She did not feel like dealing with her father right now. She took a big gulp of wine. Aywin grabbed Samara's wine and chugged it.

"Hey!" Samara said, and punched Aywin in the shoulder.

Aywin gave her the wine glass back. "I've told you before: if you put that stuff near me, imma drink it," he teased.

Samara sighed angrily and got up. She went to the kitchen, grabbed another bottle of wine, and brought it to the living room. She poured herself a glass, and she and Aywin took turns sipping the wine glass together. Luna noticed how close she was sitting to Darick and decided it would be best to move away from him. If her father came in and saw that, he would freak out.

"So, I hear we are going to the base tomorrow?" Aywin asked.

Samara nodded. "Yep, although I'm not sure if you're going. Do you even know how to fight?"

Aywin rolled his eyes. "Duh, I do. What a dumb question. I grew up with Arin; do you seriously think he didn't train his ONLY son how to fight? If he trained Luna, which he did, then he trained me. You should know that, you basically grew up with us."

Luna burst out laughing. Aywin shot her daggers. "Come on now, brother… we both know you are horrid at fighting," Luna said playfully.

Aywin sighed. "Just because I'm shit, doesn't mean I don't know how to."

This time both Luna and Samara began to laugh. Darick sat there and stared at the three of them. He was not used to this much laughter; he never grew up with it. Everything had always been so serious it seemed.

With a loud crack, the front door opened. Luna's father came in; his eyes narrowed and stern. The testosterone in the room had just gotten ten times higher. Everybody paused. The laughter quickly dissipated. Arin was a huge man, and just his presence could take a person's breath away. He walked into the living room, never taking his eyes off from Darick.

Instinctively, Darick stood up from the couch. Darick wasn't small; he was big as well, but his muscles weren't as bulky as Luna's father's. The two men looked like they were going to tear each other apart. When they stood just a foot apart, Luna watched in horror as her father's hand came out with a small blade and stabbed Darick right in the abdomen. Darick grimaced but didn't seem surprised at the manoeuvre. Luna knew Darick could easily kill her father. Well… maybe not easily, but Darick was much quicker. Samara and Aywin gasped. Darick grabbed the blade's handle and ripped it out. It was covered in dark blood. He wiped the blade on his pants, flipped the dagger over, then smacked the handle firmly into Arin's palm. Arin's face turned to a big grin and he began to laugh.

"Ha! Fuck, I've never seen someone take a blade to the liver and live! So, you are telling the truth? Heart out or head off. I'm Arin, if you haven't forgotten from the last time we met," Luna's father stated boldly.

The whole room let out a sigh; the tension released. Luna couldn't believe her father had just tested what Samara had told him about how to kill Vampires—what a way to figure out the truth. Arin took the blade from Darick, then sat between Darick and Luna. Luna's father gave her a side hug and placed a kiss on the top of her head. He took his hand and ruffled her hair up. She grumbled with a smile and smoothed her hair back down.

"I'm glad you're okay," he said.

Luna smiled. "I'm always careful," she said while side-eyeing Darick's stomach wound. He appeared to be fine.

Her father nodded. "I just wish I had listened to you before," he said with honesty.

Luna felt relief flood into her system at her father's words. It meant a lot for him to admit that to her. Darick's shirt had a big hole and a blood stain. He seemed perfectly content with sitting on the couch, but she was worried that he was in pain and not showing it.

The group talked for what felt like hours. The sun had gone down and the skies were dark, the only light coming from inside the home.

Arin got up from the couch. "I'm going to retire to bed." He left the house without another word.

Aywin yawned. "I'm going to go follow," he said, and left after they all said goodnight.

Luna looked over at the beds. She and Samara were going to have to sleep together. Luna hated having to sleep in the same bed as someone else; she didn't like sharing the bed sheets. Luna looked at the couch and decided it looked pretty damn comfy. Samara had already gotten up to go to the bathroom.

"I think I'll just sleep here," Luna said out loud, even though she and Darick were the only ones in the room; it didn't really matter where she slept because it had nothing to do with him.

He raised an eyebrow. "On the couch? I was going to sleep here. You ladies can have the beds," he stated.

Luna smiled. "Oh, thanks."

She got up, and as she walked past Darick on her way to bed, his hand came out and gently grabbed her arm. His hands were so large that he took her entire arm in his grasp. His touch sent shivers throughout Luna's body. She turned to him and saw the look he was giving her. She suddenly wished it was just him and her in the house right now. She opened her mouth to say something, but no words came out. They stood in silence. Luna felt dizzy from his touch. At that moment, Samara came out of the bathroom. Luna gave Darick one last look before walking over to her bed and crawling into the cool sheets. Samara went to her bed and crawled in as well. They both turned so that they were facing each other from the opposite beds.

Darick stood up and took his shirt off. Luna's eyes wandered to the spot where he'd been stabbed. There was a thin white line there. Her brain suddenly clued in to what she was looking at. Darick had a strong, muscular body. Defined and solid. He grabbed a blanket from the side of the couch, then laid it over him as he settled down and closed his eyes.

She felt the itchiness of her forearm wounds and couldn't get comfortable. She sat up and removed the bandages. It was too dark to see them, but when she felt along her arms, they were rough and scabby. She lay down again and closed her eyes. Sleep took her instantly.

***

During the night, Luna felt something crawling on her skin. She shot up from her sleep and saw a spider on her arm. She screeched and flung the spider onto the floor. The spider had been crawling on her scabbed arms. Darick's head shot up from the couch, and he peered over at her. She was sitting up in bed breathing heavily. She hated spiders with a passion.

He raised his eyebrows. "Everything all right over there?"

Luna glanced over at Samara, who grumbled and rolled over to sleep more.

"I'm fine," Luna whispered.

She looked at the time: five a.m. There was no way she was going to fall asleep now. She sighed and got up. Darick had settled his head back down onto the couch and closed his eyes. Luna went to the kitchen and made a pot of coffee. The sound of the coffee dripping eased her into a daydream. She wondered what they were going to be going over at the base today.

Would there be a strategic army plan? How would they even figure that out if the Vampires were coming from the sky? How do you fight something from above? Her brain played over all the thoughts and questions she had.

Luna poured the coffee into a mug and leaned against the counter while drinking it. Outside, the sun had come up a bit; it was a cloudy day, so not much light came into the house.

Luna settled herself in the darkness. It was quiet and calming. When Luna and Aywin were teenagers, he would make fun of her for doing things in the dark. When she woke up in the early morning, she didn't like turning the lights on, as the natural light was relaxing to her. Even at an earlier age, Luna rarely put her lights on unless she was reading a book and it was too dark to do that.

She put down her coffee and opened the pantry door in the kitchen. It was full of snacks and meals. Luna noticed the granola and pulled it out. She opened the cooler and grabbed some fresh yogurt. Luna wondered who stocked the place with food. There was even fresh goat cheese from one of the local farms. She scooped yogurt into a bowl and mixed in granola and fruit. After she put the yogurt back into the fridge, she put on a big, fluffy jacket and headed outside with her breakfast and coffee. The air was chilly high up in the mountains, and she was a baby when it came to the cold.

She sat down in the chair Darick had been sitting in the day before. He made the chair seem so small, but there was plenty of space in it when she sat down. She tucked her legs in underneath her body and smiled as she looked out at the forest and valley. It may have been a cloudy day, but it was still a gorgeous view. The smell of fresh air and the coming rain filled her nostrils. She sat outside for at least ten minutes before the front door opened and Samara came out. She had a coffee in her hands and was huddled in a blanket. She looked cozy and sleepy.

"Mornin'," Luna said.

Samara didn't smile. She had always been a night owl and did not do well in the mornings, which was surprising since the job she had required that she get up early.

"Hey," Samara said, and sat down in the other chair.

They both sat quietly, enjoying the silence and peace of nature. The wind was blowing the tree they were in, so it slightly swayed the house. This might scare some Elves, but the house was secured tightly to the tree, so there was no chance of it breaking.

"Your boyfriend's still snoozing," Samara murmured.

Luna took the last sip of her coffee. "He's not my boyfriend."

"I think you need to tell him that," Samara stated.

Luna rolled her eyes. "I don't think he wants a girlfriend."

Samara scoffed. "Keep telling yourself that."

The two of them sat there for another few minutes in silence. Time was going by quickly, and it was nearing six a.m. Luna could see a light in the house next to them, and she assumed her brother and dad were up, eating breakfast and getting ready. They were both early risers too. Luna got up and went into the house for more coffee. She looked over at Darick, who was still lying on the couch with his eyes closed. The sheets were pulled down to his waist, exposing his naked chest. Her face heated up just looking at him. He truly was something.

"Do you usually watch others when they sleep?" Darick asked with one eye open.

Luna poured some more coffee in her cup, doing anything to look busy. "I wasn't watching. I was just looking over to see if you were still breathing," she said as casually as she could.

She saw Darick smirk and he sat up. "What time is it?" he asked.

"Around six in the morning," Luna replied.

He grabbed his shirt from the side of the couch and slipped it on. He yawned and made his way over to Luna, who was sipping her new cup of coffee. She already felt shaky and nervous from the last cup, so this one was only added to her anxiousness. She put one hand on the kitchen island she was leaning against and started to tap her fingers on the counter. On the other side of the island, Darick reached his hand over to her side and gently took her hand in his. His hand was so warm compared to her skin, which was shocking since she had been the one holding the coffee cup.

"Do you need to feed again today?" she asked.

Darick shook his head. "I'm fine." He let go of her hand, and Luna eyed him. It must've been the wrong thing to say because she noticed his moody expression came back. Maybe it made him feel too vulnerable.

"Where's Samara?" he asked.

"She's outside," Luna replied. She felt exposed now. He obviously figured out that she enjoyed his touch and company. Did she seem needy to him? She wasn't asking him to drink from her for that reason; she was just worried about him and his energy levels. She didn't want him having hunger pains and discomfort because he was too afraid to ask her to feed.

Samara came into the house with her empty coffee cup. "Let's skedaddle. Everyone's awake. Your dad and Aywin are below saddling up the horses. Wear a rain jacket. Looks like it's going to pour," she said.

Luna nodded and grabbed her rain jacket. She didn't really need anything else. Darick didn't even have a rain jacket, but apparently, the cold didn't affect him the same way. As they walked to the horses, Luna could feel the rain droplets starting to fall. Aywin waved at Luna, and she gave him the middle finger.

"Good morning to you too," Aywin grumbled sarcastically.

He was already on his horse. Luna's father was on his as well. Samara hopped onto her horse. Luna looked over at Darick, who was mounting the horse that they had shared the previous day. His gold eyes found hers. Luna ignored him and mounted Samara's horse instead.

They all started trotting down the trail towards the base. The wind and rain picked up, hitting the side of them hard. Luna could barely see straight. She wondered how Samara could ride with such low visibility. The rain was painful when it hit her face, the ice-cold water like razors. A lightning bolt flashed across the sky, and a few seconds later, a crack of thunder echoed from above, shaking the ground beneath them. Luna glanced behind her to see how Darick was holding up. She could barely make out his silhouette, but he was keeping up fine. She felt bad that he wasn't even wearing a jacket; he was going to be soaked, though the thought of a wet shirt clinging to him wasn't the worst image Luna had imagined.

"Almost there!" Samara yelled from ahead.

The wind had picked up so much that Luna had a hard time hearing past it. The lightning flashes were getting more frequent, and the thunder coming quickly after the bolts, meaning the storm was directly above them now. Luna could see lights in the distance. The base was surrounded by a sixty-foot stone wall. It reminded Luna of the castles that the Elves used to build a long time ago. The horses were running hard against the wind and rain; mud coated their hooves.

Out of nowhere, a lightning bolt struck the ground right in front of them. The flash was so bright that Luna thought she had been blinded. The horse reared back and flung Samara and Luna off. Luna landed hard, her ass hitting the ground first before her head swung back and hit last. The impact took Luna's breath away. Shocked, Luna didn't feel any pain right away, but after a few seconds, her tail bone began to throb as well as her neck and head. She didn't feel any sharp pain, so she didn't think she broke anything. The rain was coming down so hard that she had to keep trying to blink to get a good look at her surroundings. She could taste the coppery tang of blood in her mouth.

She heard voices nearby and tried to look for Samara. Her mouth wouldn't work; no words could come out. She was still out of breath and trying to take in air. She rolled onto her side and began to cough. Soon, her chest and lungs stopped having a hissy fit, and she was able to take some normal breaths.

"Luna, are you all right?!" Darick's voice was beside her now; he sounded worried.

She felt his hands grip around her waist and pull her into a seated position. He was assessing her to see if she had broken any bones.

"How's your head? Do you feel any pain anywhere?" he questioned sternly.

Luna made eye contact with Samara, who was above ten feet away and getting helped by Aywin and her father. Samara was standing up now. Luna sighed in relief—her friend was okay.

"Luna?" Darick asked.

Luna's eyes snapped back to his. "Oh, no, it's fine. I'm fine. I'm sore, but I don't think I broke anything."

She started to try and stand up, and Darick assisted her, his strong hands supporting her body. Once she stood up, she felt okay. She was going to feel this in the morning. Her body was pressed against his cold chest. His T-shirt was completely soaked through, and his skin was visible through it. How was he not cold? She was shivering. Darick wrapped himself around her in a hug to warm her up, but it didn't help, considering he was just as wet. Luna's teeth chattered.

Samara hobbled over. "You all right?" she asked.

Luna broke the hug with Darick. "Yeah, you?"

"I'll live," Samara stated.

They gave each other a quick hug. Luna's father came over with the horse that had bucked them off. "Are you all right, Luna?" her father asked.

Luna nodded and forced a smile. "I'm okay, Dad. Let's get moving."

Aywin gave Luna a tight squeeze. "Don't ever do that again! I thought you two had died," he said. His hair was mated to his face, and he looked quite dishevelled, which was a hard look for him considering Aywin had the family genes of beauty. No matter the look, he seemed to pull it off.

Everyone mounted their horses again. Luna noticed that Darick was being extra quiet. His eyes had been on her the entire time; he hadn't even checked to see if Samara was okay. Luna's legs felt a little shaky, but she knew she'd be fine; it was still the adrenaline racing through her. They began to ride again, and the rain seemed to be letting up. The skies were still dark, and the thunder still roared. They arrived at the front gate of the base, where they were met by a few Warrior Elves who didn't seem to be enjoying the rain either. They were soaked and miserable. It made Luna giggle a bit just looking at the young fellows. Samara spoke with the boys, who recognized her and let them all in.

The base was built in a square shape. There were multiple stone buildings on the inside for training, offices, and weapon storage as well as a bunker underneath the base. There were lots of Warriors, on foot or riding horses. It was busy for a rainy, muddy day. Samara and Luna were at the front of the group. Samara led them to a tall, circular tower.

"This is the main headquarters for war planning. This is where we are meeting everyone this morning before doing some training this afternoon," Samara said. Luna nodded and regretted it instantly because her neck began to throb badly.

Everyone dismounted. A few Warrior Elves took their horses from them and brought them to the stables. Samara made a "follow me" motion with her hand as she walked towards the door of the tower. She opened it, and they all stepped inside.

The warmth hit Luna's skin, and she felt ten times better. There was a fireplace somewhere here that she would love to stand by for hours. Samara led them down a dark hallway, to a staircase that curved up. They continued to follow her up the staircase. Luna's knee was giving her some pain; she probably tweaked it when she fell. When they got to the top, Luna gasped.

The room was large with big windows and tall ceilings. In the centre of the room were benches set up in half-circles, and they were full of Elves all dressed in their best attire. It made Luna feel insecure, with her clothes clinging to her body like a second skin. She spotted a fire crackling at the far left of the room.

Among all the unfamiliar faces, Torion stood up. "Ah, you've arrived." He beamed; then his face sunk at the look of the five Elves, soaking wet and in a mess.

Torion flicked his wrist. "Max, could you get these people some fresh clothes? Make sure to get their sizes right," he said smoothly.

Max nodded and shyly snuck out of the room through a doorway. The group walked over to the benches and sat down across from the Elves already seated. There were so many Elves Luna didn't recognize. She was trying to figure out who was who. She recognized the Plains right away; their features were so unlike the Ancients that they were hard to miss. Their pointy, hairy ears were massive, and their faces were shaped as if they were part cat.

When Torion sat down, a tall, lean male stood up. He had white hair that reminded Luna of Shaela's. He had tanned-brown skin and wore clothes that Luna hadn't seen in a long time, which were off-white, made of cotton, and hung loosely on his lean frame. She peered down and noticed he wasn't wearing any shoes. His ears stretched out wide, and Luna could see a long tail flickering behind him.

"I'm Basil, leader of the Plains," he stated.

Luna raised her eyebrows. Their tribe weren't as advanced as the Ancients, despite the Ancients trying to share their technology with them. The Plains had always refused. Basil appeared nice. He had a calming demeanour that relaxed Luna. Basil sat down slowly, and a male voice spoke up. Luna's eyes wandered until she found who it was: a large, burly man with brown hair and a beard. She recognized him right away. It was Lee, the head of the Warrior Elves and Samara's boss.

"Glad you made it here; it was pouring rain out there. I wasn't sure if you were going to ride in that storm," Lee said.

Samara smiled. "Well, sir, you know me, always taking the risk."

He gave her a small smile back, and his eyes went to Darick. "You must be the Vampire," he said. His tone turned serious and intimidating. Darick was sitting next to Luna and Samara in the front row. Her father and Aywin were behind them.

Darick leaned his body towards Lee. "I am," he said coldly.

Luna cursed inside. Why did he have to be so ominous?

"We are choosing to trust you," Lee responded, his eyes never leaving Darick's.

Darick leaned back into the bench, and Luna swore she saw his lips curve into a smile.

"Our battle plans have been set based on these Vampires coming from the sky. This morning, we sent troops into each community to move Elves into their community halls; this way they will be protected from the Vampires. It's impossible to know where they will come from. The Plains have set up their own troops and plan. However, if the Vampires choose to attack them first, we will go and assist them, and vice versa. We have educated the Warriors on how to kill the Vampires. Our Warriors are strong; they are the best of the best. We have also told the community Elves how to kill the Vampires. Any Elf in the community that wants to fight has been given the right to. From your perspective, Vampire, anything you would like to add?" Lee asked, although his question seemed to be a tease; he really didn't care what Darick thought.

"Darick," Luna blurted to Lee.

All eyes looked to her. Lee stared at her like as if she was a child.

"Excuse me?" Lee asked.

"His name is Darick, not Vampire," she stated. She heard her father clear his throat behind her. Lee glared at Luna before diverting his attention back to Darick. She felt Darick's thigh rub against hers.

"Vampires are faster than your kind. They're stronger. They have been in many wars and know how to fight. Strategy will win the war for your planet. Allowing community Elves to fight will just end in more bloodshed… and more blood means more food for the Vampires," Darick replied.

Lee's face had a look of shock on it. Luna realized that nobody knew about the blood thing.

She elbowed Darick's side. "The blood," she whispered. He looked at her questioningly for a second, then clued in.

"We drink blood to live. If you injure a Vampire during the fight, he will find a food source and heal instantly. He will still survive without drinking the blood, but it just speeds up the healing process… unless you chop our heads off or take our hearts out, which is a lot harder than you would think," Darick explained.

Lee gulped. Clearly the blood thing disturbed him. Luna noticed the other Elves around him were appalled by the blood thing too, except for Torion.

"All right then. No untrained Elves on the field," Lee stated.

Luna heard a door creak open and turned to see Max carrying a backpack of what she assumed was clothes. Torion nodded towards the benches where Luna was sitting. Max brought the backpack over to Samara, who thanked him.

"Your group should change into something dry. We have some food coming in a few minutes. Bathrooms for changing are over there to the left," Torion said.

Most of the Elves got up from the benches. The only ones who stayed were Lee, Torion, Max, and a few other Elves that Luna presumed were high up in the army or political chain. Samara had taken out a clean top and pants from the bag. Luna did the same and passed it to Darick. They all took turns going to the bathroom and changing.

Once Luna put her new clothes on, she felt so much better. She knelt by the fire and enjoyed the heat. She was wearing pants that fit a bit too big and a top that was a little snug in the shoulders, but she wasn't going to complain. Her shoes were off and drying by the fire with her socks as well as the rest of the group's clothes.

Food was brought in by some female Elves. They all made googly eyes at Darick as they came in. Luna couldn't blame them; he was an extremely attractive guy. On large tables that lined the right side of the room, they set up the food: an assortment of fresh fruits, crackers, and cheeses with coffee, tea, and water. Luna walked over and poured herself some herbal tea. Samara had got a coffee and went over to speak with Lee. They were in deep conversation. Her father was speaking with Torion. Darick stood by the window alone, looking out at the base.

Aywin nudged Luna's side. "Everything all right, L?" he whispered.

Luna sipped her tea. "I'm not sure. I'm scared we aren't going to win this. Aren't you?"

Aywin munched on some cheese and crackers. "Try not to worry until we are actually dying." He smirked.

Luna rolled her eyes. "Wow, great advice," she said sarcastically.

He winked. "I'm known for my advice."

"Honestly, though, aren't you scared?" she questioned seriously.

Aywin sighed, his cheerful complexion gone. "Luna. If these Vampires truly invade planets for a living, I guarantee you they will be prepared. And if Darick left them to come and tell us, they'll know, so they are going to be extra prepared. A short summary of where my head is at is that we are probably fucked," Aywin replied.

Luna's chest ached because she knew Aywin was right.

Chapter X

L una finished up her second cup of tea. The stormy clouds had disappeared from the sky, and the sun had come out. It shone brightly through the large windows and lit up the room in glory. Darick had been standing alone for a long time now while everyone else chatted. She wondered what thoughts were going through his mind. Did he think that they could win this war? Luna awkwardly made her way over to Darick. She didn't want to disturb him if he was deep in thought. As soon as she stood by the window next to him, his eyes met hers, his expression tight and stern.

"Is this place different than the other planets?" Luna asked softly.

She had already gotten his attention, might as well converse with him. Darick looked out the window again. Luna waited patiently for a response from him. He tended to think a lot before speaking; something that most people didn't do. The silence between sentences became unbearable at times for her.

"It is. From what I remember of the planet I was on before, it had trees and plants like this one, but they looked different. Same colours, though. Most of the animals that I've seen on your planet are bigger than the ones on ours. Our horses don't have long legs like yours, but their hair on their body is longer than the ones you have. Small differences. I suppose enough to make it foreign to me," Darick answered.

Luna leaned her forehead against the coolness of the window. The fireplace had gotten to her now as well as the tea, and she was feeling warm. Or maybe it was because she was so close to Darick. She saw that he was watching her again. The shirt that he had on now was white with long sleeves. The V-neck showed just the right amount of his muscular chest. He had dark-grey cargo pants on that fit snuggly around his thighs.

"You are truly one of the most divine women I've ever seen," Darick said out of nowhere.

Luna's eyes snapped up to Darick's. He had smirk on his face now, the seriousness gone. Luna hadn't been expecting him to say that. Did he really think that about her? She hesitated, not knowing what to say to that. Does one say thank you in response? She decided she would smile first, so at least he didn't think she was stroking out. Darick let out a deep chuckle before looking out the window again. His smile continued. Luna turned around to see if everyone else was still busy. They were all chatting; nobody was paying her or Darick any attention. Luna stepped closer to Darick. She could feel the heat of his body against her skin. Goose bumps prickled across her arms. Enough time went by that she decided to change the subject.

"Are you going to fight?" she whispered.

He faced her. The smile was gone; replaced with a concerned look. "I will," he said.

"Aren't they your friends? Your family? Why are you willing to kill your kind for us?" Luna questioned.

She never had thought about how much Darick was willing to sacrifice when he came here. Everything he ever knew was gone. He was in a world where the Elves welcomed him by beating him and putting him into a prison. The patience, perseverance, and humble nature of Darick bewildered Luna.

"Because they're in the wrong. And they won't listen to me," Darick replied.

Luna grasped Darick's hand in hers. Her small feminine fingers stroked his palm. She felt his body shiver at her touch.

"You were willing to risk it all. How did you even know we would listen?" Luna asked.

Darick sighed. "Luna, it doesn't matter."

"You were willing to DIE. Do you have a death wish?" she asked. Luna wondered what this all came down to.

"When you've seen enough death, you are willing to sacrifice yourself to save others," Darick responded shakily.

Luna could see the emotions fluttering within him. He was hurting. He'd seen horrible things. She stroked her hands up his arms and back down again. She wished she could hug him here, but she didn't want the others to think wrongly of her. She was beginning to care for Darick, and it scared her.

She stepped away. "I'm sorry," she murmured.

She could feel tears stinging in her eyes. She wasn't completely sure what she was apologizing for. Was it for pushing him to break, or because she was getting too emotionally connected to him? She left him at the window and went over to Samara and Lee.

"When are we training?" Luna interrupted.

Samara and Lee both turned and looked at her.

"You aren't going into the battle," Lee stated.

Luna's anger flared up. "I am trained to fight, so I will fight. I'm not a regular civilian," she stated authoritatively.

Lee looked at Samara.

"It's okay. She can fight," Samara said to Lee, "because I sure as hell know that if we tell her she can't fight, she's going to be out there fighting anyways. At least, this gives us time to show her some tricks with a sword." Samara gave Luna a quick wink when Lee wasn't watching.

"Okay, fine. You can fight. But that means Samara is your babysitter. You guys can head to the training yard. It looks like it has stopped raining," he said.

Luna smiled and gave Samara a pat on the shoulder as a thank-you gesture.

Samara stood up. "Let's go, people!" she shouted.

Luna's father came over to her. He'd overheard the conversation with Lee. "I'm worried about you going into battle. I wish you wouldn't," he whispered, hoping no one else would listen into the conversation.

Luna appreciated that; her father knew she didn't like to appear weak. "I'm going to fight no matter what. I'm not one to sit back and watch while everyone else sacrifices something. Are you going to join us in training?" she asked.

He shook his head. "I train with a sword any chance I get at home and at the base sometimes. I'm an old man, so I have to keep my strength up." He gave her a pat on the back. "Go kick some ass."

Luna, Samara, Aywin, Darick, and Lee made their way down the stairs and back outside. They followed Lee down a concrete pathway that winded between buildings. Eventually, the path came out to a large yard full of everything one would need to practise fighting. There were a few Warriors already practising together. Lee went and grabbed a few fake wooden swords. He tossed one to each of them.

"Let's see what you've got, Vampire boy?" Lee threatened.

Darick smirked and went into the middle with Lee.

Luna was already swinging her wooden sword around; it was as heavy as a real sword. She heard a grunt and turned to look at Darick and Lee, who had begun fighting. Their wooden swords clanged against each other loudly. Both men were strong and using a lot of force against one another. Luna couldn't help but notice how seemingly smooth Darick reacted to Lee's blows. He didn't even seem tired. He swung and moved swiftly. He almost appeared... bored. Meanwhile, Lee was putting in all his effort; his face was red with fury, and his skin slick with sweat. Darick finally decided he was done playing around and easily knocked Lee's sword to the ground and pointed his own at Lee's chest, conveying it would've been a death blow. Lee stumbled back, stunned. Luna expected him to freak out and have a man hissy fit, but instead, he began to laugh. He reached a hand out, and they shook hands awkwardly. Clearly, people didn't shake hands where Darick was from.

"I don't think I've ever come across a fighter like you," Lee stated.

Darick's glared at Lee, and Luna wondered why he suddenly looked so pissed off; Lee had just complimented him. Darick put his sword down, then left the practice area, disappearing down a random pathway.

Lee frowned at Darick for a second before turning to the rest of them. "Who's next? How 'bout you, Aywin?" he said, and pointed his wooden sword at Luna's brother.

Aywin gulped. "Uh, sure."

Luna watched as her brother struggled with fighting.

"Let's practise too," Samara said to Luna.

Luna couldn't help but look over Samara's shoulder to where Darick had run off to.

"Hey, Nexus to Luna? Don't worry about your man. He seems... grumpy," Samara stated.

Luna nodded. "Yeah, okay, let's fight."

The two of them squared off. Luna had never fought Samara before, but she knew Samara was one of the best fighters the Elves had. Samara swung first, and Luna blocked the blow and stepped to the side. Luna readjusted her grip and thrust the wooden sword out with her right arm. Samara smirked and slid forward to deflect the blow, then took a swing at Luna's left arm. Luna felt the sword hit her arm, but it wasn't hard. Samara had slowed the sword down so it wouldn't hurt her. They kept at it, untangling their swords, ducking, and slashing. By the time they stopped, Luna's arms and shoulders felt like they were going to fall off. Her knee was aching even worse from the fall off the horse, and her neck was killing her. She felt like she was eighty years old. Samara walked a bit stiffly too, and Luna suspected that she was feeling sore.

Luna and Samara looked over at Lee and Aywin. Poor Aywin was struggling for his life. He was sweating, disordered, and red in the face.

"I think if you keep going, your face is going to match your hair colour," Luna called out playfully.

Lee and Aywin stopped fighting. Lee sauntered over, and Aywin limped. The look on his face was priceless. He held up his middle finger at Luna.

"I love you too," Luna said, and grinned.

They went back to the tower to freshen up and eat some more food. Darick was still nowhere in sight.

"You were decent at fighting," Samara said to Luna. The two of them sat by the fire, eating bread and butter.

"You should see me hand-to-hand; I'm much better," Luna said, and stuffed some bread into her mouth.

Samara laughed. "Well, you are no trained Warrior Elf, but you'll hold your own, Luna. Just remember to be careful. When we go into battle, I want you and Aywin to be with me and my troops," Samara said.

Luna gave her best friend a side hug. "Ah, I'm not worried."

Samara raised her eyebrows. "Says the one who is worrying ninety-nine percent of the time," she replied with a grin.

Luna shrugged. "They say that worrying keeps you on your guard."

"Nobody has ever said that," Samara said, and smacked Luna on the shoulder.

They both shared a laugh that had Luna's belly hurting. She ate her last piece of bread before standing up and announcing to Samara, "I'm going to go and look for Darick."

Samara winked. "Don't let me find you making out in a corner."

***

Luna left the tower and walked around the base. The sun was bright and shining. It was a gorgeous day out after all that morning rain. There was little to no wind and only a few clouds in the blue sky. As Luna strolled along, she felt the anxiety brewing around the base. She could feel the nervousness of the Warriors about the Vampire situation. Everybody was on edge. The Warriors were puttering about, getting prepared for battle, which was fair, given that their planet was about to face their impending doom.

Luna continued to scout the base in search of Darick. He couldn't be that hard to find; it was not like he fit in there. Sure enough, Luna found him, but in a place where she least expected him to be. The base had a garden full of lush plants. Throughout the garden were stone statues of famous Warrior Elves. Darick was sitting in a carved marble gazebo draped in grape vines. Luna strode over to him and sat down. He was doing the stern, staring thing again, where his eyes just looked out at the distance for no particular reason. He was in his head more than any other male Luna had ever known.

"Everything all right?" she asked, her voice coming out as a whisper.

His eyes narrowed. "Why are you so concerned with me?" He turned to her. With the sun shining down on them, his gold irises were brilliant. Luna didn't know how to respond to his question. He had made it clear earlier, after the fight with Lee, that something was wrong before he disappeared.

"I think you are bad at hiding your emotions and bad at communicating them," Luna stated boldly.

His eyes darkened. "You'd be surprised at what I can hide."

Luna raised a brow. "I'm not sure I know what that means, but don't try and change the subject. Can't you just talk normally to me? Give me something at least."

He shrugged and became serious again. "So, what if I am? There's nothing to talk about anyways."

Luna sighed. "You are so frustrating sometimes."

Darick eyed her. "Frustrating?"

"YES. With a capital F. Actually, I should say fucking frustrating. Double F. How's that?" she replied.

Darick raised an eyebrow at her, and she grumbled.

"Dammit, Darick, can you just open up to me once without getting all sensitive?" she snapped.

Darick reached out his hands and pulled her onto his lap. He was so strong that he made the transition seem smooth. His hands held her around the waist. Luna's breath hitched as he dipped his mouth down to her lips and kissed her softly. Her hands came up and cupped his face as they kissed.

"Darick," she said against his lips.

"What?" he murmured back.

161

"I told you to stop changing the subject," she replied with a smile.

He kissed her again, more intensely, and pulled her body against his. She could feel his smile against her mouth. Luna broke the kiss. They sat there, breathing heavy and looking at each other with a passion Luna hadn't felt in a long time. Darick's grip loosened on her hips.

"We should probably get back," Luna blurted.

He didn't seem pleased with her comment, but he agreed nonetheless. They got up and headed back to the tower. Samara and Aywin were waiting for them. Lee had gone off to do "bossy" stuff apparently. Luna wasn't sure if she liked the guy or not.

"Ah, he's alive!" Aywin said with a big grin as Luna and Darick strolled in.

"I'm hard to kill," Darick responded.

Aywin laughed nervously. "So I hear."

"In all seriousness, how hard is it to chop a Vampire's head off?" Aywin asked.

Samara and Luna silently watched the two men interacting.

"Harder than it is to chop an Elf's head off," Darick said plainly.

Aywin put his hands on his hips. "You don't even know how difficult that is. You've never done it."

Darick stepped closer to Aywin. "Would you like me to give it a try?"

Samara burst out laughing, while Luna stood there in horror.

"Enough, let's get going, you two," Luna said.

Darick sent Aywin a glare before going to the fireplace and snatching his clothes up.

"It was a simple question," Aywin grumbled to himself.

Luna went over to the fireplace as well and grabbed her clothes, which were now nice and dry. She went to the bathroom and changed. Everybody else did the same thing. She felt much better in something that was meant for her body. Her legs were long, and it was impossible to find pants that fit her properly. Luna then followed Samara down the stairs and outside.

"You're going already?" she heard her father's voice boom.

Luna looked around, trying to find him in all the people milling about. Her eyes caught his red hair. He trudged over.

"Yeah, we're going to head back," Luna replied once he got close enough so that she didn't need to yell.

"I'm going to stay at base camp. Torion's given me leadership of one of the troops, and I need to stay to get them organized," he said.

Samara nodded. "I can ride back with you later if you'd like? I have to go and see my troops."

Arin raised his eyebrows. "Troops?" he repeated.

Samara nodded. "I have multiple units. But when we go to war, I will have my main troop. I still need to make sure the other ones are all set; they will have their own leaders. Who knows, maybe you'll be a leader of one of my units?" she replied with a smile. Arin nodded.

"All right let's go then," he said.

Samara waved down a Warrior Elf. He came over quickly, then bent down at the knee in front of her. "What can I do for you," he asked with his head bowed.

Samara motioned to Luna, Aywin, and Darick. "Find these three some horses," she stated. Then she gave Luna a side-hug. "I'll see you later tonight."

The Warrior Elf got up and strode quickly to the stable while Samara and Arin left down a pathway. Luna felt an arm move around her head and pull her into a playful choke hold. She knew it was her brother. Aywin took his fist from his other arm and rubbed it on top of her head, messing up her hair. He used to do this all the time when they were children. Aywin had a growth spurt early on as a child, and he had been taller and lankier than all the other kids, but most importantly, taller than his sister. Still much taller than her now, he continued to use that to his advantage. She elbowed him in the side of the gut, then sunk back against him to slip out of the choke hold. By the time she got out, they were both shaking with laughter and having trouble breathing. Luna's hair was sticking straight up.

"You look like one of those alpacas from Mom's friend's farm," Aywin said. His eyes were tearing up from all the giggling.

Luna took her hands and combed through her hair. "Better?" she asked, and did a pose.

"Now, I'm not sure if it's a bad hair day or just your hair," Aywin chuckled.

She smacked his arm. Darick was leaning up against a stone wall, watching the two of them. Luna could see a smirk tugging at the sides of his mouth.

"What? Got something to say?" Luna questioned Darick.

He shook his head. "Anything I'll say will likely get me punched," he replied with an amused expression.

"Good call. L's a violent one," Aywin snickered.

Luna smacked his arm again. "Am not!" She glared.

"Then stop hitting me!" Aywin protested.

The Warrior Elf came over with two horses; they were different horses than this morning. One was white, and the other grey. They were beautiful animals.

The man pointed to the white one. "This is Angel," he said, and gave the horse to Darick.

He gave the grey one to Aywin. "This is Storm."

Luna sighed. It looked like she was going to have to ride with someone again.

"Thank you," Luna said to the Warrior Elf, who nodded and walked away.

Aywin jumped up onto Storm.

Darick's eyes met Luna's. "Riding with me?" he asked.

Luna shrugged. "Sure, why not?"

Darick bent down and lifted her up by the waist. She let out a screech that caught a Warrior Elf's attention. Darick placed her on top of the horse. Her face was red with embarrassment from the accidental scream.

Aywin was laughing. "You sounded like a bird squawking."

Luna rolled her eyes. Darick jumped up. She froze as his body contacted hers and pressed against her. He was so warm and made her feel things she couldn't think about right now. His head leaned down to her ear, and she could feel his breath tickle her neck.

"Ready?" he whispered. All she could do was nod.

The two horses took off, trotting through the base and back through the gates to leave. The weather was so much nicer this round that Luna could enjoy the warm breeze on her face. This time she was in front of Darick and could see the landscape.

Aywin and Darick urged their horses forward and they galloped across the field towards their homes. Luna caught herself grinning ear to ear. She closed her mouth before a bug flew in the throat. The horses eventually slowed down to a trot, and she began to see the cluster of trees where the houses were ahead. They were still too far away to see the actual structures. Aywin and his horse were a bit behind Darick and Luna. He seemed to be daydreaming; it ran in Luna and Aywin's family.

"How did you learn to fight so well?" Luna asked Darick.

"My father," he stated, but he didn't sound proud about it.

"Was your father... cruel?" Luna questioned.

Darick let out a humourless laugh. "Cruel is an understatement."

Luna's chest tightened. What had Darick been through? She didn't want to keep asking him about his negative memories; she could tell they were bothering Darick. His body wasn't relaxed and pressed against hers anymore. Instead, he sat upright and rigid.

"Do you have any good memories?" Luna inquired.

"Sure, I do," Darick replied coarsely.

With that comment came an unbearable silence. After a few minutes of Luna trying to be patient, she exhaled annoyingly. She wished he would talk more.

"I'm trying to make conversation, Darick. Could you at least try?" She glowered.

Darick shifted his weight more towards her. "Tell me about your childhood," he said.

It was another diversion, but if he was willing to talk, Luna would go along with it. She thought for a moment. She wasn't sure what memories she should bring up; she had so many.

"My childhood was ninety-nine percent good. I mean, my father was hard on us, but, like, not in a super bad way. My mom has always been super protective, but, like, at the end of the day, my parents did a good job at raising Aywin and I.

"I was the troublemaker for sure. Aywin was Mr. Goody-Two-Shoes, doing well in school, and he never got into trouble unless it was with me. I did well in school too; I just caused problems. I got distracted in class and got detention at times. But, like, overall, I wasn't that bad. I was artistic as well as athletic, so I spent time doing sports while also painting or drawing. I love reading, as you know. Aywin does too, though. My mom is an amazing cook, and Aywin likes to cook. He makes the best food. I didn't inherit that." Luna decided to stop talking; she realized she was babbling away and was probably starting to sound annoying. Her cheeks reddened.

"I'm sorry. I just don't do well with silence," Luna said.

"Don't be sorry. I like hearing about your life," Darick replied genuinely.

Luna leaned into Darick. She felt safe with him. The rest of the way, they rode in silence, which didn't make Luna uncomfortable. She didn't feel pressured to talk to Darick like she did before; maybe it was because she was feeling more at home in his presence. The achiness in her chest caused by Edric was still present, but she pushed it further down and focused on the present moment.

They dismounted their horses and put them into the little barn area near their home. There was plenty of hay left, but the horses could use some fresh water. A creek ran behind the trees, which was perfect, as they could get some water there instead of going to the river, which was quite a walk away. Aywin was limping still from the practice fighting. Luna watched him as he picked up a wooden bucket.

"Aywin, Darick and I got this. You go and maybe take a nap?" Luna said.

Aywin smiled. "I'm honestly okay. It's just soft tissue; nothing broken," he replied.

Luna shrugged. "Eh, that's all right. You still go and nap, mister." She lightly pushed him towards the ladder to his house. He rolled his eyes and did as he was told. He must be hurt pretty good to not put up more of an argument. Luna was sore, but she could deal with the pain. Luna tossed a pail to Darick, who caught it with ease, even though he hadn't been looking.

Luna gave him a dirty look. "How can you be so good at everything? Even things that shouldn't be easy, you make them look like child's play," Luna teased.

Darick shrugged. "I don't know what you're getting at," he replied.

Luna groaned. "Oh, come on. You made catching a bucket look good. Why are you so… elegant?"

Darick chuckled. "Elegant?"

Luna grinned and did a graceful dance in front of him as they walked to tease him. "Yeah, elegant like this," she said as she finished the dance.

Darick shook his head. "I'm not sure I'd describe that as elegant." His tone was serious, but his expression showed that he was joking around.

"You don't think I'm a good dancer?" Luna questioned. She had thought the dance was pretty good, considering she never took dance lessons as a child.

"Your words, not mine," Darick replied.

Luna liked this version of him: less grumpy, more fun. He was opening to her. They got to the creek just beyond the trees, and Luna dipped her bucket in first, filling it with fresh, cold mountain water. Darick filled his next. The buckets were large. Luna struggled as they walked back. She had to use two hands and carry it in front of her. She also had to take breaks every minute or two.

Darick carried his with ease. "Do you—" he started.

Luna cut him off. "I'm good."

She didn't want help; that was one thing she hated. She was independent and did not need anyone's help. At least, that was what she told herself. Maybe that was why she was still currently single.

They finally got back and poured the buckets into the horses' water trough. The horses drank the water right away.

Luna and Darick climbed up the ladder and went into the house, which was warm but not as warm as outside. A few windows had been left open to allow the breeze to air out the home. The two of them plopped themselves onto the couch with a sigh. It had been a long day. It felt like

169

they'd been gone forever, even though it had only been a little while. Luna massaged her neck, which was still sore from the fall. Darick saw her doing so and scooted next to her. He took over the massage by gently placing her hands down onto her lap before kneading her shoulders and back.

Luna closed her eyes. For a man with strong hands, he was gentle with her. He massaged her for a long time, perhaps close to an hour; Luna wasn't sure because she fell asleep halfway through. When she woke up, she had snuggled onto his lap, and he was reading a book. She wondered where she got the book from since she hadn't noticed any in the house. She yawned and looked up at him before realizing the situation. She quickly sat up and moved off him. Darick lifted his eyes off his book slowly and glanced at her with amusement. Instead of commenting on her strange behaviour, he continued to read his book.

Luna got off the couch and went to the kitchen for some food. It was getting close to dinner time, and she was starving. She grabbed a nut mix and some handpicked veggies from the cooler, then sat down on the couch and munched on her food. She bit down on a crisp carrot, and noticed Darick's eyes flicked off the book with a glare; the sound of her munching in a quiet room must be irritating him. She smiled sheepishly before continuing to chew on the carrot.

Just then, Samara opened the front door and strode in. Wind blew her short hair in all directions, but somehow, she pulled it off. "Thank God. I thought I was going to walk into you two having sex or something," she said, and wiped her forehead off.

Luna unintentionally spat out her carrot. It flew across the room and hit the wall. Samara snorted. Darick casually picked up his book and began to read again.

"I sense a tense energy," Samara said carefully.

She made purposely slow movements around the kitchen while grabbing food to eat. Luna leaned back on the couch and rested her feet on the coffee table. The energy in the room revolved around her awkward feelings with Darick. She didn't even want to have feelings for him, but she did. And he was attracted to her, but she wasn't clear on his intentions. He was a different species, so that added a complication. Luna thought it would probably be better for them to be friends. Although so far, they had been friends with benefits: blood drinking and kissing benefits.

Luna motioned for Samara to come and join her on the couch. Samara looked from side to side, pretending like she didn't know Luna was pointing at her; then Samara pointed at herself. "Oh, me! Gotcha!" She said with a grin.

Luna flung her head back with irritation. "Samara!" she complained, more dramatically than she needed to.

Samara laughed and came over to the couch. "So, Darick dearest, what are you reading?" she asked. Luna exhaled; Samara was something....

Darick put the book down and looked at Samara with pinched lips and eyes like daggers. He was clearly wanting peace and quiet, but that was impossible when it came to the two female Elves in the room.

Samara brought her hands together for a clap. "Well then. I see the moodiness has returned full force."

Luna couldn't help but let out a giggle.

"I'm not moody," Darick retorted.

Luna crossed her arms. How Darick could say he wasn't moody when all her interactions with him had been an emotional roller coaster. Luna interrupted Samara before she could reply to his comment. "Oh, I see, then what are you?" Luna quizzed.

"Usually hungry," Darick growled. Luna gulped.

Samara exchanged a look with Luna and then her eyes widened. "Wait, like now? Do you—He needs… Oh. Okay, I should probably go for a few minutes, right? Are you like hungry now? Am I reading the room right?" Samara babbled. She stood up and left through the front door without Luna or Darick responding to her.

Luna's eyes snapped back to Darick with anger. "You could have just said something to me earlier!" she said abruptly.

Darick cursed under his breath. "Being dependent on someone as your source of food is not the most exciting thing in the world. Besides, I didn't realize I would have to feed this often," he said.

Luna bit the inside of her lip as she thought about what he said. He was probably embarrassed about having to feed from her, and he probably hated asking her. She took a few deep breaths. "Okay, fine. That's fair. But if we're going to try and make this blood-drinking thing work, you have to tell me when you're hungry before you rip someone's head off," she voiced.

His scrunched face eased up to a less pissed-off expression. Luna scooted herself closer to him on the couch and lifted her neck towards him. She moved her hair to the

172

side to expose her unscathed skin. Darick lowered his head down; his fangs found her flesh and pierced into it. The site of his bite felt warm, and soon, the warmth spread throughout her body in a heated, pleasurable blaze. She shuddered in his arms as he sucked mouthfuls of her blood into his body. Luna moaned softly as her energy began to ween. In that moment, Darick let go and licked her neck softly to heal the marks.

He stood up and went to the kitchen while Luna rested on the couch, feeling a bit dizzy. Darick came back over and handed her a cup of milk and a jar of juice. She smiled weakly and took the milk first. It was likely fresh milk from one of the farms, and she loved nothing more than a cool glass of it. After downing the whole thing, she felt much better within a few minutes. Darick watched her with a stern face.

"Feel better?" she asked. She could see his skin appeared healthier and wondered what he would look like after going weeks without feeding.

He gave her a slight nod. "I do, thank you," he replied.

The front door creaked open a crack. "I hear talking. Are you guys… decent?" Samara called.

Luna smirked. "You can come in," she yelled back.

"Oh, thank goodness. It was getting chilly out there," she said, and came in. She looked between Luna and Darick. "He drinks your blood often then?" Samara asked as she strode over to the couch and sat next to Luna.

Luna nodded, not sure how to respond to the comment.

Samara examined Luna with her eyes. "Where's the bite mark?" she asked.

"He heals it," Luna said.

Samara's eyes widened. "Shit! You can heal wounds? Do you think you could do that if someone got stabbed or something?" Samara asked.

Darick shrugged. "Depends on the severity of the wound. To be honest, I've never really tried healing anything other than a bite I've left on someone."

Luna's guts rolled at his remark—he had probably fed from hundreds of other women and men before. She was just another one of his feedings. She wondered if they had all felt the same pleasure from the experience. Annoyance took over her mood.

"Does it hurt?" Samara asked Luna.

"Doesn't feel like anything," Luna replied harshly.

Samara frowned. "Okay…"

Darick also looked at Luna with a questioning look, which pissed Luna off even more.

"How many women have you bit?" Luna asked. She couldn't help herself; she was on a roll tonight.

Darick blinked a few times. "I-I'm not sure," he said.

His voice wasn't as gruff as usual. He sounded disgusted with the question she was asking, as if he hated himself for even biting several women.

Luna exhaled. "I'm sorry. I just… I don't know. I must be tired. I should go to bed," she said.

She got up and went to the bathroom. There were a few unused toothbrushes, so she took one out and brushed her teeth. She suddenly felt like having a shower. She peered into the cupboard and found a clean, folded towel. She turned the shower on. The water wasn't heated, so its coldness shocked her once she stripped and stepped in. She washed her hair and body swiftly, rinsed everything off, then turned off the water. After drying herself and getting back into her clothes, she left the bathroom.

Samara and Darick were playing cards. The two of them looked up at Luna as she crossed the room and went over to the bed without muttering a single word or making eye contact.

"Goodnight," Samara said sweetly.

Luna grumbled and pulled the sheets higher with vexation. Luna noticed that Aywin had never showed up; he must've been too tired.

Chapter XI

Luna felt like she rolled around in bed all night. She couldn't help but feel slightly jealous about Darick. When it came to men, so far Luna hadn't had the best luck, and he was likely just another one of those bad-luck guys. However, once morning arrived, when she finally decided to open her eyes, she felt less irritable.

She got up to the sound of Samara lightly snoring. Playing cards were scattered over the coffee table. Luna speculated that they had stayed up late. Darick was sprawled out on the couch. Most of his body was exposed from the small blanket wrapped mainly around his waist. He was wearing a dark pair of boxers, and they made his skin appear paler than usual. His large legs stuck out across the couch. Luna could see that he had some sort of serpent creature with wings tattooed on his thigh. She'd never noticed it before now. She decided to stop staring at the half-naked dude and went into the kitchen.

She grabbed some milk and poured herself a bowl of cereal. A guy in town made the cereal as well as the granola and granola bars; his food was super healthy. Luna crunched away at her cereal, purposely being loud, while she stared at

Darick. He appeared so peaceful in his sleep. One wouldn't think he drank blood as a hobby. Luna finished her cereal, then made herself a cup of coffee.

The sky outside had lightened from the sun slowly rising—it was Luna's favourite part of the day. She went outside with a blanket and snuggled into one of the chairs. The birds weren't chirping yet. The forest and field around her were tranquil. The fresh scent of earth filled her nostrils. The sky had a few clouds in it this morning, and they were lit up with oranges, yellows, and pinks. Luna wished she had her painting supplies with her. She often painted sunrises or sunsets. The air was chilly again this morning; the cooler season was making itself known. Soon, she would wake up to a frost. The frosts didn't last long, though; sometimes it snowed and they would go a few months without fresh food. But that was why Elves liked to can their food—they canned everything, from fish, fruits, berries, veggies, soups, and so on.

The front door opened, and Darick came out. He was dressed now. Luna glared at him before shifting her gaze to the sunrise as she sipped her coffee. He sat in the chair next to her. His body emitted waves of heat; Luna could feel it through her blanket. Darick reached out and gently grasped her left hand. Her right hand held her coffee cup. She put her cup down and looked over at him. Her hands were freezing despite holding the coffee cup; his hands felt like he'd just been by a fire. He stroked her hand gently to warm it up.

"W-what are you doing?" Luna asked, baffled.

He was holding her hand. "You seemed cold," he stated, and yawned.

He was clearly not a morning person… or a morning Vampire—however you want that sentence to go.

Luna's heart melted. He had been so kind to her. She was being an ass hole. She reached her other hand over and he grabbed it too. They sat there for a few moments together, holding hands. It should have felt more intimate, but it didn't. He somehow made it feel normal to her, like they had been doing this for years, and it gave her a sense of repose.

"Did you sleep okay?" Luna asked. She removed her hands from his and grabbed her coffee to sip from. He relaxed his hands down the sides of the chair.

"It was… all right. I was dreaming about my life before, remembering more things. I often feel as if I don't know myself," he admitted with a look of concern.

"How will you know when all your memories come back?" Luna asked.

Darick shifted in his seat, his large body making the chair groan. "Right now, I can grasp the areas where there are memories missing. I'm not sure how to describe it. So, until those voids are filled, I'll know that I haven't gotten them all back," he explained.

"Do you remember anything more that would help us?" she questioned.

Darick shook his head. "Not really. I know that the ships they take to the other planets are massive, and I can recall what they look like."

"Darick, if you guys have all this crazy technology, wouldn't you think you'd have more than just swords?" Luna pondered out loud. That thought had been bugging her. What sort of weapons did these beings have?

Darick's face paled. Luna could see he had been thinking about this too. "Remember how I said they prefer to use their mouths to kill? It's true. I know that during most battles, they fight hands on. For some reason, I can't recollect if there's something else they use. It's been driving me mad. I can feel the memory pinching in my temple," he said with frustration.

"If they know you came here to warn us, I feel like they'll be making sure they have whatever weapons they need. They know we won't be taken off guard," Luna voiced.

Darick exhaled. "Honestly, Luna, I don't know how this battle is going to turn out. All I know is, when I fought Lee yesterday, it felt easy. Too easy. And if he's one of the best fighters you guys have, then your fucked," Darick stated.

Luna's stomach felt sick, but she refused to give into the negativity. "Darick, this is our home, our planet. Elves are strong. Elves are fighters. We aren't going to back down. EVER," she said with more confidence than she felt.

Darick's gold eyes studied her. "I hope you're right," he murmured. "Can I show you something?"

Luna raised an eyebrow. "Sure…"

He sat up straighter in his chair and looked out at the field. Luna's eyes went to the field too, wondering what the hell he was going to do. Suddenly, the wind began to pick up, and the once semi-clear sky was now a dark cloud. The wind became so strong that Luna could feel it pushing against her chair. She gasped and made eye contact with Darick. His eyes had changed from gold to dark black. And then, like nothing ever happened, it all stopped: no sign of darkness, no wind, and no feeling of impending doom in the pit of Luna's stomach.

She stared at Darick with a look of disbelief. His eyes were gold again, and a smirk was plastered to his face.

"Could you do that the entire time?" Luna asked, still in a state of shock.

"Technically, yes, but I had to remember it first before I knew I could do it," he replied.

"So, what else can you do?" Luna questioned.

Darick chuckled. "Why? Is that not enough?"

"That's not what I meant. You know, we could totally use that power against the Vampires," she said, suddenly feeling more hopeful.

Darick nodded. "Yes, I will use it. The other thing I can do is not helpful. It doesn't work on Vampires," Darick explained before he paused and looked out at the field again. "I can persuade others to do things."

Luna cleared her throat. "Excuse me? You can make me do whatever you want me to do? Have you ever done that to me before?" Luna asked abruptly. She suddenly felt exposed and vulnerable. There were so many ways he could misuse that ability.

Darick's face looked hurt, then angry. "I have never used it against you. But I did use it on those guards that day that I fed from you for the first time. It was the first time that I'd tried to use that ability after my head injury. During one of my visions, I'd seen myself doing it, so I thought I would try," he replied.

Luna's eyes widened. It all made sense now. That was why he'd called himself a "smooth talker." Luna relaxed back into her chair; she hadn't realized that she'd gotten so worked up that she was practically on the edge of her seat. "I'm sorry. I didn't mean for it to come out like that. I'm just surprised that you can… do that," she said softly.

"Hey, Luna!" she heard a male voice yell from below.

Luna got up and peered over the edge of the deck. It was Fin. It had felt like ages since she'd seen him, even though it hadn't been that long ago. She smiled down at him and waved.

"Want to come up?" she called back.

He was on a horse. His long dark hair had been tied back in a bun, and his goatee was more of a short beard now. "I can't. I'm heading to the base, but I'll meet you guys there," he replied, and with that, he took off with his horse.

"Can you guys try and be quiet? Why are you out here yelling at six in the morning?" Aywin protested.

Luna looked over and saw Aywin's head poking out the window of the house he and her dad were staying in. "Oh, sorry, I forgot you need your beauty sleep," Luna replied dryly.

Aywin smoothed back his hair. "I don't need sleep for my beauty, but I need it for sanity. So, keep it down over there." He raised up his middle finger, then tucked his head back through the window and shut it.

Luna laughed and shook her head. Aywin had suddenly decided he wasn't a morning person today. Luna grabbed her coffee cup and said, "I'm heading inside."

Darick followed her in. Samara was awake now. She was leaning against the island counter, eating an apple. Her hair was wet, meaning she just got out of the shower. Luna could smell the orange-citrus shampoo in the air. Luna joined Samara by the island, and Darick began to clean up the cards.

"I'm heading to the base early this morning," Samara said.

Luna thought about how Aywin wanted to get a bit more sleep. "I'll wait until Aywin is up. He's... grumpy this morning," Luna said, and rolled her eyes.

Samara took the last bit out of the crispy apple she was eating. The juice from the apple hit Luna's cheek. She took the sleeve of her shirt and wiped her face, which now smelled sweet.

Samara finished chewing. "I'll meet you there then." She put the rest of the apple in the compost, then went out the door after grabbing a jacket.

Luna turned to look at Darick, who had made himself comfortable on the couch. "Want to go for a hike?" she asked.

"A hike?" he repeated.

"I'm starting to think that you take after a parrot," Luna mumbled. "Yes, a hike. Like a walk up a mountain," she said more clearly.

"That sounds horrible," Darick replied.

"It's good exercise," Luna said with a frown.

"There are better ways to exercise," Darick said under his breath.

Luna sighed. "You don't have to come if you don't want to. I was just inviting you."

She reached up and tied her hair into a high ponytail. While she was doing so, Darick walked over to her. His hands wrapped around her waist, and he pulled her into his hard, strong body. Luna could've stopped it, but why when his touch felt so good. His head leaned down to her face as if he was going to kiss her. His breath was warm and minty.

"I'll go for a hike, but only because you're going," he said.

He let go of her waist and went out the front door. Luna, still shocked from unexpected intimate moment, took her a minute to gather up her thoughts. She took a deep breath before following him out the door.

***

Once they climbed down the ladder, Luna peered up at the mountain behind them. It was massive; there was no way they would climb the whole thing, but they could at least hike up to a good lookout.

She started to trek through the forest and past the creek. Darick followed just behind her. Both had long, athletic legs, so their strides were similar. Luna's legs were too long for her body, although Samara had always said she was jealous of Luna's figure; apparently, long legs were a good thing. Samara had a longer torso than Luna, and she was more petite than her. Luna had insecurities, but she felt lucky and healthy in her own body and figured that no matter what body she'd have, she'd always hate certain parts of it. That was how the mind worked, right? You want what you don't have. Girls in school wanted Luna's long, thick red hair, her perfect, sharp facial features, and the cute freckles under her eyes. Luna liked the thought of having dark hair but would never dye her own.

The pair hiked up the mountain in silence. Soon, the ground became rocky and slippery moss. Luna had to be careful not to slip; it was a good thing she had great balance. They climbed above the trees, and the wind was cool and refreshing against her back. The sun had risen, but the sky was overcast. It was still a magnificent view. Luna found a rock with a flat service big enough for both her and Darick to sit on. She sat down first, followed by Darick, who was grinning.

"I guess hiking is worth the exercise," he said.

She nodded. It was more peaceful up in the mountain than down by the house. The solitude of being some- where where nobody else was felt exhilarating for Luna. Sometimes, she felt she could live alone in the forest her entire life. She was an introvert after all.

"It's beautiful," Luna whispered.

Darick put his hand around her waist, a spot that he seemed to like. "It is," he said, his gold eyes looking at her.

She leaned against his body. She wasn't sure what type of relationship they had, but in the moment, he was exactly what she needed. She lifted her head up and met her lips with his. He kissed her gingerly, with a tenderness that made her yearn for more. Instead, they broke the kiss and enjoyed holding each other while staring off in the distance. After gazing out at the world for almost an hour, they headed back down the mountain.

This time, Darick had to catch Luna twice from slipping. The rocks were dangerous, and Luna still felt a little dizzy from the moment they had shared together. When they finally made it over the deadly, moss-covered rocks and back through the forest, Aywin and Arin were waiting. Luna went over to her father and gave him a hug. His facial expression had seemed sad, and she wondered how much this impending war was stressing him out. Luna had been keeping herself in a state of denial, where she deliberately chose to disassociate from the thought of the war until the Vampires came. And when they did, she bet she would have a small panic attack.

Her father squeezed her tightly, then broke away from the hug. He smelled like cigars and home, and it made Luna miss her mother.

"Will Mom be safe?" Luna asked.

Her father smiled and nodded. "Of course, she is. I didn't want her anywhere near here, so that's why she didn't come."

Luna nodded but what if she never saw her mom again? What if they all died? Those thoughts started to panic her, so Luna instantly shut her mind off and focused on the present moment.

"Let's get to the base," Arin stated with a gruff voice.

They all agreed and hopped on their horses. The sky was still cloudy. The greyness of the clouds made her think back to what Darick had done: Could he control the weather? What was his gift exactly?

The ride went smoothly. They got to the gates and dropped their horses off with one of the Warrior Elves. Samara was nowhere in sight, so Luna wondered if she'd be busy for most of the day.

They were walking towards the tower when a few Warrior Elves surrounded Darick, who didn't seem surprised. In fact, he had a look of contentment on his face, mixed with boredom. Torion strode over, from behind one of the Warrior Elves.

"Darick, when were you going to tell us that your father is the one who's in charge of the Soul Empire?"

Luna narrowed her eyes. "What are you guys talking about? Darick lost his memories, and he doesn't owe anything to you. You're lucky he is even helping us."

She noticed Aywin and Arin looked bewildered too. Did the Warrior Elves know something Luna didn't? What the hell was the Soul Empire?

"Let's go upstairs, shall we?" Torion suggested.

Darick still appeared calm, but Luna was freaking out. She had no idea what was going on, and she did not like that the Elves had begun to close in on them. It set off her fight-or-flight response. Instead of making any moves, she agreed to go into the tower. Her facial expression was a mixture of being pissed off and being confused at the same time.

They went into the tower and to the same room as the day before. The Warriors surrounded Darick, although they all had a healthy fear of him. If he really wanted to escape, there would be no stopping him. Torion motioned for everyone to sit. So, they did. Luna's face was red with fury. Aywin put his hand on his sister's arm.

"It's okay, Luna. It'll make sense in a minute," he assured.

Luna raised her eyebrows. "Are you part of this? Are they putting him in prison again?"

Aywin shook his head. "I'm not part of this. I've been helping with something else. Torion will explain," he said softly, but his words just aggravated Luna more.

"Someone tell me what the fuck is going on here?" Luna pushed.

Torion gave off his most genuine smile. "Luna, the Elves have always known about the Vampires. But it has been hundreds of years since our planet has mingled with the others. In our records, it's written that we had an alliance with the Vampires before Darick's father, Leon, took over the Soul Empire.

"The Elves used to have magical abilities, but we gave them up for peace with the Wizards. The Wizards had strict rules for all the planets to follow in order to avoid a rebellion. But they backfired. We thought we had avoided the conflict, but here it is… back to haunt us. You see, the planets of our galaxy used to meet with each other: the Wizards, the Vampires, the Pure Humans, and the Elves. There are other planets too, but their blood does not come from human origin. Our planets used to have a truce.

"The Wizards, like I said, were the most powerful and made most of the intergalactic decisions regarding trade and so forth. However, this all changed when a Witch had a child with a Vampire. Leon was born, and Leon became one of the most powerful beings in existence. He was seen as an outcast, never truly belonging anywhere. He ended up residing with the Vampires, as the Wizards wouldn't have him. Eventually, his powers surfaced and not a single Vampire on their planet could say a word against him—he became their ruler. And he had a death wish for the other planets. That was when their attacks started. From what we know, they killed the entire population of Wizards. We have a spaceship in the Science Base, which was gifted to us by the Wizards, but we haven't used it for a long-time.

"Since then, the Elves created a movement for environmental awareness, and we refuse to take part in building things that may jeopardize our planet. During the days when we used to space travel, upon request, a Warrior Elf collected Leon's DNA. Since Leon is a powerful Vampire, we were curious about what ran through his blood. When Darick arrived, we took his blood and put it through our system. Today, the results came back.... His blood matches with Leon's, which means he carries an unimaginable amount of power," Torion explained.

Luna was shocked. She had never dreamed the Elves would know so much about life beyond their planet. As far as she knew, Elves were mostly peaceful creatures, keeping to themselves and nature.

"What do you intend to do with Darick?" Luna asked.

Torion let out a humourless chuckle. "We can't trust him anymore," he stated.

"But why?! He came here to warn us," she said.

"We don't know that, Luna. You see... Leon and his wife, Thana, had two sons: one powerful, and the other invincible. The stories say, the one who is powerful is the eviler one of the brothers, and the one who is invincible is the good guy. The question is, what brother are you, Darick?" Torion pondered.

Luna knew for a fact he was the good guy. It was clear as day. How could the other Elves not see that?

"If he was evil, don't you think he would've killed us all by now?" Luna asked.

Torion grinned. "Not if he's been trying to trick us. And now he has no power anyways. The base has a protective ring of magic surrounding it, which doesn't allow other magic to be used within its walls."

Aywin reached out and held Luna's hand. She looked up at him, tears stinging in her eyes. "Did you know about this?" she asked.

"I was recently told the history when Darick arrived on the planet. I wasn't allowed to speak of it to anyone. I didn't know then that Darick is Leon's son. Because I work at the Science Base, I was part of the group who was testing Darick's blood," Aywin explained.

Luna threw her hands up in response to everything she'd learned the past few minutes. "So, all along, you've been pretending to want Darick's advice when you know exactly how to kill Vampires?" Luna questioned Torion.

Torion scratched the back of his neck. He appeared to be deep in thought. Almost like he didn't want to give the reasoning for his lies. "Luna, we cannot trust his kind. Our records are... damaged. Some are hard to decipher. That's why we asked him... to clarify information we have," he said.

"How did Samara not know this? Shouldn't the Warrior Elves, out of anyone, know these secrets?" Luna retorted.

"The higher-ups do. Samara may be charge of her troops, but she is young like you and does not have the security-level access to highly classified information unless necessary," Torion answered smoothly. He sighed. "We will have to lock him in a warded cell, somewhere where he can't use his powers."

Luna almost burst into tears. Her body was shaking with a rage she had never felt before. It was worse than how she had felt after Edric. The hollowness in her chest filled with something bright blue and flaming. She felt a string there, pulling her towards it, something she'd never felt before. It burned but it didn't hurt. It called to her, begging her to pull at it and release the barrier. Her fists were clenched as she scowled at Torion and the Elves who had lied to her and who were making a huge mistake in taking Darick. Darick was a good man. He was here to help, and they couldn't see that.

Luna took a calming breath, but as she did, she tugged the string and felt a warm, tingling feeling take over her entire body. It was electrical but not uncomfortable.

Torion's eyes widened. The Warrior Elves began to back up.

"Oh shit," she heard Aywin whisper.

Luna peered down at herself. Her skin was glowing a bright-blue colour.

Darick smirked. "Looks like the protective ring has some... issues."

Luna was flabbergasted. Why was she glowing? Instead of having a panic attack, she focused her eyes on Torion. "Let him go," she said with authority.

Torion and all his men had backed away unintentionally, leaving Darick free and alone. Darick strode over to Luna and her brother and father.

"W-what are you?" Torion questioned.

Luna didn't know what she was or what this meant, but she knew that if she unleashed this power on him, it would kill him.

"Let us leave. When the war comes, we will fight for the Elves—not for you," Luna replied darkly.

Torion didn't respond.

"Luna, you can't do this," Arin said. Luna turned to face her father, who stared at her in disbelief. "You can't leave your kind for… him. He's not worth it," he finished.

Luna exhaled. "Dad, he's the only way we are going to win this. I'm not letting them lock him up again," she stated coldly. She loved her father, but if he disagreed with her on this, she wasn't going to budge.

"I'm with you, L. Dad, we love you, but it's wrong what they want to do to him. You must see that," Aywin stated.

Luna's heart warmed to her brother. She glanced back at her father. He wasn't going to back down, and she could see that. It hurt her chest more and made her skin glow brighter. "I love you, Dad. I always will."

She left the room with Aywin and Darick. Her skin stopped glowing by the time they reached the bottom of the stairs.

"We have to find Samara," Luna said.

"She'll come back to the house. If we keep wandering around here, they're going to come looking for us again. And if you can't glow again like you did back there, we are going to be imprisoned," Aywin responded.

Luna nodded in acknowledgement. Her head was achy and pressured from whatever she had just done. She looked down at her arms and gasped. Her scabs were gone, the ones that had covered her arms. There wasn't even a trace of white or pink scars to show for it. Darick saw her looking down, and he realized it too. His eyebrows furrowed, and his eyes narrowed.

"What are you?" he whispered.

Chapter XII

They got back to the house and tied up the horses. Aywin and Darick went and got water for the horses while Luna went upstairs to lie down. Her head had been throbbing the entire horse ride, and she just needed to lie down and relax. She grabbed a glass of water and plopped down onto the couch with a sigh. After a couple minutes of staring off into space, she fell asleep.

"Luna!" Samara's voice yelled out.

Luna's eyes shot open in panic. Samara was hovering over her, her face full of worry.

"What's going on?" Luna mumbled. She rubbed her sleepy eyes, feeling much better after the power nap.

Samara sat next to her. "What do you mean, what's going on?! The fact that you fucking glowed, threatened the Elf leader, and disobeyed orders, and now you're just chillin'?" Samara replied.

"Did you know their plan? The fact that they knew all along what Darick was?" Luna asked.

Samara held Luna's hand in hers. "I had no idea. Can you not change the subject, though. Why were you glowing?"

Luna sat up from her position. Her hand squeezed Samara's. "I don't know. It just kind of happened… out of nowhere. Like I could feel an energy, and then I held onto the feeling and then bam! Glowing blue!" Luna explained.

Samara knit her brows together and tapped a finger on her chin. "You didn't unleash it then…. Why don't we go outside, and you can do it and release that energy?" Samara suggested.

Luna thought about how she had just gotten her energy back, but this was more important than being tired. She stood up. "Sure, let's do it."

They went outside. The weather was still cloudy, and the air had a chill to it. Luna noticed Darick and Aywin were on Aywin's deck, chatting and laughing. Luna smiled. She was glad that they got along. Darick caught her eye, and he watched her as she went out into the field with Samara.

Samara rubbed Luna's back soothingly. "You got this," she said, and then she backed away, which was smart because Luna had no idea where the power came from and what she could do with it.

Luna closed her eyes and began to try and focus. Her mind was dragging her around fluidly; she couldn't seem to relax herself. She paused and took some deep breaths. She felt her heart rate slow down and her stiff muscles release tension. Instead of focusing on being calm, she tried to find the same anger she felt earlier since that had brought the string alive. She dug deep. Her chest became heavy and tight, and then she felt it: the string, the burning. It was faint, but there just enough that she could feel its warmth. She reached for it, grasping onto the warmth and allowing it to consume her. She felt her body heat up instantaneously, electrical currents firing through her nerves. She heard Samara gasp and clap her hands. She also could hear Darick's and Aywin's voices; they were behind her too. She looked down at her glowing skin, bright blue and blinding. She wasn't sure how to direct the energy. She felt an instinct to outstretch her hand, so she did. She lifted her right arm up and reached out with her hand, envisioning all the power going through that part of her body and out. She felt a zap go through her, and a large bolt of blue lightning shot from her hand and out towards the sky. It thundered and cracked. She stopped the energy, and just like that, the lightning stopped, but she was still glowing since she hadn't set the string free yet.

Even though her energy had faded with that bolt, she felt good. The power was incredible. In that moment, she knew she could do much more. She was just going to have to practise. She took a breath and relaxed the string, and her body stopped glowing. The group came running over to her.

"I can't believe you just did that!" Samara said with astonishment.

Aywin patted her on the back. "Well, well, sister, I don't recall what side of the family that comes from," he joked.

Darick was eyeing Luna. Luna caught his gaze and stared right back.

"Someone from your family is half Wizard," Darick stated.

The group went silent. Samara and Aywin exchanged looks.

"My mother or father? Wouldn't they know?" Luna asked.

Darick shook his head. "Not necessarily. Your power was dormant, and you somehow got access to it."

Luna pointed at Aywin. "Could Aywin have it too?"

Darick shrugged. "He could, or it could have passed him, and all the power had gone to you. By the looks of it, you can conjure electrical currents. Every Wizard has different abilities. I don't remember a whole lot about it, only from very… broken up pieces in my memories. But I recall something about water magic being connected to electrical power; it has healing properties as well. Earth and plant magic have properties of healing and growth too. I think there is fire and air magic too. There are more things that I can't recollect." Darick's face was pinched in pain, as if it hurt him to try and dig into his memories.

Luna placed her hand on his chest. "Don't worry about it. You'll remember when you can," she spoke softly. She was excited about her powers. She didn't even know magic existed until today. Darick placed his hand over hers.

"Hate to ruin your little lovey-dovey moment, but I think I see Fin," Aywin stated, and then pointed behind them.

Fin was getting off his horse, his dark hair blowing in the breeze. A large sword was in a sheath on his back. Luna could see small daggers around his belt. There was a large bag on his horse. He picked it up and placed it on the ground; it appeared to be heavy, and if it was heavy to him, then it must be really heavy. After he put it down, he glanced up and waved. Samara was the only one who waved back. Everybody else was confused with why he was here. He strolled over to the group.

"Hey, guys, thought I'd bring you some weapons since you seemed to have gotten yourselves banned from the base." He grinned.

His smile faded when he made eye contact with Darick. His eyes narrowed, but he didn't say anything. Instead, the two men had a silent stare-down that had the field reeking of testosterone.

"Okay, this is getting ridiculous. Darick, this is Fin. Fin, this is Darick," Samara said.

Fin brushed some hair away that had blown into his face. "I don't know you, nor do I trust you. But if Samara does, then that's enough for me," he said coldly, then put his hand out as a greeting.

Darick glared down Fin's hand. Luna sighed, thinking that Darick was going to refuse it. Instead, he surprised her and grasped onto Fin's hand with a fierce grip. They shook, then released.

"Do you fight?" Fin asked.

Darick gave him a dark smile. "Of course," he answered.

Fin nodded and gave him a crooked grin. "Good, let's see how well then."

He reached into the bag, took out a sword in a sheath, and threw it to Darick, who caught it with ease. The rest of the bag was left open for the rest of the group to rummage through. Luna found two machetes that fit well in her hands, and they felt light enough to swing with ease. That was, if she had any skill to begin with; she knew she had some, but she was not as talented as Samara.

Aywin found a long, thin sword that had a beautiful turquoise handle. Samara already had weapons and didn't need any. The last few items in the bag were some daggers and another sword. Aywin and Luna took the daggers. Luna strapped one onto her upper thigh and calf, and Aywin tucked his in his belt.

Darick and Fin walked a distance out into the field. They circled each other with predatory glares. Fin swung his sword around with an artistry, making his movements look like a dance. His finesse was mind-boggling. Fin charged Darick first; the only sound was his footsteps on the crunchy grass. At the last moment, Darick drew his sword up and swung it down towards Fin's neck. Fin brought up his sword, rotating it sideways so that the handle was high, blocking Darick's sword. Darick's sword bounced off. He sidestepped to dodge Fin's next swing. The men faced each other again. This time, Darick attacked first. He made a quick shuffling motion, then a snapping cut in the direction of Fin's legs. Fin hopped up into the air over the sword. Darick quickly drew back his sword and stepped away. When Fin landed, he launched straight into another attack. Darick turned left, then right, twisting away before he closed in again on Fin on a downswing. Fin met Darick's sword with his own. The force of the two swords colliding sent Fin skidding back. Fin was becoming breathless now. Luna could see his chest rising and lowering in a pant. His face was scowling. The two men stared grimly at each other. Luna saw a flash of hope across Darick's face and he smiled. It was a genuine smile, something Luna rarely saw from him. Darick did not appear bored in this fighting match. Instead, he was engaged and alert. He wasn't breathing as hard as Fin, but it didn't appear to be easy for him either.

Fin rushed Darick with his sword low. When he got close enough, he brought his sword up and swiped it to the left of Darick. Darick's sword slashed against Fin and caused Fin to stumble from the vibration. This gave Darick an opening—and that was all he needed to win. He reached his hand out and grabbed Fin's arm that held the sword. He twisted the arm, releasing of the sword from Fin's grasp. The sword dropped to the ground with a loud thud. Darick raised his sword and pointed it at Fin's neck. Fin brought his hands together and clapped, sweat beading on his forehead. Darick withdrew his sword and put it in the sheath strapped onto his back, like Fin. Fin picked up his sword and did the same.

"I'd have to say, you are an excellent fighter," Darick commented.

Fin wiped his sweat with the bottom of his shirt. "I used to be the best fighter. Looks like you are now," he replied with a grin.

"Now that you two are done showing off, let's go back into the house and get something to eat," Samara said.

They went into the house. Aywin took out chicken breasts and marinated them in some oil and spices before grilling them. Samara chopped vegetables, and Luna made a fresh garden salad. Aywin made a salad dressing and dip for the veggies. Darick and Fin were put in charge of setting the table. Once the food was ready, they all sat down and ate. Luna didn't eat meat very often, so it was a treat to have her brother make it since he was such a good cook. Luna often overcooked chicken so that it was dry and stringy. Aywin's chicken was moist and full of flavour. Darick joined them at the table but did not eat anything. Instead, he chatted with Fin. They seemed to have become close after fighting each other. Obviously, it was a bonding moment for them.

"What's the plan?" Aywin asked as he took a bite of his salad.

"We wait. There isn't much else we can do," Samara explained.

"Are you still in charge of the troops?" Luna asked Samara.

She nodded. "Yes, so when the alarm bells go, I have to head to the base with Fin. Luna, you and Darick are banned, so you can't come along, but Aywin can. Instead, you guys should meet us in battle."

"That sounds like a good plan," Aywin replied.

The rest nodded in agreement. They finished their meal. Fin offered to do dishes since he didn't help with the cooking. The rest of them sat on the couch.

Aywin stretched out his arms. "Okay, to keep our minds off the possible destruction of our planet, let's play a game," he said.

Luna yawned and exchanged looks with Samara.

Darick raised an eyebrow. "A game, like cards?"

Aywin folded his hands in his lap. "Not like cards, but you are right. Cards is a type of game. Let's play a guessing game," Aywin suggested.

Luna shrugged. "Sure, why not."

Aywin grinned, then went over to a desk drawer and pulled out a bunch of blank paper. He folded the pieces of paper in half and then took out some ink for writing. Aywin had always liked to play games. He had even made up a few himself.

"Okay, so we will split into two teams. Unfortunately, we have an odd number, so we might have—" Aywin was interrupted by a knock on the front door. The group snapped their heads towards the door. Fin strolled over and opened it.

"Baby, I told you it was too dangerous to come out here, as much as I'm happy to see you," Fin said to Shaela.

Shaela stood at the door, her curly white hair poking out from underneath a brown hooded cloak. Her petite frame was covered. She took the cloak off to reveal a grey shirt and tight black pants. She wore shiny diamond earrings that sparkled when she turned her head.

"Hey, guys!" she said with a grin. Before she came over to greet everybody, she jumped into Fin's arms, wrapping her body around him and giving him a passionate kiss. Her body was so tiny compared to his.

"Ew, get a room, you two," Samara teased.

Fin put Shaela down, giving her butt a squeeze before placing her feet on the floor.

"Nice to see you," Luna said, although she was worried about Shaela being here and getting in the way. Fin was right; Shaela shouldn't be here. She wasn't skilled in fighting, and quite frankly, she was weak and more of a burden than anything. She was not meant for battle. She would die within a minute of being out there. Luna knew Fin would keep her safe, but she didn't want him babysitting when he should be fighting.

The couple walked over to the couches and snuggled in. Luna was squished up against Darick, which she didn't mind. His thigh pressed against hers, and she liked the heat of him. Samara sat next to her, and then Aywin.

"Okay, this is good; now we have six! So, three per team," Aywin said.

Shaela scratched her head. "Um… what team?" she asked, her voice high and feminine.

"We are playing a game," Samara answered.

Shaela nodded. Her pretty eyes turned and met Darick's. Her face paled, and Luna saw her gulp. Fear overtook her features; Darick tended to have that effect on people.

Luna smiled. "Shaela, this is Darick. I'm not sure what you know about him, but he's on our side. He's here to help."

Shaela leaned towards Fin. "Oh, okay. I haven't heard much…." Her sentence trailed off, making Luna think that Shaela had heard a lot more about him than she was letting on.

Luna took Darick's hand in hers as a gesture to show Shaela that she trusted him, but also to show Darick that she didn't mind showing her affection around the others. Darick squeezed her hand in return and kept holding it.

Aywin cleared his throat. "Okaaayyy, let's get started. Darick, Luna, and Samara will be on one team, and Fin, Shaela, and I will be on the other team. Each team will pick three words to write down on separate pieces of paper, and those words will go to the other team. The word must be a person, place, or thing." Aywin paused and handed everybody blank pieces of paper.

Everybody wrote down their words.

"Now, don't let anyone see the word you wrote. Place it face down to the opposite team," Aywin said.

Luna put hers on the side of the table where Aywin sat. After everyone put the papers face down in two piles, Aywin began to speak again. "Each team chooses a guesser. So, we'll have one guesser and two hinters. The hinters will take one of the papers with a word on it and look at it without showing the guesser what it is. They have to give one-word hints to the guesser; the hints can't obviously be what the object is. You get twenty seconds to give hints. The guesser only has one guess. One team goes at a time. Once everyone's been the guesser, the game is done. Any questions?" Aywin said.

"Is it one point if you guess right then?" Fin asked.

Aywin nodded. "Yes. So, whoever has the most points in the end wins," he explained.

"Let's do this," Luna said, and gave off a playful, evil grin.

Luna's team decided that she was going to be the first guesser. Darick and Samara pulled out a paper and looked at it. Samara snickered, and Darick looked at the paper like it had personally offended him. Luna couldn't help but wonder what the hell the paper said. Aywin pressed "go" on the timer.

Samara spoke quickly. "Skin, sex, part, um… man…"

Luna raised her eyebrows and started to laugh. She peered over at Darick, who seemed to have his tongue tied. Samara was stuttering on some other words, as if she couldn't think of what else to say, although Luna was pretty sure she knew what it was. The timer went off.

Samara smacked Darick's arm. "What's wrong with you! You couldn't help or what?" Samara was competitive. Darick glared at her and said nothing.

"What's your guess, Luna?" Aywin asked.

"Penis?" Luna said.

"Yesssss!" Samara said, and pounded her fist up. "Penis!" she yelled.

Everyone started laughing, except Darick.

"Who the hell put 'penis' on the card?" Luna asked, wiping the tears from her eyes.

Aywin snorted. "Me, obviously."

"Okay, next! Who's the guesser?" Samara asked.

Aywin put his hand up. "Hold on a sec; we go next. It's a back-and-forth thing."

Samara rolled her eyes. "Fine."

Shaela was chosen as the guesser, and Luna turned the timer on. "Go!" she barked.

Fin spoke first. "Water, large, cold…"

Aywin butt in right. "Swim, fish…"

Fin looked at Aywin, and they both paused, trying to think of another word. The timer was almost up when Aywin put the last word in: "Fresh."

The timer went off and Luna stated, "Okay, what do you guess, Shaela?"

Shaela chewed on her bottom lip and took a deep breath. "Umm… the ocean?"

Aywin groaned, "Noooo."

Fin held Shaela's hand. "It was a good guess, baby, but the answer was 'lake.'" He spoke to her so softly in comparison to everyone else.

Aywin crossed his arms. "Hence the word 'fresh'… not 'salt,'" he mumbled under his breath.

Luna giggled; her brother was also competitive with certain things, and games were one of those things. Samara became the next guesser. Luna thought it would probably be best to save Darick for last so that he could at least get used to the game. He had been awfully quiet. Luna flipped the paper over for her and Darick to see. The word was "zucchini." Luna sighed. This one was going to be tough. Darick frowned and looked at Luna. He probably didn't even know what a zucchini was. Aywin started the timer.

To Luna's surprise, Darick spoke first. "Green, vegetable, seeds, long…"

Luna nodded; those choices weren't too bad. She spoke next. "Stem, edible…" She stopped, not knowing what else to say. Darick had used the words she wanted to use.

The timer dinged. Samara answered optimistically, "Cucumber!" She grinned.

Luna and Darick shook their heads, and Samara's brows furrowed. "Zucchini," Luna said.

Samara smacked her forehead. "Ugh, I wasn't even thinking of that."

Aywin was the guesser next, and he guessed right on the word "bow." Darick became the last guesser for his team and guessed correctly on the word "blood." Luna wondered if Fin wrote that one. Fin ended up guessing wrong on the word "frozen," which gave Luna's team the win. Luna had to hand it to her brother; he always seemed to make things fun.

The group stayed up awhile longer, chatting. It was getting late, and the sun had gone down. Aywin, Fin, and Shaela went back to the house Aywin was staying at since Luna's father was no longer there. Samara crawled into bed and turned onto her side while Luna and Darick sat together on the couch.

Luna wasn't sure what her relationship was with Darick, but at this point, they were more than friends. She leaned herself up against him, enjoying his masculine scent. His arm was draped around her back and holding her waist. She lifted her head so that her lips touched his collar bone. His golden eyes bore into hers. He dipped his head down and kissed her hard on the lips. His hand gripped her hips.

Luna broke the kiss and looked at him with soft eyes. "What is this, Darick?"

Darick gave her a blank look. "What is what?" he asked, his voice deep and low.

Luna sighed. "Us? What are we to each other?" Luna didn't want things to keep going on like this; it was awkward at times. She wasn't sure how affectionate she should be around him.

"I already told you, you are mine. I've chosen you," he said.

The words sent a pleasurable shiver through Luna's body. Her heart heated up, and her chest ached. This man had claimed her as his own, and he barely knew her.

"How can you choose me when you don't even know me and I hardly know you? You barely know yourself," she whispered.

His free hand clasped around her hands. He rubbed her sensitive palm with his thumb. "I know you," he stated boldly.

Luna brought his hand to her lips and kissed it softly. "I won't argue with that," she said with a smile.

Luna ended up falling asleep on the couch with Darick.

Chapter XIII

L una's body shot up. The sound of alarms blaring filled the room. Red lights flashed, reminding Luna of the prison. Next to her, Darick was already up, looking around with confusion. Luna turned back to Samara's bed, but she was already up, getting dressed.

"Get dressed, you two! And hurry the fuck up. They're here!" Samara yelled over the alarms.

Luna got up and dressed into her battle clothes. She strapped on her weapons and tied back her hair. Luna turned to Darick, who wore similar clothes to hers and Samara's. They wore grey armour bound with leather and chain mail.

Luna opened the front door. It was still dark outside. Luna forgot to look at the time, but she assumed it was somewhere between two and four a.m. Her heart dropped at the sight of the object in the sky. Darick came out the door behind her, followed by Samara. They both saw the object and stopped as well. Luna's legs felt shaky, and she almost had to sit down.

The thing in the sky looked like nothing she'd ever seen before. Made of dark, shiny metal, the spacecraft was the size of half the valley and had red, white, and yellow lights all over it. It was oval in shape but had a pointed nose. Luna could hear alarms screaming from all over, and she could see red lights flashing everywhere.

"I've gotta go!" Samara said.

Luna looked over and saw Aywin, Fin, and Shaela climbing down the ladder from their place. They met Samara on the ground before they all got on their horses and took off towards the base.

"Do you think they've come down from... that thing yet?" Luna asked Darick once her breath returned. The shock was still vibrating her body. Her hands were trembling, so she tucked them behind her back so Darick didn't see.

"It's a spaceship. No, they haven't come down yet," he replied. His tone had changed. He had a deadly look in his eyes.

"What do we do?" Luna asked.

Now that the time had come to fight, she wasn't sure what their role was. Do they wait for the Vampires to come to them?

"We stand here and look at the ship. There's going to be a way that they need to get down. I'm thinking, they'll use smaller ships to get the troops down. So, once we see them letting out those smaller vessels, we will head in the same direction," Darick explained.

Luna nodded. She took a few deep breaths to calm herself down. She never got the chance to say good-bye to her brother. She hoped he fought smart; she didn't want to lose him. After a few minutes of staring at the ship, Luna saw an explosion on the outside of it, and then another. She frowned and looked around to see what could be causing it. She noticed there were objects being thrown at the ship from the ground. It must be some sort of weapon the Warrior Elves had; they were shooting the weapons from the base.

The ship's lights flickered, and smaller vessels started dropping to the ground. They landed near the base.

"Come on!" Darick said.

They both climbed down the ladder and ran to the horse. Luna sat in the front while Darick sat behind her. His face was caught up in a look so ominous that Luna tried to keep herself from meeting his fiery eyes. Luna had never ridden a horse so fast; the horse galloped like its life depended on it.

When they arrived at the base, all hell had broken loose. Troops had already stormed through the gates and were fighting. To the right side of the base, Luna could see blood and the slashing of swords off the slope of the mountain. A blood-curdling scream caught Luna's attention, and she turned to see a Vampire tearing an Elf's throat out and slurping up the blood. Luna's stomach curdled. She held in the vomit and got off the horse with Darick.

"Stay close to me!" Darick ordered.

She followed him into the fray. She had no problems staying close to him; he was a weapon on his own. Darick reached out his arm and sent a couple Vampires flying into the air with the wind he created. There were hundreds of them. The Warrior Elves were doing a decent job so far; there were lots of decapitated Vampires lying around. Luna stepped over a few heads. The smell of blood hung thick in the air. Luna continued to follow Darick, who used his sword to slash the head off any Vampire that crossed his path. She felt something wet spray on her face. She reached her hand up to wipe it and then brought her hand down. The liquid was berry red and thick and smelled like iron.

She turned to the left and spotted Edric in battle. His face was pulled into a scowl as he brought his blade down onto a Vampire's skull. The crack brought bile into her throat. The sound of swords crashing echoed around her. The moon in the sky lit up the battlefield. A storm of arrows shot past Luna and into a few Vampires in front of them. The arrows did nothing except aggravate the creatures. They bared their fangs and charged at them. Darick fought one of them in front of Luna, but another one snuck behind him and towards her. She couldn't keep standing there, doing nothing. She raised her two machetes and charged the monster. It matched her machete with a sword and snarled when she blocked its sword.

Wailing and cries of pain rolled through the forest. Luna pulled at the string inside of her. A surge of power vibrated through her veins and her skin began to glow. She pushed the energy through her arm and fingertips and it shot out, killing the Vampire she was fighting. It dropped to the ground, charred and sizzling. Apparently, lightning kills them too.

The ground had become slippery with gore. Luna took on another Vampire. Its sword cut her arm. The creature stepped away from her and brought the tip of the sword to its lips. The man licked the blade wet with her blood, then smiled, his fangs gleaming. Luna scowled and swung her weapons at him. He was too fast. Too strong. He elbowed her jaw, making her dizzy, and she fell to the ground. Her vision blurred. She reached for the power within her again but was too disorientated to focus. The Vampire dropped its sword and leaned over her with its mouth open wide. At that moment, out of nowhere, someone chopped its head off, the blood splattering all over Luna's body. Samara came into view covered in thick red sludge. She reached her hand out and helped Luna up.

More Vampires came at the two of them. Luna glanced over and saw Aywin as well as Fin. Aywin's skin glistened with sweat and blood. He had a bite mark on his forearm; Fin had slashes across his arms. All around Luna, swords were clinking and clashing under the churning sky. And the Vampires kept coming.

Luna looked around for Darick as he had disappeared. She fought off another Vampire with her lightning bolts, frying two at once. She had to be careful about how much magic she used; it drained her energy quickly. A horde of Vampires came out from one of the small metal vessels, hollering with their swords raised. Luna saw a flash of movement from her side, and she snapped her head towards it to see bodies flying. Darick was ripping heads off and tossing them. The sounds of bones breaking and popping flooded Luna's ears; she felt sick to her stomach. She lurched forward and threw up. She didn't have time to be weak. Unfortunately, her body didn't handle blood and guts too well.

She wiped her face and charged another Vampire heading her way. She swung her machete, trying to catch its neck. It countered her and stepped to the side with inhuman speed.

Its fangs came for her neck. Luna knew she was going to die. She tensed up, fear stunning her muscles. The teeth never made contact. The Vampire's neck snapped to the side and ripped off, showering Luna with a jet of blood from its arteries.

"What the—" Luna whispered.

She turned and saw Darick behind her, maybe fifty yards back with his hand outstretched. He'd used his powers. She hadn't realized how powerful he truly was. More vessels came down from the ship. Luna looked around… so many bodies, so many dead. The septic smell of death was putrid. A horror scene. Luna heard a manly scream; she turned and saw that Fin's arm had been cut off. The Vampire was on top of him, drinking his blood. Luna screamed. Anger rising in her, she threw lightning at the Vampire, killing it instantly, then ran over to Fin, tears staining her cheeks. He lay on the ground motionless. Only his eyes moved as he looked at her. Blood gushed from his arm, and the wound on his neck. He was going to die; there was no saving him. Luna knelt beside him. The acrid taste of blood rose up into her mouth as she grasped onto his only hand.

"It's okay, Fin. I'm going to stay here with you," she whispered to him. His eyes closed, and his body went limp.

"Luna, watch out!" Aywin's voice yelled out to her.

She turned and saw a plague of Vampires coming towards her. She squinted, focusing on the man in leading the group. He looked so familiar. He had grey eyes, bronze skin, and hair darker than the night; it was curly and fell just past his ears. He looked like Darick, except not.… He was around the same height, but maybe slightly taller and leaner; his thighs weren't thick like Darick's. He was gorgeous. He walked with arrogance, and had a smug look on his face. When his eyes met hers, she saw a flash of something—recognition? How could he know her?

She watched as he sniffed the air. The group was close now. She got up. Aywin and Samara came to either side of her, their swords raised. The man smiled and put his sword down to lean on it. Darick came from behind Luna. He stepped in front of her and let out a low growl.

The other man snickered. "Ah, brother, fancy meeting you here," he said, and winked.

Darick tightened his grip on his sword. "Leave this planet. You don't need it," he replied.

The other man raised an eyebrow. "I was never planning on taking the planet, Darick. I'm just here to take you. So, if you'd kindly come with me, we will leave this place," he retorted.

Darick glared. "That's why I came here, to warn them! You're lying!" he snapped.

The other man narrowed his eyes and studied Darick. A few seconds of silence went by. "Mmm, interesting," he said. His silver eyes turned bright blue for a few seconds before fading back to their original colour.

Darick screamed in pain and fell to his knees. His body shook and his hands reached for his head.

Luna's heart pounded. "No, stop!" she cried.

The other man's eyes met hers. "It's okay. I'm giving him his memories back... all of them," the man stated coolly.

Luna frowned. Why would he do that?

Darick stopped screaming. His body was trembling, tears burning the corners of his eyes. "Impossible," Darick croaked.

The other man gave off an uneven smile. "Ah, see, little brother? Now you get it."

Darick shook his head. "I-I can't—that's not right. You're wrong!" Darick shouted.

Luna was confused. She stared at the scene before her, unsure of what was going on. "Stop the fighting then! No more bloodshed!" Luna hurled.

While they were here having a moment, Vampires were still fighting the Elves. The other man held his hand up and time froze. Luna frowned and looked around.

"What the fuck?" Samara said from beside her.

Aywin shook his head. "What's going on?" he whispered.

Darick's brother strode up to Darick, who was still trembling. He flicked his hands in a strange motion, and dark wisps surrounded Darick, then formed cuffs on his wrists and ankles. The cuffs had unusual ruins on them, which Luna didn't recognize. Darick tried to fight out of the chains but was met with a shock of pain. He screamed out and toppled to the ground.

"Take him…." the brother ordered, and the two Vampires behind him grabbed Darick and dragged him towards the vessel. The brother eyed Luna. His eyes bore into her soul, but she felt a warmth in them. She pushed that aside and allowed herself to awaken the lightning insider her. She sent it out towards the brother, who lifted his hand and, with ease, deflected the lighting out into the dark sky. Luna stood there, shocked, wondering who this guy was.

"Huh, I'm running into a lot of surprises today," the brother said with curiosity. He rocked onto his heels and rubbed his fingertips together. Chains and cuffs suddenly appeared on Luna, Samara, and Aywin.

"Let's take them too. In the meantime, call all troops back and let's get the fuck off this planet," the brother growled.

His eyes never left Luna's. The trance broke once the Vampires grabbed onto them and started taking the three of Elves into the vessel. Luna struggled against the chains but felt a shock of pain with every move. It was the most pain she'd ever experienced. She blacked out and sagged against the Vampire holding her.

***

When Luna opened her eyes, a brain splitting migraine racked her temple.

She grimaced. "Ah, fuck," she moaned, and rolled over.

"You're not wrong. I would rather be doing that right now," a male voice said from the darkness.

Luna sat up and looked around. Her eyes adjusted to the dim room—or, more like, prison. It wasn't like any prison she'd ever seen, though. It was a metal box with a clear glass front. The inside smelled of metal, which brought her back to the battle and all the blood. Her stomach lurched in response, but she had nothing to throw up. Darick's brother stood on the other side of the glass, his head cocked to the side. She looked around the room. Samara was there too as well as Aywin. They were passed out on the ground. There was no sign of Darick. She rushed to them, feeling their necks for a pulse.

"Oh, thank goodness," Luna said under her breath. They were alive. She faced the man that had spoken to her.

"Who are you?" she questioned; her voice sounded weak and raspy. She needed water and food. Her stomach rolled with nausea.

The man chuckled. "I have a hard time believing that you don't know who I am." He clenched his jaw, and his grey eyes switched to shining blue.

She felt a singe of pain in her temples again and shot a bolt of electricity at the glass. It disappeared once it hit it.

The man shook his head. "Feisty thing, you are. I like it."

Luna charged the glass and hit it. Nothing happened. It just felt like hitting a wall. If she tried to smash it, she was going to break her hands. She could see the man better now. He had crescent-moon eyebrows, thin and narrow, unlike Darick's thick ones. He carried an imperious manner; his angular cheekbones carved down towards a square-cut jawline. His eyes were back to a bright-silvery colour, with shiny speckles of blue in them, and they darted constantly.

"So, you're Darick's brother? What did you do with him! I need to see him!" Luna protested.

The man smirked. "I'm Zane, not merely Darick's brother. What an awful title that would be. You won't be seeing my dear younger brother anytime soon. He's... busy at the moment," Zane said while crossing his arms and leaning up against the glass.

Luna felt a surge of anger go through her body as he got closer to her. She backed away. "Let us go back home! You don't need us. Leave our planet alone," Luna said sternly. Her energy began to build within her once again. Despite being drained, her skin blazed with anger. She thought of Fin. She thought of all the dead Elves, and her body shook with grief and vexation.

Zane raised his eyebrows at her, then winked. "You do carry some powers there, don't you? Must've had some Wizards in your bloodline. Wonder what your blood tastes like?" Zane said.

The thought of his fangs breaking her skin made Luna shiver. She growled. "You won't be getting near me, EVER," She spat.

"So, what did my brother tell you about us... Vampires?" Zane asked casually. He had a small smile on his face, but Luna could see the ticking of his jaw.

"Why does that matter? Just let me and my friends go home," Luna replied. Her skin hadn't stopped glowing.

"Your home is safe now. Like I said, I had no intention of taking it anyways," Zane replied.

"For fuck's sake, there's no point in lying. Darick told me your plan. He told me your history! I know about your father," Luna retaliated.

Zane's body moved from the glass, and she heard him growl, "You know nothing!" He snarled.

Darkness cramped the room and fear poured into Luna's throat. She gasped and took a step back. If she thought Darick was intimidating... she was wrong. This man was the definition of danger. Frost formed on the glass before her. He held the same darkness that Darick did, except his was suffocating. She hadn't seen him lose his cool yet. As much as he scared her, she liked that she could get on his nerves.

"I know that you guys invade other planets and kill innocent people. I know you enjoy the hunt, and the killing. I know that Darick stood up for the people, and now he is a prisoner because you guys want the killing to continue! You want death and destruction! And that's what makes YOU a monster," Luna hurled, her skin glowing even brighter than before.

Zane clenched his fists. The darkness in the room was overwhelming. It poured towards Luna. Zane exhaled with narrowed eyes. He turned away from her abruptly, leaving the room. The pressure and energy once felt dissipated. The frost on the glass began to melt. She heard metal shutting and then silence.

Luna took a deep breath, her body relaxing now that she no longer had to deal with Zane. She looked out the glass and saw a hallway with three cells across from her, all empty. The hallway had three cells per side, and at each end was a set of big metal doors.

Luna began to pace back and forth in the cell. Her legs and arms were sore from battle, and her energy levels were depleted. Her stomach growled with hunger. She sighed and slid down the cold metal wall. She hoped Aywin and Samara would wake up soon. She could feel herself panicking. She took some deeper breaths and tried to focus on different things in her environment. She noticed that she was wearing dark-grey clothing: matching joggers and a shirt. The material was alien to her, but it felt soft and comfortable. Her skin was clean as well, no sign of battle other than the cuts and bruises. She peered over at Aywin and Samara, who also wore the same clothing. It disturbed

Luna. She wondered who had stripped them of their clothes and dressed them. She wasn't wearing a bra or underwear. She was thankful for the new clothing, though; the other clothes would have been repulsive to wear, and after a day of having them on, they would have started to rot. Even the thought of rotting blood made Luna's stomach turn.

She sat up against the wall for what felt like hours; she wouldn't know since there was no way to tell time. She studied the room. There were four small single beds against the walls and an open toilet in the back, which would suck because that meant going to the bathroom in front of Aywin and Samara.

She heard a moan and saw that Aywin had sat up. He had his hand on his forehead. His eyes were squinted and adjusting to his new surroundings.

"Aywin!" Luna beamed. She crawled over to him.

He opened his eyes fully. "W-where are we?" he murmured.

As he asked the question, Samara began to stir beside him. Instead of being slow like Aywin, her whole body shot up and she was gulping in air. Her eyes were wild and searching the room.

Luna gently grabbed her arm. "Samara, it's okay. It's Luna."

Samara met her eyes and nodded. Her chest heaved up and down but slowed after a few seconds.

"We are locked up. The Vampires have us," Luna stated.

Aywin stood up and stretched his lean body. His head almost touched the roof in the cell. He put his hands up and started feeling around the metal room. Samara and Luna sat on the ground, watching him.

"What are you doing?" Samara questioned.

Aywin rolled his eyes. "Searching for a way out, dumb ass," he retorted.

"No need to be rude, gosh," Samara said.

Luna smiled. As much as she wished that they weren't in this situation, she was happy to have them here with her. Aywin continued to scan the room. Within a couple minutes, he threw his arms above his head with a big sigh.

"No way out, huh?" Luna said with a raised brow.

"At least, I was trying," Aywin grumbled.

"What do the Vampires want with us anyways? Why bring us here?" Samara asked.

Luna shrugged. She had thought about that question a lot in the last couple hours. "I'm not sure. When I woke up, Darick's brother, Zane, was outside the cell. He asked me about what Darick had told me about them. I don't know why that's important, but maybe they're worried Darick said something he shouldn't have? He also said he wasn't interested in invading our planet, which I called bullshit on. Why come to a planet with a massive spaceship full of an army and attack the people there if you weren't planning an attack?" Luna said.

"Makes absolutely no fucking sense," Samara responded.

"He's just trying to get us to trust him," Aywin said, his face stuck in a grim expression.

"Well, that's not going to work," Luna stated. The other two agreed with nods.

"Do you think they're going to… torture us?" Aywin asked. He sat down on one of the beds, which squeaked under his weight.

"Probably," Samara said coldly.

Luna's stomach dropped, and she closed her eyes. "Can we not talk about torture, please?" she asked smoothly.

"I'm just preparing you guys. Torture isn't all that bad," Samara said with a shrug.

Aywin glared at her. "Says that one who gets tortured aaalll the time," Aywin said sarcastically.

Samara frowned. "It's just pain. In training, we teach ourselves to be one with the pain. It's just your nervous system's response."

Aywin crossed his arms. "We aren't all cold-stone killers like you," he said ruthlessly.

Samara stood up and went over to one of the other beds. Luna got up as well and went to one of the empty beds in the back. "Maybe Darick will escape and get us out," Luna said.

Aywin scoffed. "Hate to burst your little love bubble, but Darick is likely dead. If he betrayed these creatures, I could see them ripping him apart."

A sadness washed over Luna. He couldn't be dead. Zane had said he was alive still, that he was "busy." The bed Luna sat on was made of some strange, soft material that indented when she placed weight on it. When she took the weight off, the indent went away. She wasn't sure what it was, but it was comfortable. Luna looked over at Aywin, who was picking at something on his arm. She remembered the Vampire bite that she'd seen on him.

"Does that bite hurt?" Luna asked.

Aywin chewed his bottom lip. "It burns a bit. The Vampire tore some skin out in the process. It looks like it has dried out a bit." While continuing to look at the wound, he asked, "How long were we out for? I feel like it shouldn't be this dried out already."

Luna pondered for a few seconds. "I'm not sure," she replied. She looked at her wounds. They hadn't scabbed over yet, meaning it hadn't been longer than three or four days. She'd never tried to use her magic to heal the ones she had from the battle. She would have to try later once she felt better. She was hungry; the gnawing sensation in her stomach worsened the more she thought about food and water.

"Holy shit," Aywin said, his voice bouncing off the walls of the room.

Luna and Samara sat up and looked at him.

"Fin's dead," he stated.

Luna felt deep grief and sadness. It melted her firm barrier, causing tears to sting in the corners of her eyes. Her chest tightened. The room fell silent again. Fin was dead. The Vampires killed him.

"They will pay," Samara said, her voice full of pent-up anger.

Time went by slowly. The three were lying on their beds, chatting about random things occasionally. The sting of Fin's death still filled the air and caused Luna's chest to tighten when she thought about him, especially how much Shaela was going to cry. He was her soulmate; they were in love.

The three Elves heard a creaking sound, then a heavy clunk. Footsteps were coming down the hallway. They remained in their beds. An unfamiliar man came into view, holding trays of food. He reached out through the glass, placed the trays on the floor, and then left. Samara burst towards the glass and tried to get out, but it was glass again.

"How did he do that?" Samara asked, with a frustrated tone.

"I don't know, but I need food," Aywin said, and grabbed a tray. They all got their trays and sat down on their beds.

There was a soup-looking substance and a bun as well as a box that read "orange juice." A container filled with water was also on the tray; the container made crunchy sounds when they held it and it had a paper wrapped around it saying it was water. It was the strangest thing Luna had ever seen. Why did Vampires have to label their things? It was not like they ate food.

Luna ate her food. It was better than she had expected, a bit salty but not bad. The buns weren't as good as the Elves' bread. The buns were white and had no seeds or grains in them.

Luna patted her stomach full of food. "Well, that was decent."

Aywin and Samara nodded in return. Samara finished off the rest of her soup by slurping it down. They placed the dirty trays over by the glass.

"I have to pee," Samara said, and smiled sheepishly. They all turned and looked at the open toilet.

"Go pee then. Don't worry, I won't look," Aywin teased.

Samara sighed. "I just don't want you guys to listen. Can you, like… sing or something?" she suggested.

Luna snorted. "Sing? I'm not singing."

Samara went over to the toilet. "Just talk loudly! I don't know. Just don't listen!"

Aywin and Luna laughed but followed directions and talked loudly to each other. Once she was done, she strode over and sat on her bed.

"Better?" Luna asked with a grin.

"Much," Samara replied.

Eventually, the three of them fell asleep after doing some jumping jacks and watching Samara do a random flip off the wall to get out some energy. Luna fell asleep last. She could hear the subtle sounds of Aywin and Samara snoring. She closed her eyes and felt her body drift away.

Chapter XIV

A soft tapping noise woke Luna up. She was a light sleeper; a mouse scurrying across the floor would wake her from REM sleep. She sat up and rubbed her heavy eyes. Fear struck her when she saw a dark figure standing on the other side of the glass. By how it was standing, she could tell it was Zane. He stood as if he owned the place, which he probably did.... Luna looked over at her sleeping friends. They were still snoring away, their bodies cocooned in blankets, unaware of the evil that lurked by the glass. Luna got up and walked over to the glass. Once she got close enough, she could see the smirk on his face.

"Are you usually this creepy and watch people sleep?" she asked.

"Just the pretty ones," he replied.

"Bite me," Luna retorted.

"Love too," Zane said with a wink.

Luna grumbled. "Why are you here?"

"Checking in on you, making sure nobody ate you," Zane replied with a smug expression.

His grey eyes danced over her, making her feel like a piece of meat. She shivered. Who knew what this man was capable of? He killed entire planets with his father.

"Please. You'll be the first one to kill us, judging by your history," Luna said cruelly. She had no remorse for this man.

Zane lifted his hand to his heart. "You wound me," he said playfully.

"That's too bad. I was hoping to kill," Luna replied harshly, her eyes shooting daggers into his.

His face darkened and his jaw tightened before he gave her a slanted smile. "I came to ask you some questions. But you need to be alone, so you're going to come and walk with me. Promise me you'll behave?" He winked.

Goose bumps prickled Luna's skin. She felt safe in this cage, away from him, but being out there with him, where he could snap her neck? No way. But what if she tried to escape? She could kill him and then free her friends and find Darick.

"Okay, let's go then," Luna replied, her face remaining expressionless.

Zane reached in and grabbed her shirt, then pulled her out of the glass. He snapped his fingers and cuffs appeared on her wrists. Luna cursed under her breath.

He put his arm out for her to take. "Shall we?" he asked with a wicked smile; she realized he knew he had just ruined her plan for escape.

She glared at him and did not take his arm. He shrugged and began to walk; she felt a force push her to stay beside him. She could feel her hands trembling with fear, but she held her head up high and tried to be strong. They went through the metal doors and into an area that led to multiple hallways. In front of them sat an elevator—which Luna had never seen before. She studied it with a look of worry. Zane reached over and pressed a button next to the door. The door slid open, and the two of them walked inside.

Inside the elevator was tiny, maybe enough for another two or three people. There were buttons all up one side of the door with different symbols on them. Zane pressed one of the symbols, and the doors closed. The elevator began to move. Luna felt her heartbeat speed up.

"No need to worry," Zane stated, as if he sensed her hysteria.

"I'm not," Luna snapped.

Zane chuckled. "You should learn how to lie better. The smell is basically radiating off you."

Luna frowned. "Smell?" she questioned, but didn't mean to say it out loud.

Zane pointed to his perfect nose. "Yeah, that's how you say it in Elven language right: SMELL. The thing you do with your nostrils."

Luna narrowed her eyes at him. "I know what a smell is! How can you smell fear? That doesn't even make sense," Luna stated.

Zane raised a brow. "Ah, you really know nothing about Vampires, do you? We can pick up the hormones you release when you're scared"—he paused to lean in closer—"and when you're… aroused," he said, practically whispering the word.

Luna's cheeks reddened. She backed away from Zane and gave him a death stare. He had done that on purpose, just to get a reaction out of her. She calmed herself down and took some breaths. She wasn't going to respond. From the corner of her eye, she saw him smirk before looking forward again. She was not even close to feeling aroused; she hated him. All her feelings from the battle had been homed in on Zane and his death wish against innocent lives. Instead of Luna having to think about the corpses that had covered the blood-soaked ground, she focused her emotions on Zane. He infuriated her, and she would get him back, somehow, for what he'd done to her planet, to the innocent Elves that resided there and were now dead.

Something in the elevator dinged and the doors opened. They stepped out into a massive room. The architecture was unlike anything Luna had ever seen. The ceilings were high, and sculptures were carved into the walls. The walls themselves were covered in paintings. Luna brought her head back down and saw all the painting supplies. There were stands with half-finished paintings everywhere. The room was a dream to her—a place she could sit and explore for hours. Zane went over to a couch and sat down. She had to sit down next to him; her cuffs burned her skin if she tried to disobey.

"What is this? Where are we?" she asked, curious. Why was this room here? She assumed they were still in the spaceship.

"My painting room. I like to have one when we travel in space. I have one back home too. I thought this would be a more… peaceful place for an interrogation," Zane responded casually.

Luna's jaw dropped. She couldn't believe he'd painted all the art in the room—it was gorgeous. His style of painting was like Luna's. Quite a few paintings were of dark skies filled with stars and other colours and shapes she didn't recognize. Zane saw her studying one of them.

"That's one of my favourites. Those are galaxies, beautiful from far away," he murmured.

She saw no paintings of battle, nothing gory. The hatred towards him tremored slightly, but she kept the wall up. "You don't paint the wars?" she asked.

Luna saw a flash of pain in Zane's eyes. She furrowed her brows, wondering why he responded that way.

His face changed back to his arrogant self. "War isn't pretty," he stated with little emotion in his voice.

"Well, if you're a monster, don't you like gruesome things?" Luna said abruptly. She certainly saw him as a monster. Her friend was dead because of him.

Zane smirked. "Monster, huh? You haven't even seen or experienced the true monsters in this life. The atrocious and unspeakable things that I've seen would trump what you think a monster is. Darling, there's no such thing as monsters—evil is the only awful thing that you should fear," he said with a sneer.

Luna didn't know how to respond to that. He was probably right. She knew nothing of other worlds and monsters; she was sheltered. She thought for a moment before replying. His silvery-grey eyes had brightened with speckles of blue.

"Death," she said.

Zane strummed his fingers along the side of the couch. "Death?"

Luna nodded. "Death is the worst thing I've seen," she said. Because it was true. The spine-chilling feeling of watching someone die in front of you was the most monstrous, evil thing, and death itself was scary.

Zane chuckled. "Death is but a brief moment of darkness; death is the escape from the monstrosity they call life."

It was the most depressing statement Luna had ever heard. It made her wonder what had happened to this man? What had he seen? What did he know? "How long until we get to your planet?" Luna asked, deciding to change the subject.

Zane leaned back on the couch, relaxing his posture. "Now, now, I'm the one that's supposed to be asking the questions. But I don't mind it when the girl takes the lead," he said with a wink.

Luna grumbled. This man was constantly flirting, and it was getting on her nerves. She remained silent. She could tell that, unlike Darick, Zane hated silence.

Zane sighed and rolled his eyes dramatically. "You are so stubborn. We aren't heading to my planet. We don't own planets other than our own," he explained.

Luna frowned. "I thought you took over planets?"

"We used to. The place where we are going is called Earth. And we share it. Anyways, enough about that. I need to find out some stuff from you and your… friends," Zane said.

Luna could tell that Zane was a good liar. He had all the characteristics of a good liar and a narcissist. He was attractive, personable, easy to talk to, and he acted like everything wasn't a big deal, but Luna had seen the darkness in him. She had felt it. He had an immense amount of power, and his temper could snap.

"What are you to my brother? His scent is all over you," Zane stated coldly. His expression had changed to a stern, serious look that reminded Luna of Darick.

"I'm... a friend? I don't know. What do you mean, I smell of him?" she asked.

Zane growled, "Never mind." He paused and scanned the room quickly before resuming the conversation. "What happened when Darick showed up?"

Luna had been fidgeting with her nails. This man made her nervous, and she wished he hadn't taken her into such a personal room. It made him seem more human when he was clearly the enemy. Just the thought of him being the enemy made Luna's anger flair up once again. She would like to say that she wasn't an angry person, but lately, that statement felt false. Even with Zane's gorgeous exterior, he still made her skin crawl and her blood set on fire.

She leaned in close to him with her face scrunched up in annoyance. Her skin began to glow blue. "Why should I tell you anything? I'm not helping you. You killed one of my closest friends as well as hundreds of Elves. And then you left the planet because you decided you didn't want it. And you abducted me and my friends for NO REASON. Why the hell would I help you?" Luna snapped.

Her emotions had broken free, and her true anger and feelings were coming out. She just wanted to know if Darick was okay. Zane watched her carefully, his eyes studying her like she was a rare species. She felt a pressure around her, as if something was dampening the energy that sizzled inside her.

"Where's Darick? I want to see him. I want to know he's alive!" she spat. Her face had reddened to the colour of a tomato, and she was moving towards Zane. The cuffs on her wrists started burning her skin. She sat back and the cuffs lessened; the pain diminished. She glared at Zane, waiting for a response. If she tried to use her powers against him, he would kill her. Instead, Zane shook his head. He exhaled and got up. His playful attitude had vanished, and Luna was left with a creature she feared.

The room had gotten colder, and Luna could see frost forming on the walls. She gulped. Her body had to follow Zane, because of whatever powers he wielded. He went back to the elevator, and they went down to the prison area again. Luna was confused with Zane's choice to not speak; it made her uncomfortable. Usually when a person yelled at another, some sort of argument followed, but he gave her nothing. Maybe he had better control of himself than Luna previously thought. He was silent the entire walk down the hallway to the glass. An invisible force pushed Luna through the glass and into the prison where her friends still slept. The cuffs on her wrists disappeared, and she whipped around to face Zane.

He had a strange expression on his face. His pupils were dilated, his nostrils flared, and his jaw was so clenched that Luna was afraid he'd break his teeth. "Darick is alive," he stated before turning away and striding down the hallway.

Relief washed over Luna. Zane hadn't been lying. She smiled and took some deep breaths. A warmth filled her chest and lungs, and a weight lifted off her shoulders. She crawled into bed. Exhaustion took her.

***

Luna couldn't tell if it was the morning due to the lack of a clock, but she woke up and felt energized. Who knew sleeping in a prison cell would be so good for her sleep schedule? Samara and Aywin were giggling. Luna sat up and rubbed her eyes.

"Good morning, sleepy head," Aywin said, and waggled his eyebrows. He was eating cut-up fruit from a food tray. Samara sat beside him on his bed, and she was drinking something out of a strange-looking mug.

"When did you guys get up?" Luna asked with a groggy voice.

"Like two hours ago. You've been snoozing away. Breakfast came about a half an hour ago, though, so your eggs will be cold," Samara said, and pointed to a tray by the glass.

"Is there coffee?" Luna wondered out loud.

"Oh yeah. And it has good flavour." Samara grinned.

Luna nodded and got up to get her tray. She brought it back to her bed and drank her coffee. It was warm enough to still comfort her. Luna took a fork full of eggs and put them in her mouth. They were cold, but it didn't bother her. The flavour was good enough that she continued to eat them. She was silent as she ate. Samara and Aywin kept chatting, but they could tell something was up with Luna.

Luna finished her food and got up and put the tray by the glass. Then she leaned her forehead against the glass. The coolness brought her anxious mind back to reality and grounded her. She took a deep breath and closed her eyes.

"You okay?" Samara asked. She had quietly walked up beside Luna.

Luna lifted her head off the glass. Her eyes burned with anger and confusion about the situation at hand. "Zane talked to me last night," Luna said.

Samara's eyes widened. "Are you okay? Did he do anything?" she asked with a worried tone.

Aywin overheard and came over. "What's going on?"

Luna held her hands up. "He didn't hurt me. I'm fine. He was asking about Darick and was wondering what sort of stuff Darick had told me. He also said that we are heading to a place called Earth. He said something about sharing it? I'm not sure what that means. Maybe there's other people there," Luna explained.

"Why didn't you wake us up?" Aywin questioned, with his eyebrows drawn together.

"He took me to another room. I guess I didn't really think to wake you up before he took me. I wanted to know why he has taken us prisoner, but I still don't know," Luna replied.

Samara nibbled on her bottom lip, which Luna knew meant she was deep in thought. "Maybe he took us because of Darick; that would make the most sense. I'm not sure what's going on between them, but they obviously don't like each other, and us three were right there when Darick showed up," she speculated.

Luna and Aywin nodded in agreement. The sound of a loud door slamming startled them. They backed away from the glass. Zane and another man that they didn't recognize showed up. The other man was shorter than Zane; Luna estimated he was around six feet. He had golden-blonde hair and stunning green eyes. His hair was practically shaved on the sides and gradually got longer along the top of his head. It reminded her of Edric's hairstyle, which sent a shiver down her spine in revulsion. He had some red-blonde stubble on his face. Zane scanned the inside of the cell. His eyes met Luna's and the corners of his lips turned up.

"Good morning, sunshine," he said. His dark curls fell around his face. It should have looked messy, but with his features, it just made him look even more badass. Luna hated how good-looking he was.

Her nose crinkled. "What do you want?" she asked coldly.

Zane's mouth twitched. "A lot of things." He raised his eyebrows and paused before continuing. "Today, we get to do something fun," he stated. His silver eyes flickered with mischief.

Luna felt her blood run cold. He snapped his fingers and cuffs appeared on Luna, Samara, and Aywin.

"Ah, shitpancake," Aywin complained.

"What?" Samara snickered at Aywin's vulgar comment.

The three suddenly fell silent when they noticed Zane and the man giving them deadly looks.

Luna grumbled. "You don't have to chain me. It's not like we're more powerful than you."

Zane smirked. "What can I say? I like my girls tied up."

Samara let out a little laugh; Luna glared at her, so Samara covered it up with a cough. An invisible force pushed the Elves through the glass and towards Zane and the other man.

"Mmm, how rude of me. I didn't introduce you to my friend. This is Karn," he said. Karn's face remained stern.

"We don't care about your stupid friends, asshole," Luna growled.

Aywin nudged her side as a warning to calm down. Zane's eyes narrowed. He sized her up before letting out a chuckle. Karn laughed as well. Luna frowned; she wasn't sure why her comment was so funny.

"That's got to be my favourite derogatory term you Elves use. The Earth humans use it too. Whoever came up with that? To call a person the hole in your butt?" Zane laughed.

"I'm going to start calling you a nostril or an ear-hole," Karn joked with Zane.

Luna, Samara, and Aywin exchanged looks.

"Anyways, back to business, I suppose. We are going to go into hyperspeed soon. So, I need to take you to a safer room specifically used to damper the force of travelling where we can strap you in so you don't get injured," Zane explained.

He led the group down the hallway. The door in front of him opened by itself, and the group continued to stride through. Instead of going into the elevator, Zane turned left and went further down the hallway. They passed many doors along the hallway until, finally, a door on their right opened to a room with a few seats in it. The seats were welded to the floor and had belts on them. Luna had never seen anything like this. The seats were metal but were padded in the area where one would sit. As they walked further into the room, Luna's jaw went slack. The room had a massive window to the outside. As the spaceship moved through space, she could see a multitude of stars and some floating rocks; Luna wondered what the floating rocks were.

"Please... sit," Zane ordered calmly.

His invisible power forced the three Elves to the seats, sat them down, and buckled them up. Their cuffs remained on. Zane and Karn went to the remaining seats in the front of the Elves, and they buckled up too.

Zane pulled out a handheld device from his pocket. "We're ready," he said into it.

A few silent minutes passed. Luna wasn't sure what was happening, but she assumed it was going to be rough if they had to be strapped in. Suddenly, a loud buzzing noise filled the room. The spaceship stopped abruptly, causing Luna's body to fall tight against the belts. Out of nowhere the ship went full speed. It was so fast that all Luna could see was a blur of stars through the window. After a few seconds, the stars disappeared into a bright light. A force, so intense, pressed against Luna's body. It felt like her skin was going to peel off and like a heavy weight was sitting against her chest, making it hard to breathe. Luckily, it only lasted a few seconds before stopping. The spaceship continued back to its regular speed, and the stars outside appeared normal again.

Zane and Karn got out of their seats. Luna looked over at Aywin when she heard him throwing up. Luna didn't blame him; she felt nauseated as well. Samara's face was pale, and she had her eyes closed.

"First times a bitch," Karn stated.

"What… happened exactly?" Samara asked groggily. She opened her eyes slowly.

"It's called hyperspeed, or 'jumping.' It's a way to travel thousands of miles in mere seconds, but you can only go so far at a time or else it can kill you, even with the shielding methods we use. We won't make another jump for at least another day or two. And then we will be a few days from Earth," Zane explained nonchalantly.

The buckles came off, but Luna had a hard time standing. The crushing weight earlier had made her dizzy and sore. Luna was surprised when Zane and Karn allowed them to sit and rest for a few minutes before forcing them back into the prison. Zane and Karn went over to the window and stared out at the cosmos.

"I can't believe that we are travelling in a spaceship," Aywin said in awe.

Samara nodded. "Yeah, who knew? I wouldn't have guessed that this was going to happen. I mean, a murderous Vampire arrived on our planet not too long ago, so really, I've had to start expecting the unexpected."

Luna's smile faded. She thought about Darick and wondered what they were doing to him. Luna willed herself to stand. She wobbled slightly but was able to keep on her own two feet. Samara and Aywin joined her in standing. Zane turned around from the window. His striking features were shaded in the darkness; his jaw was clenched. Luna could see the wheels turning in his head. She wondered what he was thinking about. She watched him exhale.

"All right. Back to the cell," he ordered.

Samara gave Zane the stink eye, and Aywin glared. Luna pinched her lips. She wanted to say something snarky, but she couldn't get the words out. Zane's eyes almost begged her to try and protest. After a second of silence, she watched as a smirk displayed itself on Zane's lips. Her brows knitted into a scowl. Zane and Karn walked ahead of them outside the room. Again, his force pushed them forward. They continued down the hallway, then back into the cell. Once they went through the glass, the cuffs evaporated. A dark mist lingered, and Luna swiped it away. Zane and Karn remained outside the glass. Karn had his arms crossed, and Zane had that same cocky grin that Luna had come to hate.

"When do we get to shower?" Luna asked dryly.

Zane shrugged. "I'm not sure. Depends on how good you're going to be. You still haven't answered any of my questions about Darick."

Aywin stepped in front of Luna. "We aren't helping you. Darick's our friend. He warned us about you. You can stick all your questions up your ass," he retorted.

Samara's and Luna's jaw dropped. Aywin wasn't one to lash out; he'd always been the non-aggressor. Obviously, he had more anger in him than the two women thought.

Zane and Karn chuckled. "Again, with the ass," Karn joked.

Zane stepped closer to the glass. His silver eyes glowed as the cell began to vibrate. A strange compressing feeling came over the three Elves, as if they were being squeezed.

Fear struck their systems. Zane stepped back and the force disappeared. Luna's chest lightened, and she was able to breathe again.

"Let's not forget to be polite," Zane threatened. His usual casual demeanour had changed to a twisted mouth and dark, narrowed eyes.

The three Elves stepped further away from the glass, their bodies pumping adrenaline and begging for them to escape. Zane's expression relaxed, as if he was proud of the fear that he'd just imposed on them. A Vampire that Luna didn't recognize came from the hallway with food trays and placed them through the glass on the floor, then left right away, not even glancing at the Elves.

Luna and Samara sat on Luna's bed while Aywin sat on his. They watched Zane and Karn as they whispered amongst themselves. Luna pondered on what they could be talking about. The two Vampire men gave the Elves one last look before leaving. Their absence allowed the group to relax again.

"Well, shit," Samara muttered.

"He's fucking crazy," Aywin whispered.

Luna nodded. "Yeah. He's also a lot more powerful than we think. Like I feel like he could just think about snapping our necks and it would happen. He wouldn't even have to be in the room to do it." She shivered at the thought.

Samara hunched against the cold metal wall. "Why don't we just give him what he wants? Darick could be dead for all we know. And it's not like we have anything super secretive to say. Darick's memory was gone. He didn't know much, so he couldn't tell us much," Samara said calmly.

Luna chewed her bottom lip. "I guess we could." The idea of giving Zane any information made her blood boil, though. "I just can't stand the guy," Luna muttered under her breath.

Aywin scratched the back of his neck. "If we give him what he needs, maybe he'll let us go. Now that I think of it, it's not that big of a deal. Like Samara said, if they want Darick dead, he's going to be dead whether we are here or not."

Aywin's comment made Luna's heart ache. She wanted to see Darick.

"Okay, that settles it then. Next time Zane comes around, we give him what he wants. There's no harm in doing it," Samara decided.

They got up and looked at their lunches. It still felt too early to eat. Still full from breakfast, Luna didn't eat any of her food, whereas Samara and Aywin mowed down their meals. The rest of the day went by slowly. They spent a lot of time doing nothing. To pass the time, Luna and Samara exercised and practised hand-to-hand combat, which Luna was good at due to working as a prison guard. She felt much better fighting with her hands than she did with any weapons.

Once night came, the three of them lay down and fell asleep. Luna had nightmares about the battle. The dead bodies haunted her mind. She kept seeing the life draining out of Fin as she watched him die. Luna woke up at one point to use the bathroom. She had been afraid that Zane would be there, but he never showed up. She was thankful for that.

***

By morning, she was the first person to wake up; her eyes were heavy with lack of sleep. Samara woke up not too long after, as did Aywin. Luna sipped her coffee and talked with Samara.

"Do you think I could spit and hit the glass from here?" Samara asked. They were sitting on her bed, which was the closest to the glass.

Luna eyed the distance. "I don't think so," she stated honestly.

Samara swished the saliva around in her mouth, then shot it out. It landed just before the glass. Luna and Samara raised their hands and grinned.

"So close!" Luna cheered. The two women began to giggle.

Aywin rolled his eyes. "Can you two not spit. It's not like they clean this place. I already have to shit and piss in the open. I don't want to be slipping on saliva too," Aywin grumbled.

Luna laughed. "We are just finding ways to pass the time."

"I'm sure there are many other ways to pass time that don't involve spitting contests," Aywin responded.

Samara got up and wiped up her spit with a leftover paper towel. Just as she came and sat down, the sound of the metal door in the hallway opening and shutting put them on alert. They sat on their beds, waiting for whatever was coming.

Two men and a woman appeared at the glass. One of the men was huge and had a shaved head. The other guy had short brown hair and wild eyes. The woman was gorgeous. She had night-black hair that was straight and thick and flowed down to her hips. Her eyes were the colour of storming ocean water, and her skin was bronzed as if she had spent time in the sun. She was tall and slim, and had a fierce look on her face, which made Luna nervous.

"Garrett, you can have the red head. I'll take the other one," the large man with the bald head said.

Garrett snorted. "No way, Cade. She looks feisty. You're bigger than me. You take her."

The woman rolled her eyes. "How about you two stop arguing about who gets who, and we just go in," she said with a snarky tone.

"Sure thing," Cade answered, a deadly grin splayed across his face.

"Get behind me," Luna ordered to Aywin and Samara.

Samara narrowed her eyes. "I can fight just as well as you can."

Luna clenched her fists as the three Vampires came through the glass. "Yeah, but you guys don't have lightning," she replied.

She reached in and felt her body begin to glow. With a flash, she shot out a bolt of lightning. The Vampires dodged it with ease, as if they'd expected her to strike. The female grabbed Aywin, and Garrett took a hold of Samara. They had moved so fast that Luna had no time to comprehend their movements.

The girl laughed, her fangs shining bright white in the dim lighting. She stood behind Aywin. Her tongue flicked out and licked the side of his neck. Aywin's face grew pale, and Luna could see a bead of sweat dripping down his forehead. Garrett had Samara in a tight grip. He snapped his jaws beside her ear. Cade stood in front of Luna. He was terrifying. He wore a black muscle shirt that showed off the sleeve tattoos covering both arms, and his right eyebrow was pierced. He reminded Luna of some of the prisoners she had taken care of, and the thought repulsed her.

She narrowed her eyes. "I can kill you," she snapped.

Cade let out a deep chuckle. "And then we kill your friends. I mean, as much as I don't want to die, it'd be great to know you had to watch your friends die because of your choice," he replied darkly.

Luna's anger faded, and she felt a sharp prick of fear in her chest. There was no way they could win against these Vampires.

Cade moved in on her. "Just give us want we want. We just need... a little snack," he said smugly. "I'll even make it feel good if you're a good girl." Cade grinned.

Luna lifted her lip in disgust. What had she envisioned was going to happen? It was not like she didn't know Vampires drink blood. She knew this would happen because she knew how Darick had a hard time resisting the urge. Cade licked his bottom lip and walked towards her. At that moment, Luna heard the door in the hallway open. The female Vampire left the room in a flash, but Garrett and Cade stayed. Aywin ran over to Luna. Samara let out a scream when Garrett's body was pulled away from her and flung over to the opposite wall. Cade's body followed. A force pushed them up against the wall. Their faces were grimacing in pain. Cade let out an agonizing moan.

Zane strode into the cell through the glass. His face ruthless; nostrils flared, jaw tight and ticking.

"I swear, man, we weren't going to hurt them. We were just messing around," Garrett pleaded. He opened his mouth to say more, but something snapped his jaw shut.

The corners of Zane's lips crept up into a devilish smile. "'Man'? I think you mean 'lord,'" Zane stated coldly.

Zane paced back and forth and stared down the men. Luna, Samara, and Aywin had gone to the back of the room and pressed themselves against the metal wall while they watched the scene play out in front of them. Luna felt like her heart was going to give out. Zane had referred to himself as lord…. Lord of what? Was his father king and he technically a lord of whatever planets they owned?

"So, you think you can just come into this area without asking me?" Zane asked. He sounded calm, but his face said otherwise. His body was practically trembling with rage.

"W-we," Cade started.

Zane held his hand up. "I never said you could talk," he growled.

Cade shut his mouth. Zane put more force on the men's bodies, torturing their insides with the pressure. "The question is… do I let you live?" Zane pondered as he paced. He leaned towards the men, his eyes blazing with fire.

After a few scary seconds of listening to the sound of heavy breathing as the men were being tormented against the wall, Zane snapped his fingers and the men fell to the ground, gasping for more air.

"Leave. If I ever see you down here again, you're dead. You're lucky that nobody drew blood," Zane said.

The men got up; they were unsteady on their feet, but Luna had never seen a person run so fast out of a room— other than how the woman had left. Zane peered over at the three Elves. He opened his mouth as if he wanted to say something but then snapped it shut. He grumbled to himself before leaving the room.

Luna was too shocked to say anything; she bet Samara and Aywin felt the exact same way. They stood there for a while; the only sound, the quiet hum of the spaceship.

"Why did he save us?" Aywin finally asked, his voice still shaky.

"I don't think he saved us in the way you think he did; he still needs us. He doesn't want us dead," Luna said, her voice coming out stronger than she felt.

Samara said nothing. She went over to her bed to lie down. Aywin went to his and did the same.

Luna slid her back against the wall to the floor. The coldness felt good; it woke her up. She closed her eyes and leaned her head back. She thought of Darick and how he'd stood up for her when Edric had forced himself on her. She wished she could see him. Her bottom lip trembled. She held in the tears and took a deep breath.

"It'll be okay," she told herself quietly.

Chapter XV

Luna took a fork full of rice and chicken from the plate on her lunch tray. She had already eaten the green beans, which were her least favourite vegetable. She reflected on the day before when the three Vampire attacked them. Zane had been pissed. She'd seen him mad a few times now, but his anger towards those Vampires was terrifying.

"Hey, are you even listening?" Aywin asked Luna.

Luna blinked a few times. "Huh?" she responded.

Aywin sighed. "You never listen to me."

"Yes, I do. I was just... thinking," she replied with a shrug.

"Ugh," Aywin said, and put down his empty tray onto the floor near the glass wall.

"What were you saying then?" Luna asked. Samara let out a chuckle from her bed as she watched the interaction.

"I was SAYING that we need Zane to come by again so we can talk to him about Darick," he said.

Luna nodded. "Yeah, but we can't exactly force him to come here, can we?"

Samara got up and went to the glass and began to yell Zane's name repeatedly. Luna got up and grabbed the back of Samara's shirt and pulled her. "Shush," she said.

Aywin laughed. "Can we not just take a moment to appreciate how loud Samara's voice is?"

Samara smirked. "That could be taken in so many different ways."

Luna made a gagging motion.

Aywin's cheeks flushed. "I didn't mean it that way. I—" He didn't have a chance to finish before Zane appeared by the glass with his hands in his pockets.

He wore slim-fitting black pants and a collared T-shirt. Luna hadn't seen him without his trench coat on. She noticed his left arm was tattooed down to the wrist. She couldn't see his upper arm, but assumed he had a full sleeve. It looked like the tattoos were of animals and maybe forest scenes; she couldn't tell from where she stood.

He raised his brow. "You called?"

Samara nodded. "We are ready to talk to you about Darick."

Zane yawned, then rubbed the corners of his eyes. "This isn't some sort of escape plan, right?" he questioned with an annoyed expression.

Aywin shook his head. "Nope."

Zane smirked. "Good, because I was going to come into the cell anyways. I don't feel like taking you guys anywhere," he stated, and then stepped in through the glass.

Luna and Samara backed up.

Zane's eyes met Luna's. "You scared?" he asked, then winked at her.

Luna scoffed but said nothing. She didn't want him to have the satisfaction of knowing that he frustrated her. He leaned his back up against the glass wall, which seemed to stay in place when he wanted it to.

"Go on," he said, and made a motion with his hands.

Aywin and Luna exchanged looks. "We aren't sure where you want us to start," Aywin admitted.

Zane sighed. "Who spent the most time with him?"

Samara and Aywin pointed at Luna.

Zane chewed his bottom lip. "Mmm. Let's start back to what I had asked you a few days ago. What happened when Darick showed up to your planet?"

Luna sat down on Samara's bed. She felt like this was going to take a while, and she wanted to be comfortable. She watched as Samara leaned up against the wall next to her; Aywin stayed seated on his bed.

"I saw an object come down from the sky. I went to investigate and saw a man come out of it. The Elven Warriors were there, and he attacked them. My understanding is that he killed a few of them," she explained.

Zane nodded. "Makes sense; he was practically dead," he muttered.

Luna raised her brows. "Dead?"

Zane gave her an arrogant shrug. "He was on the verge of starvation. He'd been lost in orbit for almost two years. We didn't get a reading on the vessel until it hit your planet. Then we knew where he ended up," he explained.

Luna paused, taking in the information. "Wouldn't two years kill him without food?" Luna questioned.

Zane shrugged. "It basically puts us into a state of hiber-nation, and then we die when our body has fully depleted."

Luna nodded. Zane motioned for her to keep speaking. She exhaled. "Anyways… he killed some of our men, so they locked him up in our prison. He'd had a head injury, so he'd lost his memories; the only thing he remembered was his name. Occasionally, snap shots of his past would come to him. He and I became friends, and when he escaped, he came to my place and stayed with me. He'd had a vision of wars going on, and in his mind, he knew that the Vampires invaded other planets. So, he knew that you guys were going to come to our planet to kill us," she finished.

Zane let out a chuckle and shook his head.

Luna glared. "What's so funny?"

He smirked. "Nothin'. Is that all you have to tell me?"

Luna's eyebrows furrowed. "I guess." She narrowed her eyes. "You aren't going to let us go, are you?"

Zane crossed his arms. "No, I'm certainly not."

Aywin let out a puff of air. "We told you what you wanted to know! Why won't you let us go?"

Zane's body went through the glass and out the other side. "You don't know what I want," he said frankly.

Samara spoke up. "Tell us what you want then. We need to go home."

Luna could sense the emotions building up inside her. Zane ran his hands through his hair and looked around the other cells, as if he was bored of the conversation.

"What do you want!" Luna barked.

At the sound of her voice, his head snapped over to meet her eyes. "You."

Luna was bewildered. "Me?" she squeaked. She wished her voice had come out stronger.

"I'll explain once we get to Earth. Let's get you guys back to the hyperspeed room," Zane said.

Karn walked over to Zane. Luna wondered if he'd been there the entire time. Zane turned and began to walk down the hallway. Cuffs appeared on the Elves wrists before they were dragged through the glass and down the hall. They went the same room as the one they'd been in a few days prior. Zane's power pulled them into the seats and secured the belts around them. When Zane and Karn put their seat belts on, Zane spoke into a device to signal that they were ready.

Luna held her breath. She was not looking forward to the amount of force that travelling at hyperspeed did to her Elf body. The ship took off. The window changed to a smudge of bright lights before the ship returned to its regular speed.

Zane and Karn stood up. "Well, only a few more days to go until we get to Earth," Zane said.

The three Elves stood up, their bodies shaking and swaying. This time, Zane and Karn gave them no time to recover but led the way back to the cell. Once the three of them got into the cell, they went directly to their beds to lie down. Luna could feel the nausea rolling through her stomach. Zane and Karn left them there. Luna rolled over onto her back and stared up at the dark metal ceiling. She wondered what her life would be like if she hadn't met Darick. She'd still be working in a prison. She'd be content but, deep down, wishing for more. She exhaled.

"I can smell your thoughts; they're stinky," Samara said from her bed.

Luna flipped back onto her stomach and hugged her pillow underneath her chest to help prop her head up to talk with Samara. "I just wish I could see Darick," Luna said softly.

Samara was sitting cross-legged on her bed with her blanket overtop of her. "Do you love him?" she asked.

"Ugh, could do two not talk about boyfriend stuff while I'm here," Aywin murmured.

Samara glared at him. "Just put your pillow around your ears and mind your own business."

Aywin rolled over in the bed and did what Samara said. Luna rested her face on the pillow. "I don't think I love him, but I care for him more than I've ever cared for a man. Other than River, he is the only guy I've ever really cared for," she replied.

Samara gave Luna a genuine smile, but the smile dwindled. "I'm sorry."

Luna raised a brow. "For what?"

"That you started to really care for someone, and all this happened," Samara replied.

Luna's forehead creased. "That seems to be my luck," she said.

"I wish it weren't," Samara replied with a concerned expression.

"You deserve love too," Luna said softly.

The room fell silent as Samara pondered. "I don't think I'll ever find it," Samara said truthfully.

"You will. It's just a matter of when," Luna replied. She flopped onto her back again and closed her eyes.

Sleep took her into a journey of dreams.

***

The next few days were long and torturous for Luna. She did lots of exercising and combat fighting with Samara to pass the time. Aywin had talked Zane into getting him some reading material about space, but it was in a different language; the Soul Empire's language of the Vampires.

Luna thought she could hear a slight accent in the Vampires' voices, but it was so subtle that she could only hear it if she paid close attention. They spoke more brashly and had a harder time pronouncing certain words. For example, Luna had recognized that Zane often made t's sound like d's, or pronounced e's as u's. Darick hadn't been as obvious with his pronunciations, but Luna wondered if that had to do with his head injury. Zane had told Aywin that the Vampires didn't speak their "old" language anymore. Zane explained that he could understand the language, but he had a difficult time speaking it himself; he could read the language well.

Zane still wouldn't tell Luna about Darick. In fact, he refused to talk about Darick at all. He also refused to talk about the plan of their imprisonment. Thankfully, he had given them more supplies to take care of themselves, like hairbrushes, toothbrushes, different clothes, and so on. He even let them shower. There were shower locker rooms in the spaceship's gym. Luna had a good look at the gym, and the equipment appeared much different than on her planet.

It was made of shiny metal and looked a lot more complicated than the stuff from Nexus. She saw some stuff with black ropes too.

During this time, Luna continued to have nightmares every night. She would wake up sweating and trembling. She wondered if she had a problem… if the battle had taken something from her that she would never get back.

It was a quiet afternoon, and Luna took a handful of raw nuts that had been given to them to snack on if they needed to. She could feel herself losing weight; she usually ate more. Even Aywin looked skinnier. Samara was a smaller Elf, so she looked about the same. Karn was standing by the glass, talking to Samara. He had been speaking to her quite often for the past two days and it was beginning to bug Luna. Luna munched on her nuts while glaring at Karn.

"Samara," she called in the middle of chewing.

Samara glanced over at her. "Yes?"

"I want to talk to you," Luna stated.

Samara raised her eyebrow. "Okay…" She stared at Luna, waiting for her to talk.

Luna sighed. "Alone!" she retorted.

Samara said bye to Karn, then came over to Luna, who was sitting on her bed. Aywin was busy, trying to learn the Vampires' language, so he wasn't paying attention. Karn walked out of view, and Luna could hear a metal door open and close.

"What?" Samara asked.

"Is he flirting with you?" Luna questioned, eyeing Samara.

"No, of course, not. We are just talking about different types of fighting styles. He's a Warrior too," Samara answered.

Luna chewed her bottom lip. "Okay, just don't get too close. We can't trust them," she stated.

Samara's face twisted. "Luna, you don't have to warn me. I'm not stupid."

Luna felt a pang of guilt; she wasn't trying to belittle Samara, but obviously she had. "I'm sorry, I didn't mean it like that. I just worry," she admitted.

Samara put her hands on her hips and raised her brow. "You worry too much."

"I know," Luna responded.

Aywin suddenly jumped up in his bed, startling Luna and Samara. "Ah-ha!" Luna and Samara both turned and looked at him. His smile beamed. "I figured out a sentence!" he exclaimed.

"What's the sentence?" Luna asked.

"'The cosmos consists of thousands of galaxies, with thousands of planets,'" Aywin read.

Samara's eyes lit up. "Thousands? That seems like a hell of a lot of other planets. Are they all inhabited?" she asked.

Aywin sighed with irritation. "I don't know. I've only understood one sentence. This entire book is about space." He flipped through the hundreds of pages dramatically.

The heavy thundering of multiple footsteps approaching silenced the group and they turned towards the glass. Darick and Zane approached from the other side. Luna practically leapt out to the glass; her heart was stammering in her chest, feeling like it was going to explode. She had never felt such relief. Darick's gorgeous gold eyes stared back at her. She had expected him to be smiling, but instead, his face was tight. Zane stood beside Darick with a smirk on his face.

Luna frowned. She could tell that something was off about Darick. She reached out towards the glass and placed her palms against it.

"Darick, are you okay? What did they do to you?" she asked with concern.

Zane scoffed and shook his head. Darick's eyes narrowed at his brother before returning his gaze to Luna. "I'm fine," he replied. No emotion took over his features; he looked empty.

Luna's chest tightened with worry. Before she could respond, Zane spoke up. "We're approaching Earth. We're going to put you guys onto some smaller ships to head down and land on the planet. We aren't taking this massive thing. It's not exactly stealthy," Zane explained.

Samara and Aywin were standing at the glass as well. "I thought you said that the Earth people know we are coming?" Aywin asked.

"Only the government of one country does. From my understanding, the governments of the other countries of Earth don't know about us," Zane responded.

"Countries?" Aywin questioned.

Zane sighed. "I'm not going over everything with you. Just follow me," he replied in a grumpy tone.

Luna noticed that Darick wasn't cuffed. Zane snapped his fingers and the glass disappeared. The brothers started walking down the hallway, while Luna, Samara, and Aywin remained in the cell, staring at where the glass should've been.

Zane turned around and looked at them with a raised brow. "You coming, or what?"

They all exchanged looks. Samara shrugged, then stepped out of the cell and began to follow the two brothers. Luna was boggled that Zane hadn't put any cuffs on them. She and Aywin followed Samara.

They entered the elevator, which felt too tight with all of them in it. Luna was pretty sure the elevator had a weight limit because the weight it could hold was written on the wall inside the elevator: only three to four people should be in it at a time. Worried, Luna focused on the numbers displaying the levels they were passing. Finally, they reached the lowest floor level.

When they stepped out, they were in a bright room with dark-blue walls and approximately twenty metal sliding doors around its perimeter. The room was filled with a few other Vampires. Luna recognized one as Pierce, the woman who had attacked them and had gotten away with it. Pierce made eye contact with Zane and walked over to him, her hips swaying back and forth. Her dark thick hair was pulled back into a high ponytail showing off her alluring features. Luna rolled her eyes at the female; she couldn't help it. When Pierce got close enough to Zane, her lush red lips curved up into a seductive smile.

"Zane," she purred, then placed a hand on her hip and glanced over at Luna, Samara, and Aywin. Pierce gave them a threatening glare before returning her attention to Zane. Zane wasn't paying much attention to her, despite the fact she was right in front of him. He was focused on the room and who was getting into what ship. "Are you coming with us?" Pierce asked.

Zane's jaw ticked as he examined the room. He glanced over at Luna and the other Elves before answering Pierce. "We better go into our own ship. We'll meet you down there," he said. Pierce nodded and walked away; there was clear disappointment on her face, which made Luna smile inside.

"That one has a resting bitch face, but I'm pretty sure it's an active bitch face too," Aywin whispered to Luna.

Luna couldn't help but let out a giggle. Zane gave Luna a once-over glance before motioning for them to follow him. Luna glared at Zane; she didn't like to be gestured at like a dog. If it was anybody else, it probably wouldn't have bugged her so much. He began to walk down the centre of the room before turning to the left to a big metal sliding door. The door opened to reveal a small spacecraft with room for ten people.

Led inside, Luna noticed rows of seats at the back of the vessel, with two seats in the front facing a big window, likely the place where the pilots would sit. The Elves chose the seats in the back row and sat down.

Luna eyed Darick, who hadn't even stolen a glance at her. She shot eye daggers at the back of his head, hoping he would turn around. She felt Samara nudge her side. "You're going to burn a hole in him," she muttered.

Luna grumbled. "Maybe if I do that, he'll start thinking straight again. There's something wrong with him."

Samara chewed on the inside of her lip. "He could've been tortured, for all we know."

The anger in Luna began to boil again, her protective nature clawing at the surface. She scanned the room. Zane and Darick sat at the front of the ship, and Karn had just walked in and sat in the first row of seats. She had the sudden urge to escape, but there was no smart way of doing it. She didn't know how to drive the ship, and even if she did, they wouldn't make it back to her planet. She took a couple deep breaths to calm down. She closed her eyes and exhaled. When she opened them, Zane was standing right in front of her. She jumped back in her seat and almost fell out the other side.

The corners of his mouth curved up into a mischievous smile. "Something on your mind?" he asked, then winked.

"Just about how much I want to kill you," she retorted.

Zane smirked and crossed his muscular arms over his chest. "Aw, here I was hoping that you were going to say something else."

Luna tightened her features. "Too bad my thoughts are on murder."

"How exactly were you planning on accomplishing that?" he asked.

Luna leaned back in her chair. She was trying to pretend that her heart wasn't pounding a million miles per minute. "I would never tell you my plan," she replied with her eyebrows up.

Zane let out a chuckle before turning and walking back to the front. Luna relaxed her scrunched up face. "Fasten your belts. It's going to be a bumpy ride," he announced before buckling in.

They did as he asked, and thank goodness they did because the ride was worse than Luna anticipated. In one of the pilot seats, Zane was pressing buttons, lightening up the front of the screen, while Darick manoeuvred the vessel. The spacecraft soon detached from the larger ship.

Luna's eyes widened with awe at seeing a planet from space for the first time; it was Earth. Earth appeared to be a lot larger than her planet, but she had never seen her planet from space. The planet was made up of blue and white marble swirls, and parts of it looked brown, yellow, and green. It was the most breathtaking thing Luna had ever seen.

As their ship progressed towards the planet, the closer they got, the rougher the ride. At one point, they were going so fast, the vessel caught on fire and she felt a compressing force against her body. As the craft plummeted towards the planet, Luna was too busy trying not to pass out to pay attention to their landing. Darick slowed the craft down and they hovered in the clouds above ground.

It took a few seconds for Luna to clear her shakiness. Once she felt stable, she opened her eyes and gasped. Now around twenty thousand feet in the air, they were moving over what appeared to be mountains and forested landscape. The ship moved with ease, as if they weren't moving at all. Zane pressed a button and the view from the window of the ship blurred for a moment.

"Why'd you do that?" Aywin asked. He had been enjoying the entire ride. Aywin, of course, had worked on the Elves' old spacecraft in the Science Base on their planet but had never been on one before. The Vampires' spacecraft was much higher tech.

Zane and Darick seemed too busy to answer, but Karn turned around in his seat and explained, "It cloaks us. Light reflects off it in a way that makes us appear to be our surroundings. It mirrors the things around the ship."

Aywin's jaw went slack in awe.

"Yeah, but why do that?" Samara questioned further. Her face was still pale from the ride down.

"We don't want certain people to know we are here," Karn stated before turning around to face the front again.

Samara and Luna exchanged confused looks. "I wonder what he means by that," Luna whispered.

"That was my exact thought too," Samara answered.

The ship descended lower and lower until they landed softly into a small meadow in a forest. All the passengers remained seated and watched as a few more vessels landed around them. Their view out the window was clear enough to see the other vessels, although all were cloaked, the spacecrafts were close enough for Luna to detect them. If she had been outside walking and only quickly looked up at the sky, she wouldn't have noticed them, but because she was studying the sky very closely, she could pick them out by the shimmering look of heat waves across the body of each vessel: a rippling distortion of reality.

Zane clapped his hands as he stood up. Darick stretched as well as Karn. The group of Elves stood warily, scared that they might fall over. Thankfully, they all had recovered from the ride and were steady. From outside the window, a few large semi-trucks drove in. The Elves had never seen vehicles before and wondered what they were.

They followed the Vampires outside. Luna took a deep breath of air. Her nose twisted at the smell of it. The air on the planet was... different: it smelled off and wasn't as fresh as the air on her planet. It was also warm, and she felt a slight breeze. The grass under her feet reminded her of the grass at home, except this grass was thinner and not as tall. The trees here were different too, but similar enough for her to know they were trees. The planet still had beauty to it.

"Hey, Earth to Luna." Zane waved his hand in front of Luna's face.

She had completely zoned out, staring at the mountains in the distance. She blinked a few times before swatting his hand away with a frown. "I don't even know what that means," she retaliated.

Zane smirked. "Just a sayin' here that I picked up," he murmured.

Aywin huddled close to Luna. "It's like when we say Nexus instead of the word Earth. Obviously."

Luna rolled her eyes. "I know that, Aywin. I was being sarcastic," she whispered back harshly.

Zane pointed towards a semi-truck. "Time to go."

Samara and Aywin went ahead of Luna, walking beside Karn. Darick was in the back of the truck already. The box door was open, and there were benches along its sides. Vampires from the other ships were filling up the other trucks. Luna followed Zane and jumped into the back. She didn't want to sit beside him, but it was the only spot left. Her eyes caught Darick's. He had been looking at her. His face fell back to the ground. Luna exhaled sadly, then scooted in beside Zane. She didn't understand what was going on with Darick. When they got to wherever they were staying, she was going to talk to him alone. She needed to know what had changed.

A man remained on the grass by the back door. He was intimidating and gave off Vampire vibes. Luna hadn't seen his teeth but assumed that he had sharp fangs. "Let's get going. We have about an hour ride," he stated gruffly. He closed the door of the semi and left them in complete darkness. Luna gulped.

***

She felt a rumble from the vehicle, and it began to move. The ride was not smooth but bumpy as hell and hurt her ass. Her left thigh kept rubbing against Zane's thigh and it was making her angry. She didn't want to be near him. She almost called out to Samara but held back. Her throat felt like it was tightening the longer she spent in the darkness. There was chatting going on around her that helped ease her panic, but she felt like the walls were coming in on her even though she couldn't see them.

Why was she so panicky? Maybe it was the fact that she'd seen all that blood and gore in the small battle on her planet. She never thought something like that would affect her, but it did. Badly.... The dreams had been proving that to her lately. She could work in a prison; she was tough. But when it came to death... Actually, when it came to ripping apart limbs, that was where the line was drawn in her sanity.

"Your heart rate is high. Don't like the dark?" Zane's deep, joking voice snapped her out of her terrible daydream.

Luna shook her head and tried to relax her clenched fists. "No," she said, her voice coming out shaky. She could feel Zane lean towards her even though she couldn't see him.

"Boo," he said suddenly. She almost jumped from the unexpected loudness and nearness of his voice.

A small smile crept across her face. She exhaled and tried to get rid of it. There was no way she was going to give him the comfort of knowing he'd made her smile. Somehow, his little joke to scare her gave her comfort.

"You can't scare me," she said matter-of-factly. She could feel his chest rumble with a chuckle.

"I've scared you lots. You just hide it well," he answered arrogantly.

"Keep telling yourself that. Whatever makes you think more highly of yourself, although I don't think it's possible for you to get any more egotistic," Luna replied brusquely.

Zane's lips turned up. "Ouch."

Luna shrugged. "I only speak truth. You think you're better than everybody else."

Zane went silent. Luna wondered if she'd finally hit a nerve. "Your statement couldn't be more incorrect," he muttered more to himself than to Luna.

Luna's brows knitted. She wasn't sure what to say to that and, instead, fell silent for a minute or two.

"What did you do to Darick?" she finally asked. Her mind had been wandering, threatening to fall into another panic attack, so she decided to distract herself and talk to Zane.

"Nothing he didn't deserve," Zane replied.

Luna's face heated, and she shifted her legs away from Zane. "He's different, and I know it's because of you."

"I gave him his memories back. Why don't you talk to him about it if you're so concerned." His tone was edgy.

"Why is he helping you? Do you have some sort of brain-washing abilities?" she retorted. Her words were coming out angry, but she tried to keep herself quiet so the others wouldn't overhear the conversation.

"Actually, I do. Well, kind of. I can persuade others, just like Darick can. He can't do it to Vampires, but I can. But I didn't brainwash him. He's choosing to help me, because to win this, I'm going to need all the help that I can get," he explained.

"To win what? I won't be helping you invade and kill another planet," Luna said.

Zane scoffed. "I'm not INVADING this fucking planet. Can you stop saying that? I'll tell you more once we get to a safer place."

Luna was taken aback by the sharpness of his voice. She could feel that he was stressed. Was that also fear? She wasn't sure. She couldn't imagine Zane fearing anything; he had a lot of power. She snapped her mouth shut. She was finished with their conversation. Obviously, he wasn't going to answer any more of her questions. But would she actually believe any of his answers anyway?

The hour in the semi-truck went by faster than Luna had anticipated. The truck stopped, and the back door opened. The light from outside shone in and hurt Luna's eyes. Her pupils adjusted and her vision cleared.

It wasn't sunny outside but cloudy. Everyone got out of the truck. Luna looked around. A huge stone wall encircled about seven to ten acres, with a massive brick mansion standing near its centre. The mansion had big ornate wooden doors and large windows, and looked only a couple years old. From what Luna could tell, it had three floors. Quite a few other Vampires were milling around outside the mansion. In front of the home was a paved circular driveway with gardens all around and a luscious, mowed green grass yard.

"Well shit, nice place," Aywin commented.

Chapter XVI

The semi-trucks left the group, driving through a large metal gate leading out of the grounds. The gate was guarded by multiple Vampires holding weapons that were unfamiliar to Luna. The other Vampires from the trucks had already walked into the house.

"How many people can live in there?" Aywin asked, pointing to the house.

"A lot," Zane replied.

"What? No way, what a specific answer," Aywin muttered sarcastically.

"There are a few more underground floors with living quarters," Zane said.

"Where's the rest of the Vampires? There's got to be more than what I've seen so far. What about your ship in space?" Samara asked.

"Full of so many questions, aren't you?" Zane's jaw ticked. "Most of us live on our own planet. I wouldn't bring our entire civilization onto a spaceship and then to this planet. There's just a select group of us here," Zane explained. He strolled ahead towards the open front door. He was done with the interrogation.

The rest of the group followed him. Luna hung back with Darick. She brushed up beside him and noticed he flinched when she tried to touch his arm. When he sped up to be ahead of her, her heart ached.

They all stepped inside the mansion. The first-floor ceilings arched all the way up to the third floor. The floors above were open in a circle with railings around them. Doors lined the open hallways. The floor of the foyer was a night-black marble stone with white swirls. Luna had never seen a building like this before. She was used to the life of an Elf; they kept things simple.

Extravagant paintings of nature—trees, animals, mountains, and waterfalls—covered the ceilings and walls. A large set of stairs branched up to the different floors.

"Follow me," Zane stated authoritatively.

He didn't go up the stairs but passed them. They winded through a hallway. Luna's shoes tapped against the floor, the clicking sound echoing throughout the house. They walked into a room with a large table surrounded by chairs in the centre. The room smelled like old books; the aroma sent Luna's thoughts back to her own home. A large crystal chandelier hung from the ceiling; she could imagine each crystal on the chandelier as being smooth. A projector screen covered the back wall.

Luna squinted her eyes at the sunlight that came in through the windows on the side wall. Karn had already went over and began to shut them. Flakes of dust floated into the air from the movement. The group began to choose chairs to sit on at the table. Zane remained standing; he strode over to the projector screen and flicked it on to reveal an overhead view of a town. Luna got comfortable in her chair; it was softer than the truck ride to the mansion, to which she was thankful.

"So. As you… Elves have made it known, you have many questions. Let me do the talking. No more questions. Whatever I don't tell you, you don't need to know," he stated plainly. His lean, muscular build rested against the wall next to the screen. His silver eyes scanned the Elves for any opposition. When he was satisfied with the lack of objection, he began to talk.

"As you already know, we are on the Planet Earth." The screen slowly showed different pictures of scenery and cities. Luna couldn't help but notice the round ears of what she assumed were the people that inhabited the planet. They wore clothes that looked alien to Luna.

"These are the humans that live here. The main language they speak in the area we are in is English, which you already know. You speak it but with an accent. There are lots of other languages on this planet, but don't worry about learning them, as you won't be here long. The humans on Earth track the years that they've inhabited the planet. The meaning of the year isn't very significant, but it's important to understand just in case it comes up.

"I came here with a few Vampires a couple years ago. We contacted leaders from the United States of America and made a deal with them. Now we can come and go as we please. We have a few organizations on the planet now. We run some private medical companies, mainly blood dona- tion stuff. The humans here do not know we exist. At least, they don't know where we are from or that we are a different species. Apparently, the government here wants to keep it that way. In other words, we can live here as long as we don't ever say who we really are.

"Unfortunately, our presence has been made known to other creatures that inhabit this planet. They can… smell us. This is a recent discovery within the last month. These other creatures are called Werewolves. Most of the time, they look like regular Earthly humans, but they aren't. They can transform when needed into a creature that looks like a wolf on steroids.

"The government here did not tell us about them, and now they refused to get in the middle of the issue, which is that the Werewolves don't want us here. Their pack leader has made that known. Unfortunately, we found out that a bite from them can kill a Vampire."

Aywin raised his hand. Zane glared at him and raised his dark brow. "What are steroids?" Aywin questioned sheepishly.

Zane sighed. "Was I not clear on the question-asking part?"

"Just answer…" Karn murmured.

"They're a drug… that enhances muscle growth. Just think of a wolf but much larger," Zane explained. He waited for Aywin to nod before going on. "Werewolves are deadly; faster than us when shifted and stronger. My powers drain quickly with them. I don't know why. If I use my powers too much, I… Anyways, it doesn't matter. Luna, we need your powers. We need your help to fight them. They won't reason with us. They just… kill. It's like they have an innate sense to kill us, and they aren't backing down. We just need to take out their army," Zane finished. His jaw were clenched, and his eyes cut holes into Luna's.

"It's their planet," Luna stated. She heard Karn sigh angrily across from her.

"No, it's not. They don't own it. They just live here like we do now. We've done nothing wrong. There's literally nothing we've done to them. They attacked us first, and we need to show them that they can't do that. We built this fortress around this house within a week because they had snuck in one night and tore women from their beds, leaving their bodies mangled and gutted in their rooms. They killed over twenty Vampires, but fucking Darick here had to show up on our radar again after two years, so instead of avenging their death, we went to get him. Now that we're back, we must deal with these things because they aren't playing fair—they're dirty," Karn snapped.

From the way his face flushed and his lower lip trembled slightly, Luna realized Karn must have lost someone he cared about. His eyes glistened with tears, but he didn't let them fall. Instead, his face took on a scowl and his nostrils flared. His fangs flickered in the light.

"I'm sorry," Luna said, surprising herself with the empathy she felt towards the man.

Karn seemed taken aback too because his face softened and his posture relaxed.

Luna turned to Zane and stated, "I'll help, but you need to promise me that you will let us go back to our own planet once we're done."

Zane nodded. "I promise."

Shock struck Luna. She was prepared to lash out and fight for herself and her friends to go home, but Zane just agreed. She picked up her jaw from the floor and clamped her mouth shut. She gave Zane a curt nod.

Zane smirked and turned to Darick. "Brother dearest has already agreed to help. Let's show you all to your rooms that you'll be in for the time being."

They got up and followed him back through the hallway, then up the stairs to the second floor. After passing a few doors, Zane stopped at one, opened it, and said, "Luna this is your room."

Luna was amazed by the fanciness of the room. It had high, arched ceilings and more nature scenes adorned the wall opposite the door, which also had several large windows to let in lots of natural lighting. The bed was massive; it was a king-sized bed with a beautifully carved wooden frame. There were dressers and carpets and even a fireplace in the room.

Zane snapped his fingers and the fireplace lit. "Clothes have been brought for you. They're in the dressers. But there's also a walk-in closet to the right. You have your own bathroom on that side too. There are shoes as well. You'll find all that you need. If there's anything missing, just let me know," Zane explained, and with that he continued down the hallway with the others. Samara was in the room next to Luna's, and Aywin was a bit further down the hallway where Karn's and Darick's rooms were.

After everyone was given a bedroom, Luna stepped into hers and closed the door. The warmth of the fire hit her cold skin and took away the goose bumps. She had the sudden need to explore everything. She went through all the drawers in the dressers and bathroom. She found the walk-in closet and was stunned with the amount of clothes. The clothes weren't what she was used to. She assumed these were what humans on Earth wore, and she knew wearing them would help her blend in better.

She decided to change into clothes that reminded her of home. She found pants that kind of looked like the cargo pants from home and a hoodie as well. She put on a pair of army boots that were stiff from never being worn. She went to the bathroom and brushed her long, thick hair while staring at herself in the mirror. Her purple-blue eyes were going to stand out on Earth as well as her appearance. It would be the same for the other Elves, and even the Vampires. From the pictures she'd seen, humans weren't as flawless as Elves and Vampires. They also weren't nearly as attractive either. To be honest, they looked a bit plain in comparison to them. Luna had an otherworldly beauty.

A knock on her bedroom door disturbed her thoughts. She left the bathroom and opened the door. Samara and Aywin stood there, grinning. Samara wore a pair of tight black pants and a tight tank top. Aywin wore a pair of jeans and a salmon-coloured T-shirt.

"Do you have like a gazillion outfits too?" Samara asked, and peered behind Luna into her room.

"Yeah. Do you know where we can get food in this place?" Luna asked. She walked into the hallway and closed her bedroom door behind her.

"Vampires only drink blood, right? What if they don't have any… normal food here," Aywin questioned. Luna's nose crinkled as she thought about how someone could drink gross, thick human blood.

"We aren't going to starve you guys," Karn said with a smirk. He strode down the hallway towards them. His blonde hair was wet from a recent shower.

Samara put her hand on her hip. "So, where's the food then?"

"This way." He continued past them.

Luna shrugged, and the three Elves followed him. They went back down the stairs and through another hallway that opened into a humongous kitchen all in black, from the cupboards to the appliances (which Elves were not familiar with) to the countertops. The only thing that wasn't black was the white-and-grey marbled tile floor and matching backsplash.

Karn opened a glass pantry door to reveal a tonne of food—mostly food the Elves weren't familiar with, but they dug in anyways. Luna munched on some cracker chips she found and grabbed some veggies out of the fridge. Aywin shared Luna's food. Samara ate some canned fruit and trail mix. Karn gave them all a quick overview of the appliances in the kitchen so that they knew how to use them. He said they had to listen carefully so that they didn't "burn down the building." After he went over everything, they went back to eating.

"How'd they know to buy all this?" Luna asked between her chews.

They all sat at the dining-room table, looking through the large window in front of them, which overlooked the yard.

"Zane just asked our workers to bring a variety of things," Karn said.

"Workers?" Samara asked.

Karn nodded. "Yeah. We pay people to take care of the property and clean the house."

"Like people, people?" Aywin asked.

Karn laughed. "I'm not sure what you mean."

"Like Earthly people?" Aywin clarified.

"Yes, Earth people," Karn replied.

"Sooo, they don't… realize the weirdness? Or do they know you're Vampires?" Luna asked.

"They don't know, and we aren't that weird." Karn chuckled.

Luna scoffed. "Says the guy who drinks blood."

"Hey, it tastes better than you think," he replied.

"I've licked my finger with a cut that's bleeding, and let me just say, that it does not taste good enough to drink entire cups of—especially if it's not yours. That's nasty," Aywin said.

"We must have different taste buds then," Karn said with a grin.

"Obviously," Aywin murmured.

"Won't they notice our… ears?" Aywin questioned.

Karn shrugged. "Maybe, we aren't too concerned about it."

Luna stuffed some more crackers into her mouth. She hadn't been able to snack on food for a while, which was her favourite thing to do. Karn scooted himself out of the dining-room chair. "Come on, let me show you the other cool parts of this place," he said with a wink.

They put their food away before exploring the rest of the mansion. Karn took them to a few different rooms. Luna couldn't believe how large the building was. Just when she thought they'd seen it all, he'd show them something else. So far, they'd seen the library, the gym, a bar/dancing room, a movie theatre (the Elves had no idea what movies were), and an indoor swimming pool.

Karn opened a bright-red door, which reminded Luna of blood and made her stomach lurch. Once she saw what was inside the room, all the sickness vanished—she was in heaven. The room was a painting room filled with a variety of drawing and painting supplies. Luna couldn't help but let out a little squeal. She had been happy to see the library, but this room was even better.

"You guys sure have everything here," she said with a beaming smile.

Karn gave off a bored shrug. "This is Zane's doing. He's the only one who paints. Anyways, that concludes our tour. You guys can hang out wherever you want. The attack plan on the Werewolves is still in development, so it may take a few days of planning before that happens. Feel free to help yourselves to what you want and let us know if you need anything."

Aywin began to walk away, down the hall. "Well, I'm going to go and find out what movies are," he stated, and disappeared around a corner.

Luna walked further into the painting room. She peered over at Samara, who was chatting with Karn. "Samara, I'm going to hang out in here awhile. I think I feel like painting something," she said.

Samara surveyed the room before giving Luna a slight nod. "Okay, sounds good. I'll give you some peace and quiet then," she replied with a smile.

She and Karn walked away together down the hallway, talking away. Luna could feel something was developing between the two, but she wasn't going to continue to ask Samara about it. Obviously, Samara had strong feelings against the Vampires, just like Luna did, but Samara was an adult and Luna wasn't going to try and plan out her love life.

Luna strolled over to a blank canvas. Her mind was already bustling with ideas to paint. Painting supplies was available in front of her. She squirted a bunch of different colours onto a wooden palette, then imagined space and how Earth looked from it. She began to paint.

***

It felt like hours had gone by as she painted. But that didn't matter—painting soothed her soul, so she continued. By the time she finished, her right hand had started to cramp. She stood back and stared at the canvas. The painting had turned out even better than she'd expected. The white swirls on the planet combined with the other colours created something exquisite.

After she cleaned up her paint brushes and palette, she left the room. Her head began to feel spacey from spending too much time alone in her own mind, or maybe it was from the paint fumes. The paint on Earth was different than what she was used to. However, the head spaciness also often happened when she read too many books. At those times, she'd feel like she was in a separate reality, living a life she wasn't supposed to be living, and every problem in life would suddenly seem smaller and less important.

She was walking back to her room and staring down at the floor when she ran into something hard. She bounced back and looked up. It was Darick. His hair was cut shorter and no longer ruffled. He must've gotten a haircut in the last couple hours; it looked good on him, making his already strikingly handsome features stand out even more. His expression was stern as he stared at her.

"Uh, um, h-hi," Luna stuttered. She was taken aback by how emotionless he was.

He had his hands tucked into a pair of dark jeans. "Hi," he replied dryly.

The insecure feelings that had been overwhelming Luna burst out. She noticed her skin begin to glow blue as she let her emotions run wild. "You know what?" she barked. "You have been a little rude since we left Nexus. I was worried about you, Darick; I was scared. I thought they'd killed you, and I would have done anything to try and save you. But now you are suddenly back and you give me nothing. Not even a smile, not even a 'Oh, I'm happy to see they never killed you.' NOTHING. Do you even care? What did he do to you, Darick?"

Darick's eyes flickered with guilt, his large body relaxed. "I should never have dragged you into any of this. You shouldn't even be here. Zane did nothing terrible to me. He had me in a cell and questioned me, but then let me go. There was no torture, no brainwashing, nothing. All that he did was give me my memories back," Darick explained. His tone of voice had softened.

Luna could see his former self breaking through. She reached out and grabbed his hands.

He tore them away from her and backed up. "We can't… we can't do this. I can't do this," he stammered.

Luna's eyebrows knit together, and a pain she'd never felt tore at her heart. "I'm trying to help you, Darick. I care about you," she pleaded. Her eyes welled up with tears.

Darick shook his head. "I'm sorry," he said quickly before his large body disappeared in a flash.

She had forgotten how speedy Vampires could be. Luna didn't know how to handle her emotions. Her skin felt like it was on fire; it was burning a bright blue. She was mad—mad at Darick for saying the words she knew he didn't mean, mad at Edric for what he'd done, and mad at the fact that Fin was dead and hundreds of other Elves.

She wiped the tears from her cheeks and took a few breaths to calm herself down. Eventually, her skin dimmed and she felt more stable. Her heart still ached, and she wasn't sure how to fix that problem. She went back to her room and had a bath.

She let the warm water consume her and scrubbed off all the emotional filth. She wasn't going to let another man cause her pain like Edric had. She was confident in herself. She was strong. She had never needed a man before, so she didn't need one now. River had broken her, and that pain was where these feelings were stemming from…. At least, that was what she told herself.

After bathing, she dried off, put on a shirt with some loose shorts, and got ready for bed. She crawled in under the sheets, which felt silky against her skin, and tried not to think about Darick. Instead, before she drifted off to sleep, she thought about how she was going to work on her powers more to help the Vampires win the war against the Werewolves so that she could go home to her family. She missed her parents. She missed her house.

Chapter XVII

Luna woke up to the sound of someone banging on her bedroom door. She grumbled and tucked her face further into the soft, feathery pillow.

"Luna!" the voice called. It was Samara.

"Go away," Luna replied.

The door swung open, and Samara strolled in wearing an exercise outfit. "Get up. Let's go do some training," Samara ordered.

Luna sat up in the bed, not wanting to leave the warm, cozy sheets; her hair stuck out in all directions. "Aren't I the one that usually has to wake you up?" Luna asked groggily.

Samara laughed. "Sometimes. Now, come on. I've been thinking about that gym all night," she said, and waggled her eyebrows.

Luna groaned while getting out of bed. She went to her dresser and pulled out a pair of leggings and a stretchy tight-fitting tank top with a built-in bra. They didn't have built-in sports bras on Nexus; she liked them. She went to the bathroom and changed into her new clothes. She did her morning routine of brushing her hair and teeth and washing her face. She opened the bathroom door to find Samara sitting on the end of her bed, fiddling with her nails.

"Ugh, finally. You take forever," Samara said as she stood up.

"I had to get beautiful," Luna teased, and flopped her ponytail to one side while batting her eyelashes. Samara rolled her eyes with a laugh as they left the room.

They arrived at the gym. It was six thirty in the morning, and Luna had expected the place to be empty, but it wasn't. Darick was in there, of course....

The Earthly gym equipment was foreign to Luna and Samara. Thankfully, each machine had instructions and an image to explain what it was used for. Darick was in the middle of a set of chest presses, so he didn't look up when the Elves entered the gym.

Luna and Samara decided that they were going to do some back and bicep exercises and then, for the last fifteen minutes of their workout, practise some hand-to-hand combat on the mats to raise their heart rates. They took turns switching from machine to machine. Luna used dumbbells for her bicep curls. She kept sneaking glances at Darick, who hadn't even said "good morning" or acknowledged them. It made Luna push harder; Luna didn't want to admit that she was also sneaking glances because of how good Darick looked. He wore a loose sleeveless shirt and a pair of jogging pants. His muscles were pumped and shining from sweat. They rippled and flexed with every move he made. She swallowed her pooling saliva.

"He really shouldn't be allowed to walk around like that. He's going to distract people," Samara whispered jokingly, then added a wink at the end of her sentence.

Luna's face blushed, but she continued to do some more curls. Darick grabbed the small towel he'd been carrying around and wiped his forehead with it. He swung the towel over his shoulder and sauntered towards the exit of the gym, his golden eyes remaining down at the floor.

"Good morning!" Luna called out.

Darick paused. His head went up, and he turned around to face her, a serious expression on his face. "Mornin'," he answered, then gave her a curt nod before leaving.

Luna let out a frustrated sigh.

"Looks like it's time to do some combat fighting," Samara stated.

The two women went over to the mats on the far side of the gym. The mats smelled of salt and stale sweat. There were large mirrors on the walls around the mats. Samara and Luna squared off against one another. Luna threw the first punch, which Samara blocked with her forearm. Samara reared to the side and elbowed Luna's chin. Luna took a few steps back, shocked from the blow; her chin felt numb. She grinned and circled around Samara. Samara kicked at Luna, who ducked, then stepped in and punched Samara in the gut. Samara countered back quickly with a snap kick to Luna's leg. Luna stumbled forward. Samara swung her body around and grabbed Luna's head into a choke hold. The two women struggled on the ground, Luna desperately trying to get out of the hold. Samara's grip was too tight. Luna tapped Samara's side to let her know she'd won that round. They both started laughing, their chests heaving up and down from the work.

"Next time if you fumble, go backwards, not towards me," Samara said.

"Okay," Luna replied. They did a few more rounds until they had both drawn blood and were sweating so much that the mats were slimy.

Luna heard clapping from the other side of the gym. Zane strolled over with an uneven smile plastered on his face.

"How long were you being a creep and watching?" Luna asked in an edgy tone. She would help with the Werewolf thing, but it didn't mean that she suddenly liked or trusted Zane.

"Does the length of the watching increase the creepiness? Do I get extra bonus points and become better stalker material?" he asked with a smirk.

Luna's eyes narrowed. "Stalker. Definitely a stalker," she retorted.

"Aw, and here I thought some girls liked to be watched," he said.

Samara burst out laughing, but Luna muttered some curses under her breath. "Did you need something?" Luna asked abruptly.

Zane crossed his arms and put his hand under his chin in a thinking gesture. He went silent for a minute, only tapping his foot. "Ah!" His eyes lit up. "That's what it was. Sorry, I was so caught up with my stalking that I forgot why I came here. We need to work on your powers. I need to see what you're capable of to finish the plan of attack against the Werewolves."

"I'm pretty busy," Luna replied heartlessly.

Samara sighed. "Oh my gosh. Just go. It's fine. You need to work on your lightning energy stuff anyways. I'll meet up with you later." Samara nudged Luna's side, then strode past Zane, leaving only Luna and Zane in the quiet gym.

The humming of the air conditioner was the only sound cutting through the awkwardness. Zane's eye's never left Luna's. She had to remove her gaze from his before she caught herself showing weakness.

She lifted her head high. "Let's go then."

Zane nodded and gestured with his hand for her to follow him. They walked down a few hallways and then through a sliding glass door that led out to the backyard of the property. The morning air was cool against Luna's skin, but it felt good to be outside. Being inside made her feel stuffy and headachy sometimes.

Zane stepped to the side. "Show me what you've got," he said with a raised brow.

Luna called up the energy within herself and pulled it out. Her skin began to glow and heat. She shot a few lightning bolts out towards the sky. When she was finished, she relaxed her body and let the energy hide back inside her. Zane chuckled. Luna frowned and stared at him with disbelief and embarrassment.

"What's so funny?" she asked ruthlessly.

"Luna. You can manipulate electrical currents. Shooting a few lightning bolts is nothing compared to what I can teach you to do with your powers," Zane replied. He stepped close to her, and she could feel his body heat radiating off him in waves. Luna wasn't sure what he meant, but she was curious.

"Our bodies have electrical currents. Think about your nervous system… about your muscles. There are tiny electrical signals going through us all the time. You could use them. Try to control me. Manipulate me. See what happens." His voice lowered to a whisper.

Luna gulped. He was so close to her, and she really didn't trust him, but if she could do more with her powers, she wanted to know how to, and he really was the perfect candidate to teach her. His powers went beyond anything she'd ever seen. She nodded her head and pulled up her energy again, then focused it on Zane. She watched as a grin splayed across his face.

"I can feel you," he murmured.

She made it so he moved his arms up and down. She gasped—she'd just made him move. "Oh shit!" she exclaimed.

Zane smirked. "Told you. Now, don't do this to me, but I bet you can mess up someone's brain waves too. Try it in battle. Our powers come easily to us once we know what we are capable of."

Luna let her energy die down and took her hold off Zane. "Anything else that you think I could do?" Luna inquired.

Zane took a few steps away from her. His lack of body heat left her feeling cold. "You could try creating an electrically charged barrier around yourself. Like a shield. Also, I notice that you are using your own electrical energy. It probably drains you faster, leaving you exhausted. But since there's electrical currents all around you, you could use those. Like from the sky or the ground or another living creature. I also bet you can heal yourself faster. Your body's cells use currents like that to heal, so you may be able to accelerate the process. You can also create fire. Honestly, Luna you're more powerful than you can even comprehend right now. You'll get better at what you do, but you may be able to control others minds like me—in a way where you can read their thoughts, their memories, their deepest secrets," he said.

The words sent a chill over Luna. She thought of how the first time she'd used her powers, she had healed the wounds on her arms instantly. What was Zane capable of?

"If you can read minds, why didn't you just read mine or Samara's or Aywin's to get what you wanted from us?" she asked. Her body felt frozen and on edge.

"I can't read minds," he stated frankly.

"How did you give Darick his memories back?"

"I healed the part of his brain that was damaged. I could sense something was wrong with him," he replied.

Luna felt relief washing over her system. Her body loosened. "He heals with the intake of blood. Why wouldn't his brain heal?" Luna asked curiously.

Zane shrugged. "I'm not sure. Maybe it was because he wasn't drinking pure human blood, or maybe it was because he didn't drink a sufficient amount of blood after starving for two years."

Luna's face blushed at Zane's comment.

Zane's eyes narrowed and his jaw clenched. "Wait.... No. No way," Zane said in shock. "He was feeding from you?"

At that moment, Luna really wondered if Zane could read minds because he had read hers perfectly. Luna smiled sheepishly. "I mean… y-yeah, he was. But like, I don't see why that's an issue." Luna didn't understand why Zane looked mad; his nostrils had flared and his eyes blazed.

"Did he hurt you?" Zane asked.

The question caught Luna off guard. Darick would never hurt her. He had drained her a bit too much blood the first time, but it was nothing terrible or life-threatening to her.

"No, of course, not. He'd never do that," Luna objected.

Zane let out a humourless laugh. "You'd be surprised."

"What's that supposed to me?" Luna questioned brusquely.

"It doesn't matter…." Zane muttered angrily. He snapped around and went back towards the sliding door.

"Wait a minute!" Luna barked.

Zane stopped and slowly turned back towards her, his eyes flashing with darkness.

"Where are you going?"

He shook his head, then turned away from her and went into the house.

Luna stood outside alone in confusion. Had Zane just had a hissy fit? She began to laugh out loud, because if that was true, it was the most obscure thing ever.

***

Luna spent more time outside with her powers. She began practising conjuring up electrical currents from the sky and ground. She even brought in a lightning storm from the cloudy sky above. After some time, her stomach growled with hunger, and she realized she hadn't had a proper meal in a while.

She decided to go up to her room first to shower and change into a different pair of clothes. She noticed a laundry hamper in the bathroom that opened to a laundry chute, and she put her dirty clothes in it. Then she knocked on Samara's bedroom door but got no answer. So, she went down to the kitchen and found some ingredients to make pancakes.

Luna sat at the dining table alone, eating her pancakes with butter and some canned peaches. The food was heavenly to her empty stomach. When she finished the plate, she sat at the table for a while, staring out at the green grass outside. It had begun to rain and small puddles were forming on the grass.

The peaceful moment was interrupted by a loud crash erupting through the mansion and her body winced. She burst out of her seat and headed towards the sounds of arguing coming from above. She continued up the stairs, following a loud voice that she could only presume was Zane's. When she reached the top floor, Luna found Darick and Zane squaring off in a living room-like area. There was a couch turned over on one side of the room and a glass coffee table smashed in the centre. Something in the air smelled like burnt hair. What were the two of them doing?

"I had no fucking memories, Zane. How was I supposed to know? And why are you so pissed about it? It's not like you haven't done it before," Darick said sternly.

Zane's fists were clenched, and his chest heaved up and down with anger. Luna's stomach dropped once she noticed all the furniture in the room was now hovering a few inches off the ground. A static-like feeling filled the room, and ice was slowly forming up the walls and ceiling.

"You would have fucking felt it once you fed. And yet you still did it," Zane snarled.

"I was hungry, and… she offered." Darick was trying to speak calmly, but Luna could see the frustration in his eyes.

Zane lashed out, pushing Darick up to the wall with an invisible force.

"Stop!" Luna screamed.

Zane's threatening expression softened, but he didn't let Darick go and continued to push him against the wall. He crossed his arms. His jaw clicked; then his eyes lifted to meet hers, and they burned like coals.

"You need to leave," Zane stated simply.

"No! You'll kill him if I leave," Luna snapped. Her skin was now glowing bright blue; she was prepared to use her power against Zane if needed.

"I won't kill him. If I wanted him dead, he'd be dead," Zane replied heartlessly.

Luna flinched at the words. What was wrong with him? Why was he acting like this? "Let him go," Luna said boldly.

This time, her energy filled the room. She zapped Zane with a shock of electrical current. Zane winced, and a smirk played across his lips. He dropped Darick back down onto the floor. The rest of the objects in the room crashed to the floor too.

"Darick will fill you in," Zane stated coldly before leaving the room.

Luna ran over to Darick as he stood up shakily. Luna tried to help him, but he put up his hands. "Don't," he said coldly.

Luna scowled. "Oh, okay, I get it. Don't want to touch the gross Elf. I get that you don't want... to be more than friends, but can we at least be friends? Is that even possible for you? And what was that fight all about?"

"Can you not talk so loudly? Just let me get ahold of myself for a second," Darick answered dryly.

Luna snapped her mouth shut. She almost commented on how rude he was being, but she took a once-over look at Darick and saw how tired he was. He walked over to the couch and flipped it back up. Then he let out a groan as he sat on it. Luna wasn't sure what she was supposed to do, so she joined him in sitting, except she sat in a rocking chair across from him, and gave him a few minutes to get ahold of himself.

He stared off at a wall for what felt like forever. Luna was becoming impatient, but she knew Darick well enough to know that silence was when he was having his deepest thoughts, and it was better to not talk and allow him to ponder.

"I'm going to tell you a bunch of things that I've been meaning to talk to you about," Darick said softly. He looked defeated.

Luna just nodded, not saying a word.

"I'm not a good guy, Luna. I killed my father right before I fled to your planet. I did it because I wanted to be the leader of the Soul Empire, but Zane wouldn't let me. He knew what I was capable of. I knew I couldn't beat him—he has more power—so that's why I left. Zane knows what I am. I did terrible things, Luna.... I killed hundreds upon hundreds of people. Maybe even thousands. I couldn't keep track. But I tried. I liked to keep count of the numbers. I liked the pain I would inflict while I drank. I'm like my father. I have a craving for blood that's difficult to control. I always have. I just want... more of it. Every Vampire has to control their feeding, but I chose not to control it and let it control me. It makes it hard to be around you, especially now that I have my memories back," Darick explained. He took a break and stared at the floor, his eyes refusing to meet Luna's.

"I don't understand. Zane is the one killing the humans. He's the one who enjoys invading other planets. He wanted to come and take over my planet. You aren't making sense," Luna replied softly.

Darick let out a defeated sigh. "With my injury, I was discombobulated. I was mixing myself up with my brother. I'm the monster, Luna."

Luna began to shake her head. Her lower lip trembled. "No, you're wrong. That's not who you are, at least not anymore," she said.

"I still have the urges. But you're right. I'm different than what I was before. But I know that part is in me and it tries to come out at times. I'm trying... but I'm not safe." Darick drummed his fingers against the side of the couch.

"So, you're the brother who is powerful, but he's the invincible brother that Torion was talking about—the good one who wants peace?" Luna asked rhetorically.

"Zane has always been the one doing things for the greater good, and he hated our father. He hated me, too, for it."

"Why wouldn't he kill your father then?"

"That's a question for him, I suppose," Darick replied carefully.

He stood up and began walking towards the exit, brushing past Luna, who reached out and grabbed his arm. Darick allowed the touch to linger for longer than he should have. He exhaled and pulled his arm from her grasp.

The feeling of his warm, soft skin remained on hers, leaving her feeling empty. She allowed the loneliness she felt to seep into her pours and change her perception of him. He was troubled, and she couldn't save him. He didn't want saving, anyways. Her body felt light as she stood up to return to her bedroom.

***

Her legs felt like lead as she made her way up the stairs. She peered up at the massive clock on the wall and noticed it was only eleven.

She ran into Aywin in the hallway. He held a bowl of white puffy things in his hand. Luna frowned. "What's that?" she asked. The smell of the food was to die for. Her mouth watered.

Aywin offered the bowl out to her. "It's called popcorn! Apparently, humans eat it when they watch movies, and that's what I've been doing for most of the morning," Aywin replied with a grin on his face.

Luna grabbed a handful of the popcorn and put it into her mouth. It melted on her tongue and tasted of salt and butter. "Damn, that is good," she murmured between munches.

Aywin's eye's widened. "Oh! Here, take this," he said, giving Luna a flat, handheld black device. "Karn gave me yours because he couldn't find you. They're called phones. There's no password for yours. They use them to communicate here, kind of like the radios we use on our planet, and they also have music on them. You can put more on your phone. It's called downloading. Oh, and games too! Here, I'll show you."

Luna and Aywin stood in the hallway for an hour or two, going over the phone's features. At first, Luna struggled to understand all the things. Aywin had always been the high-tech guy; with his purely objective mindset, he could figure out anything. Luna's mind didn't work the same way. She eventually got a hang of things and figured out how to text, call, listen to music, download free apps, take pictures, and so on.

The music wasn't the same as what she was used to from her planet; the music on Earth was even better. It had a lot of other instrument sounds in it, and there were so many genres. After Aywin left to go back and watch movies, Luna stayed in the hallway, listening to different musical artists. Music had always been a source of comfort for Luna; she just never learned how to play an instrument. So, having the ability to just listen to it whenever she wanted to was making her soul sing.

She listened to songs that made her want to dance or fight or do something energetic and then to ones that made her sad, relaxed, or even angry… but in a good way. She noticed that while she listened to some of the calmer songs, the tightness she had been feeling in her chest lately began to loosen. Maybe she was beginning to worry she had an illness that she wasn't aware of…. Luna continued to scroll on the device. She was so caught up in what she was doing that she didn't hear Samara sneak up on her.

"You got one too?" Samara asked as she peered over Luna's shoulder.

Luna screamed and dropped the phone onto the ground. She panicked, hoping it didn't break. She picked it up and didn't see any cracks, then faced Samara with narrowed eyes. "Where have you been?"

"Ermm… just… exploring the mansion," Samara replied. A blush spread across Samara's upper cheeks.

Luna gasped. "You didn't…." Luna said in shock.

Samara raised her hands. "Whoa now, don't be jumping to conclusions. It wasn't like that. Karn and I were literally hanging out and talking. Did you know that the only reason they attacked us was because they thought Darick had persuaded us to attack them? That's why they didn't strike first. They had no idea what they were walking into. Karn also told me about Darick…. Luna, he's—"

Luna interrupted Samara mid-sentence. "Samara, I know what he is. Or what he was. He's not that man anymore," Luna defended.

Samara's forehead creased. "Luna… just be careful. I'm being careful too. I obviously don't completely trust these guys, but Karn seems genuine. He even admitted his past to me. He grew up with Darick and Zane; the three of them have known each other their entire lives. Apparently, what Zane's done in the past two years has been life-changing to the Soul Empire. Now they drink blood from blood bags and not the actual people. Kids are being taught how to control their blood lust at an early age. He's worked hard to change what his father made normal for their society."

Luna started to feel guilty with the way she had been treating Zane. If Zane truly was who everyone said he was, then she should be ashamed with what she had said to him. "Why didn't Zane tell me any of this?" Luna asked coarsely.

Samara gave Luna's shoulder a soft, comforting squeeze. "Girl, all you've done is yell at him. You haven't even allowed him to open up to you, so why would he?" Samara said plainly.

The words were like a shot to Luna's stomach. Samara was right: Luna had been so walled off against Zane that she never allowed herself to listen to any possible truth. "Thank you," Luna said kindly to Samara.

The reason that Luna loved Samara so much was because their friendship was strong enough that they could be brutally open and honest with each other. And sure, there were days that they hurt each other's feelings, but they were always able to come back from it.

"Do you want to go swimming?" Samara asked.

Luna felt her body wince from even the thought of more exercise. She was so tired from the morning, and all the power she'd used.

"Not really," Luna replied.

"Oh, come on. You can sit in the hot tub? It might ease your achy muscles," Samara said as she nudged Luna's side.

The sound of sitting in a warm hot tub did seem relaxing. "All right, let's do it," Luna answered.

"Yay! I'll change into a bathing suit, and I'll meet you back here," Samara said before she speed walked to her room.

Luna walked over to her bedroom and went in. The sun was shining brightly through the windows; it had finally decided to peak out of the clouds. Luna smiled and began her search for a bathing suit. She found a bikini similar to the ones she had at home but a bit more... revealing. Luna slid it on anyways; it was just going to be her and Samara. She took a towel and wrapped it around herself for the walk down, then slid on a pair of open-toed shoes.

Samara was already in the hallway. She wore a large shirt that covered her body and held a towel in her hand. They made their way down to the swimming pool.

Windows that were open to the backyard surrounded the indoor pool. Thankfully, nobody was outside gawking in. There was a six-person hot tub in the front right corner of the room, and the pool took up the rest of the space. Luna and Samara placed their towels on a towel rack. Samara took off the large, baggy shirt to reveal a yellow bikini underneath that complemented her skin tone and jet-black hair. Luna had chosen a red bikini. She pulled at the back of her bikini bottoms.

"Do these seem... small to you?" Luna questioned as they dipped into the hot tub.

The warm water felt euphoric against her cold bruised skin. The Elves had hot springs, but not hot tubs, and their "pools" were lakes and oceans.

"Yeah, they are on the small side," Samara replied.

They sat in the hot tub for a long time in silence. Luna closed her eyes and leaned her head back. She let out a moan as she sunk deeper to the water. She felt the spray of the bubbles as they popped around her face.

"Ah, my favourite sound," Zane said.

Samara snorted and let out a laugh. Luna popped her eyes open and sat up straighter in the water. Zane was standing by the swimming pool entry way with Karn. He was wearing slim black pants and a dark-blue top that had the sleeves rolled up, revealing part of his tattoo. The two men strode over to the Elves. They stopped just in front of the hot tub and stared down at them.

Zane raised a brow. "No comment? You usually have something snarky to say." Zane smirked.

Luna narrowed her eyes. "I guess it's your lucky day."

He winked at her, then looked from one woman to the other. "Tonight, we are hosting a party. Thought it'd be nice to do, considering our… history. That way, you can get acquainted with some of the other Vampires. You will be fighting next to them at some point. We were thinking around six," Zane said.

"What do we wear?" Samara asked.

"Dress to impress," Karn commented, and gave Samara a seductive grin.

Luna rolled her eyes at the interaction, but she was happy for Samara, even though she knew the fling couldn't possibly last long. They were going to go back home at some point. The two men left the room, and soon after, Luna and Samara got out of the hot tub. It was nearly four in the afternoon, and they needed to get ready for the special dinner.

***

Samara brought a bunch of dresses into Luna's room, and they got ready together. Luna curled her hair and put on makeup. She didn't enjoy getting "dolled up"; it had never been her thing. She often found that she'd become uncomfortable, and so she would usually choose to wear something that didn't make her feel the need to suck in her stomach. How unfortunate for women to feel that way when dressing up.

She slid into a long sparkly red dress that hugged her curves beautifully. The dress had a slit that came up to her upper thigh. She felt slightly scandalous, but it looked so good on her that she didn't care. Besides, she wanted to show Darick what he was missing; she was still frustrated with him. Samara wore a silky emerald-green dress that fell just past her mid-thigh.

"You look amazing," Luna said in awe, and she wasn't lying; Samara was a gorgeous woman.

Samara spun around in a circle, then said, "Gee, thanks."

By the time Luna and Samara left the room, it was a quarter to six. "Do you think Aywin's still in his room?" Luna asked.

Samara shrugged. "Not sure, let's check."

They walked over to his room, their high heels clicking against the stone floor. Luna knocked on the door. She heard footsteps approach the door before it swung open. Aywin's red hair was combed to perfection. He wore a pair of black dress pants that reminded Luna of what Zane wore on a day-to-day basis, a grey vest, and a white shirt.

"Someone cleans up nicely," Samara said, and smiled.

Aywin curtsied in a silly manner. "Madam," he stated formally.

Luna frowned. "What does that mean?"

Aywin laughed as he came out and closed the door behind him. "It's an Earth thing. From watching the movies, I think it's a way to address a woman in a polite way," he explained.

They took off down the hallway. Luna forced a yawn. "Sounds boring," she said, then grinned at her brother, who rolled his eyes.

"Hey, you'd be surprised with how much I've learned about Earth culture by watching their movies," he replied. "It's crazy how different and similar we are. Like, we are on a planet millions of miles away and we speak one of the most common languages here, though we have a bit of an accent. And our language obviously isn't called English; it's Elven. But my point is, it's so similar."

As they walked to the dining hall, Aywin continued to ramble on about the different movies he'd watched without boring Luna too much. She did find some of what he was talking about interesting.

They walked into an enormous dining hall with tall, arched ceilings and multiple crystal chandeliers hanging from them. The room had quite a few people in it already. Luna was shocked by the number of Vampires around. She hadn't seen any when she'd been exploring the mansion and wondered if they all stayed downstairs.

Along the back of the room was a table set with food. The rest of the room was composed of smaller standing-height cocktail tables with different types of drinks of them. Luna felt bile rise in her throat when she noticed that most of the drinks were red. She realized that they were the only non-Vampires there, so, of course, the party was mostly going to cater to the Vampires' needs. Soft piano music was playing in the background; Luna recognized the instrument.

She caught Aywin staring at the blood. "Ew," he whispered. His face was scrunched up with disgust.

Samara sighed. "You two are so sensitive."

Just as Luna was about to comment, Karn strode over and grabbed Samara by the waist. He looked handsome in a full light-grey suit and green tie.

"Mmm, how'd you know I'd wear the green one?" she asked with her lips pursed.

He chuckled. "Because you love green."

"Fair point," she replied with a giggle.

Karn turned towards Aywin and Luna. "Welcome. Please enjoy yourselves. We have some food for you guys in the back, and there are a variety of drinks there as well. The other drinks here… well, I'm sure you've figured out what those are." He smirked and grabbed a champagne glass full of thick blood.

Karn then pulled Samara over to the dance floor; they rocked back and forth slowly together and talked. Samara's smile was the widest Luna had ever seen it. A pink tinge covered her cheeks, giving her a glow that made Luna happy.

"When did they get so… close?" Aywin asked.

"Recently. What do you think about the combo?" Luna asked her brother.

Aywin shrugged. "As long as he doesn't cannibalize her, I think it's great."

Luna burst out laughing. "Really? Your standards are so low," she teased.

Aywin eyed the food at the back. "Speaking of low, my body's running low on food. I've only been eating popcorn today and need to get some other stuff in me," he said before heading to the food table.

Luna stood against the wall awkwardly, surveying the room and taking in all the Vampires she didn't know. Her eyes landed on Pierce, who wore a tight, sheer silver dress that showed off her boobs. She was talking with Zane. He held a glass of blood in his right hand while his left was tucked into his pocket. He was stunning. His curly dark hair glistened in the light, as if he'd put some hair product in it. The thought made Luna laugh. She couldn't imagine him doing that. Pierce batted her lashes at him and nibbled her bottom lip; she was hard-core flirting with him. Luna snorted. She had just laughed twice now while standing alone—if anybody was watching her, they'd probably think she was crazy.

"You look… nice," Darick's deep voice said from behind her.

She turned to face him and his large, overwhelming figure. He was wearing a navy-blue suit tailored for his body. His expression was stern, but Luna could see a small smile tugging at the corner of his mouth.

"Thank you," she said, and twirled.

He looked out towards the Vampires mingling. "You should go and talk to someone and get to know them," he said.

"That sounds exactly like something I don't want to do," Luna replied jokingly. She hoped to see Darick smile but instead he exhaled.

"Yeah, me too."

"Do you want to dance?" Luna asked.

Darick raised a brow at her. "No," he said frankly.

Luna rolled her eyes. "Oh, come on, live a little. Besides, I've never danced to piano music; it's kind of nice," she said, and swayed her hips.

Darick chewed at the inside of his mouth for a moment. Luna could see the wheels spinning in his mind. "Okay, fine," he stated.

She smiled widely and grabbed his hand, leading him to the dance floor, where a few others were slowly dancing. He placed his large warm hands on her waist, and she reached up and put her arms around his shoulders. She was too short to reach around his neck. Being intimate with him again made her feel at peace. The way their bodies swayed and moved with one another felt so right. His rigid body loosened the more they danced. A few songs went by, but they never let go.

"Darick," Luna whispered. His gold eyes flicked to hers. "It's okay," she said softly. She regretted saying the words because his body immediately tightened and he let go of her waist.

"I can't do this. I already told you I don't want to get involved with you, Luna," he stated.

Luna dropped her hands from his shoulders and stepped back. Anger boiled under her skin, and it took everything within her to stop from glowing blue. She thought they'd just shared a moment together, and now, she'd had enough of feeling this way. Had it all been in her mind only? Had he never truly cared about her? Moments of silence went by as they continued to stare at one another. Someone nearby cleared their throat, and she wondered if it was Zane; he was probably enjoying the scene.

She tried to calm herself, but she couldn't help it. Her mouth opened and the words burst out. "You know what, you're right, Darick. I can't do this either. I'm done trying. I've been going back and forth in my head about my feelings towards you, but now, I've decided it doesn't matter because you don't even want to consider MY feelings. Fuck you," she said fiercely, then left the dance floor.

She was officially done with him and his games with her. She knew he was going through a hard time, but what hurt her was that he wasn't willing to talk to her about it. He just kept pushing her away, and she wasn't going to chase him anymore. She calmed her emotions and tried to let the turmoil go. She was going to a fun night.

Luna strode over to the food table and downed a glass of… well, she wasn't sure what it was, but there was alcohol in it. She put the empty glass down, then chugged another drink and placed that one down before snatching one more to sip on. She hadn't had anything to eat yet, so within ten minutes, she was feeling not only buzzed but confident enough to approach some of the mingling Vampires.

From there, the evening went better than anticipated. Luna got to know quite a few of the Vampires; she enjoyed talking to them. They were all personable and friendly—well, except for Pierce. Her dark-blue eyes had been glaring at Luna the entire evening. She had also been sticking to Zane like a leech, which pissed Luna off. Aywin had found a group of guys that did the mechanical work on the space-ships, so he was engulfed in a conversation with them. Samara and Karn spent the entire evening together, going from dancing to chatting and then to mingling.

Towards the end of the night, Luna decided to finally approach Pierce and Zane. She strolled over to them, making sure to walk like she owned the floor. She wasn't sure why she felt so competitive with Pierce. Maybe it was the active bitch face Pierce had. Luna held her head up high; she knew she was an alluring woman, but she never took advantage of that in her movements. Tonight, she did.

Zane's eyes met hers, and the smirk on his face darkened, his eyes burning with something Luna couldn't quite name. She stood right in front of them and gave a fake smile to Pierce. "Ah, nice to officially meet you outside of the cell. I mean, we'd run into each other earlier, before coming down to Earth, but you seemed... distracted," Luna said, pretending to be nice.

Pierce stepped closer to Zane; her luscious red lips curved up into a sneer. "Luna, so great to see you. Zane, would you be so kind to grab us ladies some drinks?" she asked while batting her lashes at him.

Zane looked from one woman to the other, then shrugged. "Why not?" he said, and left them.

"I'd have to say, Luna… that dress sure attracts some attention, not to mention flies," Pierce said with a beaming white smile that showed off her fangs.

"Huh, you did a great job of combing your hair. It's impressive how you're able to hide the horns," Luna replied with a frown.

Pierce let out a mocking laugh. "Oops, my bad. I could have sworn I was talking to an adult."

"I'm an acquired taste. If you don't like me, acquire some taste," Luna responded.

Pierce applied some more red lipstick on her lips, acting like she was bored with the conversation. "Somewhere out there is a tree that produces oxygen for you; you owe it an apology," Pierce said coldly. Her mood had changed, and Luna could tell she had irritated her. This made Luna smile even wider.

"You really should come with a warning label," Luna retorted.

Pierce forced a terrifyingly fake smile. "Do you accidentally wipe your face after taking a shit?"

Luna shrugged. "Sorry, I was just trying to look like you today."

With that comment, Pierce growled, but Zane walked over with two drinks just in time.

Luna held her perfectly friendly smile, but she could see Pierce was having a hard time keeping things together. Luna took her drink from Zane. "Thank you," she said kindly.

He raised his brow at her as if he could sense her strange behaviour.

Pierce took the glass of blood and downed it. "I think I might need some fresh air, would you come with me?" she asked Zane.

He nodded and gave Luna a small wave before leaving with Pierce.

After her conversation with Pierce, Luna felt more accomplished than she should have. It was childish for sure, but that didn't mean it didn't feel good. She finished the evening with more fun, dancing with Samara and even Karn. Once she felt she had too much to drink, Luna decided to make her way back to her room before she couldn't make it.

She was about to turn down the hallway that led to her room when she heard a giggle. It was definitely a Pierce laugh; she could pick out that woman's annoying voice from anywhere. Luna took off her high heels and tip-toed down another hallway to track down where the giggle was coming from. She saw a door slightly open and she peered in.

Zane was sitting at the edge of a bed, flipping through a ancient looking book. He had a glass of blood in his other hand. Pierce was across the room, trying to talk to Zane about something, but he wasn't paying attention. This made Luna smile. Pierce kept walking closer to Zane. She had pushed her dress down to show more of her breasts so that they were practically busting out. "Zane," she purred.

Zane's eyes slowly looked up to her. She bit her bottom lip and stepped towards him. She looked at him with seductive eyes; her luscious lips pouted out. She placed her hands on his knees and pushed his legs apart roughly. She leaned towards him. Her right hand stroked his thigh, going higher and higher. Luna felt guilty for watching, but she was also mad. Why would Zane go for Pierce? Luna studied Zane's features, trying to figure out how much he liked what Pierce was doing. His expression seemed bored.

Pierce licked her lips, her hand going even higher, but Zane grabbed her wrist and stated, "We have company."

Luna realized the meaning of his words. Just before Pierce turned to look at the door, Luna fled. Her face blushed bright pink with embarrassment. She ran to her room, her bare feet thudding against the tile. She opened her door and shut it. Her heart was racing, and she suddenly didn't feel so drunk anymore. Had Zane known it was her watching? Or did he just know that someone was at the door?

She stripped off her dress and showered before getting ready for bed. She tucked herself in the sheets and hoped that there wouldn't be a knock on her door. Thankfully, there wasn't.

Chapter XVIII

*L*una woke up to a knock on her door. She pulled her phone off the charger and checked the time: nine thirty a.m. She had slept in quite a bit. She sat up and did a quick mental scan of herself.

She wasn't hungover, which was surprising, considering the amount she'd had to drink. At least, she remembered everything and didn't black out. Her stomach was feeling slightly off but not too bad.

She walked over to the bathroom and quickly brushed her hair and washed her face. Her T-shirt hugged her body and just covered the top of her cheeky underwear bottoms. The person at the door knocked again, louder this time. Luna sighed. She strolled over to the door and opened it, expecting Samara. Instead, it was Zane.

His eyes dropped down to her braless breasts first, then to her underwear. A smirk splayed across his face. The worst part wasn't even the fact that she was wearing little to no clothing; it was what he held in his hands: her heels, the ones that she had accidentally left just outside his bedroom door last night.

"Yours?" he questioned with a raised brow and a grin that showed off his fangs.

Luna grumbled and snatched the heels from his grasp. "Thanks."

She stepped back to close the door, but he placed his hand on it and leaned against the frame. Luna gave him a glare and crossed her arms across her chest. It was chilly, and the last thing she needed was her nipples poking out from underneath her shirt.

"Can I help you?" she inquired.

"Listen, I get we got off on the wrong start, with you thinking I'm a psychopathic murderer and all, but let me make it up to you. Let's go and work on your powers and then do some painting. I noticed you painted something in there already," Zane suggested with a genuine, closed-mouth grin.

There was no sign of arrogance, and it threw Luna off. She eyed him carefully. She purposefully allowed a few seconds to go by, as she knew Zane hated silence in conversations. Judging by the tapping of his foot on the ground and the clenching of his jaw, she had done a good job in irritating him.

"Sure. Give me ten," Luna said, then shut the door in his face.

She wasn't keen on hanging out with Zane, but she did want to work on her powers. She hopped in the tub and had a speedy two-minute shower. She blow-dried her hair until it was semi-dry; it was so thick that it would take longer than ten minutes to dry it. Then she changed into a pair of black leggings and a soft silky blue shirt. Luna opened the bedroom door and found Zane sitting on the ground, leaning up against the wall. It made her think of all the times she did that while watching Darick at the prison. So many things had happened in the last few weeks that it felt surreal.

Zane got up and dusted off his pants. He held a trench coat in his arms.

"Why do you wear dress pants and fancy shirts all the time?" Luna asked as she closed her bedroom door and followed Zane down the hallway.

Zane let out a low chuckle, which surprised Luna. She didn't know if she'd ever heard him laugh like that before. "Well, since you're asking, I do like to dress in style, unlike my baby brother. I don't always dress like this. I wear jeans and joggers sometimes... if I must."

Luna burst out laughing.

Zane frowned. "What?"

The look on his face made Luna laugh more. "It's just... you don't seem like the type to care so much about your looks. I guess you clearly do, by how you dress and how your hair's always perfect even when it shouldn't be," Luna replied.

They got to the bottom of the stairs and continued down another hallway to the art room. Zane's smirk came back. "So, you think my hairs perfect?" he asked.

Luna rolled her eyes. "Of course, that's the part you pick from what I just said."

He shrugged. "I can't help that I'm devastatingly attractive."

Luna held up her hands. "Whoa now, nobody said you were attractive," she teased.

Zane laughed, then opened the red door to the art room. The air was cold, as if the heater didn't reach this room. The bottom of each window along the side of the room was covered in moisture. Outside, the sun hid behind some clouds, but some blue sky was visible. Luna breathed in the smell of paint and other art supplies—her favourite smell other than the smell of old books, of course.

"I thought we were working on my powers first?" she questioned as she brought an empty canvas to easel.

"I got distracted," Zane stated, and did the same thing.

They both went through their own routines of setting up their stations before going to work. Luna wasn't sure what she wanted to paint, but she started anyways.

"How long have you been painting for?" Zane asked.

Luna looked up from her canvas and noticed his silvery-blue eyes looking at her. "A long time. Started when I was a kid," Luna answered, then went back to painting before she realized she was being rude and should have asked him the same thing. "What about you?" she asked brightly. She had told herself she was going to at least try and be nicer to the guy. She'd been a bit of a bitch to him—maybe "a bit" was a slight understatement.

"I've loved art since I could hold a pencil. I started mainly sketching, but then began to paint as I got older," Zane replied before looking intently at what he was doing, and they continued to paint in silence for another couple minutes.

Luna noticed her painting was slowly turning into the outside of the prison from home.

"Did you know you chew your bottom lip a lot when you paint," Zane stated.

Luna's brows furrowed at the strange comment. "Um, thanks? I thought I told you to stop being a creep," Luna said without looking up.

"Says the one who was watching me in my room last night," Zane replied with a smirk.

Luna felt a blush break out across her pale features. "To be fair, the door was open and Pierce laughs like a hyena," Luna retorted.

Zane chuckled but didn't respond with any snarky comment.

A few hours went by quickly, during which they made the odd comment but were mostly silent. The sound of the fan in the room created a peaceful white noise. Luna put the last touches on her painting, then began to clean up her supplies. Zane got up and did the same thing with his.

He walked over and looked at her painting. The realism in her work was inspiring. She watched as Zane's face looked impressed. "Not too bad, Elf Luna. Didn't think you had it in you," he remarked jokingly.

Luna rolled her eyes. "Please, let's not pretend like you didn't know I was good. Let's see your piece."

Zane strolled over to his painting and turned it towards her. Luna's jaw dropped—it was her. And it wasn't just her; it was the most stunning portrait she'd ever seen. There was so much detail.... Even her freckles were perfectly placed. He got the right the shade of her cheeks when she blushed and the right colour of her lips and eyes. Her purple-blue eyes. She was at a loss for words. How had he done that in only a few hours? Why had he painted her? To prove that his realism was better than hers, or as a friendly gesture? If it was to prove a point, she couldn't even be mad; he did such a stunning job.

"Wow," she said dumbfounded.

To Luna's surprise, he didn't try and brag. Instead, he replied casually, "Thanks." He placed the canvas back down. "Now, let's go and work on your powers."

They left the art room and headed over to the glass sliding door that they had gone to last time. The air was warmer than the day before. The sun had come out from behind the clouds and was shining brightly down on them.

Luna closed her eyes and lifted her face up, feeling the heat of the rays against her cheeks. The sun made her think of her father; he was always outside doing something if he wasn't at work, and he always said he enjoyed spending time in the sun. Thinking about him made her sad. She tried to push the thoughts away so that she could focus on learning her powers. When she fluttered her eyes open, the tears beginning to form made her thick dark eyelashes stick to each other. Luna never knew why she had dark eyelashes since she had red hair, but she did, and her eyebrows were a bit darker too. She caught Zane looking at her with an expression she couldn't read. He leaned himself up against the side of the house.

"Well, go on," he said with a wink.

Luna shook her arms and legs as if she was warming up for a run. "What should I do?" she asked as she bent her leg up to her abdomen to stretch her thigh.

"You could try creating and controlling fire," Zane suggested.

Luna widened her legs out into a ready stance and drew up energy from the plants and earth. She felt the flicker of electrical energy around her, then pinpointed the energy into a single spot in front of her and intensified it. Her skin burned bright blue, and she could feel the warmth spreading out around her. A flame sparked, and Luna fuelled it even more. She made sure to keep the fire controlled. It wasn't easy. The more she put into it, the bigger it got, and the more difficult it was to keep it contained. She played with the fire in the air, letting it drift from side to side, then flung it around while also keeping a burning flame on the ground.

Luna didn't know how long she practised, but at least an hour had gone by. She practised controlling the fire until her energy began to diminish and she started to become fatigued. When her mind began hurting and her body became wobbly, she extinguished the flame. Her legs felt like they were going to give out on her. She was grateful to see that she'd learned to conjure her energy without anger. Although, she wasn't sure if her anger really left her system these days. At least, she didn't need to focus on it when she pulled the string of magic, which came seamlessly to her now.

"Are you all right?" Zane asked. He hurried over to her and reached out an arm.

Luna put her hand up to let him know she was fine. She took a few deep breaths and focused on not puking. She had never used her powers for that long without stopping and starting, and it had taken a toll on her body. A splitting headache spiked, and she regretted her decision in pushing herself.

"I've never seen someone use powers like that for that long without stopping. It must have something to do with you pulling the energy from the ground," Zane said with astonishment. He was studying her like she was a science project, but a softness to his features betrayed that he was nervous about her fatigue. "I'll go grab you some water. Do you want something to eat?" he asked.

Luna decided to ground herself and try using the energy from the earth for nothing but her own benefit. This seemed to work because Luna could feel her body beginning to rejuvenate; her nausea was going away and her muscles were gaining their strength. She stood up straight and stretched her neck. "Yeah, I could use some food. Let's go to the kitchen," she said, and forced a smile.

Zane raised his eyebrow. "You sure you're good?"

Luna nodded as she walked to the sliding door. "When did you become so worried?" she teased.

The corner of his lips curved up. "Only for you," he replied with a wink.

Luna rolled her eyes as the two of them walked into the house.

***

When they made their way to the kitchen, they found Aywin, Samara, Karn, and Darick sitting at the dining table. Karn and Darick were drinking mugs of what Luna assumed was blood. Samara and Aywin were eating a stir fry.

"Hey! How are you? I went to your room, but you weren't there. Aywin made a stir fry; there's some for you on the counter if you want it," Samara said with a smile.

Luna eyed her. She looked too happy, like the "I just had sex" happy. Luna glanced at Samara and Karn. "Thanks. I was just practising my powers," she replied, and went over to grab the stir fry. She sat down next to Aywin.

He peered up at her. "Everything okay? You look... tired," he said quietly while Samara and Karn chatted.

Luna noticed Darick was sipping his blood and just staring out the window. "I'm fine. Using my powers drains me," she murmured back.

Aywin gave her back a rub. "Don't overdo it."

She smiled at her brother before she dug into the stir fry he'd made. He was the best cook, and it tasted heavenly.

Zane sat next to Luna with a glass of blood. He hadn't even tried to hide it, like Karn and Darick. He took a long swig, then began to talk to Karn. "I was thinking we should set a plan for when we are going to attack. I'm not waiting for them to come for us again. I know we've been running different scenarios, but I think going at night to avoid any humans and to take the Werewolves off guard would be the best option. We have to wait until a few more vessels come down from our main ship. They should all be down by the end of tomorrow," Zane explained.

Darick leaned into the conversation. "So, the plan is to attack tomorrow night?" he questioned.

Zane took another sip of blood, then placed his glass down. "I suppose so. There is no other reason to wait longer. It just gives them more time to come at us."

Karn shifted in his seat. Luna could feel the nervousness from across the table. They were all on edge. The Werewolves must be scary if these guys were sweating.

Darick rubbed a hand over his face. "So, how long do you think our magic will last?"

Zane took a breath and exhaled it out. His eyes darted from Luna to Darick. "Somehow using magic against the Werewolves takes away energy quicker. Today, Luna lasted an entire hour, so against the wolves, she could probably stand at least forty to fifty minutes without rest. I drained my magic fast last time, but now that I know that, I'll be smarter about it. No one can say how long exactly. If we are strategic with our magic, we could use it for a while—all depends on how often we use it and whether we are resting. If we catch the Werewolves off guard, we can take more out without expending too much. And my thoughts are that when they're in their human form, they will be easier to kill."

Darick chugged the rest of his blood before standing up and leaving the room without a word. Luna didn't know if that was a good or bad sign from him. Really, she couldn't read him anymore; his emotions were too hidden, except perhaps his anger. His expression was back to how she'd known him at the very beginning: stern and serious, nothing more. She rolled her eyes at herself for thinking about him so much again. She took a few more bites of her stir fry, finishing it off.

"You guys have weapons we can use right?" Samara asked.

Zane let out humourless chuckle. "Sorry to break it to you, sweetheart, but you and Aywin won't be fighting."

Samara's face darkened into the Elf Warrior Luna knew her to be. "Sorry to break it to YOU, handsome, but we go where Luna goes," she threatened.

Luna's eyes widened. Samara had been quite chill for the last while with Zane, but her feisty side was making an entry. Zane's jaw clenched for a few seconds before he loosened it with an exhale through his nose. "Aw, you can't just cheer us on?" he asked, with a smirk tugging at his full lips.

"If by 'cheer you on,' you mean a high-five in the face… with a chair. Then, yes, sure," Samara replied, a brow raised.

Zane was full on smiling now, fangs showing. He gave Samara a slight nod. "Touché. Have it your way then," he stated casually, then looked over at Karn. "Why don't you show the Elves where the weapons are kept, and they can choose their poison."

Karn nodded. The group watched Zane as he got up and left the room the way Darick had gone. Aywin and Samara were finished with their food, so Luna took their plates with hers and washed them in the sink.

"Everything all right?" Samara asked, startling Luna, who had been so zoned out washing dishes that she hadn't even heard Samara come up behind her.

"Yeah," Luna lied. She didn't feel like talking at the moment; her mind was tired.

Samara leaned against the counter and closer to Luna. "Talk to me," she whispered.

Luna sighed and peered back at Karn and Aywin, who were in a serious discussion about something.

"Darick was an ass last night," Luna said, and dragged her hands through her hair. She finished washing the last plate and stuck it in the drying rack as Samara waited patiently for her to go on. "I thought he cared more about me, but he basically told me to go away. I may have over-reacted a bit… but I thought him and I had something. We were friends. Now he doesn't even want to be friends. It's just frustrating," she explained.

Samara chewed her bottom lip while thinking of what to say. "Luna, you deserve someone who loves you and cares for you. You don't need someone who you have to chase and who is insecure with themself, or has whatever else going on. I know it's hard. I'm sorry. You guys were so close to forming a loving relationship. Like, I don't know what happened between you exactly…."

Luna smirked. "We never… you know, if that's what you mean, but we were close. I probably felt more for him than he did for me. Speaking of doing the nasty, did you and Karn?" Luna murmured.

Samara made a "you caught me" expression and grinned.

Luna smiled excitedly. "How was it?"

Samara couldn't help but let out a laugh. "Good, really good. I know you told me to be careful, and I kind of thought I would be able to stay away from him, but he and I are so alike. He's easy to talk to and makes me laugh all the time. I haven't even known him that long, and it feels like it's been a lifetime," Samara replied.

Luna reached out and squeezed her friend's hand. "I'm just protective. I don't want him to walk all over you. Not that that's possible because you'd kick his ass, but still."

"Are you girls done talking over there?" Karn interrupted from the dining table. "We should go and look at the weapons."

"Yeah, we're coming," Samara replied.

***

The four of them headed to the weapons room, which was one level down. Luna hadn't been downstairs yet, and instead of the stairs, they decided to take an elevator.

The first floor down wasn't as creepy as Luna had imagined it would be. It was modernly decorated and had lots of lights to bright up the hallways. They turned down a few hallways before Karn opened a big metal door and led them into a massive room full of every weapon imaginable.

Most of the weapons weren't familiar to Luna. She knew swords, daggers, spears, and bows, but there were lots of guns here. She noticed the bullets for the guns were lined with silver. Apparently, Werewolves were sensitive to it; they didn't heal from shot with a silver lead bullet. The room smelled of gunpowder and steel. Karn took them through the gun area and showed off the weapons. He gave them a quick review on how to load and handle the guns. Most were bolt action or semi-automatic, so they were easy to load.

Samara got the hang of the guns quickly, while Luna and Aywin still didn't feel confident in shooting them since they hadn't practised. Samara chose to a sword and a Glock 19 handgun, which was nice and small and fit nicely in the strap she wore around her thigh. Luna chose a few daggers. She grabbed two medium-sized swords she fit on her back in a beautiful black sheath case. The swords themselves were a piece of art; their silvery handles were carved into what Karn described as dragons. Aywin chose a large sword that was just as gorgeous as Luna's, except his had a dark-blue handle wrapped with leather to create a unique design. The swords were a different style than what Luna was used to. On Nexus, the swords looked like the swords from Asia on Earth: The katana or hwando. But the swords that were in the weapons room appeared medieval, with wider blades.

"Would you guys like to go to the indoor fighting arena?" Karn asked. "You could practise fencing. I think Darick and Zane might be there too; it's on this lower level, just down the hallway."

Samara jumped up. "Duh! I would love to practise some fighting! Who says no to that?" She winked at Karn.

Aywin and Luna agreed to go as well. The group left the weapons room and made their way through the intricate hallways. Luna had no idea how to get back; her sense of direction in the house was terrible. At least when she was outside, she could pay attention to the sun or certain landmarks that stood out. They turned a corner, and Luna heard music blaring.

"Must be close," Aywin stated.

Karn opened a door, and the music became even louder. Luna didn't recognize the artist. There was a deafening clash of metal on metal as Darick's sword met with Zane's. Luna watched with amazement as the two brothers battled it out. She knew that Zane would win in a battle of magic, but when it came to swords, she was clueless. Darick was smooth with his sword fighting, making it look effortless. Zane moved his feet and body more. He used his quick reflexes to throw Darick off. Darick was a big, muscular guy, so sometimes, his body couldn't move as swiftly as Zane could. Either way, both brothers seemed to have their weaknesses and strengths, balancing each other out so that neither one was winning. Nevertheless, it was a mesmerizing fight to watch. Sweat and heavy breathing was masked by the music, making the scene even more exciting.

Finally, the brothers held their hands up to let each other know they needed a break. Zane made a swooping motion with his hand and the music's volume lowered. Luna could hear her own thoughts now.

"Who wants to go next?" Karn asked.

Samara stepped up first. She was always keen on fighting. She pointed at Karn, then sized him up with her eyes. "You and me," she stated, adding a wink.

The edges of Karn's mouth curved up. "No 'accidentally' cutting my head off," he joked, forming quotation marks with his fingers when he said "accidentally."

"Which head?" Samara answered, then gave Karn a wink.

The two stepped up onto the mats as Darick and Zane joined Luna and Aywin. Darick, of course, chose to stand as far away from Luna as possible, which pissed her off even more. Zane stood beside her, but he was focused on the fight. The music turned up, and Karn and Samara began to battle.

Samara kept up with Karn well for the first little bit. Karn was one of the best fighters Luna had ever seen. He wasn't as good as Darick and Zane, but he had a fluidity that the Elves didn't have. Luna decided that it must be because of the Vampires' speed and ability; they seemed extra in touch with their mind-body connection. Really, they were on another level of athleticism; Luna had no idea how to explain it.

Karn eventually got the upper hand and took Samara down. But they didn't stop there. They went on for a few more rounds until Samara's pixie cut was drenched with sweat. Finally, they stepped off the fighting mat area, and it was Luna and Aywin's turn. Luna usually marvelled at the thought of beating up her brother, but she felt nervous and pressured from all the good fighters in the room. She was by no means good with a sword. Samara had said that Luna was better than she thought, but still; she wasn't near the Samara's level. Luna could sense Aywin's nervous energy too; he had never been a fighter either. He didn't enjoyed it and wasn't interested in actually doing it—he was a science nerd. Luna let the music pump her up, and she pretended that nobody was around.

"It's okay. Let's just have fun," Luna mouthed to her brother.

He smiled and gave her a slight nod in return to show he understood. They circled around each other for a second before bursting into action. Luna had more fun than she thought she would. Once they were a few minutes into fighting, she completely forgot that everyone was watching. It just felt like she and her brother were spending time with one another.

Luna was faster than Aywin, and she took him down quite a few times. He didn't mind, though; he didn't have male pride when it came to fighting a girl. He knew he wasn't good at fighting and being beat by a woman meant nothing to him, so he laughed and smiled the entire time. Eventually, Luna held her hand up after she felt like she was going to throw up from exhaustion; the swords were heavy.

Her skin felt sticky as she walked over to Samara and the men. Zane turned the music down so that they could all hear each other speak. Luna could feel his eyes on her. She was still breathing hard and could feel her heart pounding in her ears.

"How many times have you used a sword?" Zane asked while the others chatted amongst themselves.

Luna shrugged. "Not many times. I was never really trained in sword fighting at all. My father showed me some stuff as a child," she answered honestly. She was embarrassed about her skill level, but she couldn't blame herself. It wasn't like she needed to be able to use a sword as a prison guard.

He smirked. "That explains it then."

Her jaw dropped, and she punched his shoulder. He flinched and stared at her in disbelief. "Did you just hit me?" he asked. His shock faded into a smug look.

"Oh sorry, I must have hit you too hard; you've lost your memory," Luna taunted.

Zane raised a brow. "So feisty."

Luna rolled her eyes. "You're just not used to people giving you sass. Not everyone bows down to the all and powerful one, Lord Zane."

He crossed his arms. "All and powerful one? Wow, I haven't heard that before. You do realize that people don't worship me, right?"

Luna snorted. "Oops, did I forget to say that the person I'm referring to is you?"

His eyes flickered with mischief, and Luna regretted her teasing. His jaw clenched before it relaxed as his lips curved into a grin.

"What?" Luna asked shortly.

He shook his head silently, the grin still present and getting bigger, showing off his fangs. "Oh nothing, sweetheart," he said.

The comment sent an electrical feeling down Luna's back and into her stomach. She pushed it aside and held her head up high. "Call me 'sweetheart' again, and I won't just be punching your arm," she retorted.

He leaned in closer to her. "Good, I like it rough."

Luna's face turned bright pink while Zane casually spun around and budged into Karn and Darick's conversation. "Let's go speak with the others," he murmured.

Darick and Karn nodded. Luna had tip-toed over to Samara and Aywin. Her face was still blushing, and she was annoyed with Zane's flirty comments. She didn't understand why he had to infuriate her every second he got.

"We have to go. You know how to get back upstairs?" Karn asked Samara.

"Yeah, we're good," Samara replied.

Luna hoped that Samara's comment actually meant that she knew how to get back because Luna had no freaking clue. Karn, Zane, and Darick left the room. With their presence gone, Luna could breathe more; the power that radiated off Darick and Zane was overwhelming at times, especially Zane's. Sometimes, she swore she could feel another string inside herself that almost felt painful when Zane was around. He got on her nerves.

"Let's go watch some movies!" Aywin suggested.

Samara and Luna exchanged looks. Luna had no idea what a movie was, but she decided she was willing to give it a try. "Can we shower first?" Luna asked.

Aywin sighed. "Yeah, you do stink pretty bad, L."

Luna slapped his arm. "Hey!"

They headed to their rooms and showered.

***

After changing into new clothes, they met outside Samara's room and made their way down to the theatre. The room was dark and had rows of comfy chairs and couches surrounding a black screen. Aywin turned the screen on and selected a movie called Harry Potter and the Philosopher's Stone.

They spent the rest of the day watching the Harry Potter movie. Luna loved it. Apparently, there were quite a few Harry Potter films. They just watched the first one. The next thing they watched was a TV show. Luna learned that TV shows have things called "episodes" and "seasons." Aywin had apparently started one called The Witcher. Luna thought the show was the coolest thing ever, mainly because of the clothes in the show, which reminded her of home. She wondered how much the humans on Earth knew about other planets. They must know something or else they wouldn't have been able to create stuff so similar. Her favourite character was Yennifer since Yennifer's eyes were like hers, although Luna's had speckles of blue. There were even Elves in the show, but their ears were smaller than actual Elves' ears.

They watched as many episodes as possible before Luna felt tired. She needed to go to bed; a good sleep that night was a must for her. Her eyes felt sore and heavy from sitting and watching a screen all day. She was beginning to feel nervous about the battle. The thought of having to kill another living creature wasn't something she took lightly. Even though the Werewolves had terrorized the Vampires, it still felt strange to go into battle. She was starting to over-think it all.

The group of Elves headed up to their rooms. They were about to go upstairs when Luna thought she would love to read a book before bed. "I'll see you guys in the morning; I'm going to quickly go to the library," she said.

"Sounds good," Aywin replied.

Samara smiled. "Have a goodnight." The two walked up the stairs.

Luna walked across the foyer to the other side of the house to get to the library. She planned on grabbing any book she thought looked interesting and take it up to her room to read.

She opened the library door and found the lights already on. She walked across the room to a set of large bookcases. There were aisles of them in this room. It was the biggest library she'd ever seen. She was quickly scanning the books with her fingers, feeling the leather textures on her skin, when she heard a rustling sound from beside her. Her eyes popped up from the books to see Darick nestled in a large chair, reading a book. The sound she heard was the flipping of a page.

His face looked relaxed and content, not scrunched up and serious like she had always seen it. The picture he created made her smile: a large man all cozy in a library, reading a book. She wondered if he'd noticed her and was choosing to ignore her. She snatched a random book from the shelf and turned around to head out.

As she did, she ran straight into Pierce. Pierce's striking blue eyes tore into Luna's. Her hair was braided beautifully into an updo. Luna was suddenly jealous because she had never been very good at doing her own hair.

"Hi," Luna stuttered.

Pierce was probably the most intimidating female Luna had ever known. Maybe it was due to her beauty? Pierce's eyes narrowed, and she placed her hand on her hip. "Sorry, I'm busy right now. Can I ignore you another time?" she said viciously, then walked around Luna.

"Yeah, sure, stupidity's not a crime, so you're free to go," Luna said innocently.

Pierce snapped around and gave Luna a horrible glare. "I'm just going so that I can get far away from you," Pierce said cruelly.

"Is there a reason you hate me so much?" Luna questioned with a raised brow.

Pierce flipped her hair back. "How can I not?" She whipped away from Luna and walked further into the library.

Luna laughed to herself, then left the room. She didn't know why there was a stick up Pierce's ass, but it was way up there and was not coming out.

She went up to her room and got ready for bed. She tucked into her cold, silky bed sheets and pulled out her book. The book was a novel, and she couldn't put it down; it was so good. She looked at the time, and it was nearly midnight. She needed to go to sleep or else she was going to be grumpy in the morning. She put the book down and turned off the lights. Her body felt relaxed and sore from all the fighting. She fell asleep within minutes.

Chapter XIX

Luna woke up in the morning feeling rested. She had forgotten all about the battle because of the book she had read last night. As soon as she realized what day it was, though, her body grew nervous. She felt shaky and a little nauseated.

Samara knocked on her door around eight a.m., and they both headed down to the kitchen. Aywin was already there, making eggs and hashbrowns and buttering toast. Luna and Samara helped him out. The three of them sat at the dining table, eating their food in silence. Luna felt the other two were also nervous about the battle. She had to force the food down her throat; she knew she would need the energy later.

"Anybody else have the nervous shits this morning?" Aywin asked.

Samara snorted but then nodded. Luna laughed. "No poops yet, but I feel like I'm going to throw up."

"That's just the food," Samara teased.

Aywin frowned. "Hey, fuck you too." He grinned.

Samara winked at him. Luna finished the rest of her plate and waited for the others to finish theirs. She got up with the plates and washed them in the sink as well as the dirty pots and pans. She heard footsteps coming into the room. Karn and Zane strolled in, smiling, with Darick lagging behind them. Luna could feel their powerful presence suck the breath out of her lungs. She grumbled and walked over to the dining table to join them. Karn kissed Samara softly on the lips before sitting beside her. Luna turned her gaze from the awkward kissing and found Zane's intimidating silvery eyes staring back at her.

She batted her lashes, mockingly. "Good morning, all powerful one."

Karn burst out laughing first, followed by a few snickers from Samara and Aywin.

Zane winked. "Morning, sweetheart."

Luna was hoping to get on his nerves, but instead, he got on hers. Her nostrils flared. "When my heart is sweet, it's never around you," she retorted.

Zane smirked but didn't reply. She decided that was a win for her. She leaned back in her chair and tried to relax, even though she could feel her hands shaking from the fear of the battle. She saw Zane's smile fade a second as he peered at her hands and back at her eyes again. He didn't say anything. Instead, he looked around the group.

"Today's the day. The troops are arriving shortly. We plan to arrive at the place where they conjugate just before mid-night, but it's a two-hour drive to get there," he explained.

Everyone nodded to show that they understood, except for Luna. She was terrified. Why was she so nervous? Maybe it was because Zane was dependent on her powers along with his and Darick's. She was one of the key players in winning this thing, and she had only used her powers a couple times in a battle. The good thing was that from practising, she felt confident in using her powers. They felt naturally part of her now; they came easy and didn't wear her down nearly as much as they did at first.

She was staring at the dining table, picturing the battle in her mind, when she felt a soft touch of someone's hand on her back. The hand was warm and comforting. Her eyes flicked up to Samara. Nobody else was around the dining table anymore; they had left without Luna noticing. She blinked a few times to clear her head.

"You're worried," Samara stated.

Luna clenched her shaking fists. "What if my powers don't help them?"

"They will, Luna. Stop second guessing yourself. You got this," Samara said in a stern tone.

"You have so much faith in me," Luna replied, amused. A small smile splayed across her face.

Samara pinched her lips. "Yes. And now you must have faith in yourself."

Luna chewed the inside of her mouth. She didn't meet Samara's eyes. "I'm going to go and relax for a while in my room."

"Okay, just text me if you want to hang out. I'm probably going to go and find Karn," Samara replied.

Luna got up and went back up to her room. The house was quiet and cold, making her feel lonely and lost. She didn't know how to have faith in herself. If she wasn't strong enough, would hundreds of Vampires die? She lifted her legs up the stairs, forcing herself to move. Everything felt heavy.

Her stomach suddenly lifted, and she felt the familiar presence of electricity and pressure inside her. She got up the stairs and turned to find Zane leaning against the wall next to her bedroom door. He had been studying the ground as if it was the most interesting thing he had ever seen. He had a solemn look on his face that made Luna shiver. Maybe he didn't believe in her either. The sight of him took away some of the hollowness in her chest. His head lifted slowly; the loose dark curls framing his face made him look like a dark angel.

"Hi, stalker," Luna stated; her tone sounded soft and sad when she had intended for it to be snarky.

Zane uncrossed his arms. His expression was one that made Luna uncomfortable and exposed. "You do know it'll be okay, right?" Zane said finally after far too many seconds of silence.

The hallway suddenly felt too tight and dark for Luna, making her claustrophobic. "You don't know that," Luna murmured.

He gave her a smug smile. "I know everything, remember?"

Luna could feel a lightness in her chest at the joke. "Zane... will we win?"

Zane lifted himself off the wall and leaned closer to her. His breath smelled good for a guy that drank blood. "Obviously. Don't worry, Luna," he said kindly. He brushed past her and back towards the stairs.

She stood in the hallway for a minute before going back to her room. She wasn't sure if Zane had been truthful or not, but it made her feel better. She lay down in bed and pulled out her book. She began to read and couldn't put the book down again for hours. Before she knew it, it was almost five in the afternoon. She decided to get up and do some stretching.

She lay on the floor and went through her usual routine of full-body stretching. Just over forty-five minutes of stretching had gone by when a knock interrupted her. She got up and opened her door to find Samara.

"The troops have arrived. Everyone's in the big meeting room downstairs. I was thinking we could eat dinner quickly, then go down there. There's going to be a meeting around seven thirty."

"Yeah, sounds good," Luna replied.

The two of them went down to the kitchen and cooked pasta. They made enough for Aywin, who was missing in action. Luna texted him on her phone to let him know he had a plate of food waiting for him. It was still strange for her to use the cellular device. She squinted a lot when she stared at the screen. The pair sat down at the dining table and began to eat. Their appetites were small due to their battle nerves.

"Are you feeling any better?" Samara asked.

Luna drummed her fingers on the table. "I think so. What about you? Aren't you scared?"

Samara brows knitted. "Girl, you know I love to fight. This is just another day in paradise. I am a bit nervous, but I've been trying not to overthink it. Overthinking can get you in trouble; it pushes your body into panic, and that's not something you want when fighting. You want your mind to be focused and crystal clear," she explained seriously.

Luna took a big bite of pasta. The food was good, considering Aywin hadn't made it. As if Aywin knew Luna had been thinking about him, he entered the room wearing a unique set of armour, nothing like Luna had ever seen before. The armour was a matte silver grey with mixes of gold lines around the borders. Leather straps made an X-shape across his chest, attaching to a sword sheath on his back. A gold diamond shape was at the centre of his breastplate. A soft material came up around his neck like a collar. He strolled in as if modelling and then spun around in a circle.

Samara clapped her hands. "Hot damn, where'd you score that?"

Aywin grinned. "There's more with your names on them." He sat down at the table and started to eat the plate left for him.

"Is it comfy?" Luna asked.

"It's not too bad. Better than ours. This kind is lighter, and I can move better in it," he explained.

They finished their meals, and Samara did the dishes while Luna dried them and put them away. When it was nearly seven thirty, Aywin took the girls to where the armour was displayed. A few others were already there, choosing armour and changing into it.

Luna grabbed hers, which literally had her name on it. It was tailored to her body. The breastplate had curves for her breasts so that they weren't mushed down. The armour for the females had 'skirts' sewn in. She had to hand it to the Vampires: their armour was comfy. Once Samara and Luna finished dressing, they grabbed their chosen weapons from the weapons room. Once they strapped up, they followed Aywin downstairs.

The once empty and quiet mansion was now bustling with people. It made Luna feel more human. She didn't realize how much she missed the white noise of people chatting around her. They entered the meeting room where all the Vampires were heading. Luna hadn't been in the room before. It was by far the biggest room in the building that she knew of, fitting hundreds upon hundreds of people in it. The room was shaped in a circle and had tall ceilings. There were multiple levels with stairs leading to seating areas. Two empty chairs were in the middle of a stage at the front of the room.

People were finding places to sit. Luna, Samara, and Aywin went around the room to try and find a row of three empty seats, which was harder than they thought it would be. Aywin spotted empty spots in the second row and pointed to them. They rushed over and sat down: Luna on the far side with Samara in the middle and Aywin beside her on the other side.

The Vampire beside Luna sniffed the air and turned to look at Luna. Luna gulped and faced the other way. Vampires could still make her uncomfortable. She tried to focus her attention on the front of the room so she didn't have to talk to the guy. She noticed that most of the Vampires in the room were male.

Two figures strode onto the stage. Luna could tell it was Zane and Karn. They sat down in the empty chairs. Zane adjusted a mic that was hooked onto his chest area. He also wore armour, but his was midnight black with shades of blues and made him look like a king. All talking at once, the crowd had been loud, but everyone shut up once they saw Zane.

"Thanks to all of you for volunteering to come down here and win this battle for us. Each group will have a leader assigned to them; you already know who you are," Zane said, his voice sounding authoritative and powerful. He went on to explain battle plans and details.

Luna zoned out for most of it because she had no idea what he was talking about. Samara seemed to understand. Aywin appeared to be at least trying to figure it out. Luna assumed she was going to be stuck with Zane and Darick the entire time anyways. Zane talked for almost two hours. During that time, blood was served to the Vampires. Luna could smell a strong aroma of iron in the air, and it made her feel sick. It took her back to the battle on her planet with the Vampires and the amount of blood that had been spilled there.

Finally, Zane finished his speech. He had told them to sit tight for a while before they would all go upstairs and head out into the trucks to leave. Luna watched as Zane walked off the stage and into the crowd. He was swarmed by Vampires wanting to talk to him. They liked him; Luna could see it. He must be a much better leader than his father. The time seem to slow down, and while they waited, Luna and Samara stretched a few times. None of the Vampires approached them to talk. Instead, they gave them strange looks as if they wanted to devour them.

Finally, a speaker clicked on and a voice announced, "Please make your way upstairs. We are going to be loading

the trucks up now. Grab your weapons on your way out."
The voice sounded like Karn.

Luna, Samara, and Aywin followed the crowd as they
made their way upstairs. It was slow going. When they got
outside, Luna noticed a lot of trucks in the yard loading
people in them.

"Hey! You three are coming with us," Karn yelled from
behind them.

They turned around and saw Karn, Darick, and Zane
walking towards them, all looking bad-ass. If Luna hadn't
known them, she would have been terrified to see them
approaching her. Zane had his usual arrogant smirk on his
face, which calmed Luna nerves, knowing that he could be
his normal self when they were about to go to battle.

Zane led them over to a separate vehicle that was smaller
than the rest, only able to hold ten people; it was a van, not
a truck. The six of them got in, and the driver slid the doors
closed. The side of the van had windows to look out of.
Luna sat across from Darick. His large body was hunched
over in the van, and his broad shoulders were scrunched up
against Karn. Luna's father would have had a horrible time
sitting in the van if he were here. The van began to drive;
the sound of the engine humming soothed Luna.

"We are going to be at the front line. Just stick close.
Karn's responsible for Samara; Darick, you're with Aywin,
and, Luna, you're with me," Zane stated.

"Do you want us to stay behind you when we start fighting, or how will that work?" Samara asked.

"Well, we are going to take them off guard, so my hope is
that we can find the leader first and kill him, like I explained

earlier, and maybe the rest will surrender. If not… we will have to just go for it until they do," Zane answered.

"How are we tracking the leader down?" Aywin asked.

Zane pointed at his nose and grinned. "Smell, of course."

Aywin frowned. "Smell?"

"Little did you know that Vampires have a strong sense of smell, and Karn here knows what the leader smells like, so he's going to take us to him." Zane rested his elbows on his legs and leaned forward.

They continued to ride in silence for the rest of the way. It was late at night, and Luna was sleepy. She rested her head against Samara's shoulder and felt herself falling asleep.

***

When the van stopped abruptly, she jolted awake. The light in the van went off—all was pitch black.

"Let's go. Follow me and try not to make any loud noises," Zane whispered.

They got out of the van and into the night. The moon above was bright, lighting the valley enough for Luna to see. So far, she could only trees and grass. Zane jogged ahead, and the rest followed. She kept her breathing controlled and her heartrate steady as they ran along the tree line.

The other trucks had parked further into the trees. They passed groups of Vampires, who watched them go by. It was an eerie experience. Luna had never run through a forest in complete darkness, with just the moon as her flashlight. They ran for approximately four kilometres before cresting over a hill into a valley that dipped down. Houses covered the area. The lights in the homes were out, but many had exterior lights.

Karn sniffed the air and shook his head. He made a motion for them to get closer. Karn led them now, instead of Zane. They followed him through the tall grass and along the hillside behind the houses. Karn stopped every once in a while to sniff the air. He dipped down, close to a house, and sniffed more. He then shook his head and turned to Zane.

"Something's wrong," he said in a hushed tone.

Zane's eyes narrowed. "What is it?"

"This house smells strongly of him, but he's not here. His smell is heading away now, down the street, and it's disappearing. It's like he's moving," Karn whispered back.

Zane cursed under his breath just in time for a frightening howl to erupt into the night. More howls roared. They were coming from behind them, towards the place where the other Vampires were hiding. Luna shivered as fear slid over her flesh. Whatever a Werewolf was, she really didn't want to meet one. Too bad she was about to.

Zane quickly texted someone on his phone, then sprinted down the street; the rest of them followed. The night air was becoming colder, but with all the running, Luna's skin felt numb. The road went over a hill and back into the valley where the Vampires were. Unfortunately, the scene unfolding before Luna was horrible and sickening. But the sound was the worst of it: gnashing, biting, wailing, and growling. Blood curdling screams and wet sloshing slashes filled the air.

Zane snarled and his power erupted from within him. His body vibrated with energy as he charged the Werewolves, who were massive creatures. Although they fought on all fours, when they stood, their heads reached eight feet tall.

Luna could hear more Werewolves coming from behind them, but she had to follow Zane; he was the one she had to stick with. She charged down towards Zane while she pulled at her powers. She felt them instantly, the blue glow taking over her being and filling her with rage. She drew energy from the sky and threw bolts of lightning down at the Werewolves, killing them instantly. She wished that she hadn't enjoyed it so much, but fighting with Zane felt like a dance. He tried to use his sword more than his power, but when he used his power, it shook the earth around them and killed the Werewolves in seconds.

Luna could see that Zane was trying to find the leader. He must have picked up the scent from the leader's house because he sniffed the air wildly between the killings. Luna heard a woman scream from behind her. She snapped her body around and saw Pierce lying on the ground on her back. A large dark-brown Werewolf was on top of her, trying to bite at her face, its jaws mere millimetres away. A dark thought crossed Luna's mind for a second before running over; she almost wanted to leave Pierce like that, but she knew she wouldn't be able to live with herself if she did. Luna bolted over and used fire to burn the monster. It wailed and fell to the ground in flames. The smell was sickening. Luna threw out her hand to Pierce, who took it and stood up. She looked like a warrior goddess, with her black hair moving in the breeze and her flawless skin covered with sprinkles of blood.

"Thanks," Pierce said with a small smile.

Luna nodded, then watched as Pierce jogged off to fight more Werewolves. Luna turned back to try and track down Zane again. He had moved further into the battle, so she followed him. Luna could feel her power draining the more she used it; she had to start using her sword more. She watched as a Werewolf charged Zane, jumped on his back, and tried to bite into his neck. Zane used his powers to lift it and explode it into a mush of blood and gore. The spray hit Luna's face, and she gagged. She didn't have time to vomit because a Werewolf pounced towards her. She raised her sword up and gutted it. The wolf yelped. The sword stuck into one of its ribs and was pulled from Luna's hands. The Werewolf jumped over her and, standing on two feet, pulled the sword out and tossed it on the ground before it ran into the fray.

All Luna could smell was the innards of Vampires and Werewolves, and all she could hear were their keening and choking sounds as she slipped on the sodden earth now oily with gore. It was the valley of death.

The sky thundered above, and rain began to pelt them. Luna assumed it was Darick's doing. She peered up to see the silhouette of Darick on one of the rolling hills. His body was trembling with power. A Werewolf pounced him, and as he fought it, he was too busy to notice the one creeping up behind him. Luna shot a bolt of lightning down at the wolf behind him, frying it on the spot. Darick spun around and saw the smoking corpse. His gold eyes met Luna's, and he gave her a nod before continuing to fight the beasts.

She heard bones snapping and crunching behind her and watched a Werewolf rip a Vampire in half. She picked up her sword and charged the creature. A fracturing sound echoed through the night as she brought the sword down on the Werewolf's skull. The yelps of the enemy were spine-chilling. A geyser of blood showered into the air as Vampire sliced into a Werewolf beside her. The smell of battle was ungodly, and Luna wished she didn't have to be part of it. Her heart was pounding, and sweat was slick on her fore-head. The rain helped cool her sizzling skin.

A Werewolf suddenly came out from behind her. Its snarl made her shudder, and her eyes widened at the look of its bloody teeth. She swung her sword at it but missed; these creatures were far too fast for her. It opened its mouth and went for her arm. She felt something push her out of the way. Zane let out an agonizing growl. His body dropped to the ground, and the Werewolf's teeth sunk into his neck. It tore at him, and his neck cracked. Luna winced, knowing that in a second, it was going to decapitate him. She screamed and threw all her energy at the monster. It flung back into a few other Werewolves heading their way, tumbling them to the ground.

Luna could feel tears streaming down her cheeks. She ran over to Zane, who was lying on the ground; it was the weakest and most vulnerable she had ever seen him. He was dying. His neck was torn open so bad that she could see his fractured cervical spine. If she tried to move him she would decapitate him and he'd be dead. At the sight of him, an anger she had never felt before tore at her insides. She felt a vengeance within her so potent that she didn't recognize herself. It was stronger than the anger she'd felt when she'd first discovered her powers. She tried to access her healing abilities, but the energy wouldn't come. It was too focused on killing that she couldn't make it heal. At that moment, another Werewolf came at them. She snarled, pulling at every energy string in distance before she released the energy around her. She thought the energy would kill the creature, but instead it went through all of them.

The fighting suddenly ceased as every Werewolf blinked in confusion. The large Werewolf in front of her stumbled slightly before falling to the ground. It twitched a few times before it got up again while shaking its head. It was pure white and had beautiful orange eyes. The anger within her intensified—this was the Werewolf pack leader.

The Werewolf slowly circled her as it morphed into a naked male human. He was a beautiful Asian man with bewitching bronze skin and shoulder-length hair, which was tied back.

Luna peered down at Zane, whose chest was barely moving. Panic tore at her insides. She reached out her hand to cup his face. In that moment, a charged magnetic force pulled her even closer to Zane. It radiated through her and made her feel things for him that confused her. The achiness in her chest eased, and part of the constant hollowness within her filled. She realized it was the first time she had ever touched his skin, and it set her body on fire. Her flesh burned wildly at the contact, but she needed to focus on saving him—he didn't have much time left. She needed to feed him blood or he was going to die.

She pulled out a small dagger and cut her wrist, then pressed it to his mouth. He didn't move at first, but once the blood hit his tongue, he snarled and bit into her wrist.

She flinched at the pain, but it was soon replaced with a euphoric feeling, a feeling unlike anything she had experienced with Darick. At that moment, something within her broke out. The connection that she had been feeling from earlier intensified and moved deep into her soul. Her body heated, and her core ached. She couldn't help but let out a moan as she felt his fangs dig in more and take more blood from her. She felt him groan against her flesh.

The Werewolf watched with narrowed glowing-orange eyes. Luna was thankful he didn't come over; she needed Zane to heal fully. She watched as his neck knit itself back together, the more blood he drank. Luna's body sagged against his. All her energy and powers were gone as she allowed him to take everything she had left. When he was done, Zane sat up and held her in his lap. She heard him yell for someone, but she was so sleepy that she couldn't understand what he was saying. He held her tightly. Was he crying? Her vision remained clear as she watched the naked man walk towards them.

"You can stay the fuck back," Zane snarled.

The man held his hands up in defence and went down on his knees. He let out a howl into the night, and hundreds of other Werewolves howled back in response. "We aren't going to hurt you anymore," the man said. His voice was rich and deep.

Zane let out a humourless chuckle. "Says the guy who's been tearing apart my people."

The man shook his head sadly. "You don't understand. We were possessed." He pointed at Luna, "She saved us.

Whatever magic she holds zapped us out of it. Thank you…. We are so sorry."

Zane's eyes narrowed, and his expression darkened. He rested Luna softly on the ground and stood up. His body was trembling with anger. "I promised myself that I wouldn't kill you if you surrendered. But now that it's happening, it's harder than I thought, so you better get the fuck back before I do something I don't want to do," Zane growled.

The man nodded and backed away. "They are coming for you. And you'll need us when they do," the man stated. With that, he morphed back into a Werewolf and ran towards the houses. The rest of the Werewolves followed.

"I don't know what that means, but it doesn't sound good," Zane said more to himself than to Luna.

His strong arms wrapped around her and picked her up. She could barely make out the Vampires swarming them to help before her eyes fluttered closed and darkness overtook her.

***

Luna woke up in a bright room with monitors around her. She sat up and regretted it instantly. Her head throbbed. An IV was in her arm, and she noticed a blood bag hanging from an IV pole. She looked up and saw Samara and Aywin sitting in chairs across from her bed, snoozing.

"What happened?" Luna asked.

Their eyes fluttered open and widened at the sight of her. "Oh, thank God," Samara said, and jumped up to run to her side. Aywin got up too and went to the other side of the bed.

"You lost a lot of blood; this is your fourth unit. I don't even know how you're still alive," Aywin said, his voice trembling. Luna could see he was fighting back tears. She frowned. There was no way Zane had taken that much blood, right?

"Is… is everyone okay?" Luna asked groggily.

"Lots of Vampires died. They've been taking their bodies and burning them ceremonially. Apparently, it's something the Vampires do to respect their dead. Karn and Darick are alive, though, if that's what you mean," Samara answered. Her expression remained flat; she looked exhausted. Both of them did.

"How long have I been out?" Luna wondered out loud.

"A full day," Aywin answered.

Luna peered down at her wrist. No sign of any fang marks. Zane must've healed her. Samara saw that Luna was studying her wrist.

"Did you save him?" she asked.

Luna nodded. "I think so. He was going to die."

"You could have died," Aywin snapped. His disappointment was clear on his face.

Luna dropped her wrist and held her brother's hand. "But I didn't. It's okay, Aywin," she said softly.

His lip quivered, and he bent down and hugged her. Her chest tightened with emotion, and she let herself cry. Samara bent down too, and the three of them held each other for as long as they needed. Their tears streamed down their faces, making everything damp. After a while, they released the hug. Luna heard a knock. The three of them looked over to see Darick standing by the open door, his body taking up the frame. His skin was paler than usual.

"Can I come in?" he asked.

Luna nodded. Samara and Aywin left the room to give them some privacy. He strode over to the bed. His golden eyes stared at her with a sorrow so strong than Luna winced. "I thought I'd lost you," he said after the silence was unbearable.

He reached out his large hand and grasped hers. His comment felt more intimate than friendly. He bent down and hugged her tightly. She froze with surprise. He had been acting so emotionless lately that she'd thought he hated her. He clearly didn't. She rested her hands on his back but didn't feel the same butterflies that she used to for him. She cared for him but not in a romantic way anymore, which was okay—it was for the best. She'd used Darick as her fallback after Edric. Darick had been the one to defend her, so all her emotions had gone to him; she realized now the mistake in that. Darick needed to figure himself out before he tried to love someone else. Luna saw that.

"If you don't mind, brother, I'd love it if you took your fucking hands off my mate," Zane's vain voice growled from the door.

Darick released his hold and took a step away from Luna, who frowned. Zane was leaning against the doorframe with the side of his lips curved up into a smirk. Just seeing Zane made Luna's body heat and think things that made her face blush. She was so glad to see him alive and well. There was no scar or sign of the wound on his neck. The familiar string inside her body begged to be released.

"Did you just say 'mate'?" she asked.

Zane smirked. "Whoops, must have slipped out."

Darick looked pissed off. Luna's frown remained. She had no clue what a "mate" was. Zane stepped further into the room. His presence caused frost to form up the corner walls.

He exhaled before speaking. "Right now, us being mated is the least of our concerns. Turns out Wizards aren't extinct. Apparently, they have a vendetta against us Vampires. Also, I think I found out where dear old mother's been hiding…. Turns out she had magic in her too…."

The Soul Empire Series

The Ancient Nexus
Book I

Coming Soon!
Goblet Of Blood Book II

Make sure to follow me to get updates on book release dates!

Instagram: paige.ra.morgan_author

Tiktok: @paigemorgan409